run with the hunted
a charles bukowski reader

charles bukowski

....

run with the hunted
a charles bukowski reader

edited by John Martin

ecco

An Imprint of HarperCollinsPublishers

A hardcover edition of this book was published in 1993 by HarperCollins Publishers.

HarperCollins books may be purchased for educational, business, or sales promotional use. For information please write: Special Markets Department, HarperCollins Publishers, Inc., 10 East 53rd Street, New York, NY 10022.

First Ecco Edition published in 2003.

Designed by C. Linda Dingler

Library of Congress Cataloging-in-Publication Data

Bukowski, Charles.
   Run with the hunted / Charles Bukowski ; edited by John Martin. — 1st ed.
    p. cm.
   ISBN 0-06-016911-7 (cloth)
   1. Martin, John, 1930– . II. Title.
PS3552.U4A6   1993
811'.54—dc20   92-53353
                                r92

ISBN 0-06-092458-6 (pbk.)
  04 05 06 07 SP / RRD 30 29 28 27 26 25 24

For William Packard

Acknowledgments

The material in this reader is reprinted from the following books published by Black Sparrow: *The Days Run Away Like Wild Horses over the Hills* (1969), *Post Office* (1971), *Mockingbird Wish Me Luck* (1972), *South of No North* (1973), *Burning in Water, Drowning in Flame* (1974), *Factotum* (1975), *Love Is a Dog from Hell* (1977), *Women* (1978), *Play the Piano Drunk* (1979), *Ham on Rye* (1982), *Hot Water Music* (1983), *You Get So Alone at Times It Just Makes Sense* (1986), *The Rooming-house Madrigals* (1988), *Hollywood* (1989), *Septuagenarian Stew* (1990), and *The Last Night of the Earth Poems* (1992).

Editor's Note

The material in this Bukowski reader is taken from the more than twenty novels, books of short stories, and volumes of poetry that Bukowski has published with Black Sparrow Press over the past twenty-five years. Sometimes autobiographical and sometimes the result of Bukowski's wonderful gift for observation, these poems and prose pieces, taken together, serve to chronicle this writer's inner and outer life, from childhood to the present—and an astonishing and heroic life it is. So long as there are intelligent and courageous readers neither Bukowski's work nor his life, interwoven as they are, will soon be forgotten.

1

. . . .

ᘒ the great white horses come up
ᘒ lick the frost of the dream

• •

The first thing I remember is being under something. It was a table, I saw a table leg, I saw the legs of the people, and a portion of the tablecloth hanging down. It was dark under there, I liked being under there. It must have been in Germany. I must have been between one and two years old. It was 1922. I felt good under the table. Nobody seemed to know that I was there. There was sunlight upon the rug and on the legs of the people. I liked the sunlight. The legs of the people were not interesting, not like the tablecloth which hung down, not like the table leg, not like the sunlight.

Then there is nothing . . . then a Christmas tree. Candles. Bird ornaments: birds with small berry branches in their beaks. A star. Two large people fighting, screaming. People eating, always people eating. I ate too. My spoon was bent so that if I wanted to eat I had to pick the spoon up with my right hand. If I picked it up with my left hand, the spoon bent away from my mouth. I wanted to pick the spoon up with my left hand.

Two people: one larger with curly hair, a big nose, a big mouth, much eyebrow; the larger person always seeming to be angry, often screaming; the smaller person quiet, round of face, paler, with large eyes. I was afraid of both of them. Sometimes there was a third, a fat one who wore dresses with lace at the throat. She wore a large brooch, and had many warts on her face with little hairs growing out of them. "Emily," they called her. These people didn't seem happy together. Emily was the grandmother, my father's mother. My father's name was "Henry." My mother's name was "Katherine." I never spoke to them by name. I was "Henry, Jr." These people spoke German most of the time and in the beginning I did too.

The first thing I remember my grandmother saying was, "I will bury *all* of you!" She said this the first time just before we began eating a meal, and she was to say it many times after that, just before we began to eat. Eating seemed very important. We ate mashed potatoes and gravy, especially on Sundays. We also ate roast beef, knockwurst and sauerkraut, green peas, rhubarb, carrots, spinach, string beans, chicken, meatballs and spaghetti, sometimes mixed with ravioli; there were boiled onions, asparagus, and every Sunday there was strawberry shortcake with vanilla ice cream. For breakfasts we had french toast and sausages, or there were hotcakes or waffles with bacon and scrambled eggs on the side. And there was always coffee. But what I remember best is all the mashed potatoes and gravy and my grandmother, Emily, saying, "I will bury *all* of you!"

She visited us often after we came to America, taking the red trolley in from Pasadena to Los Angeles. We only went to see her occasionally, driving out in the Model-T Ford.

I liked my grandmother's house. It was a small house under an overhanging mass of pepper trees. Emily had all her canaries in different cages. I remember one visit best. That evening she went about covering the cages with white hoods so that the birds could sleep. The people sat in chairs and talked. There was a piano and I sat at the piano and hit the keys and listened to the sounds as the people talked. I liked the sound of the keys best up at one end of the piano where there was hardly any sound at all—the sound the keys made was like chips of ice striking against one another.

"Will you stop that?" my father said loudly.

"Let the boy play the piano," said my grandmother.

My mother smiled.

"That boy," said my grandmother, "when I tried to pick him up out of the cradle to kiss him, he reached up and hit me in the nose!"

They talked some more and I went on playing the piano.

"Why don't you get that thing tuned?" asked my father.

—*HAM ON RYE*

ice for the eagles

• •

I keep remembering the horses
under the moon
I keep remembering feeding the horses
sugar
white oblongs of sugar
more like ice,
and they had heads like
eagles
bald heads that could bite and
did not.

The horses were more real than
my father
more real than God
and they could have stepped on my
feet but they didn't
they could have done all kinds of horrors
but they didn't.

I was almost 5
but I have not forgotten yet;
o my god they were strong and good
those red tongues slobbering
out of their souls.

• •

I had begun to dislike my father. He was always angry about something. Wherever we went he got into arguments with people. But he
didn't appear to frighten most people; they often just stared at him,
calmly, and he became more furious. If we ate out, which was seldom, he
always found something wrong with the food and sometimes refused to

pay. "There's flyshit in this whipped cream! What the hell kind of a place is this?"

"I'm sorry, sir, you needn't pay. Just leave."

"I'll leave, all right! But I'll be back! I'll burn this god-damned place down!"

Once we were in a drug store and my mother and I were standing to one side while my father yelled at a clerk. Another clerk asked my mother, "Who *is* that horrible man? Every time he comes in here there's an argument."

"That's my husband," my mother told the clerk.

Yet, I remember another time. He was working as a milkman and made early morning deliveries. One morning he awakened me. "Come on, I want to show you something." I walked outside with him. I was wearing my pajamas and slippers. It was still dark, the moon was still up. We walked to the milk wagon which was horsedrawn. The horse stood very still. "Watch," said my father. He took a sugar cube, put it in his hand and held it out to the horse. The horse ate it out of his palm. "Now you try it . . . " He put a sugar cube in my hand. It was a very large horse. "Get closer! Hold out your hand!" I was afraid the horse would bite my hand off. The head came down; I saw the nostrils; the lips pulled back, I saw the tongue and the teeth, and then the sugar cube was gone. "Here. Try it again . . . " I tried it again. The horse took the sugar cube and waggled his head. "Now," said my father, "I'll take you back inside before the horse shits on you."

I was not allowed to play with other children. "They are bad children," said my father, "their parents are poor." "Yes," agreed my mother. My parents wanted to be rich so they imagined themselves rich.

The first children of my age that I knew were in kindergarten. They seemed very strange, they laughed and talked and seemed happy. I didn't like them. I always felt as if I was going to be sick, to vomit, and the air seemed strangely still and white. We painted with watercolors. We planted radish seeds in a garden and some weeks later we ate them with salt. I liked the lady who taught kindergarten, I liked her better than my parents.

—*HAM ON RYE*

rags, bottles, sacks

• •

as a boy
I remember the sound
of:
"RAGS! BOTTLES! SACKS!"

"RAGS! BOTTLES! SACKS!"

it was during the
Depression
and you could hear the
voice
long before you saw the
old wagon
and the
old tired
swaybacked horse.

then you heard the
hooves:
clop, clop, clop . . .

and then you saw the
horse and the
wagon

and it always seemed
to be
on the hottest summer
day:

"RAGS! BOTTLES! SACKS!"

oh
that horse was so
tired—

white streams of
saliva
drooling
as the bit dug into
the
mouth

he pulled an intolerable
load
of
rags, bottles, sacks

I saw his eyes
large
in agony

his ribs
showing

the giant flies
whirled and landed upon
raw places on his
skin.

sometimes
one of our fathers would
yell:
"Hey! Why don't you
feed that horse, you
bastard!"

the man's answer was
always the
same:
"RAGS! BOTTLES! SACKS!"

the man was
incredibly

dirty, un-
shaven, wearing a crushed
and stained
fedora

he
sat on top of
a large pile of
sacks

and
now and
then
as the horse seemed to
miss
a step

this man would
lay down
the long whip . . .

the sound was like a
rifle shot

a phalanx of flies would
rise
and the horse would
yank forward
anew

the hooves slipping and
sliding on the hot
asphalt

and then
all we could
see
was the back of the
wagon
and
the massive mound of
rags and bottles
covered with
brown
sacks

and
again
the voice:
"RAGS! BOTTLES! SACKS!"

he was
the first man
I ever wanted to
kill

and
there have been
none
since.

• •

There were continual fights. The teachers didn't seem to know anything about them. And there was always trouble when it rained. Any boy
who brought an umbrella to school or wore a raincoat was singled out.
Most of our parents were too poor to buy us such things. And when they
did, we hid them in the bushes. Anybody seen carrying an umbrella or
wearing a raincoat was considered a sissy. They were beaten after school.

David's mother had him carry an umbrella whenever it was the least bit cloudy.

There were two recess periods. The first graders gathered at their own baseball diamond and the teams were chosen. David and I stood together. It was always the same. I was chosen next to last and David was chosen last, so we always played on different teams. David was worse than I was. With his crossed eyes, he couldn't even see the ball. I needed lots of practice. I had never played with the kids in the neighborhood. I didn't know how to catch a ball or how to hit one. But I wanted to, I liked it. David was afraid of the ball, I wasn't. I swung hard, I swung harder than anybody but I could never hit the ball. I always struck out. Once I fouled a ball off. That felt good. Another time I drew a walk. When I got to first, the first baseman said, "That's the only way you'll ever get here." I stood and looked at him. He was chewing gum and he had long black hairs coming out of his nostrils. His hair was thick with vaseline. He wore a perpetual sneer.

"What are you looking at?" he asked me.

I didn't know what to say. I wasn't used to conversation.

"The guys say you're crazy," he told me, "but you don't scare me. I'll be waiting for you after school some day."

I kept looking at him. He had a terrible face. Then the pitcher wound up and I broke for second. I ran like crazy and slid into second. The ball arrived late. The tag was late.

"You're *out!*" screamed the boy whose turn it was to umpire. I got up, not believing it.

"I said, 'YOU'RE OUT!'" the umpire screamed.

Then I knew that I was not accepted. David and I were not accepted. The others wanted me "out" because I was *supposed* to be "out." They knew David and I were friends. It was because of David that I wasn't wanted. As I walked off the diamond I saw David playing third base in his knickers. His blue and yellow stockings had fallen down around his feet. Why had he chosen me? I was a marked man. That afternoon after school I quickly left class and walked home alone, without David. I didn't want to watch him beaten again by our classmates or by his mother. I didn't want to listen to his sad violin. But the next day at lunch time, when he sat down next to me I ate his potato chips.

• • •

My day came. I was tall and I felt very powerful at the plate. I couldn't believe that I was as bad as they wished me to be. I swung wildly but with force. I knew I was strong, and maybe like they said, "crazy." But I had this feeling inside of me that something real was there. Just hardened shit, maybe, but that was more than they had. I was up at bat. "Hey, it's the STRIKEOUT KING! MR. WINDMILL!" The ball arrived. I swung and I felt the bat connect like I had wanted it to do for so long. The ball went up, up and HIGH, into left field, 'way OVER the left fielder's head. His name was Don Brubaker and he stood and watched it fly over his head. It looked like it was never going to come down. Then Brubaker started running after the ball. He wanted to throw me out. He would never do it. The ball landed and rolled onto a diamond where some fifth graders were playing. I ran slowly to first, hit the bag, looked at the guy on first, ran slowly to second, touched it, ran to third where David stood, ignored him, tagged third and walked to home plate. Never such a day. Never such a home run by a first grader! As I stepped on home plate I heard one of the players, Irving Bone, say to the team captain, Stanley Greenberg, "Let's put him on the regular team." (The regular team played teams from other schools.)

"No," said Stanley Greenberg.

Stanley was right. I never hit another home run. I struck out most of the time. But they always remembered that home run and while they still hated me, it was a better kind of hatred, like they weren't quite sure *why*.

Football season was worse. We played touch football. I couldn't catch the football or throw it but I got into one game. When the runner came through I grabbed him by the shirt collar and threw him on the ground. When he started to get up, I kicked him. I didn't like him. It was the first baseman with vaseline in his hair and the hair in his nostrils. Stanley Greenberg came over. He was larger than any of us. He could have killed me if he'd wanted to. He was our leader. Whatever he said, that was it. He told me, "You don't understand the rules. No more football for you."

I was moved into volleyball. I played volleyball with David and the others. It wasn't any good. They yelled and screamed and got excited, but the *others* were playing football. I wanted to play football. All I needed was a little practice. Volleyball was shameful. Girls played volleyball. After a while I wouldn't play. I just stood in the center of the field where nobody was playing. I was the only one who would not play anything. I stood there each day and waited through the two recess sessions, until they were over.

One day while I was standing there, more trouble came. A football sailed from high behind me and hit me on the head. It knocked me to the ground. I was very dizzy. They stood around snickering and laughing. "Oh, look, Henry fainted! Henry fainted like a lady! Oh, look at Henry!"

I got up while the sun spun around. Then it stood still. The sky moved closer and flattened out. It was like being in a cage. They stood around me, faces, noses, mouths and eyes. Because they were taunting me I thought they had deliberately hit me with the football. It was unfair.

"Who kicked that ball?" I asked.

"You wanna know who kicked the ball?"

"Yes."

"What are you going to do when you find out?"

I didn't answer.

"It was Billy Sherril," somebody said.

Billy was a round fat boy, really nicer than most, but he was one of them. I began walking toward Billy. He stood there. When I got close he swung. I almost didn't feel it. I hit him behind his left ear and when he grabbed his ear I hit him in the stomach. He fell to the ground. He stayed down. "Get up and fight him, Billy," said Stanley Greenberg. Stanley lifted Billy up and pushed him toward me. I punched Billy in the mouth and he grabbed his mouth with both hands.

"O.K.," said Stanley, "I'll take his place!"

The boys cheered. I decided to run, I didn't want to die. But then a teacher came up. "What's going on here?" It was Mr. Hall.

"Henry picked on Billy," said Stanley Greenberg.

"Is that right, boys?" asked Mr. Hall.

"Yes," they said.

Mr. Hall took me by the ear all the way to the principal's office. He pushed me into a chair in front of an empty desk and then knocked on the principal's door. He was in there for some time and when he came out he left without looking at me. I sat there five or ten minutes before the principal came out and sat behind the desk. He was a very dignified man with a mass of white hair and a blue bow tie. He looked like a real gentleman. His name was Mr. Knox. Mr. Knox folded his hands and looked at me without speaking. When he did that I was not so sure that he was a gentleman. He seemed to want to humble me, treat me like the others.

"Well," he said at last, "tell me what happened."

"Nothing happened."

"You hurt that boy, Billy Sherril. His parents are going to want to know why."

I didn't answer.

"Do you think you can take matters into your own hands when something happens you don't like?"

"No."

"Then why did you do it?"

I didn't answer.

"Do you think you're better than other people?"

"No."

Mr. Knox sat there. He had a long letter opener and he slid it back and forth on the green felt padding of the desk. He had a large bottle of green ink on his desk and a pen holder with four pens. I wondered if he would beat me.

"Then why did you do what you did?"

I didn't answer. Mr. Knox slid the letter opener back and forth. The phone rang. He picked it up.

"Hello? Oh, Mrs. Kirby? He what? What? Listen, can't *you* administer the discipline? I'm busy now. All right, I'll phone you when I'm done with this one . . ."

He hung up. He brushed his fine white hair back out of his eyes with one hand and looked at me.

"Why do you cause me all this trouble?"

I didn't answer him.

"You think you're tough, huh?"

I kept silent.

"Tough kid, huh?"

There was a fly circling Mr. Knox's desk. It hovered over his green ink bottle. Then it landed on the black cap of the ink bottle and sat there rubbing its wings.

"O.K., kid, you're tough and I'm tough. Let's shake hands on that."

I didn't think I was tough so I didn't give him my hand.

"Come on, give me your hand."

I stretched my hand out and he took it and began shaking it. Then he stopped shaking it and looked at me. He had blue clear eyes lighter than the blue of his bow tie. His eyes were almost beautiful. He kept looking at me and holding my hand. His grip began to tighten.

"I want to congratulate you for being a tough guy."

His grip tightened some more.

"Do you think I'm a tough guy?"

I didn't answer.

He crushed the bones of my fingers together. I could feel the bone of each finger cutting like a blade into the flesh of the finger next to it. Shots of red flashed before my eyes.

"Do you think I'm a tough guy?" he asked.

"I'll kill you," I said.

"You'll what?"

Mr. Knox tightened his grip. He had a hand like a vise. I could see every pore in his face.

"Tough guys don't scream, do they?"

I couldn't look at his face anymore. I put my face down on the desk.

"Am I a tough guy?" asked Mr. Knox.

He squeezed harder. I had to scream, but I kept it as quiet as possible so no one in the classes could hear me.

"Now, am I a tough guy?"

I waited. I hated to say it. Then I said, "Yes."

Mr. Knox let go of my hand. I was afraid to look at it. I let it hang by my side. I noticed that the fly was gone and I thought, it's not so bad to be a fly. Mr. Knox was writing on a piece of paper.

"Now, Henry, I'm writing a little note to your parents and I want you to deliver it to them. And you *will* deliver it to them, won't you?"

"Yes."

He folded the note into an envelope and handed it to me. The envelope was sealed and I had no desire to open it.

—*HAM ON RYE*

we ain't got no money, honey, but we got rain

call it the greenhouse effect or whatever
but it just doesn't rain like it
used to.

I particularly remember the rains of the
depression era.
there wasn't any money but there was
plenty of rain.

it wouldn't rain for just a night or
a day,
it would RAIN for 7 days and 7
nights
and in Los Angeles the storm drains
weren't built to carry off that much
water
and the rain came down THICK and
MEAN and
STEADY
and you HEARD it banging against
the roofs and into the ground
waterfalls of it came down
from the roofs
and often there was HAIL
big ROCKS OF ICE
bombing
exploding
smashing into things
and the rain
just wouldn't
STOP
and all the roofs leaked—
dishpans,

cooking pots
were placed all about;
they dripped loudly
and had to be emptied
again and
again.

the rain came up over the street curbings,
across the lawns, climbed the steps and
entered the houses.
there were mops and bathroom towels,
and the rain often came up through the
toilets: bubbling, brown, crazy, whirling,
and the old cars stood in the streets,
cars that had problems starting on a
sunny day,
and the jobless men stood
looking out the windows
at the old machines dying
like living things
out there.

the jobless men,
failures in a failing time
were imprisoned in their houses with their
wives and children
and their
pets.
the pets refused to go out
and left their waste in
strange places.

the jobless men went mad
confined with
their once beautiful wives.
there were terrible arguments
as notices of foreclosure
fell into the mailbox.

rain and hail, cans of beans,
bread without butter; fried
eggs, boiled eggs, poached
eggs; peanut butter
sandwiches, and an invisible
chicken
in every pot.

my father, never a good man
at best, beat my mother
when it rained
as I threw myself
between them,
the legs, the knees, the
screams
until they
separated.

"I'll kill you," I screamed
at him. *"You hit her again
and I'll kill you!"*

*"Get that son-of-a-bitching
kid out of here!"*

"no, Henry, you stay with
your mother!"

all the households were under
siege but I believe that ours
held more terror than the
average.

and at night
as we attempted to sleep
the rains still came down
and it was in bed
in the dark

watching the moon against
the scarred window
so bravely
holding out
most of the rain,
I thought of Noah and the
Ark
and I thought, it has come
again.
we all thought
that.

and then, at once, it would
stop.
and it always seemed to
stop
around 5 or 6 a.m.,
peaceful then,
but not an exact silence
because things continued to
drip
    drip
        drip

and there was no smog then
and by 8 a.m.
there was a
blazing yellow sunlight,
Van Gogh yellow—
crazy, blinding!
and then
the roof drains
relieved of the rush of
water
began to expand in
the warmth:
PANG! PANG! PANG!

and everybody got up
and looked outside
and there were all the lawns
still soaked
greener than green will ever
be
and there were the birds
on the lawn
CHIRPING like mad,
they hadn't eaten decently
for 7 days and 7 nights
and they were weary of
berries
and
they waited as the worms
rose to the top,
half-drowned worms.
the birds plucked them
up
and gobbled them
down; there were
blackbirds and sparrows.
the blackbirds tried to
drive the sparrows off
but the sparrows,
maddened with hunger,
smaller and quicker,
got their
due.

the men stood on their porches
smoking cigarettes,
now knowing
they'd have to go out
there
to look for that job
that probably wasn't
there, to start that car

that probably wouldn't
start.

and the once beautiful
wives
stood in their bathrooms
combing their hair,
applying makeup,
trying to put their world back
together again,
trying to forget that
awful sadness that
gripped them,
wondering what they could
fix for
breakfast.

and on the radio
we were told that
school was now
open.
and
soon
there I was
on the way to school,
massive puddles in the
street,
the sun like a new
world,
my parents back in that
house,
I arrived at my classroom
on time.

Mrs. Sorenson greeted us
with, "we won't have our
usual recess, the grounds
are too wet."

"AW!" most of the boys
went.

"but we are going to do
something special at
recess," she went on,
"and it will be
fun!"

well, we all wondered
what that would
be
and the two hour wait
seemed a long time
as Mrs. Sorenson
went about
teaching her
lessons.

I looked at the little
girls, they all looked so
pretty and clean and
alert,
they sat still and
straight
and their hair was
beautiful
in the California
sunshine.

then the recess bell rang
and we all waited for the
fun.

then Mrs. Sorenson told
us:
"now, what we are going to

do is we are going to tell
each other what we did
during the rainstorm!
we'll begin in the front
row and go right around!
now, Michael, you're
first! . . . "

well, we all began to tell
our stories, Michael began
and it went on and on,
and soon we realized that
we were all lying, not
exactly lying but mostly
lying and some of the boys
began to snicker and some
of the girls began to give
them dirty looks and
Mrs. Sorenson said,
"all right, I demand a
modicum of silence
here!
I am interested in what
you did
during the rainstorm
even if you
aren't!"

so we had to tell our
stories and they *were*
stories.

one girl said that
when the rainbow first
came
she saw God's face
at the end of it.

only she didn't say
which end.

one boy said he stuck
his fishing pole
out the window
and caught a little
fish
and fed it to his
cat.

almost everybody told
a lie.
the truth was just
too awful and
embarrassing to
tell.

then the bell rang
and recess was
over.

"thank you," said Mrs.
Sorenson, "that was very
nice.
and tomorrow the grounds
will be dry
and we will put them
to use
again."

most of the boys
cheered
and the little girls
sat very straight and
still,
looking so pretty and
clean and

alert,
their hair beautiful
in a sunshine that
the world might
never see
again.

•••

One night my father took me on his milk route. There were no longer any horsedrawn wagons. The milk trucks now had engines. After loading up at the milk company we drove off on his route. I liked being out in the very early morning. The moon was up and I could see the stars. It was cold but it was exciting. I wondered why my father had asked me to come along since he had taken to beating me with the razor strop once or twice a week and we weren't getting along.

At each stop he would jump out and deliver a bottle or two of milk. Sometimes it was cottage cheese or buttermilk or butter and now and then a bottle of orange juice. Most of the people left notes in the empty bottles explaining what they wanted.

My father drove along, stopping and starting, making deliveries.

"O.K., kid, which direction are we driving in now?"

"North."

"You're right. We're going north."

We went up and down streets, stopping and starting.

"O.K., which way are we going now?"

"West."

"No, we're going south."

We drove along in silence some more.

"Suppose I pushed you out of the truck now and left you on the sidewalk, what would you do?"

"I don't know."

"I mean, how would you live?"

"Well, I guess I'd go back and drink the milk and orange juice you just left on the porch steps."

"Then what would you do?"

"I'd find a policeman and tell him what you did."

"You would, huh? And what would you tell him?"

"I'd tell him that you told me that 'west' was 'south' because you wanted me to get lost."

It began to get light. Soon all the deliveries were made and we stopped at a cafe to have breakfast. The waitress walked over. "Hello, Henry," she said to my father. "Hello, Betty." "Who's the kid?" asked Betty. "That's little Henry." "He looks just like you." "He doesn't have my brains, though." "I hope not."

We ordered. We had bacon and eggs. As we ate my father said, "Now comes the hard part."

"What is that?"

"I have to collect the money people owe me. Some of them don't want to pay."

"They ought to pay."

"That's what I tell them."

We finished eating and started driving again. My father got out and knocked on doors. I could hear him complaining loudly, "HOW THE HELL DO YOU THINK *I'M* GOING TO EAT? YOU'VE SUCKED UP THE MILK, NOW IT'S TIME FOR YOU TO SHIT OUT THE MONEY!"

He used a different line each time. Sometimes he came back with the money, sometimes he didnt.

Then I saw him enter a court of bungalows. A door opened and a woman stood there dressed in a loose silken kimono. She was smoking a cigarette. "Listen, baby, I've got to have the money. You're into me deeper than anybody!"

She laughed at him.

"Look, baby, just give me half, give me a payment, something to show."

She blew a smoke ring, reached out and broke it with her finger.

"Listen, you've got to pay me," my father said. "This is a desperate situation."

"Come on in. We'll talk about it," said the woman.

My father went in and the door closed. He was in there for a long time. The sun was really up. When my father came out his hair was hanging down around his face and he was pushing his shirt tail into his pants. He climbed into the truck.

"Did that woman give you the money?" I asked.

"That was the last stop," said my father. "I can't take it any more. We'll return the truck and go home . . . "

I was to see that woman again. One day I came home after school and she was sitting on a chair in the front room of our house. My mother and father were sitting there too and my mother was crying. When my mother saw me she stood up and ran toward me, grabbed me. She took me into the bedroom and sat me on the bed. "Henry, do you love your mother?" I really didn't but she looked so sad that I said, "Yes." She took me back into the other room.

"Your father says he loves this woman," she said to me.

"I love *both* of you! Now get that kid out of here!"

I felt that my father was making my mother very unhappy.

"I'll kill you," I told my father.

"Get that kid out of here!"

"How can you love that woman?" I asked my father. "Look at her nose. She has a nose like an elephant!"

"Christ!" said the woman, "I don't have to take this!" She looked at my father: "*Choose,* Henry! One or the other! Now!"

"But I can't! I love you both!"

"I'll kill you!" I told my father.

He walked over and slapped me on the ear, knocking me to the floor. The woman got up and ran out of the house and my father went after her. The woman leaped into my father's car, started it and drove off down the street. It happened very quickly. My father ran down the street after her and the car. "EDNA! EDNA, COME BACK!" My father actually caught up with the car, reached into the front seat and grabbed Edna's purse. Then the car speeded up and my father was left with the purse.

"I knew something was going on," my mother told me. "So I hid in the car trunk and I caught them together. Your father drove me back here with that horrible woman. Now she's got his car."

My father walked back with Edna's purse. "Everybody into the house!" We went inside and my father locked me in the bedroom and my mother and father began arguing. It was loud and very ugly. Then my father began beating my mother. She screamed and he kept beating her. I climbed out a window and tried to get in the front door. It was locked.

I tried the rear door, the windows. Everything was locked. I stood in the backyard and listened to the screaming and the beating.

Then the beating and the screaming stopped and all I could hear was my mother sobbing. She sobbed a long time. It gradually grew less and less and then she stopped.

—*HAM ON RYE*

Death Wants More Death

• •

death wants more death, and its webs are full:
I remember my father's garage, how child-like
I would brush the corpses of flies
from the windows they had thought were escape—
their sticky, ugly, vibrant bodies
shouting like dumb crazy dogs against the glass
only to spin and flit
in that second larger than hell or heaven
onto the edge of the ledge,
and then the spider from his dank hole
nervous and exposed
the puff of body swelling
hanging there
not really quite knowing,
and then *knowing*—
something sending it down its string,
the wet web,
toward the weak shield of buzzing,
the pulsing;
a last desperate moving hair-leg
there against the glass
there alive in the sun,
spun in white;

and almost like love:
the closing over,

the first hushed spider-sucking:
filling its sack
upon this thing that lived;
crouching there upon its back
drawing its certain blood
as the world goes by outside
and my temples scream
and I hurl the broom against them:
the spider dull with spider-anger
still thinking of its prey
and waving an amazed broken leg;
the fly very still,
a dirty speck stranded to straw;
I shake the killer loose
and he walks lame and peeved
towards some dark corner
but I intercept his dawdling
his crawling like some broken hero,
and the straws smash his legs
now waving
above his head
and looking
looking for the enemy
and somehow valiant,
dying without apparent pain
simply crawling backward
piece by piece
leaving nothing there
until at last the red gut-sack splashes
its secrets,
and I run child-like
with God's anger a step behind,
back to simple sunlight,
wondering
as the world goes by
with curled smile
if anyone else
saw or sensed my crime

Son of Satan

• •

I was eleven and my two buddies, Hass and Morgan, they were each twelve and it was summer, no school, and we sat on the grass in the sun behind my father's garage and smoked cigarettes.

"Shit," I said.

1 was sitting under a tree. Morgan and Hass were sitting with their backs against the garage.

"What is it?" asked Morgan.

"We gotta get that son of a bitch," I said. "He's a disgrace to this neighborhood!"

"Who?" asked Hass.

"Simpson," I said.

"Yeah," said Hass, "too many freckles. He irritates me."

"That's not it," I said.

"Oh yeah?" said Morgan.

"Yeah. That son of a bitch claims he fucked a girl under my house last week. It's a god damned lie!" I said.

"Sure it is," said Hass.

"He can't fuck," said Morgan.

"He can fucking lie," I said.

"I got no use for liars," Hass said, blowing a smoke ring.

"I don't like to hear that kind of bull from a guy with freckles," said Morgan.

"Well, maybe we ought to get him then," I suggested.

"Why not?" asked Hass.

"Let's do it," said Morgan.

We walked down Simpson's driveway and there he was playing handball against the garage door.

"Hey," I said, "look who's *playing* with himself!"

Simpson caught the ball on a bounce and turned to us.

"Hi, fellas!"

We surrounded him.

"Fucked any girls under any houses lately?" Morgan asked.

"Nah!"

"How come?" asked Hass.

"Oh, I dunno."

"I don't believe you've ever fucked anybody but *yourself!*" I said.

"I'm gonna go inside now," said Simpson. "My mother asked me to wash the dishes."

"Your mother has dishes up her pussy," said Morgan.

We laughed. We moved in closer to Simpson. Suddenly I shot a hard right to his belly. He doubled over, holding his gut. He stayed that way for a half minute, then straightened up.

"My dad will be home any time," he told us.

"Yeah? Does your dad fuck little girls under houses too?" I asked.

"No."

We laughed.

Simpson didn't say anything.

"Look at those freckles," said Morgan. "Each time he fucks a little girl under a house he gets a new freckle."

Simpson didn't say anything. He just began to look more and more frightened.

"I got a sister," said Hass. "How do I know you won't try to fuck my sister under some house?"

"I'd never do that, Hass, you've got my promise!"

"Yeah?"

"Yeah, I mean it!"

"Well, here's one just so you *don't!*"

Hass shot a hard right to Simpson's belly. Simpson doubled over again. Hass reached down, grabbed a handful of dirt and shoved it down the neck of Simpson's shirt. Simpson straightened up. He had tears in his eyes. A sissy.

"Let me go, fellows, *please!*"

"Go where?" I asked. "Wanna hide under your mother's skirt while the dishes fall out of her pussy?"

"You never fucked anybody," said Morgan, "you don't even *have* a dick! You piss out of your *ear!*"

"If I ever see you *look* at my sister," said Hass, "you're gonna get a beating so bad you'll be just one *big* freckle!"

"Just let me go, please!"

I felt like letting him go. Maybe he hadn't fucked anybody. Maybe he had just been day-dreaming. But I was the young leader. I couldn't show any sympathy.

"You're coming with us, Simpson."

"No!"

"No, my *ass!* You're coming with us! *Now, march!*"

I walked around behind him and kicked him in the butt, hard. He screamed.

"SHUT UP!" I yelled, "SHUT UP OR YOU'LL GET WORSE! NOW MARCH!"

We walked him up the driveway and across the lawn and down my driveway and into my backyard.

"Now stand straight!" I said. "Hands at your sides! We're going to hold a kangaroo court!"

I turned to Morgan and Hass and asked, "All those who think this man is guilty of lying about fucking a little girl under my house will now say 'guilty'!"

"Guilty," said Hass.

"Guilty," said Morgan.

"Guilty," I said.

I turned to the prisoner.

"Simpson, you are judged guilty!"

The tears were really coming out of Simpson then.

"I didn't do anything!" he sobbed.

"That's what you're guilty of," said Hass. "Lying!"

"But you guys lie all the time!"

"Not about fucking," said Morgan.

"That's what you lie about most, that's where I learned it from!"

"Corporal," I turned to Hass, "gag the prisoner! I'm tired of his fucking lies!"

"Yes, sir!"

Hass ran to the clothesline. He found a handkerchief and dish towel. While we held Simpson he jammed the handkerchief into his mouth and then tied the dish towel over his mouth. Simpson made some gagging sounds and changed color.

"You think he can breathe?" asked Morgan.

"He can breathe through his nose," I said.

"Yeah," Hass agreed.

"What'll we do now?" Morgan asked.

"The prisoner is guilty, isn't he?" I asked.

"Yeah."

"Well, as judge I sentence him to be hanged by the neck until dead!"

Simpson made sounds from beneath his gag. His eyes looked at us, pleading. I ran into the garage and got the rope. There was a length of it neatly coiled on a large spike on the garage wall. I had no idea why my father had that rope. He had never used it as far as I knew. Now it would be put to use.

I walked out with the rope.

Simpson started to run. Hass was right behind him. He made a flying tackle and brought him to the ground. He spun Simpson over and began punching him in the face. I ran up and slammed Hass hard across the face with the end of the rope. He stopped punching. He looked up at me.

"You son of a bitch, I'll kick your god damned ass!"

"As the judge, my verdict was that this man would *hang!* So it will be! RELEASE THE PRISONER!"

"You son of a bitch, I'll kick your god damned ass good!"

"*First,* we'll hang the prisoner! *Then* you and I will settle our differences!"

"You're damn right we will," said Hass.

"The prisoner will now rise!" I said.

Hass slid off and Simpson rose to his feet. His nose was bloodied and it had stained the front of his shirt. It was a very bright red. But Simpson seemed resigned. He was no longer sobbing. But the look in his eyes was terrified, horrible to see.

"Gimme a cigarette," I said to Morgan.

He stuck one into my mouth.

"Light it," I said.

Morgan lit the cigarette and I took a drag, then holding the cigarette between my lips I exhaled through my nose while making a noose at the end of the rope.

"Place the prisoner upon the porch!" I commanded.

There was a back porch. Above the porch was an overhang. I flung the rope over a beam, then pulled the noose down in front of Simpson's face. I didn't want to go on with it any longer. I figured Simpson had suffered enough but I was the leader and I was going to have to fight Hass afterwards and I couldn't show any weakness.

"Maybe we shouldn't," said Morgan.

"This man is *guilty!*" I screamed.

"Right!" screamed Hass. "Let him *hang!*"

"Look, he's pissed himself," said Morgan.

Sure enough, there was a dark stain on the front of Simpson's pants and it was spreading.

"No guts," I said.

I placed the noose over Simpson's head. I yanked on the rope and lifted Simpson up on his toes. Then I took the other end of the rope and tied it to a faucet on the side of the house. I knotted the rope tight and yelled, "Let's get the fuck out of here!"

We looked at Simpson hanging there on tip-toe. He was spinning around ever so slightly and he looked dead already.

I started running. Morgan and Hass ran with me. We ran up the drive and then Morgan split for his place and Hass split for his. I realized I had no place to go. Hass, I thought, either you forgot about the fight or you didn't want it.

I stood on the sidewalk for a minute or so, then I ran back into the yard again. Simpson was still spinning. Ever so slightly. We had forgotten to tie his hands. His hands were up, trying to take the pressure off of his neck but his hands were slipping. I ran over to the faucet and untied the rope and let it go. Simpson hit the porch, then tumbled forward onto the lawn.

He was face down. I turned him over and untied his gag. He looked bad. He looked as if he might die. I leaned over him.

"Listen, you son of a bitch, don't die, I didn't want to kill you, really. If you die, I'm sorry. But if you *don't* die and if you ever tell *anybody,* then your ass is dead for *sure!* You *got* that?"

Simpson didn't answer. He just looked at me. He looked terrible. His face was purple and he had rope burns on his neck.

I got up. I looked at him for a while. He didn't move. It looked bad. I felt faint. Then I got myself together. I inhaled deeply and walked up the driveway. It was about four in the afternoon. I began walking. I walked down to the boulevard and then I kept walking. I had thoughts. I felt as if my life was over. Simpson had always been a loner. Probably lonely. He never mixed with us other guys. He was strange that way. Maybe that's what bothered us about him. Yet, there was something nice about him anyhow. I felt as if I had done something very bad and yet in another way, I didn't. Mostly I just had this vacant feeling and it was centered in my stomach. I walked and I walked. I walked down to the highway and back. My shoes really hurt my feet. My parents always bought me cheap shoes. They looked good for maybe a week or so, then the leather cracked and the nails started coming through the soles. I kept walking anyhow.

When I got back to the driveway it was almost evening. I walked slowly down the driveway and into the backyard. Simpson wasn't there. And the rope was gone. Maybe he was dead. Maybe he was somewhere else. I looked around.

My father's face was framed in the screen door.

"Come in here," he said.

I walked up the porch steps and past him.

"Your mother isn't home yet. And that's good. Go to the bedroom. I want to have a little talk with you."

I walked into the bedroom and sat on the edge of the bed and looked down at my cheap shoes. My father was a big man, six feet two-and-one-half. He had a big head, and eyes that hung there under bushy eyebrows. His lips were thick and he had big ears. He was mean without even trying.

"Where ya been?" he asked.

"Walking."

"Walking. Why?"

"I like to walk."

"Since when?"

"Since today."

There was a long silence. Then he spoke again.

"What happened in our backyard today?"

"Is he dead?"

"Who?"

"I warned him not to talk. If he talked, then he's not dead."

"No, he's not dead. And his parents were going to call the police. I had to talk to them a long time in order to get them not to do that. If they had called the police, it would have killed your mother! Do you know that?"

I didn't answer.

"It would have killed your mother, do you know that?"

I didn't answer.

"I had to pay them to be quiet. Plus, I'm going to have to pay the medical bills. I'm going to give you the beating of your life! I'm going to cure you! I'm not going to raise a son who is not fit for human society!"

He stood there in the doorway, not moving. I looked at his eyes under those eyebrows, at that big body.

"I want the police," I said. "I don't want you. Give me the police."

He moved slowly toward me.

"The police don't understand people like you."

I got up from the bed and doubled my fists.

"Come on," I said, "I'll fight you!"

He was upon me with a rush. There was a blinding flash of light and a blow so hard that I really didn't feel it. I was on the floor. I got up.

"You better kill me," I said, "because when I get big enough I'm going to kill you!"

The next blow rolled me under the bed. It seemed like a good place to be. I looked up at the springs and I had never seen anything as friendly and wonderful as those springs up there. Then I laughed, it was a panicked laugh but I laughed, and I laughed because the thought came to me that maybe Simpson *had* fucked a little girl under my house.

"What the hell are you laughing at?" my father screamed. "You are surely the *Son of Satan*, you are not *my* son!"

I saw his big hand reach under the bed, searching for me. When it came near I grabbed it with both hands and bit it with all the strength I had. There was a ferocious yowl and the hand withdrew. I tasted wet flesh in my mouth, spit it out. Then I knew that while Simpson was not dead I might very well be dead very soon.

"All right," I heard my father say quietly, "now you've really asked for it and by god you are going to get it . . . "

I waited, and as I waited all I could hear were strange sounds. I could hear birds, I could hear the sound of autos driving by, I could even hear my heart pounding and my blood running through my body. I could hear my father breathing, and I moved myself exactly under the center of the bed and waited for the next thing.

—*Septuagenarian Stew*

• •

The fifth grade was a little better. The other students seemed less hostile and I was growing larger physically. I still wasn't chosen for the homeroom teams but I was threatened less. David and his violin had gone away. The family had moved. I walked home alone. I was often trailed by one or two guys, of whom Juan was the worst, but they didn't start anything. Juan smoked cigarettes. He'd walk behind me smoking a cigarette and he always had a different buddy with him. He never followed me alone. It scared me. I wished they'd go away. Yet, in another way, I didn't care. I didn't like Juan. I didn't like anybody in that school. I think they knew that. I think that's why they disliked me. I didn't like the way they walked or looked or talked, but I didn't like my father or mother either. I still had the feeling of being surrounded by white empty space. There was always a slight nausea in my stomach. Juan was dark-skinned and he wore a brass chain instead of a belt. The girls were afraid of him, and the boys too. He and one of his buddies followed me home almost every day. I'd walk into the house and they'd stand outside. Juan would smoke his cigarette, looking tough, and his buddy would stand there. I'd watch them through the curtain. Finally, they would walk off.

Mrs. Fretag was our English teacher. The first day in class she asked us each our names.

"I want to get to know all of you," she said.

She smiled.

"Now, each of you has a father, I'm sure. I think it would be interesting if we found out what each of your fathers does for a living. We'll start with seat number one and we will go around the class. Now, Marie, what does your father do for a living?"

"He's a gardener."

"Ah, that's nice! Seat number two . . . Andrew, what does your father do?"

It was terrible. All the fathers in my immediate neighborhood had lost their jobs. My father had lost his job. Gene's father sat on his front porch all day. All the fathers were without jobs except Chuck's who worked in a meat plant. He drove a red car with the meat company's name on the side.

"My father is a fireman," said seat number two.

"Ah, that's interesting," said Mrs. Fretag. "Seat number three."

"My father is a lawyer."

"Seat number four."

"My father is a . . . policeman . . . "

What was I going to say? Maybe only the fathers in my neighborhood were without jobs. I'd heard of the stock market crash. It meant something bad. Maybe the stock market had only crashed in our neighborhood.

"Seat number eighteen."

"My father is a movie actor . . . "

"Nineteen . . . "

"My father is a concert violinist . . . "

"Twenty . . . "

"My father works in the circus . . . "

"Twenty-one . . . "

"My father is a bus driver . . . "

"Twenty-two . . . "

"My father sings in the opera . . . "

"Twenty-three . . . "

Twenty-three. That was me.

"My father is a dentist," I said.

Mrs. Fretag went right on through the class until she reached number thirty-three.

"My father doesn't have a job," said number thirty-three.

Shit, I thought, I wish I had thought of that.

One day Mrs. Fretag gave us an assignment.

"Our distinguished President, President Herbert Hoover, is going to visit Los Angeles this Saturday to speak. I want all of you to go hear our President. And I want you to write an essay about the experience and about what you think of President Hoover's speech."

Saturday? There was no way I could go. I had to mow the lawn. I had to get the hairs. (I could never get all the hairs.) Almost every Saturday I got a beating with the razor strop because my father found a hair. (I also got stropped during the week, once or twice, for other things I failed to do or didn't do right.) There was no way I could tell my father that I had to go see President Hoover.

So, I didn't go. That Sunday I took some paper and sat down to write about how I had seen the President. His open car, trailing flowing streamers, had entered the football stadium. One car, full of secret service agents, went ahead and two cars followed close behind. The agents were brave men with guns to protect our President. The crowd rose as the President's car entered the arena. There had never been anything like it before. It was the President. It was him. He waved. We cheered. A band played. Seagulls circled overhead as if they too knew it was the

President. And there were skywriting airplanes too. They wrote words in the sky like "Prosperity is just around the corner." The President stood up in his car, and just as he did the clouds parted and the light from the sun fell across his face. It was almost as if God knew too. Then the cars stopped and our great President, surrounded by secret service agents, walked to the speaker's platform. As he stood behind the microphone a bird flew down from the sky and landed on the speaker's platform near him. The President waved to the bird and laughed and we all laughed with him. Then he began to speak and the people listened. I couldn't quite hear the speech because I was sitting too near a popcorn machine which made a lot of noise popping the kernels, but I think I heard him say that the problems in Manchuria were not serious, and that at home everything was going to be all right, we shouldn't worry, all we had to do was to believe in America. There would be enough jobs for everybody. There would be enough dentists with enough teeth to pull, enough fires and enough firemen to put them out. Mills and factories would open again. Our friends in South America would pay their debts. Soon we would all sleep peacefully, our stomachs and our hearts full. God and our great country would surround us with love and protect us from evil, from the socialists, awaken us from our national nightmare, forever . . .

The President listened to the applause, waved, then went back to his car, got in, and was driven off followed by carloads of secret service agents as the sun began to sink, the afternoon turning into evening, red and gold and wonderful. We had seen and heard President Herbert Hoover.

I turned in my essay on Monday. On Tuesday Mrs. Fretag faced the class.

"I've read all your essays about our distinguished President's visit to Los Angeles. I was there. Some of you, I noticed, could not attend for one reason or another. For those of you who could not attend, I would like to read this essay by Henry Chinaski."

The class was terribly silent. I was the most unpopular member of the class by far. It was like a knife slicing through all their hearts.

"This is very creative," said Mrs. Fretag, and she began to read my essay. The words sounded good to me. Everybody was listening. My words filled the room, from blackboard to blackboard, they hit the ceiling and bounced off, they covered Mrs. Fretag's shoes and piled up on the floor. Some of the prettiest girls in the class began to sneak glances at me. All the tough guys were pissed. Their essays hadn't been worth shit. I drank in my words like a thirsty man. I even began to believe them. I saw Juan sitting there like I'd punched him in the face. I stretched out my legs and leaned back. All too soon it was over.

"Upon this grand note," said Mrs. Fretag, "I hereby dismiss the class . . . "

They got up and began packing out.

"Not you, Henry," said Mrs. Fretag.

I sat in my chair and Mrs. Fretag stood there looking at me.

Then she said, "Henry, were you there?"

I sat there trying to think of an answer. I couldn't. I said, "No, I wasn't there."

She smiled. "That makes it all the more remarkable."

"Yes, ma'am . . . "

"You can leave, Henry."

I got up and walked out. I began my walk home. So, that's what they wanted: lies. Beautiful lies. That's what they needed. People were fools. It was going to be easy for me. I looked around. Juan and his buddy were not following me. Things were looking up.

—*HAM ON RYE*

dinner, 1933

• •

when my father ate
his lips became
greasy
with food.

and when he ate
he talked about how
good
the food was

and that
most other people
didn't eat
as good
as we
did.

he liked to
sop up
what was left
on his plate
with a piece of
bread,
meanwhile making
appreciative sounds
rather like
half-
grunts.

he *slurped* his
coffee
making loud
bubbling
sounds.
then he'd put
the cup
down:

"dessert? is it
jello?"

my mother would
bring it
in a large bowl
and my father would
spoon it
out.

as it plopped
in the dish
the jello made
strange sounds,
almost fart-
like
sounds.

then came the
whipped cream,
mounds of it
on the
jello.

"ah! jello and
whipped cream!"

my father sucked the
jello and whipped
cream
off his spoon—
it sounded as if it
was entering a
wind
tunnel.

finished with
that
he would wipe his
mouth
with a huge white
napkin,
rubbing hard
in circular
motions,
the napkin almost
hiding his

entire
face.

after that
out came the
Camel
cigarettes.
he'd light one
with a wooden
kitchen match,
then place the
match,
still burning,
onto an
ashtray.

then a slurp of
coffee, the cup
back down, and a good
drag on the
Camel.

"ah that was a
good
meal!"

moments later
in my bedroom
on my bed
in the dark
the food that I
had eaten
and what I had
seen
was already
making me
ill.

the only good
thing
was
listening to
the crickets
out there,
out there
in another world
I didn't
live
in.

● ●

One day, just like in grammar school, like with David, a boy attached himself to me. He was small and thin and had almost no hair on top of his head. The guys called him Baldy. His real name was Eli LaCrosse. I liked his real name, but I didn't like him. He just glued himself to me. He was so pitiful that I couldn't tell him to get lost. He was like a mongrel dog, starved and kicked. Yet it didn't make me feel good going around with him. But since I knew that mongrel dog feeling, I let him hang around. He used a cuss word in almost every sentence, at least one cuss word, but it was all fake, he wasn't tough, he was scared. I wasn't scared but I was confused so maybe we were a good pair.

I walked him back to his place after school every day. He was living with his mother, his father and his grandfather. They had a little house across from a small park. I liked the area, it had great shade trees, and since some people had told me that I was ugly, I always preferred shade to the sun, darkness to light.

During our walks home Baldy had told me about his father. He had been a doctor, a successful surgeon, but he had lost his license because he was a drunk. One day I met Baldy's father. He was sitting in a chair under a tree, just sitting there.

"Dad," he said, "this is Henry."

"Hello, Henry."

It reminded me of when I had seen my grandfather for the first time, standing on the steps of his house. Only Baldy's father had black hair and a black beard, but his eyes were the same—brilliant and glowing, so strange. And here was Baldy, the son, and he didn't glow at all.

"Come on," Baldy said, "follow me."

We went down into a cellar, under the house. It was dark and damp and we stood awhile until our eyes grew used to the gloom. Then I could see a number of barrels.

"These barrels are full of different kinds of wine," Baldy said. "Each barrel has a spigot. Want to try some?"

"No."

"Go ahead, just try a god-damned sip."

"What for?"

"You think you're a god-damned man or what?"

"I'm tough," I said.

"Then take a fucking sample."

Here was little Baldy, daring me. No problem. I walked up to a barrel, ducked my head down.

"Turn the god-damned spigot! Open your god-damned mouth!"

"Are there any spiders around here?"

"Go on! Go on, god damn it!"

I put my mouth under the spigot and opened it. A smelly liquid trickled out and into my mouth. I spit it out.

"Don't be chicken! Swallow it, what the shit!"

I opened the spigot and I opened my mouth. The smelly liquid entered and I swallowed it. I turned off the spigot and stood there. I thought I was going to puke.

"Now, you drink some," I said to Baldy.

"Sure," he said, "I ain't fucking afraid!"

He got down under a barrel and took a good swallow. A little punk like that wasn't going to outdo me. I got under another barrel, opened it and took a swallow. I stood up. I was beginning to feel good.

"Hey, Baldy," I said, "I like this stuff."

"Well, shit, try some more."

I tried some more. It was tasting better. I was feeling better.

"This stuff belongs to your father, Baldy. I shouldn't drink it all."

"He doesn't care. He's stopped drinking."

Never had I felt so good. It was better than masturbating.

I went from barrel to barrel. It was magic. Why hadn't someone told me? With this, life was great, a man was perfect, nothing could touch him.

I stood up straight and looked at Baldy.

"Where's your mother? I'm going to fuck your mother!"

"I'll kill you, you bastard, you stay away from my mother!"

"You know I can whip you, Baldy."

"Yes."

"All right, I'll leave your mother alone."

"Let's go then, Henry."

"One more drink . . . "

I went to a barrel and took a long one. Then we went up the cellar stairway. When we were out, Baldy's father was still sitting in his chair.

"You boys been in the wine cellar, eh?"

"Yes," said Baldy.

"Starting a little early, aren't you?"

We didn't answer. We walked over to the boulevard and Baldy and I went into a store which sold chewing gum. We bought several packs of it and stuck it into our mouths. He was worried about his mother finding out. I wasn't worried about anything. We sat on a park bench and chewed the gum and I thought, well, now I have found something, I have found something that is going to help me, for a long long time to come. The park grass looked greener, the park benches looked better and the flowers were trying harder. Maybe that stuff wasn't good for surgeons but anybody who wanted to be a surgeon, there was something wrong with them in the first place.

—*HAM ON RYE*

love poem to a stripper

• •

50 years ago I watched the girls
shake it and strip
at The Burbank and The Follies
and it was very sad
and very dramatic

as the light turned from green to
purple to pink
and the music was loud and
vibrant,
now I sit here tonight
smoking and
listening to classical
music
but I still remember some of
their names: Darlene, Candy, Jeanette
and Rosalie.
Rosalie was the
best, she knew how,
and we twisted in our seats and
made sounds
as Rosalie brought magic
to the lonely
so long ago.

now Rosalie
either so very old or
so quiet under the
earth,
this is the pimple-faced
kid
who lied about his
age
just to watch
you.

you were good, Rosalie
in 1935,
good enough to remember
now
when the light is
yellow
and the nights are
slow.

• •

Jr. high went by quickly enough. About the eighth grade, going into the ninth, I broke out with acne. Many of the guys had it but not like mine. Mine was really terrible. I was the worst case in town. I had pimples and boils all over my face, back, neck, and some on my chest. It happened just as I was beginning to be accepted as a tough guy and a leader. I was still tough but it wasn't the same. I had to withdraw. I watched people from afar, it was like a stage play. Only they were on stage and I was an audience of one. I'd always had trouble with the girls but with acne it was impossible. The girls were further away than ever. Some of them were truly beautiful—their dresses, their hair, their eyes, the way they stood around. Just to walk down the street during an afternoon with one, you know, talking about everything and anything, I think that would have made me feel very good.

Also, there was still something about me that continually got me into trouble. Most teachers didn't trust or like me, especially the lady teachers. I never said anything out of the way but they claimed it was my "attitude." It was something about the way I sat slouched in my seat and my "voice tone." I was usually accused of "sneering" although I wasn't conscious of it. I was often made to stand outside in the hall during class or I was sent to the principal's office. The principal always did the same thing. He had a phone booth in his office. He made me stand in the phone booth with the door closed. I spent many hours in that phone booth. The only reading material in there was the *Ladies Home Journal*. It was deliberate torture. I read the *Ladies Home Journal* anyhow. I got to read each new issue. I hoped that maybe I could learn something about women.

I must have had 5,000 demerits by graduation time but it didn't seem to matter. They wanted to get rid of me. I was standing outside in the line that was filing into the auditorium one by one. We each had on our cheap little cap and gown that had been passed down again and again to the next graduating group. We could hear each person's name as they walked across the stage. They were making one big god-damned deal out of graduating from jr. high. The band played our school song:

Oh, Mt. Justin, Oh, Mt. Justin
We will be true,
Our hearts are singing wildly
All our skies are blue . . .

We stood in line, each of us waiting to march across the stage. In the audience were our parents and friends.

"I'm about to puke," said one of the guys.

"We only go from crap to more crap," said another.

The girls seemed to be more serious about it. That's why I didn't really trust them. They seemed to be part of the wrong things. They and the school seemed to have the same song.

"This stuff brings me down," said one of the guys. "I wish I had a smoke."

"Here you are . . . "

Another of the guys handed him a cigarette. We passed it around between four or five of us. I took a hit and exhaled through my nostrils. Then I saw Curly Wagner walking in.

"Ditch it!" I said. "Here comes vomit-head!"

Wagner walked right up to me. He was dressed in his grey gym suit, including sweatshirt, just as he had been the first time I saw him and all the other times afterward. He stood in front of me.

"Listen," he said, "you think you're getting away from me because you're getting out of here, but you're not! I'm going to follow you the rest of your life. I'm going to follow you to the ends of the earth and I'm going to get you!"

I just glanced at him without comment and he walked off. Wagner's little graduation speech only made me that much bigger with the guys. They thought I must have done some big god-damned thing to rile him. But it wasn't true. Wagner was just simple-crazy.

We got nearer and nearer to the doorway of the auditorium. Not only could we hear each name being announced, and the applause, but we could see the audience.

Then it was my turn.

"Henry Chinaski," the principal said over the microphone. And I walked forward. There was no applause. Then one kindly soul in the audience gave two or three claps.

There were rows of seats set up on the stage for the graduating class.

We sat there and waited. The principal gave his speech about opportunity and success in America. Then it was all over. The band struck up the Mt. Justin school song. The students and their parents and friends rose and mingled together. I walked around, looking. My parents weren't there. I made sure. I walked around and gave it a good look-see.

It was just as well. A tough guy didn't need that. I took off my ancient cap and gown and handed it to the guy at the end of the aisle— the janitor. He folded the pieces up for the next time.

I walked outside. The first one out. But where could I go? I had 11 cents in my pocket. I walked back to where I lived.

—*HAM ON RYE*

waiting

• •

hot summers in the mid-30's in Los Angeles
where every 3rd lot was vacant
and it was a short ride to the orange
groves—
if you had a car and the
gas.

hot summers in the mid-30's in Los Angeles
too young to be a man and too old to
be a boy.

hard times.
a neighbor tried to rob our
house, my father caught him
climbing through the
window,
held him there in the dark
on the floor:
"you rotten son of a
bitch!"

"Henry, Henry, let me go,
let me go!"

"you son of a bitch, I'll kill
you!"

my mother phoned the police.

another neighbor set his house on fire
in an attempt to collect the
insurance.
he was investigated and
jailed.

hot summers in the mid-30's in Los Angeles,
nothing to do, nowhere to go, listening to
the terrified talk of our parents
at night:
"what will we do? what will we
do?"

"god, I don't know . . . "

starving dogs in the alleys, skin taut
across ribs, hair falling out, tongues
out, such sad eyes, sadder than any sadness
on earth.

hot summers in the mid-30's in Los Angeles,
the men of the neighborhood were quiet
and the women were like pale
statues.

the parks full of socialists,
communists, anarchists, standing on the park
benches, orating, agitating.
the sun came down through a clear sky and
the ocean was clean

and we were
neither men nor
boys.

we fed the dogs leftover pieces of dry hard
bread
which they ate gratefully,
eyes shining in
wonder,
tails waving at such
luck

as
World War II moved toward us,
even then, during those
hot summers in the mid-30's in Los Angeles.

• •

That summer, July 1934, they gunned down John Dillinger outside
the movie house in Chicago. He never had a chance. The Lady in Red
had fingered him. More than a year earlier the banks had collapsed. Pro-
hibition was repealed and my father drank Eastside beer again. But the
worst thing was Dillinger getting it. A lot of people admired Dillinger and
it made everybody feel terrible. Roosevelt was President. He gave Fire-
side Chats over the radio and everybody listened. He could really talk.
And he began to enact programs to put people to work. But things were
still very bad. And my boils got worse, they were unbelievably large.

That September I was scheduled to go to Woodhaven High but my
father insisted I go to Chelsey High.

"Look," I told him, "Chelsey is out of this district. It's too far away."

"You'll do as I tell you. You'll register at Chelsey High."

I knew why he wanted me to go to Chelsey. The rich kids went
there. My father was crazy. He still thought about being rich. When

Baldy found out I was going to Chelsey he decided to go there too. I couldn't get rid of him or my boils.

The first day we rode our bikes to Chelsey and parked them. It was a terrible feeling. Most of those kids, at least all the older ones, had their own automobiles, many of them new convertibles, and they weren't black or dark blue like most cars, they were bright yellow, green, orange and red. The guys sat in them outside of the school and the girls gathered around and went for rides. Everybody was nicely dressed, the guys and the girls, they had pullover sweaters, wrist watches and the latest in shoes. They seemed very adult and poised and superior. And there I was in my homemade shirt, my one ragged pair of pants, my rundown shoes, and I was covered with boils. The guys with the cars didn't worry about acne. They were very handsome, they were tall and clean with bright teeth and they didn't wash their hair with hand soap. They seemed to know something I didn't know. I was at the bottom again.

Since all the guys had cars Baldy and I were ashamed of our bicycles. We left them home and walked to school and back, two-and-one-half miles each way. We carried brown bag lunches. But most of the other students didn't even eat in the school cafeteria. They drove to malt shops with the girls, played the juke boxes and laughed. They were on their way to U.S.C.

I was ashamed of my boils. At Chelsey you had a choice between gym and R.O.T.C. I took R.O.T.C. because then I didn't have to wear a gym suit and nobody could see the boils on my body. But I hated the uniform. The shirt was made of wool and it irritated my boils. The uniform was worn from Monday to Thursday. On Friday we were allowed to wear regular clothes.

We studied the Manual of Arms. It was about warfare and shit like that. We had to pass exams. We marched around the field. We practiced the Manual of Arms. Handling the rifle during various drills was bad for me. I had boils on my shoulders. Sometimes when I slammed the rifle against my shoulder a boil would break and leak through my shirt. The blood would come through but because the shirt was thick and made of wool the spot wasn't obvious and didn't look like blood.

I told my mother what was happening. She lined the shoulders of my shirts with white patches of cloth, but it only helped a little.

Once an officer came through on inspection. He grabbed the rifle out of my hands and held it up, peering through the barrel, for dust in the bore. He slammed the rifle back at me, then looked at a blood spot on my right shoulder.

"Chinaski!" he snapped, "your rifle is leaking oil!"

"Yes, sir."

I got through the term but the boils got worse and worse. They were as large as walnuts and covered my face. I was very ashamed. Sometimes at home I would stand before the bathroom mirror and break one of the boils. Yellow pus would spurt and splatter on the mirror. And little white hard pits. In a horrible way it was fascinating that all that stuff was in there. But I knew how hard it was for other people to look at me.

The school must have advised my father. At the end of that term I was withdrawn from school. I went to bed and my parents covered me with ointments. There was a brown salve that stank. My father preferred that one for me. It burned. He insisted that I keep it on longer, much longer than the instructions advised. One night he insisted that I leave it on for hours. I began screaming. I ran to the tub, filled it with water and washed the salve off, with difficulty. I was burned, on my face, my back and chest. That night I sat on the edge of the bed. I couldn't lay down.

My father came into the room.

"I thought I told you to leave that stuff on!"

"Look what happened," I told him.

My mother came into the room.

"The son-of-a-bitch doesn't *want* to get well," my father told her. "Why did I have to have a son like this?"

My mother lost her job. My father kept leaving in his car every morning as if he were going to work. "I'm an engineer," he told people. He had always wanted to be an engineer.

It was arranged for me to go to the L.A. County General Hospital. I was given a long white card. I took the white card and got on the #7 streetcar. The fare was seven cents (or four tokens for a quarter). I dropped in my token and walked to the back of the streetcar. I had an 8:30 a.m. appointment.

A few blocks later a young boy and a woman got on the streetcar. The woman was fat and the boy was about four years old. They sat in the seat behind me. I looked out the window. We rolled along. I liked that #7 streetcar. It went really fast and rocked back and forth as the sun shone outside.

"Mommy," I heard the young boy say. "What's *wrong* with that man's face?"

The woman didn't answer.

The boy asked her the same question again.

She didn't answer.

Then the boy screamed it out, *"Mommy! What's wrong with that man's face?"*

"Shut up! I don't know what's wrong with his face!"

I went to Admissions at the hospital and they instructed me to report to the fourth floor. There the nurse at the desk took my name and told me to be seated. We sat in two long rows of green metal chairs facing one another. Mexicans, whites and blacks. There were no Orientals. There was nothing to read. Some of the patients had day-old newspapers. The people were of all ages, thin and fat, short and tall, old and young. Nobody talked. Everybody seemed very tired. Orderlies walked back and forth, sometimes you saw a nurse, but never a doctor. An hour went by, two hours. Nobody's name was called. I got up to look for a water fountain. I looked in the little rooms where people were to be examined. There wasn't anybody in any of the rooms, neither doctors or patients.

I went to the desk. The nurse was staring down into a big fat book with names written in it. The phone rang. She answered it.

"Dr. Menen isn't here yet." She hung up.

"Pardon me," I said.

"Yes?" the nurse asked.

"The doctors aren't here yet. Can I come back later?"

"No."

"But there's nobody here."

"The doctors are on call."

"But I have an 8:30 appointment."

"Everybody here has an 8:30 appointment."

There were 45 or 50 people waiting.

"Since I'm on the waiting list, suppose I come back in a couple of hours, maybe there will be some doctors here then."

"If you leave now, you will automatically lose your appointment. You will have to return tomorrow if you still wish treatment."

I walked back and sat in a chair. The others didn't protest. There was very little movement. Sometimes two or three nurses would walk by laughing. Once they pushed a man past in a wheelchair. Both of his legs were heavily bandaged and his ear on the side of his head toward me had been sliced off. There was a black hole divided into little sections, and it looked like a spider had gone in there and made a spider web. Hours passed. Noon came and went. Another hour. Two hours. We sat and waited. Then somebody said, "There's a doctor!"

The doctor walked into one of the examination rooms and closed the door. We all watched. Nothing. A nurse went in. We heard her laughing. Then she walked out. Five minutes. Ten minutes. The doctor walked out with a clipboard in his hand.

"Martinez?" the doctor asked. "José Martinez?"

An old thin Mexican man stood up and began walking toward the doctor.

"Martinez? Martinez, old boy, how are you?"

"Sick, doctor . . . I think I die . . . "

"Well, now . . . Step in here . . . "

Martinez was in there a long time. I picked up a discarded newspaper and tried to read it. But we were all thinking about Martinez. If Martinez ever got out of there, someone would be next.

Then Martinez screamed. "AHHHHH! AHHHHH! STOP! STOP! AHHHH! MERCY! GOD! PLEASE STOP!"

"Now, now, that doesn't hurt . . . " said the doctor.

Martinez screamed again. A nurse ran into the examination room. There was silence. All we could see was the black shadow of the half-open doorway. Then an orderly ran into the examination room. Martinez made a gurgling sound. He was taken out of there on a rolling stretcher. The nurse and the orderly pushed him down the hall and through some swinging doors. Martinez was under a sheet but he wasn't dead because the sheet wasn't pulled over his face.

The doctor stayed in the examination room for another ten minutes. Then he came out with the clipboard.

"Jefferson Williams?" he asked.

There was no answer.

"Is Jefferson Williams here?"

There was no response.

"Mary Blackthorne?"

There was no answer.

"Harry Lewis?"

"Yes, doctor?"

"Step forward, please . . . "

It was very slow. The doctor saw five more patients. Then he left the examination room, stopped at the desk, lit a cigarette and talked to the nurse for fifteen minutes. He looked like a very intelligent man. He had a twitch on the right side of his face, which kept jumping, and he had red hair with streaks of grey. He wore glasses and kept taking them off and putting them back on. Another nurse came in and gave him a cup of coffee. He took a sip, then holding the coffee in one hand he pushed the swinging doors open with the other and was gone.

The office nurse came out from behind the desk with our long white cards and she called our names. As we answered, she handed each of us our card back. "This ward is closed for the day. Please return tomorrow if you wish. Your appointment time is stamped on your card."

I looked down at my card. It was stamped 8:30 a.m.

—*HAM ON RYE*

• •

It was like a wood drill, it might have been a wood drill, I could smell the oil burning, and they'd stick that thing into my head into my flesh and it would drill and bring up blood and pus, and I'd sit there the monkey of my soul-string dangling over the edge of a cliff. I was covered with boils the size of small apples. It was ridiculous and unbelievable. Worst case I ever saw, said one of the docs, and he was old. They'd gather around me like some freak. I was a freak. I'm still a freak. I rode the streetcar back and forth to the charity ward. Children on streetcars would stare and ask their mothers, "What's wrong with that man? Mother, what's wrong with that man's *face?*" And the mother would SHU-USSSHHH!!! That shuusssshhh was the worst condemnation, and then they'd continue to let the little bastards and bastardesses stare from over the backs of their seats and I'd look out the window and watch the buildings go by, and I'd be drowning, slugged and drowning, nothing to do. The doctors for lack of anything else called it Acne Vulgaris. I'd sit for hours on a wooden bench while waiting for my wood drill. What a pity story, eh? I remember the old brick buildings, the easy and rested nurses, the doctors laughing, having it made. It was there that I learned of the fallacy of hospitals—that the doctors were kings and the patients were shit and the hospitals were there so the doctors could make it in their starched white superiority, they could make it with the nurses too:—Dr. Dr. Dr. pinch my ass in the elevator, forget the stink of cancer, forget the stink of life. We are not the poor fools, we will never die; we drink our carrot juice, and when we feel bad we can take a pop, a needle, all the dope we need. Cheep, cheep, cheep, life will sing for us, Big-Time us. I'd go in and sit down and they'd put the drill into me. ZIRRRR ZIRRRR ZIRRRR, ZIR, the sun meanwhile raising dahlias and oranges and shining through nurses' dresses driving the poor freaks mad. Zirrrrrrr, zirrr, zirr.

"Never saw *anybody* go under the needle like that!"

"Look at him, cold as steel!"

Again a gathering of nurse-fuckers, a gathering of men who owned big homes and had time to laugh and to read and go to plays and buy paintings and forget how to think, forget how to feel anything. White starch and my defeat. The gathering.

"How do you feel?"

"Wonderful."

"Don't you find the needle painful?"

"Fuck you."

"What?"

"I said—fuck you."

"He's just a boy. He's bitter. Can't blame him. How old are you?"

"Fourteen."

"I was only praising you for your courage, the way you took the needle. You're tough."

"Fuck you."

"You can't talk to me that way."

"Fuck you. Fuck you. Fuck you."

"You ought to bear up better. Supposing you were blind?"

"Then I wouldn't have to look at your goddamned face."

"The kid's crazy."

"Sure he is, leave him alone."

That was some hospital and I never realized that 20 years later I'd be back, again in the charity ward. Hospitals and jails and whores: these are the universities of life. I've got several degrees. Call me Mr.

—*SOUTH OF NO NORTH*

• •

The ultra-violet ray machine clicked off. I had been treated on both sides. I took off the goggles and began to dress. Miss Ackerman walked in.

"Not yet," she said, "keep your clothes off."

What is she going to do to me, I thought?

"Sit up on the edge of the table."

I sat there and she began rubbing salve over my face. It was a thick buttery substance.

"The doctors have decided on a new approach. We're going to bandage your face to effect drainage."

"Miss Ackerman, what ever happened to that man with the big nose? The nose that kept growing?"

"Mr. Sleeth?"

"The man with the big nose."

"That was Mr. Sleeth."

"I don't see him anymore. Did he get cured?"

"He's dead."

"You mean he died from that big nose?"

"Suicide." Miss Ackerman continued to apply the salve.

Then I heard a man scream from the next ward, *"Joe, where are you? Joe, you said you'd come back! Joe, where are you?"*

The voice was loud and so sad, so agonized.

"He's done that every afternoon this week," said Miss Ackerman, "and Joe's not going to come get him."

"Can't they help him?"

"I don't know. They all quiet down, finally. Now take your finger and hold this pad while I bandage you. There. Yes. That's it. Now let go. Fine."

"Joe! Joe, you said you'd come back! Where are you, Joe?"

"Now, hold your finger on this pad. There. Hold it there. I'm going to wrap you up good! There. Now I'll secure the dressings."

Then she was finished.

"O.K., put on your clothes. See you the day after tomorrow. Good-bye, Henry."

"Goodbye, Miss Ackerman."

I got dressed, left the room and walked down the hall. There was a mirror on a cigarette machine in the lobby. I looked into the mirror. It was great. My whole head was bandaged. I was all white. Nothing could be seen but my eyes, my mouth and my ears, and some tufts of hair sticking up at the top of my head. I was *hidden*. It was wonderful. I stood and lit a cigarette and glanced about the lobby. Some in-patients were sitting about reading magazines and newspapers. I felt very exceptional and a bit evil. Nobody had any idea of what had happened to me. Car crash. A fight to the death. A murder. Fire. Nobody knew.

I walked out of the lobby and out of the building and I stood on the sidewalk. I could still hear him. *"Joe! Joe! Where are you, Joe!"*

Joe wasn't coming. It didn't pay to trust another human being. Humans didn't have it, whatever it took.

On the streetcar ride back I sat in the back smoking cigarettes out of my bandaged head. People stared but I didn't care. There was more fear than horror in their eyes now. I hoped I could stay this way forever.

I rode to the end of the line and got off. The afternoon was going into evening and I stood on the corner of Washington Boulevard and Westview Avenue watching the people. Those few who had jobs were coming home from work. My father would soon be driving home from his fake job. I didn't have a job, I didn't go to school. I didn't do anything. I was bandaged, I was standing on the corner smoking a cigarette. I was a tough man, I was a dangerous man. I knew things. Sleeth had suicided. I wasn't going to suicide. I'd rather kill some of them. I'd take four or five of them with me. I'd show them what it meant to play around with me.

A woman walked down the street toward me. She had fine legs. First I stared right into her eyes and then I looked down at her legs, and as she passed I watched her ass, I drank her ass in. I memorized her ass and the seams of her silk stockings.

I never could have done that without my bandage

• • •

The bandages were helpful. L.A. County Hospital had finally come up with something. The boils drained. They didn't vanish but they flattened a bit. Yet some new ones would appear and rise up again. They drilled me and wrapped me again.

My sessions with the drill were endless. Thirty-two, thirty-six, thirty-eight times. There was no fear of the drill anymore. There never had been. Only an anger. But the anger was gone. There wasn't even resignation on my part, only disgust, a disgust that this had happened to me, and a disgust with the doctors who couldn't do anything about it. They were helpless and I was helpless, the only difference being that I was the victim. They could go home to their lives and forget while I was stuck with the same face.

But there were changes in my life. My father found a job. He passed an examination at the L.A. County Museum and got a job as a guard. My father was good at exams. He loved math and history. He passed the exam and finally had a place to go each morning. There had been three vacancies for guards and he had gotten one of them.

L.A. County General Hospital somehow found out and Miss Ackerman told me one day, "Henry, this is your last treatment. I'm going to miss you."

"Aw come on," I said, "stop your kidding. You're going to miss me like I'm going to miss that electric needle!"

But she was very strange that day. Those big eyes were watery. I heard her blow her nose.

I heard one of the nurses ask her, "Why, Janice, what's wrong with you?"

"Nothing. I'm all right."

Poor Miss Ackerman. I was 15 years old and in love with her and I was covered with boils and there was nothing that either of us could do.

"All right," she said, "this is going to be your last ultra-violet ray treatment. Lay on your stomach."

"I know your first name now," I told her. "Janice. That's a pretty name. It's just like you."

"Oh, shut up," she said.

I saw her once again when the first buzzer sounded. I turned over, Janice re-set the machine and left the room. I never saw her again.

• • •

My father didn't believe in doctors who were not free. "They make you piss in a tube, take your money, and drive home to their wives in Beverly Hills," he said.

But once he did send me to one. To a doctor with bad breath and a head as round as a basketball, only with two little eyes where a basketball had none. I didn't like my father and the doctor wasn't any better. He said, no fried foods, and to drink carrot juice. That was it.

I would re-enter high school the next term, said my father.

"I'm busting my ass to keep people from stealing. Some nigger broke the glass on a case and stole some rare coins yesterday. I caught the bastard. We rolled down the stairway together. I held him until the others came. I risk my life every day. Why should you sit around on your ass, moping? I want you to be an engineer. How the hell you gonna be an engineer when I find notebooks full of women with their skirts pulled up to their ass? Is *that* all you can draw? Why don't you draw flowers or mountains or the ocean? You're going back to school!"

I drank carrot juice and waited to re-enroll. I had only missed one term. The boils weren't cured but they weren't as bad as they had been.

—*Ham on Rye*

my old man

• •

16 years old
during the depression
I'd come home drunk
and all my clothing—
shorts, shirts, stockings—
suitcase, and pages of
short stories
would be thrown out on the
front lawn and about the
street.

my mother would be
waiting behind a tree:
"Henry, Henry, don't
go in . . . he'll
kill you, he's read
your stories . . . "

"I can whip his
ass . . . "

"Henry, please take
this . . . and
find yourself a room."

but it worried him
that I might not
finish high school
so I'd be back
again.

one evening he walked in
with the pages of
one of my short stories
(which I had never submitted
to him)
and he said, "this is
a great short story."
I said, "o.k.,"
and he handed it to me
and I read it.
it was a story about
a rich man
who had a fight with
his wife and had
gone out into the night
for a cup of coffee
and had observed
the waitress and the spoons

and forks and the
salt and pepper shakers
and the neon sign
in the window
and then had gone back
to his stable
to see and touch his
favorite horse
who then
kicked him in the head
and killed him.

somehow
the story held
meaning for him
though
when I had written it
I had no idea
of what I was
writing about.

so I told him,
"o.k., old man, you can
have it."

and he took it
and walked out
and closed the door.
I guess that's
as close
as we ever got.

• •

I could see the road ahead of me. I was poor and I was going to stay poor. But I didn't particularly want money. I didn't know what I wanted. Yes, I did. I wanted someplace to hide out, someplace where one didn't have to do anything. The thought of being something didn't only appall me, it sickened me. The thought of being a lawyer or a councilman or an engineer, anything like that, seemed impossible to me. To get married, to have children, to get trapped in the family structure. To go someplace to work every day and to return. It was impossible. To do things, simple things, to be part of family picnics, Christmas, the 4th of July, Labor Day, Mother's Day . . . was a man born just to endure those things and then die? I would rather be a dishwasher, return alone to a tiny room and drink myself to sleep.

My father had a master plan. He told me, "My son, each man during his lifetime should buy a house. Finally he dies and leaves that house to his son. Then his son gets his own house and dies, leaves both houses to *his* son. That's two houses. That son gets his own house, that's three houses . . . "

The family structure. Victory over adversity through the family. He believed in it. Take the family, mix with God and Country, add the ten-hour day and you had what was needed.

I looked at my father, at his hands, his face, his eyebrows, and I knew that this man had nothing to do with me. He was a stranger. My mother was non-existent. I was cursed. Looking at my father I saw nothing but indecent dullness. Worse, he was even more afraid to fail than most others. Centuries of peasant blood and peasant training. The Chinaski bloodline had been thinned by a series of peasant-servants who had surrendered their real lives for fractional and illusionary gains. Not a man in the line who said, "I don't want a house, I want a *thousand* houses, *now!*"

He had sent me to that rich high school hoping that the ruler's atti-tude would rub off on me as I watched the rich boys screech up in their cream-colored coupes and pick up the girls in bright dresses. Instead I learned that the poor usually stay poor. That the young rich smell the stink of the poor and learn to find it a bit amusing. They had to laugh, otherwise it would be too terrifying. They'd learned that, through the centuries. I would never forgive the girls for getting into those cream-colored coupes with the laughing boys. They couldn't help it, of course, yet you always think, maybe . . . But no, there weren't any maybes. Wealth meant victory and victory was the only reality.

What woman chooses to live with a dishwasher?

Throughout high school I tried not to think too much about how things might eventually turn out for me. It seemed better to delay thinking . . .

Finally it was the day of the Senior Prom. It was held in the girls' gym with live music, a real band. I don't know why but I walked over that night, the two-and-one-half miles from my parents' place. I stood outside in the dark and I looked in there, through the wire-covered window, and I was astonished. All the girls looked very grown-up, stately, lovely, they were in long dresses, and they all looked beautiful. I almost didn't recognize them. And the boys in their tuxes, they looked great, they danced so straight, each of them holding a girl in his arms, their faces pressed against the girl's hair. They all danced beautifully and the music was loud and clear and good, powerful.

Then I caught a glimpse of my reflection staring in at them—boils and scars on my face, my ragged shirt. I was like some jungle animal drawn to the light and looking in. Why had I come? I felt sick. But I kept watching. The dance ended. There was a pause. Couples spoke easily to each other. It was natural and civilized. Where had they learned to converse and to dance? I couldn't converse or dance. Everybody knew something I didn't know. The girls looked so good, the boys so handsome. I would be too terrified to even look at one of those girls, let alone be close to one. To look into her eyes or dance with her would be beyond me.

And yet I knew that what I saw wasn't as simple and good as it appeared. There was a price to be paid for it all, a general falsity, that could be easily believed, and could be the first step down a dead-end street. The band began to play again and the boys and girls began to dance again and the lights revolved overhead throwing shades of gold, then red, then blue, then green, then gold again on the couples. As I watched them I said to myself, someday my dance will begin. When that day comes I will have something that they don't have.

But then it got to be too much for me. I hated them. I hated their beauty, their untroubled youth, and as I watched them dance through the magic colored pools of light, holding each other, feeling so good, little unscathed children, temporarily in luck, I hated them because they had something I had not yet had, and I said to myself, I said to myself again, *someday I will be as happy as any of you, you will see.*

They kept dancing, and I repeated it to them.

Then there was a sound behind me.

"Hey! What are you doing?"

It was an old man with a flashlight. He had a head like a frog's head.

"I'm watching the dance."

He held the flashlight right up under his nose. His eyes were round and large, they gleamed like a cat's eyes in the moonlight. But his mouth was shriveled, collapsed, and his head was round. It had a peculiar senseless roundness that reminded me of a pumpkin trying to play pundit.

"Get your ass out of here!"

He ran the flashlight up and down all over me.

"Who are you?" I asked.

"I'm the night custodian. Get your ass out of here before I call the cops!"

"What for? This is the Senior Prom and I'm a senior."

He flashed his light into my face. The band was playing "Deep Purple."

"Bullshit!" he said. "You're at least 22 years old!"

"I'm in the yearbook, Class of 1939, graduating class, Henry Chinaski."

"Why aren't you in there dancing?"

"Forget it. I'm going home."

"Do that."

I walked off. I kept walking. His flashlight leaped on the path, the light following me. I walked off campus. It was a nice warm night, almost hot. I thought I saw some fireflies but I wasn't sure.

—*Ham on Rye*

the burning of the dream

• •

the old L.A. Public Library burned
down
that library downtown
and with it went
a large part of my
youth.

I sat on one of those stone
benches there with my friend
Baldy when he
asked,
"you gonna join the
Abraham Lincoln
Brigade?"

"sure," I told
him.

but realizing that I wasn't
an intellectual or a political
idealist
I backed off on that
one
later.

I was a *reader*
then
going from room to
room: literature, philosophy,
religion, even medicine
and geology.

early on
I decided to be a writer,

I thought it might be the easy
way
out
and the big boy novelists didn't look
too tough to
me.
I had more trouble with
Hegel and Kant.

the thing that bothered
me
about everybody
is that they took so long
to finally say
something lively and/
or
interesting.
I thought I had it
over everybody
then.

I was to discover two
things:
a) most publishers thought that anything
boring had something to do with things
profound.
b) that it would take decades of
living and writing
before I would be able to
put down
a sentence that was
anywhere near
what I wanted it to
be.

meanwhile
while other young men chased the

ladies
I chased the old
books.
I was a bibliophile, albeit a
disenchanted
one
and this
and the world
shaped me.

I lived in a plywood hut
behind a roominghouse
for $3.50 a
week
feeling like a
Chatterton
stuffed inside of some
Thomas
Wolfe.

my greatest problem was
stamps, envelopes, paper
and
wine,
with the world on the edge
of World War II.
I hadn't yet been
confused by the
female, I was a virgin
and I wrote from 3 to
5 short stories a week
and they all came
back
from *The New Yorker, Harper's,
The Atlantic Monthly.*
I had read where
Ford Madox Ford used to paper
his bathroom with his

rejection slips
but I didn't have a
bathroom so I stuck them
into a drawer
and when it got so stuffed with them
I could barely
open it
I took all the rejects out
and threw them
away along with the
stories.

still
the old L.A. Public Library remained
my home
and the home of many other
bums.
we discreetly used the
restrooms
and the only ones of
us
to be evicted were those
who fell asleep at the
library
tables—nobody snores like a
bum
unless it's somebody you're married
to.

well, I wasn't *quite* a
bum. *I* had a library card
and I checked books in and
out
large
stacks of them
always taking the
limit
allowed:

Aldous Huxley, D. H. Lawrence,
e.e. cummings, Conrad Aiken, Fyodor
Dos, Dos Passos, Turgenev, Gorky,
H.D., Freddie Nietzsche,
Schopenhauer,
Steinbeck,
Hemingway,
and so
forth . . .

I always expected the librarian
to say, "you have good taste, young
man . . . "

but the old fried and wasted
bitch didn't even know who she
was
let alone
me.

but those shelves held
tremendous grace: they allowed
me to discover
the early Chinese poets
like Tu Fu and Li
Po
who could say more in one
line than most could say in
thirty or
a hundred.
Sherwood Anderson must have
read
these
too.

I also carried the Cantos
in and out

and Ezra helped me
strengthen my arms if not
my brain.

that wondrous place
the L.A. Public Library
it was a home for a person who had had
a
home of
hell
BROOKS TOO BROAD FOR LEAPING
FAR FROM THE MADDING CROWD
POINT COUNTER POINT
THE HEART IS A LONELY HUNTER

James Thurber
John Fante
Rabelais
de Maupassant

some didn't work for
me: Shakespeare, G. B. Shaw,
Tolstoy, Robert Frost, F. Scott
Fitzgerald

Upton Sinclair worked better for
me
than Sinclair Lewis
and I considered Gogol and
Dreiser complete
fools

but such judgments come more
from a man's
forced manner of living than from
his reason.

the old L.A. Public
most probably kept me from
becoming a
suicide
a bank
robber
a
wife-
beater
a butcher or a
motorcycle policeman
and even though some of these
might be fine
it is
thanks
to my luck
and my way
that this library was
there when I was
young and looking to
hold on to
something
when there seemed very
little
about.

and when I opened the
newspaper
and read of the fire
which
destroyed the
library and most of
its contents

I said to my
wife: "I used to spend my
time
there . . . "

THE PRUSSIAN OFFICER
THE DARING YOUNG MAN ON THE FLYING TRAPEZE
TO HAVE AND HAVE NOT

YOU CAN'T GO HOME AGAIN.

• •

I made practice runs down to skid row to get ready for my future. I didn't like what I saw down there. Those men and women had no special daring or brilliance. They wanted what everybody else wanted. There were also some obvious mental cases down there who were allowed to walk the streets undisturbed. I had noticed that both in the very poor and very rich extremes of society the mad were often allowed to mingle freely. I knew that I wasn't entirely sane. I still knew, as I had as a child, that there was something strange about myself. I felt as if I were destined to be a murderer, a bank robber, a saint, a rapist, a monk, a hermit. I needed an isolated place to hide. Skid row was disgusting. The life of the sane, average man was dull, worse than death. There seemed to be no possible alternative. Education also seemed to be a trap. The little education I had allowed myself had made me more suspicious. What were doctors, lawyers, scientists? They were just men who allowed themselves to be deprived of their freedom to think and act as individuals. I went back to my shack and drank . . .

Sitting there drinking, I considered suicide, but I felt a strange fondness for my body, my life. Scarred as they were, they were mine. I would look into the dresser mirror and grin: if you're going to go, you might as well take eight, or ten or twenty of them with you . . .

It was a Saturday night in December. I was in my room and I drank much more than usual, lighting cigarette after cigarette, thinking of girls and the city and jobs, and of the years ahead. Looking ahead I liked very little of what I saw. I wasn't a misanthrope and I wasn't a misogynist but I liked being alone. It felt good to sit alone in a small space and smoke and drink. I had always been good company for myself.

• • •

Then I heard the radio in the next room. The guy had it on too loud. It was a sickening love song.

"Hey, buddy!" I hollered, "turn that thing down!"
There was no response.
I walked to the wall and pounded on it.
"I SAID, 'TURN THAT FUCKING THING DOWN!'"
The volume remained the same.
I walked outside to his door. I was in my shorts. I raised my leg and jammed my foot into the door. It burst open. There were two people on the cot, an old fat guy and an old fat woman. They were fucking. There was a small candle burning. The old guy was on top. He stopped and turned his head and looked. She looked up from underneath him. The place was very nicely fixed-up with curtains and a little rug.
"Oh, I'm sorry . . ."
I closed their door and went back to my place. I felt terrible. The poor had a right to fuck their way through their bad dreams. Sex and drink, and maybe love, was all they had.
I sat back down and poured a glass of wine. I left my door open. The moonlight came in with the sounds of the city: juke boxes, automobiles, curses, dogs barking, radios . . . We were all in it together. We were all in one big shit pot together. There was no escape. We were all going to be flushed away.
A small cat walked by, stopped at my door and looked in. The eyes were lit by the moon: pure red like fire. Such wonderful eyes.
"Come on, kitty . . . " I held my hand out as if there were food in it. "Kitty, kitty . . . "
The cat walked on by.
I heard the radio in the next room shut off.
I finished my wine and went outside. I was in my shorts as before. I pulled them up and tucked in my parts. I stood before the other door. I had broken the lock. I could see the light from the candle inside. They had the door wedged closed with something, probably a chair.
I knocked quietly.
There was no answer.
I knocked again.
I heard something. Then the door opened.

The old fat guy stood there. His face was hung with great folds of sorrow. He was all eyebrows and mustache and two sad eyes.

"Listen," I said, "I'm very sorry for what I did. Won't you and your girl come over to my place for a drink?"

"No."

"Or maybe I can bring you both something to drink?"

"No," he said, "please leave us alone."

He closed the door.

I awakened with one of my worst hangovers. I usually slept until noon. This day I couldn't. I dressed and went to the bathroom in the main house and made my toilet. I came back out, went up the alley and then down the stairway, down the cliff and into the street below.

Sunday, the worst god-damned day of them all.

I walked over to Main Street, past the bars. The B-girls sat near the doorways, their skirts pulled high, swinging their legs, wearing high heels.

"Hey, honey, come on in!"

Main Street, East 5th, Bunker Hill. Shitholes of America.

There was no place to go. I walked into a Penny Arcade. I walked around looking at the games but had no desire to play any of them. Then I saw a Marine at a pinball machine. Both his hands gripped the sides of the machine, as he tried to guide the ball with body-English. I walked up and grabbed him by the back of his collar and his belt.

"Becker, I demand a god-damned rematch!"

I let go of him and he turned.

"No, nothing doing," he said.

"Two out of three."

"Balls," he said, "I'll buy you a drink."

We walked out of the Penny Arcade and down Main Street. A B-girl hollered out from one of the bars, "Hey, Marine, come on in!"

Becker stopped. "I'm going in," he said.

"Don't," I said, "they are human roaches."

"I just got paid."

"The girls drink tea and they water your drinks. The prices are double and you never see the girl afterward."

"I'm going in."

Becker walked in. One of the best unpublished writers in America, dressed to kill and to die. I followed him. He walked up to one of the girls and spoke to her. She pulled her skirt up, swung her high heels and laughed. They walked over to a booth in a corner. The bartender came around the bar to take their order. The other girl at the bar looked at me.

"Hey, honey, don't you wanna play?"

"Yeah, but only when it's my game."

"You scared or queer?"

"Both," I said, sitting at the far end of the bar.

There was a guy between us, his head on the bar. His wallet was gone. When he awakened and complained, he'd either be thrown out by the bartender or handed over to the police.

After serving Becker and the B-girl the bartender came back behind the bar and walked over to me.

"Yeh?"

"Nothing."

"Yeh? What ya want in here?"

"I'm waiting for my friend," I nodded at the corner booth.

"You sit here, you gotta drink."

"O.K. Water."

The bartender went off, came back, set down a glass of water.

"Two bits."

I paid him.

The girl at the bar said to the bartender, "He's queer or scared."

The bartender didn't say anything. Then Becker waved to him and he went to take their order.

The girl looked at me. "How come you ain't in uniform?"

"I don't like to dress like everybody else."

"Are there any other reasons?"

"The other reasons are my own business."

"Fuck you," she said.

The bartender came back. "You need another drink."

"O.K.," I said, slipping another quarter toward him.

We found another bar near the bus depot. It wasn't a hustle joint. There was just a barkeep and five or six travelers, all men. Becker and I sat down.

"It's on me," said Becker.

"Eastside in the bottle."

Becker ordered two. He looked at me.

"Come on, be a man, join up. Be a Marine."

"I don't get any thrill trying to be a man."

"Seems to me you're always beating up on somebody."

"That's just for entertainment."

"Join up. It'll give you something to write about."

"Becker, there's always something to write about."

"What are you gonna do, then?"

I pointed at my bottle, picked it up.

"How are ya gonna make it?" Becker asked.

"Seems like I've heard that question all my life."

"Well, I don't know about you but I'm going to try everything! War, women, travel, marriage, children, the works. The first car I own I'm going to take it completely apart! Then I'm going to put it back together again! I want to know about things, what makes them work! I'd like to be a correspondent in Washington, D.C. I'd like to be where big things are happening."

"Washington's crap, Becker."

"And women? Marriage? Children?"

"Crap."

"Yeah? Well, what do you want?"

"To hide."

"You poor fuck. You need another beer."

"All right."

The beer arrived.

We sat quietly. I could sense that Becker was off on his own, thinking about being a Marine, about being a writer, about getting laid. He'd probably make a good writer. He was bursting with enthusiasms. He probably loved many things: the hawk in flight, the god-damned ocean, full moon, Balzac, bridges, stage plays, the Pulitzer Prize, the piano, the god-damned Bible.

There was a small radio in the bar. There was a popular song playing. Then in the middle of the song there was an interruption. The announcer said, "A bulletin has just come in. The Japanese have bombed Pearl Harbor. I repeat: The Japanese have just bombed Pearl Harbor. All military personnel are requested to return immediately to their bases!"

We looked at each other, hardly able to understand what we'd just heard.

"Well," said Becker quietly, "that's it."

"Finish your beer," I told him.

Becker took a hit.

"Jesus, suppose some stupid son-of-a-bitch points a machine gun at me and pulls the trigger?"

"That could well happen."

"Hank . . . "

"What?"

"Will you ride back to the base with me on the bus?"

"I can't do that."

The bartender, a man about 45 with a watermelon gut and fuzzy eyes, walked over to us. He looked at Becker. "Well, Marine, it looks like you gotta go back to your base, huh?"

That pissed me. "Hey, fat boy, let him finish his drink, O.K.?"

"Sure, sure . . . Want a drink on the house, Marine? How about a shot of good whiskey?"

"No," said Becker, "it's all right."

"Go ahead," I told Becker, "take the drink. He figures you're going to die to save his bar."

"All right," said Becker, "I'll take the drink."

The barkeep looked at Becker.

"You got a nasty friend . . . "

"Just give him his drink," I said.

The other few customers were babbling wildly about Pearl Harbor. Before, they wouldn't speak to each other. Now they were mobilized. The Tribe was in danger.

Becker got his drink. It was a double shot of whiskey. He drank it down.

"I never told you this," he said, "but I'm an orphan."

"God damn," I said.

"Will you at least come to the bus depot with me?"

"Sure."

We got up and walked toward the door.

The barkeep was rubbing his hands all over his apron. He had his apron all bunched up and was excitedly rubbing his hand on it.

"Good luck, Marine!" he hollered.

Becker walked out. I paused inside the door and looked back at the barkeep.

"World War I, eh?"

"Yeh, yeh . . . " he said happily.

I caught up with Becker. We half-ran to the bus depot together. Servicemen in uniform were already beginning to arrive. The whole place had an air of excitement. A sailor ran past.

"I'M GOING TO KILL ME A JAP!" he screamed.

Becker stood in the ticket line. One of the servicemen had his girlfriend with him. The girl was talking, crying, holding on to him, kissing him. Poor Becker only had me. I stood to one side, waiting. It was a long wait. The same sailor who had screamed earlier came up to me. "Hey, fellow, aren't you going to help us? What're you standing there for? Why don't you go down and sign up?"

There was whiskey on his breath. He had freckles and a very large nose.

"You're going to miss your bus," I told him.

He went off toward the bus departure point.

"Fuck the god-damned fucking Japs!" he said.

Becker finally had his ticket. I walked him to his bus. He stood in another line.

"Any advice?" he asked.

"No."

The line was filing slowly into the bus. The girl was weeping and talking rapidly and quietly to her soldier.

Becker was at the door. I punched him on the shoulder. "You're the best I've known."

"Thanks, Hank . . . "

"Goodbye . . . "

—*HAM ON RYE*

The Loser

• •

and the next I remembered I'm on a table,
everybody's gone: the head of bravery
under light, scowling, flailing me down . . .
and then some toad stood there, smoking a cigar:

"Kid you're no fighter," he told me,
and I got up and knocked him over a chair;
it was like a scene in a movie, and
he stayed there on his big rump and said
over and over: "Jesus, Jesus, whatsamatta wit
you?" and I got up and dressed,
the tape still on my hands, and when I got home
I tore the tape off my hands and
wrote my first poem,
and I've been fighting
ever since.

The Life of a Bum

Harry awakened in his bed, hungover. Badly hungover.
"Shit," he said lightly.
There was a small sink in the room.
Harry got up, relieved himself in the sink, washed it away with the spigot, then he stuck his head under there and drank some water. Then he splashed water on his face and dried off with a portion of the undershirt he was wearing.
The year was 1943.
Harry picked some clothing up off the floor and slowly began to dress. The shades were down and it was dark except where the sunlight slipped in through the torn shades. There were *two* windows. A class place.
He walked down the hall to the bathroom, locked the door and sat down. It was amazing that he could still excrete. He hadn't eaten for days.
Christ, he thought, people have intestines, mouths, lungs, ears, bellybuttons, sexual parts, and . . . hair, pores, tongues, sometimes teeth, and all the other parts . . . fingernails, eyelashes, toes, knees, stomachs . . .
There was something so *weary* about all that. Why didn't anybody complain?
Harry finished with the rough roominghouse toilet paper. You can

bet the landladies wiped themselves with something better. All those religious landladies with their long-dead husbands.

He pulled up his pants, flushed, walked out of there, down the roominghouse stairway and into the street.

It was 11 a.m. He walked south. The hangover was brutal but he didn't mind. It told him he had been somewhere else, someplace good. As he walked along he found half a cigarette in his shirt pocket. He stopped, looked at the crushed and blackened end, found a match, then tried to light up. The flame didn't catch. He kept trying. After the fourth match, which burned his fingers, he was able to get a puff. He gagged, then coughed. He felt his stomach quiver.

A car came driving by swiftly. It was filled with four young men.

"HEY, YOU OLD FART! DIE!" one of them screamed at Harry.

The others laughed. Then they were gone.

Harry's cigarette was still lit. He took another drag. A curl of blue smoke rose. He liked that curl of blue smoke.

He walked along in the warm sun thinking, I am walking and I am smoking a cigarette.

Harry walked until he got to the park across from the library. He kept dragging on the cigarette. Then he felt the heat from the butt and reluctantly tossed it away. He entered the park and walked until he found a place between a statue and some brush. The statue was of Beethoven. And Beethoven was walking, head bowed, hands clasped behind him, obviously thinking of something.

Harry got down and stretched out on the grass. The mowed grass itched quite a bit. It was pointed, sharp, but it had a good clean smell. The smell of peace.

Tiny insects began to swarm about his face, making irregular circles, crossing each other's paths but never colliding.

They were only specks but the specks were searching for something.

Harry looked up through the specks at the sky. The sky was blue, and tall as hell. Harry kept looking up at the sky, trying to get something straight. But Harry got nothing. No feeling of eternity. Or God. Not even the Devil. But you had to find God first in order to find the Devil. They came in that order.

Harry didn't like heavy thoughts. Heavy thoughts could lead to heavy errors.

He thought a little bit about suicide then . . . in an easy way. Like most men would think about buying a new pair of shoes. The main problem with suicide was the thought that it might lead to something worse. What he really needed was an ice cold bottle of beer, the label soaked just so, and with those chilled beads so beautiful on the surface of the glass.

Harry began to doze . . . to be awakened by the sound of voices. The voices of very young school girls. They were giggling, laughing.

"Ooooh, look!"

"He's asleep!"

"Should we wake him up?"

Harry squinted in the sun, peeking at them through nearly-closed eyes. He wasn't sure how many there were but he saw their colorful dresses: yellow and red and blue and green.

"Look! He's beautiful!"

They giggled, laughed, ran off.

Harry closed his eyes again.

What had that been about?

Nothing so refreshingly delightful had ever happened to him before. They had called him "beautiful." Such kindness!

But they wouldn't be back.

He got up and walked to the edge of the park. There was the avenue. He found a park bench and sat down. There was another bum on the next bench. He was much older than Harry. The bum had a heavy, dark, grim feel about him which reminded Harry of his father.

No, thought Harry, I'm being unkind.

The bum glanced toward Harry. The bum had tiny blank eyes.

Harry gave him a slight smile. The bum turned away.

Then some noise came from the avenue. Engines. It was an army convoy. A long line of trucks filled with soldiers. The soldiers brimmed over, they were packed in, they hung out over the sides of the trucks. The world was at war.

The convoy moved slowly. The soldiers saw Harry sitting on the park bench. Then it began. It was an admixture of hissing, booing and cursing. They were screaming at him.

"HEY, YOU SON OF A BITCH!"

"SLACKER!"

As each truck in the convoy passed, the next truck picked it up:

"GET YOUR ASS OFF THAT BENCH!"

"COWARD!"

"FUCKING FAGGOT!"

"YELLOW BELLY!"

It was a very long and a very slow convoy.

"COME ON AND JOIN US!"

"WE'LL TEACH YOU HOW TO FIGHT, FREAK!"

The faces were white and brown and black, flowers of hatred.

Then the old bum rose up from his park bench and screamed at the convoy:

"I'LL GET HIM FOR YOU FELLOWS! I FOUGHT IN WORLD WAR I!"

Those in the passing trucks laughed and waved their arms:

"YOU GET HIM, POPS!"

"MAKE HIM SEE THE LIGHT!"

Then the convoy was gone.

They had thrown things at Harry: empty beer cans, soft drink cans, oranges, a banana.

Harry got up, picked up the banana, sat back down, peeled it and ate it. It was wonderful. Then he found an orange, peeled it and chewed and gulped the pulp and the juice. He found another orange and ate that. Then he found a cigarette lighter someone had thrown or dropped. He flicked it. It worked.

He walked down to the bum sitting on the bench, holding the lighter out.

"Hey, buddy, got a smoke?"

The bum's little eyes fastened upon Harry. They had a flat quality as if the pupils had been removed. The bum's lower lip quivered.

"You like Hitler, *don't ya?*" he said very quietly.

"Look, buddy," Harry said, "why don't you and I take off together? Maybe we can score for a drink?"

The old bum's eyes rolled in his head. For a moment all that Harry saw were the whites of his bloodshot eyes. The eyes then rolled back. The bum looked at him.

"Not with . . . *you!*"

"O.K.," said Harry, "see you around . . . "

The old bum's eyes rolled again and he said it once again, only louder:

"NOT WITH . . . YOU!"

• • •

Harry walked slowly out of the park and up the street toward his favorite bar. The bar was always there. Harry *moored* at the bar. It was his one haven. It was merciless and exact.

On the way Harry came to a vacant lot. A bunch of middle-aged men were playing softball. They were out of shape. Most had pot bellies, were small of stature, had large butts, almost like women. They were all 4-F or too old for the draft.

Harry stood and watched the game. There were many strikeouts, wild pitches, hit batters, errors, badly hit balls, but they kept playing. Almost as a ritual, a duty. And they were angry. The one thing they were good at was anger. The energy of their anger dominated.

Harry stood watching. Everything seemed a waste. Even the softball seemed sad, bouncing about uselessly.

"Hello, Harry, how come you're not down at the bar?"

It was old thin McDuff, puffing his pipe. McDuff was around 62, he always looked straight forward, he never looked *at* you but he saw you anyhow from behind those rimless glasses. And he was always dressed in a black suit and blue necktie. He came into the bar each day about noon, had two beers, then left. And you couldn't hate him and you couldn't like him. He was like a calendar or a pen holder.

"I'm on my way," Harry answered.

"I'll walk with you," said McDuff.

So Harry walked along with old thin McDuff and old thin McDuff puffed on his pipe. McDuff always kept that pipe *lit*. That was his thing. McDuff *was* his pipe. Why not?

They walked along, not talking. There was nothing to say. They stopped at traffic lights, McDuff puffing at his pipe.

McDuff had saved his money. He had never married. He lived in a two room apartment and didn't do much. Well, he read the newspapers but not with much interest. He wasn't religious. But it wasn't out of non-conviction. It was simply because he hadn't bothered to consider the aspect one way or the other. It was like not being a Republican because one didn't know what a Republican was. McDuff was neither happy nor unhappy. Once in a while he became a bit of a fidget, something would appear to bother him and for a tiny moment terror would fill his eyes. Then it left quickly . . . like a fly that had landed . . . then zoomed away for more promising territory.

Then they were at the bar. They walked in.

The usual crowd.

McDuff and Harry found their stools.

"Two beers," good old McDuff intoned to the barkeep.

"How ya doin', Harry?" one of the bar patrons asked.

"Gropin', shakin', and shittin'," Harry answered.

He felt bad for McDuff. Nobody had greeted him. McDuff was a blotter on a desk. He didn't make an impression on them. They noticed Harry because he was a bum. He made them feel superior. They needed that. McDuff just made them feel bland and they were already bland.

Not much happened. Everybody sat over their drinks, nursing them. Few had the imagination to simply get piss-assed drunk.

A stale Saturday afternoon.

McDuff went for his second beer and was kind enough to buy another for Harry.

McDuff's pipe was red hot from six hours of continuous firing.

He finished his second beer and walked out and then Harry sat there alone with the remainder of the crew.

It was a slow slow Saturday but Harry knew if he could hang in long enough he could make it. Saturday night was best, of course, for bumming drinks. But there was no place to go until then. Harry was ducking the landlady at the roominghouse. He paid by the week and he was nine days behind.

It got very deadly between drinks. The patrons, they just needed to sit and be somewhere. There was a general loneliness and a gentle fear and the need to be together and chat a bit, it eased them. All Harry needed was something to drink. Harry could drink forever and still need more, there wasn't enough drink to satisfy him. But the others . . . they just *sat*, talking now and then about whatever they talked about.

Harry's beer was getting flat. And the idea was not to finish it because then you had to buy another and he didn't have the money. He had to wait and hope. As a professional bummer of drinks Harry knew the first rule: you never asked for one. His thirst was their joke and any demand by him subtracted from their joy of giving.

Harry let his eyes drift down the bar. There were four or five patrons in there. Not many and not much. One of the not much was Monk Hamilton. Monk's biggest claim to immortality was that he ate six eggs for breakfast. Every day. He thought that gave him an edge. He wasn't good at thinking. He was huge, almost as wide as he was tall, with pale steady unworried eyes, oaktree neck, big knotted hairy hands.

Monk was talking to the bartender. Harry watched a fly crawl into the beer-wet ashtray before him. The fly walked around in there between the butts, pushed against a sotted cigarette, then it made an angry buzz, rose straight up, then seemed to fly backwards, and to the left, and then was gone.

Monk was a window washer. His bland eyes saw Harry. His thick lips twisted into a superior grin. He picked up his bottle, walked down, took the stool next to Harry.

"Watcha doin', Harry?"

"Waiting for it to rain."

"How about a beer?"

"Waiting for it to rain beer, Monk. Thanks."

Monk ordered two beers. They came along.

Harry liked to drink his right out of the bottle. Monk dumped some of his into a glass.

"Harry, you need a job?"

"Haven't thought about it."

"All ya gotta do is hold the ladder. We need a ladder man. It doesn't pay as good as upstairs work but you get something. How about it?"

Monk was making a joke. Monk thought Harry was too screwed-up to know that.

"Give me some time to think about it, Monk."

Monk looked down at the other patrons, let his superior grin loose again, winked at them, then looked back at Harry.

"Listen, all you gotta do is hold the ladder steady. I'll be up there cleaning the windows. All you gotta do is hold the ladder steady. That's not too hard, is it?"

"Not as hard as a lot of things, Monk."

"Then you'll do it?"

"I don't think so."

"Come on! Why don't ya give it a try?"

"I can't do it, Monk."

They all felt good then. Harry was their boy. The excellent fool.

Harry looked at all those bottles behind the bar. All those good times waiting, all that laughter, all that madness ... scotch, whiskey, wine, gin, vodka and all the others. Yet those bottles stood there, unused. It was like a life waiting to be lived that nobody wanted.

"Listen," said Monk, "I'm going to get a haircut."

Harry felt Monk's quiet thickness. Monk had won something somewhere. He fit, like a key in a lock that opened to somewhere.

"Why don't you come with me while I get a haircut?"

Harry didn't answer.

Monk leaned closer. "We'll stop for a beer on the way and I'll buy you one afterwards."

"Let's go . . . "

Harry emptied his bottle easily into his thirst, put the bottle down. He followed Monk out the door. They walked down the street together. Harry felt like a dog following his master. And Monk was calm, he was functioning, everything fit. It was his Saturday off and he was going to get a haircut.

They found a bar and stopped there. It was much nicer and cleaner than the one Harry usually bummed at. Monk ordered the beers.

How he sat there! A *man's man*. And a comfortable one at that. He never thought about death, at least not his own.

As they sat side by side, Harry knew he had made a mistake: an 8 to 5 job would be less painful.

Monk had a mole on the right side of his face, a very relaxed mole, a non-self-conscious mole.

Harry watched Monk pick up his bottle and suck on it. It was only something Monk *did,* like scratching his nose. He wasn't *hungry* for a drink. Monk just sat there with his bottle and it was paid for. And time was going by like shit down a river.

They finished their bottles and Monk said something to the bartender and the bartender answered something.

Then Harry followed Monk out the door. They were together and Monk was going to get a haircut.

They found the barbershop and entered. There were no other customers. The barber knew Monk. As Monk clambered into the chair they said something to each other. The barber spread the sheet and Monk's head loomed out of there, mole steady on right cheek, and he said, "Short around the ears and not too much off the top."

Harry, in agony for another drink, picked up a magazine, turned some pages and pretended to be interested.

Then he heard Monk speaking to the barber, "By the way, Paul, this is Harry. Harry, this is Paul."

Paul and Harry and Monk.

Monk and Harry and Paul.

Harry, Monk, Paul.

"Look, Monk," said Harry, "maybe I'll go down and get another beer while you're getting your hair cut?"

Monk's eyes fixed on Harry, "No, we'll get a beer after I'm finished here."

Then his eyes fixed on the mirror. "Not *too* much off around the ears, Paul."

As the world turned, Paul snipped away.

"Been getting much, Monk?"

"Nothin', Paul."

"I don't believe that . . . "

"You better believe it, Paul."

"Not from what I hear."

"Like what?"

"Like when Betsy Ross made that flag, 13 stars wouldn't have wrapped around *your* pole!"

"Ah, shit, Paul, you're too *much!*"

Monk laughed. His laugh was like linoleum being sliced by a dull knife. Or maybe it was a death-cry.

Then he stopped laughing. "Not *too* much off the top."

Harry put the magazine down and looked at the floor. The linoleum laugh had transferred into a linoleum floor. Green and blue, with purple diamonds. An old floor. Patches of it had begun to peel, showing the dark brown flooring beneath. Harry liked the dark brown.

He began counting: 3 barber chairs, 5 waiting chairs. 13 or 14 magazines. One barber. One customer. One . . . what?

Paul and Harry and Monk and the dark brown.

The cars went by outside. Harry started counting, stopped. Don't play with madness, madness doesn't play.

Easier to count the drinks on hand: none.

Time rang like a blank bell.

Harry was conscious of his feet, of his feet in his shoes, then of his toes . . . on the feet . . . in his shoes.

He wiggled his toes. His all-consuming life going nowhere like a snail crawling toward the fire.

Leaves were growing upon stems. Antelopes raised their heads from grazing. A butcher in Birmingham raised his cleaver. And Harry sat waiting in a barbershop, hoping for a beer.

He was without honor, a dog without a day.

It went on, it went by, it went on and on, and then it was over. The end of the barber chair play. Paul spun Monk so he could view himself in the mirrors behind the chair.

Harry hated barbershops. That final spin in the chair, those mirrors, they were a moment of horror for him.

Monk didn't mind.

He looked at himself. He studied his reflection, face, hair, all. He seemed to admire what he saw. Then, he spoke: "O.K., now, Paul, will you take a little off the left side? And you see that little piece sticking out there? That should be cleaned up."

"Oh, yeah, Monk . . . I'll get it . . . "

The barber spun Monk back and concentrated upon the little piece that stuck out.

Harry watched the scissors. There was much clicking but not much cutting.

Then Paul spun Monk toward the mirrors again.

Monk looked at himself.

A slight smile curled up the right side of his mouth. Then the left side of his face gave a little twitch. Self-love with only a twinge of doubt.

"That's good," he said, "now you've got it right."

Paul whisked Monk off with the little broom. Falling dead hair drifted in a dead world.

Monk dug in his pocket for the price and the tip.

The money transaction tinkled in the dead afternoon.

Then Harry and Monk were walking down the street together back toward the bar.

"Nothing like a haircut," said Monk, "makes you feel like a new man."

Monk always wore pale blue work shirts, sleeves rolled up to show off his biceps. Some guy. All he needed now was some female to fold his shorts and undershirts, roll his stockings for him and put them in the dresser drawer.

"Thanks for keeping me company, Harry."

"Sure, Monk . . . "

"Next time I get a haircut I'd like you to come along with me."

"Maybe, Monk . . . "

Monk was walking next to the curb and it was like a dream. A yellow dream. It just happened. And Harry didn't know where the compulsion came from. But he allowed the compulsion. He pretended to trip and lunged into Monk. And Monk, like a top-heavy circus of flesh, fell in front of the bus. As the driver hit the brakes there was a thud, not too loud, but a thud. And there was Monk sitting in the gutter, haircut, mole, and all. And Harry looked down. The strangest thing: there was Monk's wallet in the gutter. It had leaped out of Monk's back pocket on impact and there it was in the gutter. Only it wasn't flat on the ground, it stood like a little pyramid.

Harry reached down, picked it up, put it in his front pocket. It felt warm and full of grace. Hail Mary.

Then Harry bent over Monk. "Monk? Monk . . . you all right?"

Monk didn't answer. But Harry noticed him breathing and there was no blood. And, all of a sudden, Monk's face looked handsome and gallant.

He's fucked, thought Harry, and I'm fucked. We're all just fucked in different ways. There's no truth, there's nothing real, there's nothing.

But there was something. There was a crowd.

"Back off!" somebody said. "Give him air!"

Harry backed off. He backed off right into the crowd. Nobody stopped him.

He was walking south. He heard the ambulance siren. It wailed along with his guilt.

Then, quickly, the guilt vanished. Like an old war finished. You had to go on. Things continued. Like fleas and pancake syrup.

Harry ducked into a bar he had never noticed before. There was a barkeep. There were bottles. It was dark in there. He ordered a double whiskey, drank it right down. Monk's wallet was fat and fulsome. Friday must have been payday. Harry slipped out a bill, ordered another double whiskey. He drained half, waited in homage, then took the rest, and for the first time in a long time he felt very good.

● ● ●

Late that afternoon Harry walked down to the Groton Steak House. He went in and sat at the counter. He'd never been in there before. A tall, thin, nondescript man in a chef's hat and a soiled apron walked up and leaned over the counter. He needed a shave and smelled of roach spray. He leered at Harry.

"You come in for the JOB?" he asked.

Why the hell is everybody trying to put me to work? thought Harry.

"No," Harry answered.

"We have an opening for a dishwasher. Fifty cents an hour and you get to grab Rita's ass every once in a while."

The waitress walked by. Harry looked at her ass.

"No, thanks. Right now, I'll take a beer. In the bottle. Any kind."

The chef leaned closer. He had long nostril hairs, powerfully intimidating, like an unscheduled nightmare.

"Listen, fucker, you got any money?"

"I got it," said Harry.

The chef hesitated for some time, then walked off, opened the refrigerator and yanked a bottle out. He snapped the cap off, walked back to Harry, banged the brew down.

Harry took a long drink, set the bottle down gently.

The chef was still examining him. The chef couldn't quite make it out.

"Now," said Harry, "I want a porterhouse steak, medium-well done, with french fries, and go easy on the grease. And bring me another beer, now."

The chef loomed before him like an angry cloud, then he cleared off, went back to the refrigerator, repeated his act, which included bringing the bottle and slamming it down.

Then the chef went over to the grill, threw on a steak.

A glorious pall of smoke arose. The chef stared at Harry through it.

Why he dislikes me, thought Harry, I have no idea. Well, maybe I do need a haircut (plenty off everywhere, please) and a shave, and my face is a bit beat-up, but my clothes are fairly clean. Worn but clean. I am probably cleaner than the mayor of this fucking city.

The waitress walked up. She didn't look bad. Nothing extra but not bad. She had her hair piled up on top of her head, kind of wild, and she had ringlets hanging down the sides. Nice.

She leaned forward over the counter.

"You didn't take the dishwasher's job?"

"I like the pay but it isn't my line of work."

"What's your line of work?"

"I'm an architect."

"You're full of shit," she said and walked off.

Harry knew he wasn't much good at small talk. He found that the less he talked the better everyone felt.

Harry finished both beers. Then the steak and fries arrived. The chef slammed them down. The chef was a great slammer.

It looked like a miracle to Harry. He went to it, cutting and chewing. He hadn't had a steak in a couple of years. As he ate he felt new strength entering his body. When you didn't eat often it was a real *event*.

Even his brain smiled. And his body seemed to be saying, thank you, thank you, thank you.

Then Harry was finished.

The chef was still staring at him.

"O.K.," said Harry, "I'll have the same thing all over again."

"You'll have the same thing all over again?"

"Yeah."

The stare turned into a glare. The chef walked over and threw another steak on the grill.

"And I'll have another beer, please. Now."

"RITA!" the chef yelled, "GIVE HIM ANOTHER BEER!"

Rita came up with the beer.

"For an architect," she said, "you suck a lot of suds."

"I'm planning on erecting something."

"Ha! Like you could!"

Harry worked on the beer. Then he got up and walked to the men's room. When he got back he finished the beer off.

The chef came out and slammed the new plate of steak and fries in front of Harry.

"The job's still open if you want it."

Harry didn't answer. He began on the new plate.

The chef walked over to the grill where he continued to glare at Harry.

"You get *two* meals," the chef said, "*and* the grab."

Harry was too occupied with the steak and fries to answer. He was still hungry. When you were on the bum, and especially when you were drinking, you could go for days without eating, oftentimes not even wanting to, and then—it struck you: an unbearable hunger. You began to think of eating everything and anything: mice, butterflies, leaves, pawn tickets, newspaper, corks, whatever.

Now, working on the second steak, Harry's hunger was still there. The french fries were beautiful and greasy and yellow and hot, something like sunlight, a nourishing and glorious sunlight one could bite into. And the steak was not just a slice of some poor murdered thing, it was something dramatic that fed the body and the soul and the heart, that made the eyes smile, made the world not quite so hard to bear. Or be in. At that moment, death didn't matter.

Then he was finished with the plate. All that was left was the bone of the porterhouse and that had been stripped clean. The chef was still staring at him.

"I'll have it once more," Harry told the chef. "Another porterhouse and fries and another beer, please."

"YOU WILL NOT!" the chef screamed. "YOU WILL PAY UP AND GET THE HELL OUT OF HERE!"

He came around the grill and stood in front of Harry. He had an order pad. He scribbled angrily on the order pad. Then he tossed the check into the center of the dirty plate. Harry picked it up off the plate.

There was one other customer in the restaurant, a very round pink man with a large head of uncombed hair dyed a rather discouraging brown. The man had consumed numerous cups of coffee while reading the evening paper.

Harry stood up, dug out some bills, peeled off two and placed them down next to the plate.

Then he walked out of there.

Early evening traffic was beginning to clog the avenue with cars. The sun slanted down behind him. Harry glanced at the drivers of the cars. They seemed unhappy. The world was unhappy. People were in the dark. People were terrified and disappointed. People were caught in traps. People were defensive and frantic. They felt as if their lives were being wasted. And they were right.

Harry walked along. He stopped for a traffic signal. And, in that moment, he had a very strange feeling. He felt as if he was the only person alive in the world.

As the light turned green, he forgot all about that. He crossed the street to the other side and continued on.

—*Septuagenarian Stew*

Breakout

• •

The landlord walks up and down the hall
coughing
letting me know he is there,
and I've got to sneak
in the bottles,
I can't walk to the crapper
the lights don't work,
there are holes in the walls from
broken water pipes
and the toilet won't flush,
and the little jackoff
walks up and down
out there
coughing, coughing,
up and down his faded rug
he goes,
and I can't stand it anymore,
I break out,
I GET him
just as he walks by,
"What the hell's wrong?"
he screams,
but it's too late,
my fist is working against the bone;
it's over fast and he falls,
withered and wet;

I get my suitcase and then
I am going down the steps,
and there's his wife in the doorway,
she's ALWAYS IN THE DOORWAY,
they don't have anything to do but
stand in doorways and walk up and down the halls,
"Good morning, Mr. Bukowski," her face is a mole's face
praying for my death, "what—"
and I shove her aside,
she falls down the porch steps and
into a hedge,
I hear the branches breaking
and I see her half-stuck in there
like a blind cow,
and then I am going down the street
with my suitcase,
the sun is fine,
and I begin to think about
the next place where I'm
going to set up, and I hope
I can find some decent humans,
somebody who can treat me
better.

poem for lost dogs

• •

that good rare feeling comes at the oddest times: once, after
     sleeping
on a park bench in some strange town I awakened, my clothing
damp from a light mist and I rose and started walking east right
     into
the face of the rising sun and inside me was a gentle joy that was simply
there.

another time after picking up a streetwalker we strolled along in
the 2 a.m. moonlight side by side
toward my cheap room but I had no desire to bed her down.
the gentle joy came from simply walking along beside her in this
    confusing
universe—we were companions, strange companions walking
    together,
saying nothing.
her purple and white scarf hung from her purse—floating in the
    dark
as we walked
and the music could have come from the light from the moon.

then there was the time
I was evicted for non-payment of rent and carried my
woman's suitcase to a stranger's door and saw her vanish
inside, stood there a while, heard first her laugh, then his, then I
left.
I was walking along, it was a hot 10 a.m., the
sun blinded me and all I was conscious of was the sound of
my shoes on the pavement. then
I heard a voice. "hey, buddy, you got anything to spare?"
I looked, and sitting against a wall were 3 middle-aged bums,
    red-faced,
ridiculously lost and beaten. "how much are you
short for a bottle?" I asked. "24 cents," one of them
said. I reached into my
pocket, got all the change and handed it to him. "god damn, man,
thank
you!" he said.
I walked on, then felt the need for a cigarette, fumbled through
my
pockets, felt some paper, pulled it
out: a 5 dollar bill.

another time came while fighting the bartender, Tommy (again), in
the

back alley for the entertainment of the patrons, I was taking my
usual
beating, all the girls in their hot panties rooting for their muscular
Irish man's man ("oh, Tommy, kick his ass, kick his ass good!")
when something clicked in my brain, my brain simply said,
"it's time for something else," and I cracked Tommy
hard along the side of the head and he gave me a look: *wait, this*
isn't in the script, and then I landed another and I could see the fear
rise in him like a torrent, and I
finished him quick and then the patrons helped him up and inside
while
cursing me. What gave me that joy
that silent laughter within the self was that I had done it because
there is a limit to any man's endurance.
I walked to a strange bar a block away, sat down and ordered a
beer.
"we don't serve bums here," the barkeep told me. "I'm no bum," I
said, "bring me that beer." the beer
arrived, I took a heady gulp and I was there.

good rare feelings come at the oddest times, like now as I tell
you all of this.

we, the artists—

• •

in San Francisco the landlady, 80, helped me drag the green
Victrola up the stairway and I played Beethoven's 5th
until they beat on the walls.
there was a large bucket in the center of the room
filled with beer and winebottles;
so, it might have been the d.t.'s, one afternoon
I heard a sound something like a bell
only the bell was humming instead of ringing,

and then a golden light appeared in the corner of the room
up near the ceiling
and through the sound and light
shone the face of a woman, worn but beautiful,
and she looked down at me
and then a man's face appeared by hers,
the light became stronger and the man said:
we, the artists, are proud of you!
then the woman said: the poor boy is frightened,
and I was, and then it went away.
I got up, dressed, and went to the bar
wondering who the artists were and why they should be
proud of me. there were some live ones in the bar
and I got some free drinks, set my pants on fire with the
ashes from my corncob pipe, broke a glass deliberately,
was not rousted, met a man who claimed he was William
Saroyan, and we drank until a woman came in and
pulled him out by the ear and I thought, no, that can't be
William, and another guy came in and said: man, you talk
tough, well, listen, I just got out for assault and
battery, so don't mess with me! we went outside the
bar, he was a good boy, he knew how to duke, and it went
along fairly even, then they stopped it and we went
back in and drank another couple of hours. I walked
back up to my place, put on Beethoven's 5th and
when they beat on the walls I beat
back.

I keep thinking of myself young, then, the way I was,
and I can hardly believe it but I don't mind it.
I hope the artists are still proud of me
but they never came back
again.

the war came running in and next I knew
I was in New Orleans
walking into a bar drunk
after falling down in the mud on a rainy night.

I saw one man stab another and I walked over and
put a nickel in the juke box.
it was a beginning. San
Francisco and New Orleans were two of my
favorite towns.

2

. . . .

lay down
lay down and wait like
an animal

The Blackbirds Are Rough Today

· ·

lonely as a dry and used orchard
spread over the earth
for use and surrender.

shot down like an ex-pug selling
dailies on the corner.

taken by tears like
an aging chorus girl
who has gotten her last check.

a hanky is in order your lord your
worship.

the blackbirds are rough today
like
ingrown toenails
in an overnight
jail—
wine wine whine,
the blackbirds run around and
fly around
harping about
Spanish melodies and bones.

and everywhere is
nowhere—
the dream is as bad as
flapjacks and flat tires:

why do we go on
with our minds and
pockets full of
dust
like a bad boy just out of
school—
you tell
me,
you who were a hero in some
revolution
you who teach children
you who drink with calmness
you who own large homes
and walk in gardens
you who have killed a man and own a
beautiful wife
you tell me
why I am on fire like old dry
garbage.

we might surely have some interesting
correspondence.
it will keep the mailman busy.
and the butterflies and ants and bridges and
cemeteries
the rocket-makers and dogs and garage mechanics
will still go on a
while
until we run out of stamps
and/or
ideas.

don't be ashamed of
anything; I guess God meant it all
like
locks on
doors.

flophouse

• •

you haven't lived
until you've been in a
flophouse
with nothing but one
light bulb
and 56 men
squeezed together
on cots
with everybody
snoring
at once
and some of those
snores
so
deep and
gross and
unbelievable—
dark
snotty
gross
subhuman
wheezings
from hell
itself.

your mind
almost breaks
under those
death-like
sounds

and the
intermingling
odors:
hard

unwashed socks
pissed and
shitted
underwear

and over it all
slowly circulating
air
much like that
emanating from
uncovered
garbage
cans.

and those
bodies
in the dark

fat and
thin
and
bent

some
legless
armless

some
mindless

and worst of
all:
the total
absence of
hope

it shrouds
them

covers them
totally.

it's not
bearable.

you get
up

go out

walk the
streets

up and
down
sidewalks

past buildings

around the
corner

and back
up
the same
street

thinking

those men
were all
children
once

what has happened
to
them?

and what has
happened
to
me?

it's dark
and cold
out
here.

• •

I arrived in New Orleans in the rain at 5 o'clock in the morning. I sat around in the bus station for a while but the people depressed me so I took my suitcase and went out in the rain and began walking. I didn't know where the roominghouses were, where the poor section was.

I had a cardboard suitcase that was falling apart. It had once been black but the black coating had peeled off and yellow cardboard was exposed. I had tried to solve that by putting black shoepolish over the exposed cardboard. As I walked along in the rain the shoepolish on the suitcase ran and unwittingly I rubbed black streaks on both legs of my pants as I switched the suitcase from hand to hand.

Well, it was a new town. Maybe I'd get lucky.

The rain stopped and the sun came out. I was in the black district. I walked along slowly.

"Hey, poor white trash!"

I put my suitcase down. A high yellow was sitting on the porch steps swinging her legs. She did look good.

"Hello, poor white trash!"

I didn't say anything. I just stood there looking at her.

"How'd you like a piece of ass, poor white trash?"

She laughed at me. She had her legs crossed high and she kicked her feet; she had nice legs, high heels, and she kicked her legs and laughed. I picked up my suitcase and began to approach her up the walk. As I did I noticed a side curtain on a window to my left move just a bit. I saw a black man's face. He looked like Jersey Joe Wolcott. I backed down the pathway to the sidewalk. Her laughter followed me down the street.

I was in a room on the second floor across from a bar. The bar was called The Gangplank Cafe. From my room I could see through the open bar doors and into the bar. There were some rough faces in that bar, some interesting faces. I stayed in my room at night and drank wine and looked at the faces in the bar while my money ran out. In the daytime I took long slow walks. I sat for hours staring at pigeons. I only ate one meal a day so my money would last longer. I found a dirty cafe with a dirty proprietor, but you got a big breakfast—hotcakes, grits, sausage— for very little.

I went out on the street, as usual, one day and strolled along. I felt happy and relaxed. The sun was just right. Mellow. There was peace in the air. As I approached the center of the block there was a man standing outside the doorway of a shop. I walked past.

"Hey, BUDDY!"

I stopped and turned.

"You want a job?"

I walked back to where he stood. Over his shoulder I could see a large dark room. There was a long table with men and women standing on both sides of it. They had hammers with which they pounded objects in front of them. In the gloom the objects appeared to be clams. They smelled like clams. I turned and continued walking down the street.

I remembered how my father used to come home each night and talk about his job to my mother. The job talk began when he entered the door, continued over the dinner table, and ended in the bedroom where my father would scream *"Lights Out!"* at 8 p.m., so he could get his rest and his full strength for the job the next day. There was no other subject except the job.

Down by the corner I was stopped by another man.

"Listen, my friend . . . " he began.

"Yes?" I asked.

"Listen, I'm a veteran of World War I. I put my life on the line for this country but nobody will hire me, nobody will give me a job. They don't appreciate what I did. I'm hungry, give me some help . . . "

"I'm not working."

"You're not working?"

"That's right."

I walked away. I crossed the street to the other side.

"You're lying!" he screamed. *"You're working. You've got a job!"*

A few days later I was looking for one.

He was a man behind the desk with a hearing aid and the wire ran down along the side of his face and into his shirt where he hid the battery. The office was dark and comfortable. He was dressed in a worn brown suit with a wrinkled white shirt and a necktie frayed at the edges. His name was Heathercliff.

I had seen the ad in the local paper and the place was near my room.

> NEED AMBITIOUS YOUNG MAN
> WITH AN EYE TO THE FUTURE.
> EXPER. NOT NECESSARY.
> BEGIN IN DELIVERY ROOM AND WORK UP.

I waited outside with five or six young men, all of them trying to look ambitious. We had filled out our employment applications and now we waited. I was the last to be called.

"Mr. Chinaski, what made you leave the railroad yards?"

"Well, I don't see any future in the railroads."

"They have good unions, medical care, retirement."

"At my age, retirement might almost be considered superfluous."

"Why did you come to New Orleans?"

"I had too many friends in Los Angeles, friends I felt were hindering my career. I wanted to go where I could concentrate unmolested."

"How do we know that you'll remain with *us* any length of time?"

"I might not."

"Why?"

"Your ad stated that there was a future for an ambitious man. If there isn't any future here then I must leave."

"Why haven't you shaved your face? Did you lose a bet?"

"Not yet."

"Not yet?"

"No; I bet my landlord that I could land a job in one day even with this beard."

"All right, we'll let you know."

"I don't have a phone."

"That's all right, Mr. Chinaski."

I left and went back to my room. I went down the dirty hall and took a hot bath. Then I put my clothes back on and went out and got a bottle of wine. I came back to the room and sat by the window drinking and watching the people in the bar, watching the people walk by. I drank slowly and began to think again of getting a gun and doing it quickly—without all the thought and talk. A matter of guts. I wondered about my guts. I finished the bottle and went to bed and slept. About 4 p.m. I was awakened by a knock on the door. It was a Western Union boy. I opened the telegram:

MR. H. CHINASKI. REPORT TO WORK 8 AM TOMORROW.
R.M. HEATHERCLIFF CO.

It was a magazine publishers distributing house and we stood at the packing table checking the orders to see that the quantities coincided with the invoices. Then we signed the invoice and either packed the order for out of town shipment or set the magazines aside for local truck delivery. The work was easy and dull but the clerks were in a constant state of turmoil. They were worried about their jobs. There was a mixture of young men and women and there didn't seem to be a foreman. After several hours an argument began between two of the women. It was something about the magazines. We were packing comic books and something had gone wrong across the table. The two women became violent as the argument went on.

"Look," I said, "these books aren't worth reading let alone arguing about."

"All right," one of the women said, "we know you think you're too good for this job."

"Too good?"

"Yes, your attitude. You think we didn't notice it?"

That's when I first learned that it wasn't enough to just *do* your job, you had to have an interest in it, even a passion for it.

I worked there three or four days, then on Friday we were paid right up to the hour. We were given yellow envelopes with green bills and the exact change. Real money, no checks.

Toward quitting time the truck driver came back a little early. He sat on a pile of magazines and smoked a cigarette.

"Yeah, Harry," he said to one of the clerks, "I got a raise today. I got a two dollar raise."

At quitting time I stopped for a bottle of wine, went up to my room, had a drink then went downstairs and phoned my company. The phone rang a long time. Finally Mr. Heathercliff answered. He was still there.

"Mr. Heathercliff?"

"Yes?"

"This is Chinaski."

"Yes, Mr. Chinaski?"

"I want a two dollar raise."

"What?"

"That's right. The truck driver got a raise."

"But he's been with us two years."

"I need a raise."

"We're giving you seventeen dollars a week now and you're asking for nineteen?"

"That's right. Do I get it or not?"

"We just can't do it."

"Then I quit." I hung up.

—*Factotum*

young in New Orleans

• •

starving there, sitting around the bars,
and at night walking the streets for
hours,
the moonlight always seemed fake
to me, maybe it was,
and in the French Quarter I watched
the horses and buggies going by,
everybody sitting high in the open
carriages, the black driver, and in

back the man and the woman,
usually young and always white.
and I was always white.
and hardly charmed by the
world.
New Orleans was a place to
hide.
I could piss away my life,
unmolested.
except for the rats.
the rats in my dark small room
very much resented sharing it
with me.
they were large and fearless
and stared at me with eyes
that spoke
an unblinking
death.

women were beyond me.
they saw something
depraved.
there was one waitress
a little older than
I, she rather smiled,
lingered when she
brought my
coffee.

that was plenty for
me, that was
enough.

there was something about
that city, though:
it didn't let me feel guilty
that I had no feeling for the
things so many others

needed.
it let me alone.

sitting up in my bed
the lights out,
hearing the outside
sounds,
lifting my cheap
bottle of wine,
letting the warmth of
the grape
enter
me
as I heard the rats
moving about the
room,
I preferred them
to
humans.

being lost,
being crazy maybe
is not so bad
if you can be
that way:
undisturbed.

New Orleans gave me
that.
nobody ever called
my name.

no telephone,
no car,
no job,
no
anything.

me and the
rats
and my youth,
one time,
that time
I knew
even through the
nothingness,
it was a
celebration
of something not to
do
but only
know.

consummation of grief

I even hear the mountains
the way they laugh
up and down their blue sides
and down in the water
the fish cry
and all the water
is their tears.
I listen to the water
on nights I drink away
and the sadness becomes so great
I hear it in my clock
it becomes knobs upon my dresser
it becomes paper on the floor
it becomes a shoehorn
a laundry ticket
it becomes
cigarette smoke
climbing a chapel of dark vines . . .

it matters little

very little love is not so bad
or very little life

what counts
is waiting on walls
I was born for this

I was born to hustle roses down the avenues of the dead.

• •

My mother screamed when she opened the door. *"Son! Is that you,
son?"*

"I need some sleep."

"Your bedroom is always waiting."

I went to the bedroom, undressed and climbed into bed. I was awakened about 6 p.m. by my mother. "Your father is home."

I got up and began to dress. Dinner was on the table when I walked in.

My father was a big man, taller than I was with brown eyes; mine
were green. His nose was too large and you couldn't help noticing his
ears. His ears wanted to leap away from his head.

"Listen," he said, "if you stay here I am going to charge you room
and board plus laundry. When you get a job, what you owe us will be
subtracted from your salary until you are paid up."

We ate in silence.

My bill for room, board, laundry, etc., was so high by this time that it
took several paychecks to get even. I stayed until then and moved out
right afterwards. I couldn't afford the rates at home.

I found a roominghouse near my job. Moving wasn't hard. I only
owned enough to half fill a suitcase . . .

• • •

Mama Strader was my landlady, a dyed redhead with a good figure, many gold teeth, and an aged boyfriend. She called me into the kitchen the first morning and said she'd pour me a whiskey if I would go out back and feed the chickens. I did and then I sat in the kitchen drinking with Mama and her boyfriend, Al. I was an hour late for work.

The second night there was a knock on my door. It was a fat woman in her mid-forties. She held a bottle of wine. "I live down the hall, my name's Martha. I hear you listening to that good music all the time. I thought I'd bring you a drink."

Martha walked in. She had on a loose green smock, and after a few wines she started showing me her legs.

"I've got good legs."

"I'm a leg man."

"Look higher."

Her legs were very white, fat, flabby, with bulging purple veins. Martha told me her story.

She was a whore. She made the bars off and on. Her main source of income was the owner of a department store. "He gives me money. I go into his store and take anything I want. The salespeople don't bother me. He's told them to leave me alone. He doesn't want his wife to know I'm a better fuck than she is."

Martha got up and turned on the radio. Loud. "I'm a good dancer," she said. "Watch me dance!"

She whirled in her green tent, kicking her legs. She wasn't so hot. Soon she had the smock up around her waist and was waving her behind in my face. The pink panties had a large hole over the right cheek. Then off came the smock and she was just in her panties. Next the panties were on the floor by the smock and she was doing a grind. Her triangle of cunt hair was almost hidden by her dangling, bouncing stomach.

Sweat was making her mascara run. Suddenly her eyes narrowed. I was sitting on the edge of the bed. She leapt on me before I could move. Her open mouth was pressed on mine. It tasted of spit and onions and stale wine and (I imagined) the sperm of four hundred men. She pushed her tongue into my mouth. It was thick with saliva, I gagged and pushed her off. She fell on her knees, tore open my zipper, and in a second my soft pecker was in her mouth. She sucked and bobbed. Martha had a small yellow ribbon in her short grey hair. There were warts and big brown moles on her neck and cheeks.

My penis rose; she groaned, bit me. I screamed, grabbed her by the hair, pulled her off. I stood in the center of the room wounded and terrified. They were playing a Mahler Symphony on the radio. Before I could move she was down on her knees and on me again. She gripped my balls mercilessly with both of her hands. Her mouth opened, she had me; her head bobbed, sucked, jerked. Giving my balls a tremendous yank while almost biting my pecker in half she forced me to the floor. Sucking sounds filled the room as my radio played Mahler. I felt as if I were being eaten by a pitiless animal. My pecker rose, covered with spittle and blood. The sight of it threw her into a frenzy. I felt as if I was being eaten alive.

If I come, I thought desperately, I'll never forgive myself.

As I reached down to try to yank her off by the hair, she clutched my balls again and squeezed them without pity. Her teeth scissored midpoint on my penis as if to slice me in two. I screamed, let go of her hair, fell back. Her head bobbed remorselessly. I was certain the sucking could be heard all over the roominghouse.

"NO!" I yelled.

She persisted with inhuman fury. I began to come. It was like sucking the insides out of a trapped snake. Her fury was mixed with madness; she sucked at that sperm, gurgling it into her throat.

She continued to bob and suck.

"Martha! Stop! It's over!"

She wouldn't. It was as if she had been turned into an enormous all-devouring mouth. She continued to suck and bob. She went on, on. "NO!" I yelled again . . . This time she got it like a vanilla malt through a straw.

I collapsed. She rose and began dressing herself. She sang.

"When a New York baby says goodnight
it's early in the morning

goodnight, sweetheart
it's early in the morning

goodnight, sweetheart
milkman's on his way home . . . "

I staggered to my feet, clutching the front of my pants, and found my wallet. I took out $5, handed it to her. She took the $5, tucked it into the front of her dress between her breasts, grabbed my balls playfully once again, squeezed, let go, and waltzed out of the room.

I had worked long enough to save up bus fare to somewhere else, plus a few dollars to take care of me after I arrived. I quit my job, took out a map of the United States and looked it over. I decided on New York City.

I took five pints of whiskey in my suitcase on the bus with me. Whenever somebody sat next to me and began talking I pulled out a pint and took a long drink. I got there.

The bus station in New York City was near Times Square. I walked out into the street with my old suitcase. It was evening. The people swarmed up out of the subways. Like insects, faceless, mad, they rushed upon me, into and around me, with much intensity. They spun and pushed each other; they made horrible sounds.

I stood back in a doorway and finished the last pint.

Then I walked along, pushed, elbowed, until I saw a vacancy sign on Third Avenue. The manager was an old Jewish woman. "I need a room," I told her.

"You need a good suit, my boy."

"I'm broke."

"It's a good suit, almost for nothing. My husband runs the tailor shop across the street. Come with me."

I paid for my room, put my suitcase upstairs. I went with her across the street.

"Herman, show this boy the suit."

"Ah, it's a nice suit." Herman brought it out; a dark blue, a bit worn.

"It looks too small."

"No, no, it fits good."

He came out from behind the counter with the suit. "Here. Try the coat on." Herman helped me into it. "See? It fits . . . You want to try the pants?" He held the pants in front of me, from waist to toe.

"They look all right."

"Ten dollars."

"I'm broke."

"Seven dollars."

I gave Herman the seven dollars, took my suit upstairs to my room. I went out for a bottle of wine. When I got back I locked the door, undressed, made ready for my first real night's sleep in some time.

I got into bed, opened the bottle, worked the pillow into a hard knot behind my back, took a deep breath, and sat in the dark looking out of the window. It was the first time I had been alone for five days. I was a man who thrived on solitude; without it I was like another man without food or water. Each day without solitude weakened me. I took no pride in my solitude; but I was dependent on it. The darkness of the room was like sunlight to me. I took a drink of wine.

Suddenly the room filled with light. There was a clatter and a roar. The El ran level with the window of my room. A subway train had stopped there. I looked out into a row of New York faces who looked back. The train lingered, then pulled away. It was dark. Then the room filled again with light. Again I looked into the faces. It was like a vision of hell repeated again and again. Each new trainload of faces was more ugly, demented and cruel than the last. I drank the wine.

It continued: darkness, then light; light, then darkness. I finished the wine and went out for more. I came back, undressed, got back in bed. The arrival and departure of the faces continued; I felt I was having a vision. I was being visited by hundreds of devils that the Devil Himself couldn't tolerate. I drank more wine.

Finally I got up and took my new suit out of the closet. I slipped into the coat. It was a tight fit. The coat seemed smaller than when I was in the tailor shop. Suddenly there was a ripping sound. The coat had split open straight up the back. I took what remained of the coat off. I still had the pants. I worked my legs into them. There were buttons in the front instead of a zipper; as I tried to fasten them, the seam split in the seat. I reached in from behind and felt my shorts.

For four or five days I walked around. Then I got drunk for two days. I moved out of my room and into Greenwich Village. One day I read in Walter Winchell's column that O. Henry used to do all of his writing at a table in some famous writers' bar. I found the bar and went in looking for what?

It was noon. I was the only patron despite Winchell's column. There I stood alone with a large mirror, the bar, and the bartender.

"I'm sorry, sir, we can't serve you."

I was stunned, couldn't answer. I waited for an explanation.

"You're drunk."

I was probably hungover but I hadn't had a drink for twelve hours. I mumbled something about O. Henry and left.

It looked like a deserted store. There was a sign in the window: *Help Wanted*. I went in. A man with a thin mustache smiled at me. "Sit down." He gave me a pen and a form. I filled out the form.

"Ah? College?"

"Not exactly."

"We're in advertising."

"Oh?"

"Not interested?"

"Well, you see, I've been painting. A *painter,* you know? I've run out of money. Can't sell the stuff."

"We get lots of those."

"I don't like them either."

"Cheer up. Maybe you'll be famous after you're dead."

He went on to say the job entailed night work to begin with, but that there was always a chance to work one's way up.

I told him that I liked night work. He said that I could begin in the subway.

Two old guys were waiting for me. I met them down inside the subway where the cars were parked. I was given an armful of cardboard posters and a small metal instrument that looked like a can opener. We all climbed in one of the parked cars.

"Watch me," one of the old guys said.

He jumped up on the dusty seats, began walking along ripping out old posters with his can opener. So that's how those things get up there, I thought. People put them there.

Each poster was held by two metal strips which had to be removed to get the new poster in. The strips were spring-tight and curved to fit the contour of the wall.

They let me try it. The metal strips resisted my efforts. They wouldn't budge. The sharp edges cut my hands as I worked. I began to bleed. For each poster you took out there was a new poster to replace it. Each one took forever. It was endless.

"There are green bugs all over New York," said one of the old guys after a while.

"There are?"

"Yeh. You new in New York?"

"Yes."

"Don't you know all New York people got these green bugs?"

"No."

"Yeh. Woman wanted to fuck me last night. I said, 'No, baby, nothing doing.'"

"Yeh?"

"Yeh. I told her I'd do it if she gave me five bucks. It takes five bucks worth of steak to replace that jizz."

"She give you the five bucks?"

"Nah. She offered me a can of Campbell's mushroom soup."

We worked our way down to the end of the car. The two old men climbed off the back, began to walk toward the next subway car parked about fifty feet up the track. We were forty feet above the ground with nothing but railroad ties to walk on. I saw it wouldn't be any trouble at all for a body to slip through and fall to the ground below.

I climbed out of the subway car and slowly started stepping from tie to tie, can opener in one hand, cardboard posters in the other. A subway car filled with passengers pulled up; the lights from the train showed the way.

The train moved off; I was in total darkness. I could neither see the ties nor the spaces between them. I waited.

The two old guys hollered from the next car: "Come on! Hurry! We got a lot of work to do!"

"Wait! I can't see!"

"We ain't got all night!"

My eyes began to adjust. Step by step I went forward, slowly. When I reached the next car I put the posters on the floor and sat down. My legs were weak.

"What's the matter?"

"I don't know."

"What is it?"

"A man can get killed up here."

"Nobody's ever fallen through yet."

"I feel like I could."

"It's all in the mind."

"I know. How do I get out of here?"

"There's a stairway right over there. But you gotta cross a lotta tracks, you gotta watch for trains."

"Yes."

"And don't step on the third rail."

"What's that?"

"That's the power. It's the gold rail. It looks like gold. You'll see it."

I got down on the tracks and began stepping over them. The two old men watched me. The gold rail was there. I stepped very high over that.

Then I half-ran half-fell down the stairway. There was a bar across the street.

—*FACTOTUM*

Poem for Personnel Managers:

An old man asked me for a cigarette
and I carefully dealt out two.
"Been lookin' for job. Gonna stand
in the sun and smoke."

He was close to rags and rage
and he leaned against death.
It was a cold day, indeed, and trucks
loaded and heavy as old whores
banged and tangled on the streets . . .

We drop like planks from a rotting floor
as the world strives to unlock the bone
that weights its brain.
(God is a lonely place without steak.)

We are dying birds
we are sinking ships—
the world rocks down against us
and we
throw out our arms
and we
throw out our legs
like the death kiss of the centipede:
but they kindly snap our backs
and call our poison "politics."

Well, we smoked, he and I—little men
nibbling fish-head thoughts . . .

All the horses do not come in,
and as you watch the lights of the jails
and hospitals wink on and out,
and men handle flags as carefully
      as babies,
remember this:

you are a great-gutted instrument of
heart and belly, carefully planned—
so if you take a plane for Savannah,
take the best plane;
or if you eat chicken on a rock,
make it a very special animal.
(You call it a bird; I call birds
flowers.)

And if you decide to kill somebody,
make it anybody and not somebody:
some men are made of more special, precious
parts: do not kill
if you will
a president or a King
or a man
behind a desk—

these have heavenly longitudes
enlightened attitudes.

If you decide,
take us
who stand and smoke and glower;
we are rusty with sadness and
feverish
with climbing broken ladders.

Take us
      we were never children
      like your children.
      We do not understand love songs
      like your inamorata.

Our faces are cracked linoleum,
cracked through with the heavy, sure
feet of our masters.

We are shot through with carrot tops
and poppyseed and tilted grammar;
we waste days like mad blackbirds
and pray for alcoholic nights.
Our silk-sick human smiles wrap around
us like somebody else's confetti:
we do not even belong to the Party.

We are a scene chalked-out with the
sick white brush of Age.

We smoke, asleep as a dish of figs.
We smoke, as dead as fog.

Take us.

A bathtub murder
or something quick and bright; our names
in the papers.

Known, at last, for a moment
to millions of careless and grape-dull eyes
that hold themselves private
to only flicker and flame
at the poor cracker-barrel jibes
of their conceited, pampered
        correct comedians.

Known, at last, for a moment,
as they will be known
and as you will be known
by an all-gray man on an all-gray horse
who sits and fondles a sword
longer than the night
longer than the mountain's aching backbone
longer than all the cries
that have a-bombed up out of throats
and exploded in a newer, less-planned
land.

We smoke and the clouds do not notice us.
A cat walks by and shakes Shakespeare
        off of his back.
Tallow, tallow, candle like wax: our spines
are limp and our consciousness burns
guilelessly away
the remaining wick life has
doled out to us.

An old man asked me for a cigarette
and told me his troubles
and this
is what he said:
that Age was a crime
and that Pity picked up the marbles
and that Hatred picked up the
cash.

He might have been your father
or mine.

He might have been a sex-fiend
or a saint.

But whatever he was,
he was condemned
and we stood in the sun and
smoked
and looked around
in our leisure
to see who was next in
line.

nirvana

• •

not much chance,
completely cut loose from
purpose,
he was a young man
riding a bus
through North Carolina
on the way to
somewhere
and it began to snow
and the bus stopped
at a little cafe
in the hills
and the passengers
entered.

he sat at the counter
with the others,

he ordered and the
food arrived.
the meal was
particularly
good
and the
coffee.

the waitress was
unlike the women
he had
known.
she was unaffected,
there was a natural
humor which came
from her.
the fry cook said
crazy things.
the dishwasher,
in back,
laughed, a good
clean
pleasant
laugh.

the young man watched
the snow through the
windows.

he wanted to stay
in that cafe
forever.

the curious feeling
swam through him
that everything
was
beautiful

there,
that it would always
stay beautiful
there.

then the bus driver
told the passengers
that it was time
to board.

the young man
thought, I'll just sit
here, I'll just stay
here.

but then
he rose and followed
the others into the
bus.

he found his seat
and looked at the cafe
through the bus
window.
then the bus moved
off, down a curve,
downward, out of
the hills.

the young man
looked straight
forward.
he heard the other
passengers
speaking
of other things,
or they were
reading

or
attempting to
sleep.

they had not
noticed
the
magic.

the young man
put his head to
one side,
closed his
eyes,
pretended to
sleep.
there was nothing
else to do—
just listen to the
sound of the
engine,
the sound of the
tires
in the
snow.

• •

After arriving in Philadelphia I found a roominghouse and paid a week's rent in advance. The nearest bar was fifty years old. You could smell the odor of urine, shit and vomit of a half century as it came up through the floor into the bar from the restrooms below.

It was 4:30 in the afternoon. Two men were fighting in the center of the bar.

The guy to the right of me said his name was Danny. To the left, he said his name was Jim.

Danny had a cigarette in his mouth, end glowing. An empty beerbottle looped through the air. It missed his cigarette and nose, fractionally. He didn't move or look around, tapped the ashes of his cigarette into a tray. "That was pretty close, you son of a bitch! Come that close again, you got a fight on your hands!"

Every seat was taken. There were women in there, a few housewives, fat and a bit stupid, and two or three ladies who had fallen on hard times. As I sat there one girl got up and left with a man. She was back in five minutes.

"Helen! Helen! How do you do it?"

She laughed.

Another jumped up to try her. "That must be good. I gotta have some!"

They left together. Helen was back in five minutes.

"She must have a suction pump for a pussy!"

"I gotta try me some of that," said an old guy down at the end of the bar. "I haven't had a hard-on since Teddy Roosevelt took his last hill."

It took Helen ten minutes with that one.

"I want a sandwich," said a fat guy. "Who's gonna run me an errand for a sandwich?"

I told him I would. "Roast beef on a bun, everything on."

He gave me some money. "Keep the change."

I walked down to the sandwich place. An old geezer with a big belly walked up. "Roast beef on a bun to go, everything on. And a bottle of beer while I'm waiting."

I drank the beer, took the sandwich back to the fat guy in the bar, and found another seat. A shot of whiskey appeared. I drank it down. Another appeared. I drank it down. The juke box played.

A young fellow of about twenty-four came down from the end of the bar. "I need the venetian blinds cleaned," he said to me.

"You sure do."

"What do you do?"

"Nothing. Drink. Both."

"How about the blinds?"

"Five bucks."

"You're hired."

They called him Billy-Boy. Billy-Boy had married the owner of the bar. She was forty-five.

He brought me two buckets, some suds, rags and sponges. I took the blinds down, removed the slats, and began.

"Drinks are free," said Tommy the night bartender, "as long as you're working."

"Shot of whiskey, Tommy."

It was slow work; the dust had caked, turned into embedded grime. I cut my hands several times on the edges of the metal slats. The soapy water burned.

"Shot of whiskey, Tommy."

I finished one set of blinds and hung them up. The patrons of the bar turned to look at my work.

"Beautiful!"

"It sure helps the place."

"They'll probably raise the price of drinks."

"Shot of whiskey, Tommy," I said.

I took down another set of blinds, pulled out the slats. I beat Jim at the pinball machine for a quarter, then emptied the buckets in the crapper and got fresh water.

The second set went slower. My hands collected more cuts. I doubt that those blinds had been cleaned in ten years. I won another quarter at the pinball then Billy-Boy hollered at me to go back to work.

Helen walked by on her way to the women's crapper.

"Helen, I'll give you five bucks when I'm finished. Will that cover?"

"Sure, but you won't be able to get it up after all that work."

"I'll get it up."

"I'll be here at closing. If you can still stand up, then you can have it for nothing!"

"I'll be standing *tall*, baby."

Helen walked back to the crapper.

"Shot of whiskey, Tommy."

"Hey, take it easy," said Billy-Boy, "or you'll never finish that job tonight."

"Billy, if I don't finish you keep your five."

"It's a deal. All you people hear that?"

"We heard you, Billy, you cheap ass."

"One for the road, Tommy."

Tommy gave me the whiskey. I drank it and went to work. I drove myself on. After a number of whiskeys I had the three sets of blinds up and shining.

"All right, Billy, pay up."

"You're not finished."

"What?"

"There's three more windows in the back room."

"The back room?"

"The back room. The party room."

Billy-Boy showed me the back room. There were three more windows, three more sets of blinds.

"I'll settle for two-fifty, Billy."

"No, you got to do them all or no pay."

I got my buckets, dumped the water, put in clean water, soap, then took down a set of blinds. I pulled the slats out, put them on a table and stared at them.

Jim stopped on his way to the crapper. "What's the matter?"

"I can't go another slat."

When Jim came out of the crapper he went to the bar and brought back his beer. He began cleaning the blinds.

"Jim, forget it."

I went to the bar, got another whiskey. When I got back one of the girls was taking down a set of blinds. "Be careful, don't cut yourself," I told her.

A few minutes later there were four or five people back there talking and laughing, even Helen. They were all working on the blinds. Soon nearly everybody in the bar was back there. I worked in two more whiskeys. Finally the blinds were finished and hanging. It hadn't taken very long. They sparkled. Billy-Boy came in:

"I don't have to pay you."

"The job's finished."

"But you didn't finish it."

"Don't be a cheap shit, Billy," somebody said.

Billy-Boy dug out the $5 and I took it. We moved to the bar. "A drink for everybody!" I laid the $5 down. "And one for me too."

Tommy went around pouring drinks.

I drank my drink and Tommy picked up the $5.

"You owe the bar $3.15."

"Put it on the tab."

"O.K., what's your last name?"

"Chinaski."

"You heard the one about the Polack who went to the outhouse?"

"Yes."

Drinks came my way until closing time. After the last one I looked around. Helen had slipped out. Helen had lied.

Just like a bitch, I thought, afraid of the long hard ride . . .

I got up and walked back to my roominghouse. The moonlight was bright. My footsteps echoed in the empty street and it sounded as if somebody was following me. I looked around. I was mistaken. I was quite alone.

When I arrived in St. Louis it was still very cold, about to snow, and I found a room in a nice clean place, a room on the second floor, in the back. It was early evening and I was having one of my depressive fits so I went to bed early and somehow managed to sleep.

When I awakened in the morning it was very cold. I was shivering uncontrollably. I got up and found that one of the windows was open. I closed the window and went back to bed. I began to feel nauseated. I managed to sleep another hour, then awakened. I got up, dressed, barely made it to the hall bathroom and vomited. I undressed and got back into bed. Soon there was a knock on the door. I didn't answer. The knocking continued. "Yes?" I asked.

"Are you all right?"

"Yes."

"Can we come in?"

"Come in."

There were two girls. One was a bit on the fat side but scrubbed, shining, in a flowery pink dress. She had a kind face. The other wore a wide tight belt that accentuated her very good figure. Her hair was long, dark, and she had a cute nose; she wore high heels, had perfect legs, and wore a white low cut blouse. Her eyes were dark brown, very dark, and they kept looking at me, amused, very amused. "I'm Gertrude," she said, "and this is Hilda."

Hilda managed to blush as Gertrude moved across the room toward my bed. "We heard you in the bathroom. Are you sick?"

"Yes. But it's nothing serious, I'm sure. An open window."

"Mrs. Downing, the landlady, is making you some soup."

"No, it's all right."

"It'll do you good."

Gertrude moved nearer my bed. Hilda remained where she was, pink and scrubbed and blushing. Gertrude pivoted back and forth on her very high heels. "Are you new in town?"

"Yes."

"You're not in the army?"

"No."

"What do you do?"

"Nothing."

"No work?"

"No work."

"Yes," said Gertrude to Hilda, "look at his hands. He has the most beautiful hands. You can see that he has never worked."

The landlady, Mrs. Downing, knocked. She was large and pleasant. I imagined that her husband was dead and that she was religious. She carried a large bowl of beef broth, holding it high in the air. I could see the steam rising. I took the bowl. We exchanged pleasantries. Yes, her husband was dead. She was very religious. There were crackers, plus salt and pepper.

"Thank you."

Mrs. Downing looked at both of the girls. "We'll all be going now. We hope you get well soon. And I hope the girls haven't bothered you too much?"

"Oh no!" I grinned into the broth. She liked that.

"Come on, girls."

Mrs. Downing left the door open. Hilda managed one last blush, gave me the tiniest smile, then left. Gertrude remained. She watched me spoon the broth in. "Is it good?"

"I want to thank all you people. All this . . . is very unusual."

"I'm going." She turned and walked very slowly toward the door. Her buttocks moved under her tight black skirt; her legs were golden. At the doorway she stopped and turned, rested her dark eyes on me once again, held me. I was transfixed, glowing. The moment she felt my response she tossed her head and laughed. She had a lovely neck, and all that dark hair. She walked off down the hall, leaving the door ajar.

I took the salt and pepper, seasoned the broth, broke the crackers into it, and spooned it into my illness.

After losing several typewriters to pawnbrokers I simply gave up the idea of owning one. I printed out my stories by hand and sent them out that way. I hand-printed them with a pen. I got to be a very fast hand-printer. It got so that I could hand-print faster than I could write. I wrote three or four short stories a week. I kept things in the mail. I imagined the editors of *The Atlantic Monthly* and *Harper's* saying: "Hey, here's another one of those things by that nut . . . "

One night I took Gertrude to a bar. We sat at a table to one side and drank beer. It was snowing outside. I felt a little better than usual. We drank and talked. An hour or so passed. I began gazing into Gertrude's eyes and she looked right back. *"A good man, nowadays, is hard to find!"* said the juke box. Gertrude moved her body to the music, moved her head to the music, and looked into my eyes.

"You have a very strange face," she said. "You're not really ugly."

"Number four shipping clerk, working his way up."

"Have you ever been in love?"

"Love is for real people."

"You sound real."

"I dislike real people."

"You dislike them?"

"I hate them."

We drank some more, not saying much. It continued to snow. Gertrude turned her head and stared into the crowd of people. Then she looked at me.

"Isn't he *handsome?*"

"Who?"

"That soldier over there. He's sitting alone. He sits so *straight.* And he's got all his medals on."

"Come on, let's get out of here."

"But it's not late."

"You can stay."

"No, I want to go with *you.*"

"I don't care what you do."

"Is it the soldier? Are you mad because of the soldier?"

"Oh, shit!"

"It was the soldier!"

"I'm going."

I stood up at the table, left a tip and walked toward the door. I heard Gertrude behind me. I walked down the street in the snow. Soon she was walking at my side.

"You didn't even get a taxi. These high heels in the snow!"

I didn't answer. We walked the four or five blocks to the rooming-house. I went up the steps with her beside me. Then I walked down to my room, opened the door, closed it, got out of my clothes and went to bed. I heard her throw something against the wall of her room.

Rows and rows of silent bicycles. Bins filled with bicycle parts. Rows and rows of bicycles hanging from the ceiling: green bikes, red bikes, yellow bikes, purple bikes, blue bikes, girls' bikes, boys' bikes, all hanging up there; the glistening spokes, the wheels, the rubber tires, the paint, the leather seats, taillights, headlights, handbrakes; hundreds of bicycles, row after row.

We got an hour for lunch. I'd eat quickly, having been up most of the night and early morning, I'd be tired, aching all over, and I found this secluded spot under the bicycles. I'd crawl down there, under three deep tiers of bicycles immaculately arranged. I'd lay there on my back, and suspended over me, precisely lined up, hung rows of gleaming silver spokes, wheel rims, black rubber tires, shiny new paint, everything in perfect order. It was grand, correct, orderly—500 or 600 bicycles stretching out over me, covering me, all in place. Somehow it was mean-ingful. I'd look up at them and know I had forty-five minutes of rest under the bicycle tree.

Yet I also knew with another part of me, that if I ever let go and dropped into the flow of those shiny new bicycles, I was done, finished, that I'd never be able to make it. So I just lay back and let the wheels and the spokes and the colors soothe me.

A man with a hangover should never lay flat on his back looking up at the roof of a warehouse. The wooden girders finally get to you; and the skylights—you can see the chicken wire in the glass sky-lights—that wire somehow reminds a man of jail. Then there's the heaviness of the eyes, the longing for just one drink, and then the sound of people moving about, you hear them, you know your hour is

up, somehow you have to get on your feet and walk around and fill
and pack orders . . .

She was the manager's secretary. Her name was Carmen—but despite
the Spanish name she was a blonde and she wore tight knitted dresses,
high spiked heels, nylons, garter belt, her mouth was thick with lipstick,
but, oh, she could shimmy, she could shake, she wobbled while bringing
the orders up to the desk, she wobbled back to the office, all the boys
watching every move, every twitch of her buttocks; wobbling, wiggling,
wagging. I am not a lady's man. I never have been. To be a lady's man
you have to make with the sweet talk. I've never been good at sweet talk.
But, finally, with Carmen pressing me, I led her into one of the boxcars
we were unloading at the rear of the warehouse and I took her standing
up in the back of one of those boxcars. It was good, it was warm; I
thought of blue sky and wide clean beaches, yet it was sad—there was
definitely a lack of human feeling that I couldn't understand or deal
with. I had that knit dress up around her hips and I stood there pumping
it to her, finally pressing my mouth to her heavy mouth thick with scarlet
lipstick and I came between two unopened cartons with the air full of
cinders and with her back pressed against the filthy splintering boxcar
wall in the merciful dark.

—*Factotum*

Spring Swan

swans die in the Spring too
and there it floated
dead on a Sunday
sideways
circling in current
and I walked to the rotunda
and overhead
gods in chariots

dogs, women
circled,
and death
ran down my throat
like a mouse,
and I heard the people coming
with their picnic bags
and laughter,
and I felt guilty
for the swan
as if death
were a thing of shame
and like a fool
I walked away
and left them
my beautiful swan.

A Day

• •

Brock, the foreman, was always digging his fingers into his ass, using his left hand. He had a great case of hemorrhoids.

Tom noticed this throughout the working day.

Brock had been on his ass for months. Those round and lifeless eyes always appeared to be watching Tom. And then Tom would note the left hand, reaching around and digging.

And Brock was on his ass all right.

Tom did his work as well as the others. Maybe he didn't show quite the enthusiasm of some but he got the job done.

Yet Brock was always after him, making comments, making useless suggestions.

Brock was related to the owner of the shop and a place had been made for him: foreman.

• • •

That day, Tom finished packing the light fixture into the oblong 8-foot carton and flung it onto the pile at the back of his work table. He turned to get another fixture from the assembly line.

Brock was standing in front of him.

"I wanna talk to you, Tom . . ."

Brock was tall and thin. His body bent forward from the middle. The head was always hanging down, it hung from his long thin neck. The mouth was always open. His nose was more than prominent with extremely large nostrils. The feet were large, and awkward. Brock's pants hung loose on his skinny frame.

"Tom, you're not doing your job."

"I'm keeping up with production. What are you talking about?"

"I don't think you're using enough packing. You've got to use more of the shredding. We've had some breakage problems and we're trying to correct that."

"Why don't you have each worker initial his carton, then if there's breakage, you can trace it."

"*I'll* do the thinking here, Tom, that's my job."

"Sure."

"Come on, I want you to come over here and watch Roosevelt pack."

They walked over to Roosevelt's table.

Roosevelt was a 13-year man.

They watched Roosevelt pack the shredded paper around the light fixture.

"You see what he's doing?" Brock asked.

"Well, yes . . ."

"What I mean is, look what he's doing with the shredded paper."

"Yeah, he's putting it in there."

"Yes, of course . . . but you see how he's *picking up* that shredded paper . . . he lifts it and drops it . . . it's like playing a piano."

"That isn't really *protecting* the fixture . . ."

"Yes, it *is*. He's *fluffing* it, don't you see?"

Tom quietly inhaled, exhaled, "All right, Brock, I'll fluff it . . ."

"Do that . . ."

Brock reached his left hand around and dug in. "By the way, you're one fixture behind assembly now . . ."

"Sure I am. You've been talking to me."

"Doesn't matter, you'll have to catch up."

Brock gave it another dig, then walked away.

Roosevelt was laughing quietly. "*Fluff* it, motherfucker!"

Tom laughed. "How much shit does a man have to take just to stay alive?"

"Plenty," came the answer, "and more . . . "

Tom went back to his table and caught up with assembly. And while Brock was looking, he "fluffed" it. And Brock always seemed to be looking.

Finally, it was lunchtime, 30 minutes. But for many of the workers lunchtime didn't mean eating, it meant going down to the Villa and loading up on beer and ale, can after can, bulwarking themselves against the afternoon shift.

Some of the fellows popped uppers. Others popped downers. Many popped both uppers and downers, washing them down with the beer and the ale.

Outside the plant, in the parking lot, there were more people sitting inside old cars, each with a different party going. The Mexicans were in some and the blacks were in others, and sometimes, unlike in the jails, they were mixed. There weren't many whites, just a few silent ones from the south. But Tom liked the whole gang of them.

The only problem in the place was Brock.

That lunchtime Tom was in his own car drinking with Ramon.

Ramon opened his hand and showed Tom a large yellow pill. It looked like a jaw-breaker.

"Hey, dude, try this. You won't worry about shit. 4 or 5 hours go like 5 minutes. And you'll be STRONG, *nothing* will tire you . . . "

"Thanks, Ramon, but I'm too fucked-up now."

"But this is to *un-fuck* you, don't you get it?"

Tom didn't answer.

"O.K.," said Ramon, "I've had mine but I'll take yours too!"

He popped the pill into his mouth, raised the can of beer and took a hit. Tom watched that enormous pill, he could see it going down Ramon's throat, then it was gone.

Ramon slowly turned to Tom, then grinned, "Look, the damn thing hasn't even hit my belly yet and *already* I feel better!"

Tom laughed.

Ramon took another hit of beer, then lit a cigarette. For a man sup-posedly feeling very good he looked very serious.

"No, I'm not a man . . . I'm not a man at all . . . Hey, last night I tried to fuck my wife . . . She's gained 40 pounds this year . . . I had to get drunk first . . . I banged and banged, man, and *nothing* . . . Worst of all, I was sorry for *her* . . . I told her it was the job. And it *was* the job and it wasn't. She got up and turned on the tv . . . "

Ramon went on: "Man, everything's changed. It seems like no more than a year or two ago, with me and my woman, everything was interest-ing and funny for us . . . We laughed like hell at everything . . . Now, all that's stopped . . . It's gone away somewhere, I don't know where . . . "

"I know what you mean, Ramon . . . "

Ramon jolted straight upright as if given a message:

"Shit, man, we've got to punch in!"

"Let's go!"

Tom was coming back from the assembly line with a fixture and Brock was waiting there. Brock said, "All right, put it down. Follow me."

They walked out to assembly.

And there was Ramon in his little brown apron, with his fleck of mustache.

"You stand to his left now," said Brock.

Brock raised his hand and the machinery began. It moved the 8-foot fixtures toward them at a steady but predictable pace.

Ramon had this huge roll of paper in front of him, a seemingly end-less spool of heavy brown paper. The first light fixture off the assembly line arrived. He ripped away a sheet of paper, spread it on the table, then placed the light fixture on it. He flicked the paper together length-wise, holding it with a small piece of Scotch tape. Then he folded the left end into a triangle, then the right end, and then the fixture moved toward Tom.

Tom sheared off a length of gummed tape and ran it carefully along the top of the fixture, where the paper was to be sealed. Then with shorter lengths he tightly secured the left end, and then the right. Then he lifted the heavy fixture, turned, walked across an aisle and placed it upright in a wall rack where it awaited one of the packers. Then he went back to the table where another fixture was moving toward him.

It was the worst job in the plant and everybody knew it.

"You'll work with Ramon now, Tom . . . "

Brock left. There was no need to watch him: if Tom didn't perform his function properly, the whole assembly line stopped.

Nobody ever lasted long as second man to Ramon.

"I knew you'd need that yellow," Ramon said with a grin.

The fixtures moved relentlessly at them. Tom tore lengths of tape from the machine in front of him. It was a glistening, thick, wetted tape. He forced himself into the quick rhythm of the work but in order to keep up with Ramon, a certain caution was sacrificed: the razor-sharp edge of the tape occasionally cut long deep slices into his hands. The cuts were nearly invisible and seldom bled but looking at his fingers and palms he could see the bright red lines in the skin. There was never a pause. The fixtures seemed to move faster and faster and get heavier and heavier.

"Fuck," said Tom, "I ought to quit. Wouldn't a park bench beat this shit?"

"Sure," said Ramon, "sure, anything beats this shit . . . "

Ramon was working with a tight crazy grin, denying the impossibility of it all. And then, the machinery stopped, as it did every now and then.

What a gift from the gods that was!

Something had jammed, something had overheated. Without those machinery breakdowns, most of the workers could not have endured. Within those 2 or 3 minute breaks they pulled their senses and their souls back together. Almost.

The mechanics scrambled wildly looking for the cause of the breakdown.

Tom looked over at the Mexican girls on the assembly line. To him, they were all very beautiful. They gave away their time, their lives to dull and routine labor, but they *kept* something back, some little thing. Many of them wore small ribbons in their hair: blue, yellow, green, red . . . And they made private jokes and laughed continually. They showed immense courage. Their eyes knew something.

But the mechanics were good, very good, and the machinery was starting. The lighting fixtures were moving at Tom and Ramon again. They all were working for the Sunray Company again.

And after a while, Tom got so tired that it went beyond tiredness, it was like being drunk, it was like being crazy, it was like being drunk and crazy.

As Tom slapped a piece of tape on a light fixture he screamed out, "SUNRAY!"

It could have been his tone or the timing. Anyhow, everybody started laughing, the Mexican girls, the packers, the mechanics, even the old man who went about oiling and checking the machinery, they all laughed, it was crazy.

Brock walked out.

"What's happening?" he asked.

He got silence.

The fixtures came and went and the workers remained.

Then, somehow, like awakening from a nightmare, the day was over. They walked to the card racks, pulled their cards and then waited in line before the time clock to check out.

Tom hit the clock, racked his card, made it to his car. It started and he pulled out into the street, thinking, I hope nobody gets in my way, I think I'm too weak to put my foot down on the brake.

Tom drove back with the gas gauge sliding into the red. He was too tired to stop and pump gas.

He managed to park, got to his door, opened it and walked in.

The first thing he saw was Helena, his wife. She was in a loose dirty housegown, she was sprawled on the couch, her head on a pillow. Her mouth was open, she was snoring. She had a rather round mouth and her snoring was a mixture of spitting and gulping, as if she couldn't make up her mind whether to spit out her life or swallow it.

She was an unhappy woman. She felt that her life was unfulfilled.

A pint of gin was on the coffee table. It was ¾'s empty.

Tom's two sons, Rob and Bob, age 5 and 7, were bouncing a tennis ball against the wall. It was the south wall, the one without any furniture. The wall had once been white but now was pocked and dirty from the endless banging of tennis balls.

The boys paid no attention to their father. They had stopped banging the ball against the wall. Now they were arguing.

"I STRUCK YOU OUT!"

"NO, IT'S BALL FOUR!"

"STRIKE THREE!"

"BALL FOUR!"

"Hey, wait a minute," Tom asked, "can I ask you fellows something?"

They stopped and stared, almost affronted.

"Yeah," Bob said finally. He was the 7-year-old.

"How can you guys play *baseball,* bouncing a ball against a wall?"

They looked at Tom, then ignored him.

"STRIKE THREE!"

"NO, BALL FOUR!"

Tom walked into the kitchen. There was a white pot on the stove. Dark smoke was rising from it. Tom looked under the lid. The bottom was blackened, with burnt potatoes, carrots, chunks of meat. Tom slid the pot over and shut the flame off.

Then he went to the refrigerator. There was a can of beer in there. He took it out, pulled the tab and had a gulp.

The sound of the tennis ball against the wall began again.

Then there was another sound: Helena. She had bumped against something. Then she was there, standing in the kitchen. In her right hand she held the pint of gin.

"I guess you're mad, huh?"

"I just wish you'd feed the kids . . . "

"You just leave me a lousy $3 each day. What am I supposed to do with a lousy $3?"

"At least, get some toilet paper. Every time I want to wipe my ass I look around and there's just a cardboard roll hanging there."

"Hey, a woman has *her* problems too! HOW DO YOU THINK I LIVE? Every day, you go out into the *world,* you get to go out and see the world! I've got to sit around *here!* You don't know what that's like day after day!"

"Yeah, well, there's that . . . "

Helena took a hit of her gin.

"You know I love you, Tommy, and when you're unhappy, it hurts me, it hurts my heart, it does."

"All right, Helena, let's sit down here and calm down."

Tom walked to the breakfastnook table and had a seat. Helena brought her pint and sat across from him. She looked at him.

"Jesus, what happened to your hands?"

"New job. I've got to figure a way to protect my hands . . . Adhesive tape, rubber gloves . . . something . . . "

He had finished his beer can. "Listen, Helena, got any more of that gin around?"

"Yeah, I think so . . . "

He watched as she went to the cupboard, reached high, and got a bottle down. She came back with the pint, sat down again. Tom unpeeled the bottle.

"How many of these have you got around?"

"A few . . . "

"Good. How do you drink this? Straight?"

"You can . . . "

Tom took a good hit. Then he looked down at his hands, opening and closing them, watching the red wounds open and shut. They were fascinating.

He took the bottle, poured a little gin into one of his palms, then rubbed it around on his hands.

"Wow! This shit burns!"

Helena took another hit at her bottle. "Tom, why don't you get another job?"

"Another job? Where? There's a hundred guys want *mine* . . . "

Then Rob and Bob ran in. They skidded to a stop at the breakfast-nook table.

"Hey," said Bob, "when we gonna *eat?*"

Tom looked at Helena.

"I think I've got some weenies," she said.

"Weenies again?" asked Rob. "*Weenies?* I *hate weenies!*"

Tom looked at his son. "Hey, fellow, go easy . . . "

"Well," said Bob, "how about a fucking drink then?"

"You little bastard!" Helena yelled.

She reached out, open-handed, and slapped Bob hard on the ear.

"Don't hit the kids, Helena," said Tom, "I got too much of that myself when I was a kid."

"Don't tell me how to handle my kids!"

"They're mine too . . . "

Bob was standing there. His ear was very red.

"So, you want a fucking drink, eh?" Tom asked him.

Bob didn't answer.

"Come here," said Tom.

Bob walked over near his father. Tom handed him the bottle.

"Go on, drink it. Drink your fucking drink."

"Tom, what are you *doing?*" Helena asked.

"Go on . . . drink it," said Tom.

Bob lifted the pint, took a gulp. Then he handed the bottle back, stood there. Suddenly he looked pale, even the red ear began to pale. He coughed. "This stuff's AWFUL! It's like drinking *perfume!* Why do you *drink* it?"

"Because we're stupid. You've got stupid parents. Now, go to the bedroom and take your brother with you . . . "

"Can we watch the tv in there?" asked Rob.

"All right, but get going . . . "

They filed out.

"Don't you go making *drunks* out of my kids!" Helena said.

"I just hope they have better luck in life than we've had."

Helena took a hit from her bottle. That finished it off.

She got up, took the burnt pot from the stove and slammed it into the sink.

"I don't *need* all that god damned noise!" Tom said.

Helena appeared to be crying. "Tom, what are we going to *do?*"

She turned the hot water into the pot.

"Do?" asked Tom. "About what?"

"About the way we have to *live!*"

"There's not a hell of a lot we *can* do."

Helena scraped out the burnt food and poured some soap into the pot, then reached into the cupboard and got another pint of gin. She came around, sat down across from Tom, and peeled the bottle. "Got to let the pot soak a while . . . I'll get the weenies on soon . . . "

Tom drank from his bottle, sat it down.

"Baby, you're just an old sot, an old sot-pot . . . "

The tears were still there. "Oh yeah, well, *who* do you think *made* me this way? ONE GUESS!"

"That's easy," answered Tom, "two people: you and me."

Helena took her first drink from the new bottle. With that, at once, the tears vanished. She gave a little smile. "Hey, I've got an idea! I can get a job as a waitress or something . . . You can rest up awhile, you know . . . What do you think?"

Tom put his hand across the table, put it on one of Helena's.

"You're a good girl, but let's leave it like it is."

Then the tears were coming back again. Helena was good with the tears, especially when she was drinking gin. "Tommy, do you still love me?"

"Sure, baby, at your best you're wonderful."

"I love you too, Tom, you know that . . . "

"Sure, baby, here's to it!"

Tom lifted his bottle. Helena lifted hers.

They clicked their pints of gin in mid-air, then each drank to the other.

In the bedroom, Rob and Bob had the radio on, they had it on *loud*. There was a laugh-track on and the people on the laugh-track were laughing and laughing and laughing

and laughing.

—*SEPTUAGENARIAN STEW*

• •

Miami was as far as I could go without leaving the country. I took Henry Miller with me and tried to read him all the way across. He was good when he was good, and vice versa. I had a pint. Then I had another pint, and another. The trip took four days and five nights. Outside of a leg-and-thigh rubbing episode with a young brunette girl whose parents would no longer support her in college, nothing much happened. She got off in the middle of the night in a particularly barren and cold part of the country, and vanished. I had always had insomnia and the only time I could really sleep on a bus was when I was totally drunk. I didn't dare try that. When we arrived I hadn't slept or shit for five days and I could barely walk. It was early evening. It felt good to be in the streets again.

ROOMS FOR RENT. I walked up and rang the doorbell. At such times one always places the old suitcase out of the view of the person who will open the door.

"I'm looking for a room. How much is it?"

"$6.50 a week."

"May I look at it?"

"Surely."

I walked in and followed her up the stairway. She was about forty-five but her behind swayed nicely. I have followed so many women up stairways like that, always thinking, if only some nice lady like this one would offer to take care of me and feed me warm tasty food and lay out clean stockings and shorts for me to wear, I would accept.

She opened the door and I looked in.

"All right," I said, "it looks all right."

"Are you employed?"

"Self-employed."

"May I ask what you do?"

"I'm a writer."

"Oh, have you written books?"

"Oh, I'm hardly ready for a novel. I just do articles, bits for magazines. Not very good really but I'm developing."

"All right. I'll give you your key and make out a receipt."

I followed her down the stairway. The ass didn't sway as nicely going down the stairway as going up. I looked at the back of her neck and imagined kissing her behind the ears.

"I'm Mrs. Adams," she said. "Your name?"

"Henry Chinaski."

As she made out the receipt, I heard sounds like the sawing of wood coming from behind the door to our left—only the rasps were punctuated with gasps for breath. Each breath seemed to be the last yet each breath finally led painfully to another.

"My husband is ill," said Mrs. Adams and as she handed me the receipt and my key, she smiled. Her eyes were a lovely hazel color and sparkled. I turned and walked back up the stairs.

When I got into my room I remembered I had left my suitcase downstairs. I went down to fetch it. As I walked past Mrs. Adams' door the gasping sounds were much louder. I took my suitcase upstairs, threw it on the bed, then walked downstairs again and out into the night. I found a main boulevard a little to the north, walked into a grocery store and bought a jar of peanut butter and a loaf of bread. I had a pocket knife and would be able to spread the peanut butter on the bread and have something to eat.

When I got back to the roominghouse I stood in the hall and listened to Mr. Adams, and I thought, that's Death. Then I went up to my room and opened the jar of peanut butter and while listening to the death sounds from below I dug my fingers in. I ate it right off my fingers. It was great. Then I opened the bread. It was green and moldy and had a sharp sour smell. How could they sell bread like that? What kind of a place was Florida? I threw the bread on the floor, got undressed, turned out the light, pulled up the covers and lay there in the dark, listening.

I found a job through the newspaper. I was hired by a clothing store but it wasn't in Miami it was in Miami Beach, and I had to take my hangover across the water each morning. The bus ran along a very narrow strip of cement that stood up out of the water with no guard-rail, no nothing; that's all there was to it. The bus driver leaned back and we roared along over this narrow cement strip surrounded by water and all the people in the bus, the twenty-five or forty or fifty-two people trusted him, but I never did. Sometimes it was a new driver, and I thought, how do they select these sons of bitches? There's deep water on both sides of us and with one error of judgment he'll kill us all. It was ridiculous. Suppose he had an argument with his wife that morning? Or cancer? Or visions of God? Bad teeth? Anything. He could do it. Dump us all. I knew that if I was driving that *I* would consider the possibility or desirability of drowning everybody. And sometimes, after just such considerations, possibility turns into reality. For each Joan of Arc there is a Hitler perched at the other end of the teeter-totter. The old story of good and evil. But none of the bus drivers ever dumped us. They were thinking instead of car payments, baseball scores, haircuts, vacations, enemas, family visits. There wasn't a real man in the whole shitload. I always got to work sick but safe. Which demonstrates why Schumann was more relative than Shostakovich . . .

I was hired as what they called the extra ball-bearing. The extra ball-bearing is the man who is simply turned loose without specific duties. He is supposed to *know* what to do after consulting some deep well of ancient instinct. Instinctively one is supposed to know what will best keep things running smoothly, best maintain the company, the Mother, and meet all her little needs which are irrational, continual and petty.

A good extra ball-bearing man is faceless, sexless, sacrificial; he is always waiting at the door when the first man with the key arrives. Soon he is hosing off the sidewalk, and he greets each person by name as they arrive, always with a bright smile and in a reassuring manner. Obeisant. That makes everybody feel a little better before the bloody grind begins. He sees that toilet paper is plentiful, especially in the ladies' crapper. That wastebaskets never overflow. That no grime coats the windows.

That small repairs are promptly made on desks and office chairs. That doors open easily. That clocks are set. That carpeting remains tacked down. That overfed powerful women do not have to carry small packages.

I wasn't very good. My idea was to wander about doing nothing, always avoiding the boss, and avoiding the stoolies who might report to the boss. I wasn't all that clever. It was more instinct than anything else. I always started a job with the feeling that I'd soon quit or be fired, and this gave me a relaxed manner that was mistaken for intelligence or some secret power.

It was a completely self-sufficient, self-contained clothing store, factory and retail business combined. The showroom, the finished product and the salesmen were all downstairs, and the factory was up above. The factory was a maze of catwalks and runways that even the rats couldn't crawl, long narrow lofts with men and women sitting and working under thirty watt bulbs, squinting, treading pedals, threading needles, never looking up or speaking, bent and quiet, doing it.

At one time one of my jobs in New York City had been to take bolts of fabric up to lofts like this. I would roll my hand truck in the busy street, pushing it through traffic, then into an alley behind some grimy building. There would be a dark elevator and I'd have to pull on ropes with stained round wooden spools attached. One rope meant up, another rope signalled down. There was no light and as the elevator climbed slowly I'd watch in the dark for white numbers written on the bare walls—3, 7, 9, scrawled in chalk by some forgotten hand. I'd reach my floor, tug on another rope with my fingers and using all my strength slowly slide open the heavy old metal door, revealing row upon row of old Jewish ladies at their machines, laboring over piecework; the number one seamstress at the #1 machine, bent on maintaining her place; the number two girl at the #2 machine, ready to replace her should she falter. They never looked up or in any way acknowledged my presence as I entered.

In this clothing factory and store in Miami Beach, no deliveries were necessary. Everything was on hand. My first day I walked around the maze of lofts looking at people. Unlike New York, most of the workers were black. I walked up to a black man, quite small—almost tiny, who had a more pleasant face than most. He was doing some close work with a needle. I had a half pint in my pocket. "You got a rotten job there. Care for a drink?"

"Sure," he said. He took a good hit. Then handed the bottle back. He offered me a cigarette. "You new in town?" "Yeah." "Where you from?" "Los Angeles." "Movie star?" "Yes, on vacation." "You shouldn't be talking to the help." "I know." He fell silent. He looked like a little monkey, an old graceful monkey. For the boys downstairs, he *was* a monkey. I took a hit. I was feeling good. I watched them all working quietly under their thirty watt bulbs, their hands moving delicately and swiftly. "My name's Henry," I said. "Brad," he answered. "Listen, Brad, I get the deep deep blues watching you people work. Suppose I sing you guys and gals a little song?" "Don't." "You've got a rotten job there. Why do you do it?" "Shit, ain't no other way." "The Lord said there was." "You believe in the Lord?" "No." "What do you believe in?" "Nothing." "We're even."

I talked to some of the others. The men were uncommunicative, some of the women laughed at me. "I'm a spy," I laughed back. "I'm a company spy. I'm watching everybody."

I took another hit. Then I sang them my favorite song, "My Heart Is a Hobo." They kept working. Nobody looked up. When I finished they were still working. It was quiet for some time. Then I heard a voice: "Look, white boy, don't come down on us."

I decided to go hose off the front sidewalk.

It took four days and five nights for the bus to reach Los Angeles. As usual I neither slept nor defecated during the trip. There was some minor excitement when a big blonde got on somewhere in Louisiana. That night she started selling it for $2, and every man and one woman on the bus took advantage of her generosity except me and the bus driver. Business was transacted at night in the back of the bus. Her name was Vera. She wore purple lipstick and laughed a lot. She approached me during a brief stop in a coffee and sandwich shop. She stood behind me and asked, "Whatsa matter, you too good for me?" I didn't reply. "A fag," I heard her mutter disgustedly as she sat down next to one of the regular guys . . .

In Los Angeles I toured the bars in our old neighborhood looking for Jan. I didn't get anywhere until I found Whitey Jackson working behind the bar in the Pink Mule. He told me that Jan was working as a chambermaid in the Durham Hotel at Beverly and Vermont. I walked on over. I was looking for the manager's office when she stepped out of a room.

She looked good, like getting away from me for a while had helped her. Then she saw me. She just stood there, her eyes got very blue and round and she stood there. Then she said it, "Hank!" She rushed over and we were in each other's arms. She kissed me wildly, I tried to kiss back. "Jesus," she said, "I thought I'd never see you again!" "I'm back." "Are you back for good?" "L.A.'s my town." "Step back," she said, "let me look at you." I stepped back, grinning. "You're thin. You've lost weight," Jan said. "You're looking good," I said, "are you alone?" "Yes." "There's nobody?" "Nobody. You know I can't stand people." "I'm glad you're working." "Come to my room," she said.

I followed her. The room was very small but there was a good feel to it. You could look out the window and see the traffic, watch the signals working, see the paperboy on the corner. I liked the place. Jan threw herself on the bed. "Come on, lay down," she said. "I'm embarrassed." "I love you, you idiot," she said, "we've fucked eight hundred times, so relax." I took my shoes off and stretched out. She lifted a leg. "Still like my legs?" "Hell yes. Jan, have you finished your work?" "All but Mr. Clark's room. And Mr. Clark doesn't care. He leaves me tips." "Oh?" "I'm not doing anything. He just leaves tips." "Jan . . . " "Yes?" "The bus fare took all my money. I need a place to stay until I find a job." "I can hide you here." "Can you?" "Sure." "I love you, baby," I said. "Bastard," she said. We began to go at it. It felt good. It felt very very good.

Afterwards Jan got up and opened a bottle of wine. I opened my last pack of cigarettes and we sat in bed drinking and smoking. "You're all there," she said. "What do you mean?" "I mean, I never met a man like you." "Oh yeah?" "The others are only ten per cent there or twenty per cent, you're all there, *all* of you is very there, it's so different." "I don't know anything about it." "You're a hooker, you can hook women." That made me feel good. After we finished our cigarettes we made love again. Then Jan sent me out for another bottle. I came back. I had to.

I got hired immediately at a fluorescent light fixture company. It was up on Alameda Street, to the north, in a cluster of warehouses. I was the shipping clerk. It was quite easy, I took the orders out of a wire basket, filled them, packed the fixtures in cartons, and stacked the cartons on skids out on the loading dock, each carton labeled and numbered. I weighed the cartons, made out a bill of lading, and phoned the trucking companies to come pick the stuff up.

The first day I was there, in the afternoon, I heard a loud crash behind me near the assembly line. The old wooden racks that housed the finished parts were pulling away from the wall and crashing to the floor—metal and glass were hitting the cement floor, smashing, making a terrible racket. The assembly line workers ran to the other side of the building. Then it was silent. The boss, Mannie Feldman, stepped out of the office.

"What the hell's going on here?"

Nobody answered.

"All right, shut down the assembly line! Everybody get a hammer and nails and get those fucking racks back up there!"

Mr. Feldman walked back into his office. There was nothing for me to do but to get in and help them. None of us were carpenters. It took us all afternoon and half the next morning to nail the racks back up. As we finished Mr. Feldman walked out of his office.

"So, you did it? All right, now listen to me—I want the 939's stacked on top, the 820's next on down, and the louvers and glass on the bottom shelves, get it? Now, does everybody get it?"

There wasn't any answer. The 939's were the heaviest fixtures—they were really heavy mothers—and he wanted them on top. He was the boss. We went about it. We stacked them up there, all that weight, and we stacked the light stuff on the bottom racks. Then we went back to work. Those racks held up the rest of the day and through the night. In the morning we began to hear creaking sounds. The racks were starting to go. The assembly line workers began to edge away, they were grinning. About ten minutes before the morning coffee break everything came down again. Mr. Feldman came running out of his office:

"What the hell's going on here?"

Feldman was trying to collect his insurance and go bankrupt at the same time. The next morning a dignified looking man came down from the Bank of America. He told us not to build any more racks. "Just stack that shit on the floor," was the way he put it. His name was Jennings, Curtis Jennings. Feldman owed the Bank of America a lot of money and the Bank of America wanted its money back before the business went under. Jennings took over management of the company. He walked around watching everybody. He went through Feldman's books; he checked the locks and the windows and the security fence around the parking lot. He came up to me: "Don't use Sieberling Truck Lines any more. They had four thefts while running one of your shipments through Arizona and New Mexico. Any particular reason you been using those boys?" "No, no reason." The agent from Sieberling had been slipping me ten cents for each five hundred pounds of freight shipped out.

Within three days Jennings fired a man who worked in the front office and replaced three men on the assembly line with three young Mexican girls willing to work for half the pay. He fired the janitor and, along with doing the shipping, had me driving the company truck on local deliveries.

I got my first paycheck and moved out of Jan's place and into an apartment of my own. When I came home one night, she had moved in with me. What the fuck, I told her, my land is your land. Shortly thereafter, we had our worst fight. She left and I got drunk for three days and three nights. When I sobered up I knew my job was gone. I never went back. I decided to clean up the apartment. I vacuumed the floors, scrubbed the window ledges, scoured the bathtub and sink, waxed the kitchen floor, killed all the spiders and roaches, emptied and washed the ashtrays, washed the dishes, scrubbed the kitchen sink, hung up clean towels and installed a new roll of toilet paper. I must be turning fag, I thought.

When Jan finally came home—a week later—she accused me of having had a woman here, because everything looked so clean. She acted very angry, but it was just a cover for her own guilt. I couldn't understand why I didn't get rid of her. She was compulsively unfaithful—she'd go off with anyone she met in a bar, and the lower and the dirtier he was the better she liked it. She was continually using our arguments to justify herself. I kept telling myself that all the women in the world weren't whores, just mine.

—*Factotum*

fire station

● ●

(For Jane, with love)

we came out of the bar
because we were out of money
but we had a couple of wine bottles
in the room.

it was about 4 in the afternoon
and we passed a fire station
and she started to go
crazy:

"a FIRE STATION! oh, I just love
FIRE engines, they're so red and
all! let's go in!"

I followed her on
in. "FIRE ENGINES!" she screamed
wobbling her big
ass.

she was already trying to climb into
one, pulling her skirt up to her
waist, trying to jacknife up into the
seat.

"here, here, lemme help ya!" a fireman ran
up.

another fireman walked up to
me: "our citizens are always welcome,"
he told
me.

the other guy was up in the seat with
her. "you got one of those big THINGS?"

she asked him. "oh, hahaha!, I mean one of
those big HELMETS!"

"I've got a big helmet too," he told
her.

"oh, hahaha!"

"you play cards?" I asked *my*
fireman. I had 43 cents and nothing but
time.

"come on in back," he
said. "of course, we don't gamble.
it's against the
rules."

"I understand," I told
him.

I had run my 43 cents up to a
dollar ninety
when I saw her going upstairs with
her fireman.

"he's gonna show me their sleeping
quarters," she told
me.

"I understand," I told
her.

when her fireman slid down the pole
ten minutes later
I nodded him
over.

"that'll be 5
dollars."

"5 dollars for
that?"

"we wouldn't want a scandal, would
we? we both might lose our
jobs. of course, I'm not
working."

he gave me the
5.

"sit down, you might get it
back."

"whatcha playing?"
"blackjack."

"gambling's against the
law."

"anything interesting is. besides,
you see any money on the
table?"
he sat down.

that made 5 of
us.

"how was it Harry?" somebody asked
him.

"not bad, not
bad."

the other guy went on
upstairs.

they were bad players really.
they didn't bother to memorize the
deck. they didn't know whether the
high numbers or low numbers were left. and basically they hit too high,
didn't hold low
enough.

when the other guy came down
he gave me a
five.

"how was it, Marty?"
"not bad. she's got . . . some fine
movements."

"hit me!" I said. "nice clean girl. I
ride it myself."

nobody said
anything.

"any big fires lately?" I
asked.

"naw. nothin'
much."

"you guys need
exercise. hit me
again!"

a big red-headed kid who had been shining an
engine
threw down his rag and
went upstairs.

when he came down he threw me a
five.

when the 4th guy came down I gave him
3 fives for a
twenty.

I don't know how many firemen
were in the building or where they
were. I figured a few had slipped by me
but I was a good
sport.

it was getting dark outside
when the alarm
rang.

they started running around.
guys came sliding down the
pole.

then she came sliding down the
pole. she was good with the
pole. a real woman. nothing but guts
and
ass.

"let's go," I told
her.

she stood there waving goodbye to the
firemen but they didn't seem
much interested
any more.

"let's go back to the
bar," I told
her.

"ooh, you got
money?"

"I found some I didn't know I
had . . . "

we sat at the end of the bar
with whiskey and beer
chaser.
"I sure got a good
sleep."

"sure, baby, you need your
sleep."

"look at that sailor looking at me!
he must think I'm . . . a . . . "

"naw, he don't think that. relax, you've got
class, real class. sometimes you remind me of an
opera singer. you know, one of those prima d's.
your class shows all over
you. drink
up."

I ordered 2
more.

"you know, daddy, you're the only man I
LOVE! I mean, really . . . LOVE! ya
know?"

"sure I know. sometimes I think I am a king
in spite of myself."

"yeah. yeah. *that's* what I mean, somethin' like
that."

I had to go to the urinal. when I came back
the sailor was sitting in my
seat. she had her leg up against his and
he was talking.

I walked over and got in a dart game with
Harry the Horse and the corner
newsboy.

• •

The Hotel Sans was the best in the city of Los Angeles. It was an old hotel but it had class and a charm missing from the newer places. It was directly across from the park downtown.

It was renowned for businessmen's conventions and expensive hookers of almost legendary talent—who at the end of a lucrative evening had even been known to give the bellboys a little. There also were stories of bellboys who had become millionaires—bloody bellboys with eleven inch dicks who had had the good fortune to meet and marry some rich, elderly guest. And the *food*, the LOBSTER, the huge black chefs in very tall white hats who knew everything, not only about food but about Life and about me and about everything.

I was assigned to the loading dock. That loading dock had *style:* for each truck that came in there were ten guys to unload it when it only took two at the most. I wore my best clothes. I never touched anything.

We unloaded (they unloaded) everything that came into the hotel and most of it was foodstuffs. My guess was that the rich ate more lobster than anything else. Crates and crates of them would come in, deliciously pink and large, waving their claws and feelers.

"You like those things, don't you, Chinaski?"

"Yeah. Oh yeah," I'd drool.

One day the lady in the employment office called me over. The employment office was at the rear of the loading dock. "I want you to manage this office on Sundays, Chinaski." "What do I do?" "Just answer the phone and hire the Sunday dishwashers." "All right!"

• • •

The first Sunday was nice. I just sat there. Soon an old guy walked in. "Yeah, buddy?" I asked. He had on an expensive suit, but it was wrinkled and a little dirty; and the cuffs were just starting to go. He was holding his hat in his hand. "Listen," he asked, "do you need somebody who is a good conversationalist? Somebody who can meet and talk to people? I have a certain amount of charm, I tell gracious stories, I can make people laugh."

"Yeah?"

"Oh, yes."

"Make me laugh."

"Oh, you don't understand. The setting has to be right, the mood, the *decor*, you know . . . "

"Make me laugh."

"Sir . . . "

"Can't use you, you're a stiff!"

The dishwashers were hired at noon. I stepped out of the office. Forty bums stood there. "All right now, we need five good men! Five *good* ones! No winos, perverts, communists, or child-molestors! And you've got to have a social security card! All right now, get them out and hold them up in the air!"

Out came the cards. They waved them.

"Hey, I got one!"

"Hey, buddy, over here! Give a guy a break!"

I slowly looked them over. "O.K., you with the shit stain on your collar," I pointed. "Step forward."

"That's no shit stain, sir. That's gravy."

"Well, I don't know, buddy, looks to me like you been eatin' more crotch than roast beef!"

"Ah, hahaha," went the bums, "Ah, hahaha!"

"O.K., now, I need *four* good dishwashers! I have four pennies here in my hand. I'm going to toss them up. The four men who bring me back a penny get to wash dishes today!"

I tossed the pennies high into the air above the crowd. Bodies jumped and fell, clothing ripped, there were curses, one man screamed, there were several fistfights. Then the lucky four came forward, one at a time, breathing heavily, each with a penny. I gave them their work cards and waved them toward the employee's cafeteria where they would first be fed. The other bums retreated slowly down the loading ramp, jumped off, and walked down the alley into the wasteland of downtown Los Angeles on a Sunday.

Workmen For Industry was located right on the edge of skid row. The bums were better dressed, younger, but just as listless. They sat around on the window ledges, hunched forward, getting warm in the sun and drinking the free coffee that W.F.I. offered. There was no cream and sugar, but it was free. There was no wire partition separating us from the clerks. The telephones rang more often and the clerks were much more relaxed than at the Farm Labor Market.

I walked up to the counter and was given a card and a pen anchored by a chain. "Fill it out," said the clerk, a nice-looking Mexican boy who tried to hide his warmth behind a professional manner.

I began to fill out the card. After address and phone number I wrote: "none." Then after education and work abilities I wrote: "two years L.A. City College. Journalism and Fine Arts."

Then I told the clerk, "I ruined this card. Could I have another?"

He gave me one. I wrote instead: "Graduate, L.A. High School. Shipping clerk, warehouseman, laborer. Some typing."

I handed the card back.

"All right," said the clerk, "sit down and we'll see if anything comes in."

I found a space on a window ledge and sat down. An old black man was sitting next to me. He had an interesting face; he didn't have the usual resigned look that most of us sitting around the room had. He looked as if he was attempting not to laugh at himself and the rest of us.

He saw me glancing at him. He grinned. "Guy who runs this place is sharp. He got fired by the Farm Labor, got pissed, came down here and started this. Specializes in part-time workers. Some guy wants a boxcar unloaded quick and cheap, he calls here."

"Yeah, I've heard."

"Guy needs a boxcar unloaded quick and cheap, he calls here. Guy who runs this place takes fifty per cent. We don't complain. We take what we can get."

"It's O.K. with me. Shit."

"You look down in the mouth. You all right?"

"Lost a woman."

"You'll have others and lose them too."

"Where do they go?"

"Try some of this."

It was a bottle in a bag. I took a hit. Port wine.

"Thanks."

"Ain't no women on skid row."

He passed the bottle to me again. "Don't let him see us drinking. That's the one thing makes him mad."

While we sat drinking several men were called and left for jobs. It cheered us. At least there was some action.

My black friend and I waited, passing the bottle back and forth.

Then it was empty.

"Where's the nearest liquor store?" I asked.

I got the directions and left. Somehow it was always hot on skid row in Los Angeles in the daytime. You'd see old bums walking around in heavy overcoats in the heat. But when the night came down and the Mission was full, those overcoats came in handy.

When I got back from the liquor store my friend was still there.

I sat down and opened the bottle, passed the bag.

"Keep it low," he said.

It was comfortable in there drinking the wine.

A few gnats began to gather and circle in front of us.

"Wine gnats," he said.

"Sons of bitches are hooked."

"They know what's good."

"They drink to forget their women."

"They just drink."

I waved at them in the air and got one of the wine gnats. When I opened my hand all I could see in my palm was a speck of black and the strange sight of two little wings. Zero.

"Here he comes!"

It was the nice-looking young guy who ran the place. He rushed up to us. "All right! Get out of here! Get the hell out of here, you fuckin' winos! Get the hell out of here before I call the cops!"

He hustled us both to the door, pushing and cursing. I felt guilty, but I felt no anger. Even as he pushed I knew that he didn't really care what we did. He had a large ring on his right hand.

We didn't move fast enough and I caught the ring just over my left eye; I felt the blood start to come and then felt it swell up. My friend and I were back out on the street.

We walked away. We found a doorway and sat on the step. I handed him the bottle. He hit it.

"Good stuff."

He handed me the bottle. I hit it.

"Yeah, good stuff."

"Sun's up."

"Yeah, the sun's up good."

We sat quietly, passing the bottle back and forth.

Then the bottle was empty.

"Well," he said, "I gotta be going."

"See you."

He walked off. I got up, went the other way, turned the corner, and walked up Main Street. I went along until I came to the Roxie.

Photos of the strippers were on display behind the glass out front. I walked up and bought a ticket. The girl in the cage looked better than the photos. Now I had 38 cents left. I walked into the dark theatre eight rows from the front. The first three rows were packed.

I had lucked out. The movie was over and the first stripper was already on. Darlene. The first was usually the worst, an old-timer come down, now reduced to kicking leg in the chorus line most of the time. We had Darlene for openers. Probably someone had been murdered or was on the rag or was having a screaming fit, and this was Darlene's chance to dance solo again.

But Darlene was fine. Skinny, but with breasts. A body like a willow. At the end of that slim back, that slim body, was an enormous behind. It was like a miracle—enough to drive a man crazy.

Darlene was dressed in a long black velvet gown slit very high—her calves and thighs were dead white against the black. She danced and looked out at us through heavily mascaraed eyes. This was her chance. She wanted to come back—to be a featured dancer once again. I was with her. As she worked at the zippers more and more of her began to show, to slip out of that sophisticated black velvet, leg and white flesh. Soon she was down to her pink bra and G-string—the fake diamonds swinging and flashing as she danced.

Darlene danced over and grabbed the stage curtain. The curtain was torn and thick with dust. She grabbed it, dancing to the beat of the four man band and in the light of the pink spotlight.

She began to fuck that curtain. The band rocked in rhythm. Darlene really gave it to that curtain; the band rocked and she rocked. The pink light abruptly switched to purple. The band stepped it up, played all out. She appeared to climax. Her head fell back, her mouth opened.

Then she straightened and danced back to the center of the stage. From where I was sitting I could hear her singing to herself over the music. She took a hold of her pink bra and ripped it off and a guy three rows down lit a cigarette. There was just the G-string now. She pushed her finger into her bellybutton, and moaned.

Darlene remained dancing at stage center. The band was playing very softly. She began a gentle grind. She was fucking us. The beaded G-string was swaying slowly. Then the four man band began to pick up gradually once again. They were reaching for the culmination of the act; the drummer was cracking rim-shots like firecrackers; they looked tired, desperate.

Darlene fingered her naked breasts, showing them to us, her eyes filled with the dream, her lips moist and parted. Then suddenly she turned and waved her enormous behind at us. The beads leaped and flashed, went crazy, sparkled. The spotlight shook and danced like the sun. The four man band crackled and banged. Darlene spun around. She tore away the beads. I looked, they looked. We could see her cunt hairs through the flesh-colored gauze. The band really spanked her ass.

And I couldn't get it up.

—*FACTOTUM*

The Night They Took Whitey

bird-dream and peeling wallpaper
symptoms of grey sleep
and at 4 a.m. Whitey came out of his room
(the solace of the poor is in numbers
like Summer poppies)

and he began to scream *help me! help me! help me!*
(an old man with hair as white as any ivory tusk)
and he was vomiting blood
help me help me help me
and I helped him lie down in the hall
and I beat on the landlady's door
(she is as French as the best wine but as tough as
an American steak) and
I hollered her name, *Marcella! Marcella!*
(the milkman would soon be coming with his
pure white bottles like chilled lilies)
Marcella! Marcella! help me help me help me,
and she screamed back through the door:
you polack bastard, are you drunk again? Then
Promethean the eye at the door
and she
sized up the red river in her rectangular brain
(oh, I am nothing but a drunken polack
a bad pinch-hitter a writer of letters to the newspapers)
and she spoke into the phone like a lady ordering bread and eggs,
and I held to the wall
dreaming bad poems and my own death
and the men came . . . one with a cigar, the other needing a shave,
and they made him stand up and walk down the steps
his ivory head on fire (Whitey, my drinking pal—
all the songs, Sing Gypsy, Laugh Gypsy, talk about
the war, the fights, the good whores,
skid-row hotels floating in wine,
floating in crazy talk,
cheap cigars and anger)
and the siren took him away, except the red part
and I began to vomit and the French wolverine screamed
you'll have to clean it up, all of it, you and Whitey!
and the steamers sailed and rich men on yachts
kissed girls young enough to be their daughters,
and the milkman came by and stared
and the neon lights blinked selling something
tires or oil or underwear

and she slammed her door and I was alone
ashamed
it was the war, the war forever, the war was never over,
and I cried against the peeling walls,
the weakness of our bones, our sotted half-brains,
and morning began to creep into the hall—
toilets flushed, there was bacon, there was coffee,
there were hangovers, and I too
went in and closed my door and sat down and waited for the sun.

the soldier, his wife and the bum

I was a bum in San Francisco but once managed
to go to a symphony concert along with the well-
dressed people
and the music was good but something about the
audience was not
and something about the orchestra
and the conductor was
not,
although the building was fine and the
acoustics perfect
I preferred to listen to the music alone
on my radio
and afterwards I did go back to my room and I
turned on the radio but
then there was a pounding on the wall:
"SHUT THAT GOD-DAMNED THING OFF!"

there was a soldier in the next room
living with his wife
and he would soon be going over there to protect me from Hitler so
I snapped the radio off and then heard his

wife say, "you shouldn't have done that."
and the soldier said, "FUCK THAT GUY!"
which I thought was a very nice thing for him
to tell his wife to do.
of course,
she never did.

anyhow, I never went to another live concert
and that night I listened to the radio very
quietly, my ear pressed to the
speaker.

war has its price and peace never lasts and
millions of young men everywhere would die
and as I listened to the classical music I
heard them making love, desperately and
mournfully, through Shostakovich, Brahms,
Mozart, through crescendo and climax,
and through the shared
wall of our darkness.

the tragedy of the leaves

I awakened to dryness and the ferns were dead,
the potted plants yellow as corn;
my woman was gone
and the empty bottles like bled corpses
surrounded me with their uselessness;
the sun was still good, though,
and my landlady's note cracked in fine and
undemanding yellowness; what was needed now
was a good comedian, ancient style, a jester
with jokes upon absurd pain; pain is absurd

because it exists, nothing more;
I shaved carefully with an old razor
the man who had once been young and
said to have genius; but
that's the tragedy of the leaves,
the dead ferns, the dead plants;
and I walked into a dark hall
where the landlady stood
execrating and final,
sending me to hell,
waving her fat, sweaty arms
and screaming
screaming for rent
because the world had failed us
both.

You and Your Beer and How Great You Are

Jack came through the door and found the pack of cigarettes on the mantel. Ann was on the couch reading a copy of *Cosmopolitan.* Jack lit up, sat down in a chair. It was 10 minutes to midnight.

"Charley told you not to smoke," said Ann, looking up from the magazine.

"I deserve it. It was a rough one tonight."

"Did you win?"

"Split decision but I got it. Benson was a tough boy, lots of guts. Charley says Parvinelli is next. We get over Parvinelli, we get the champ."

Jack got up, went to the kitchen, came back with a bottle of beer.

"Charley told me to keep you off the beer," Ann put the magazine down.

"'Charley told me, Charley told me' . . . I'm tired of that. I won my fight. I won 16 straight, I got a right to a beer and a cigarette."

"You're supposed to stay in shape."

"It doesn't matter. I can whip any of them."

"You're so great, I keep hearing it when you get drunk, you're so great. I get sick of it."

"I am great. 16 straight, 15 k.o.'s. Who's better?"

Ann didn't answer. Jack took his bottle of beer and his cigarette into the bathroom.

"You didn't even kiss me hello. The first thing you did was go to your bottle of beer. You're so great, all right. You're a great beer-drinker."

Jack didn't answer. Five minutes later he stood in the bathroom door, his pants and shorts down around his shoes.

"Jesus Christ, Ann, can't you even keep a roll of toilet paper in here?"

"Sorry."

She went to the closet and got him the roll. Jack finished his business and walked out. Then he finished his beer and got another one. "Here you are living with the best light-heavy in the world and all you do is complain. Lots of girls would love to have me but all you do is sit around and bitch."

"I know you're good, Jack, maybe the best, but you don't know how *boring* it is to sit around and listen to you say over and over again how great you are."

"Oh, you're bored with it, are you?"

"Yes, goddamn it, you and your beer and how great you are."

"Name a better light-heavy. You don't even come to my fights."

"There are *other* things besides fighting, Jack."

"What? Like laying around on your ass and reading *Cosmopolitan?*"

"I like to improve my mind."

"You ought to. There's a lot of work to be done there."

"I tell you there are other things besides fighting."

"What? Name them."

"Well, art, music, painting, things like that."

"Are you any good at them?"

"No, but I appreciate them."

"Shit, I'd rather be best at what I'm doing."

"Good, better, best . . . God, can't you appreciate people for what they are?"

"For what they *are?* What *are* most of them? Snails, bloodsuckers, dandies, finks, pimps, servants . . . "

"You're always looking down on everybody. None of your friends are good enough. You're so damned great!"

"That's right, baby."

Jack walked into the kitchen and came out with another beer.

"You and your goddamned beer!"

"It's my right. They sell it. I buy it."

"Charley said . . . "

"Fuck Charley!"

"You're so goddamned great!"

"That's right. At least Pattie knew it. She admitted it. She was proud of it. She knew it took something. All you do is bitch."

"Well, why don't you go back to Pattie? What are you doing with me?"

"That's just what I'm thinking."

"Well, we're not married, I can leave any time."

"That's one break we've got. Shit, I come in here dead-ass tired after a tough ten rounder and you're not even glad I took it. All you do is complain about me."

"Listen, Jack, there are other things besides fighting. When I met you, I admired you for what you were."

"I was a fighter. There *aren't* any other things besides fighting. That's what I am—a fighter. That's my life, and I'm good at it. The best. I notice you always go for those second raters . . . like Toby Jorgenson."

"Toby's very funny. He's got a sense of humor, a real sense of humor. I like Toby."

"His record is 9, 5, and 1. I can take him when I'm dead drunk."

"And god knows you're dead drunk often enough. How do you think I feel at parties when you're laying on the floor passed out, or lolling around the room telling everybody, 'I'M GREAT, I'M GREAT, I'M GREAT!' Don't you think that makes me feel like an ass?"

"Maybe you are an ass. If you like Toby so much, why don't you go with him?"

"Oh, I just said I liked him, I thought he was *funny,* that doesn't mean I want to go to bed with him."

"Well, you go to bed with me and you say I'm boring. I don't know what the hell you want."

Ann didn't answer. Jack got up, walked over to the couch, lifted Ann's head and kissed her, walked back and sat down again.

"Listen, let me tell you about this fight with Benson. Even you would have been proud of me. He decks me in the first round, a sneak right. I get up and hold him off the rest of the round. He plants me again in the second. I barely get up at 8. I hold him off again. The next few rounds I spend getting my legs back. I take the 6th, 7th, 8th, deck him once in the 9th and twice in the 10th. I don't call that a split. They called it a split. Well, it's 45 grand, you get that, kid? 45 grand. I'm great, you can't deny I'm great, can you?"

Ann didn't answer.

"Come on, tell me I'm great."

"All right, you're great."

"Well, that's more like it." Jack walked over and kissed her again. "I feel so good. Boxing is a work of art, it really is. It takes guts to be a great artist and it takes guts to be a great fighter."

"All right, Jack."

"'All right, Jack,' is that all you can say? Pattie used to be happy when I won. We were both happy all night. Can't you share it when I do something good? Hell, are you in love with me or are you in love with the losers, the half-asses? I think you'd be happier if I came in here a loser."

"I want you to win, Jack, it's only that you put so much emphasis on what you do . . . "

"Hell, it's my living, it's my life. I'm proud of being best. It's like flying, it's like flying off into the sky and whipping the sun."

"What are you going to do when you can't fight anymore?"

"Hell, we'll have enough money to do whatever we want."

"Except get along, maybe."

"Maybe I can learn to read *Cosmopolitan*, improve my mind."

"Well, there's room for improvement."

"Fuck you."

"What?"

"Fuck you."

"Well, that's something you haven't done in a while."

"Some guys like to fuck bitching women, I don't."

"I suppose Pattie didn't bitch?"

"All women bitch, you're the champ."

"Well, why don't you go back to Pattie?"

"You're here now. I can only house one whore at a time."

"Whore?"

"Whore."

Ann got up and went to the closet, got out her suitcase and began putting her clothes in there. Jack went to the kitchen and got another bottle of beer. Ann was crying and angry. Jack sat down with his beer and took a good drain. He needed a whiskey, he needed a bottle of whiskey. And a good cigar.

"I can come pick up the rest of my stuff when you're not around."

"Don't bother. I'll have it sent to you."

She stopped at the doorway.

"Well, I guess this is it," she said.

"I suppose it is," Jack answered.

She closed the door and was gone. Standard procedure. Jack finished the beer and went over to the telephone. He dialed Pattie's number. She answered.

"Pattie?"

"Oh, Jack, how are you?"

"I won the big one tonight. A split. All I got to do is get over Parvinelli and I got the champ."

"You'll whip both of them, Jack. I know you can do it."

"What are you doing tonight, Pattie?"

"It's 1:00 a.m. Jack. Have you been drinking?"

"A few. I'm celebrating."

"How about Ann?"

"We split. I only play one woman at a time, you know that, Pattie."

"Jack . . ."

"What?"

"I'm with a guy."

"A guy?"

"Toby Jorgenson. He's in the bedroom . . ."

"Oh, I'm sorry."

"I'm sorry, too, Jack, I loved you . . . maybe I still do."

"Oh, shit, you women really throw that word around . . ."

"I'm sorry, Jack."

"It's o.k." He hung up. Then he went to the closet for his coat. He put it on, finished the beer, went down the elevator to his car. He drove straight up Normandie at 65 m.p.h., pulled into the liquor store on Hollywood Boulevard. He got out and walked in. He got a six-pack of Michelob, a pack of Alka-Seltzers. Then at the counter he asked the clerk for a fifth of Jack Daniels. While the clerk was tabbing them up a drunk walked up with two six-packs of Coors.

"Hey, man!" he said to Jack, "ain't you Jack Backenweld, the fighter?"

"I am," answered Jack.

"Man, I saw that fight tonight, Jack, you're all guts. You're really great!"

"Thanks, man," he told the drunk, and then he took his sack of goods and walked to his car. He sat there, took the cap off the Daniels and had a good slug. Then he backed out, ran west down Hollywood, took a left at Normandie and noticed a well-built teenage girl staggering down the street. He stopped his car, lifted the fifth out of the bag and showed it to her.

"Want a ride?"

Jack was surprised when she got in. "I'll help you drink that, mister, but no fringe benefits."

"Hell, no," said Jack.

He drove down Normandie at 35 m.p.h., a self-respecting citizen and third ranked light-heavy in the world. For a moment he felt like telling her who she was riding with but he changed his mind and reached over and squeezed one of her knees.

"You got a cigarette, mister?" she asked.

He flicked one out with his hand, pushed in the dash lighter. It jumped out and he lit her up.

—*SOUTH OF NO NORTH*

cancer

● ●

I found her room at the top of the
stairway.
she was alone.
"hello, Henry," she said, then,

"you know, I hate this room, there's
no window."

I had a terrible hangover.
the smell was unbearable,
I felt as if I was going to
vomit.

"they operated on me two days ago,"
she said. "I felt better the next
day but now it's the same, maybe
worse."

"I'm sorry, mom."

"you know, you were right, your father
is a terrible man."

poor woman. a brutal husband and
an alcoholic son.

"excuse me, mom, I'll be right
back . . . "

the smell had seeped into me,
my stomach was jumping.
I got out of the room
and walked halfway down the stairs,
sat there
holding on to the railing,
breathing the fresh
air.

the poor woman.

I kept breathing the air and
managed not to
vomit.

I got up and walked back up the
stairs and into the room.

"he had me committed to a mental
institution, did you know
that?"

"yes. I informed them
that they had the wrong person
in there."

"you look sick, Henry, are you all
right?"

"I am sick today, mom, I'm going
to come back and see you
tomorrow."

"all right, Henry . . . "

I got up, closed the door, then
ran down the stairs.
I got outside, to a rose
garden.

I let it all go into the rose
garden.

poor damned woman . . .

the next day I arrived with
flowers.
I went up the stairway to the
door.
there was a wreath on the
door.
I tried the door anyhow.
it was locked.

I walked down the stairway
through the rose garden
and out to the street
where my car was
parked.

there were two little girls
about 6 or 7 years old
walking home from school.

"pardon me, ladies, but would you
like some flowers?"

they just stopped and stared at
me.

"here," I handed the bouquet to the
taller of the girls. "now, you
divide these, please give your
friend half of them."

"thank you," said the taller
girl, "they are very
beautiful."

"yes, they are," said the other
girl, "thank you very
much."

they walked off down the street
and I got into my car,
it started, and
I drove back to my
place.

The Death of the Father

• •

My mother had died a year earlier. A week after my father's death I stood in his house alone. It was in Arcadia, and the nearest I had come to the house in some time was passing by on the freeway on my way to Santa Anita.

I was unknown to the neighbors. The funeral was over, and I walked to the sink, poured a glass of water, drank it, then went outside. Not knowing what else to do, I picked up the hose, turned on the water and began watering the shrubbery. Curtains drew back as I stood on the front lawn. Then they began coming out of their houses. A woman walked over from across the street.

"Are you Henry?" she asked me.

I told her that I was Henry.

"We knew your father for years."

Then her husband walked over. "We knew your mother too," he said.

I bent over and shut off the hose. "Won't you come in?" I asked. They introduced themselves as Tom and Nellie Miller and we went into the house.

"You look just like your father."

"Yes, so they tell me."

We sat and looked at each other.

"Oh," said the woman, "he had so *many* pictures. He must have liked pictures."

"Yes, he did, didn't he?"

"I just love that painting of the windmill in the sunset."

"You can have it."

"Oh, can I?"

The doorbell rang. It was the Gibsons. The Gibsons told me that they also had been neighbors of my father's for years.

"You look just like your father," said Mrs. Gibson.

"Henry has given us the painting of the windmill."

"That's nice. I *love* that painting of the blue horse."

"You can have it, Mrs. Gibson."

"Oh, you don't mean it?"

"Yes, it's all right."

The doorbell rang again and another couple came in. I left the door ajar. Soon a single man stuck his head inside. "I'm Doug Hudson. My wife's at the hairdresser's."

"Come in, Mr. Hudson."

Others arrived, mostly in pairs. They began to circulate through the house.

"Are you going to sell the place?"

"I think I will."

"It's a lovely neighborhood."

"I can see that."

"Oh, I just *love* this frame but I don't like the picture."

"Take the frame."

"But what should I do with the picture?"

"Throw it in the trash." I looked around. "If anybody sees a picture they like, please take it."

They did. Soon the walls were bare.

"Do you need these chairs?"

"No, not really."

Passersby were coming in from the street, and not even bothering to introduce themselves.

"How about the sofa?" someone asked in a very loud voice. "Do you want it?"

"I don't want the sofa," I said.

They took the sofa, then the breakfastnook table and chairs.

"You have a toaster here somewhere, don't you, Henry?"

They took the toaster.

"You don't need these dishes, do you?"

"No."

"And the silverware?"

"No."

"How about the coffee pot and the blender?"

"Take them."

One of the ladies opened a cupboard on the back porch. "What about all these preserved fruits? You'll never be able to eat all these."

"All right, everybody, take some. But try to divide them equally."

"Oh, I want the strawberries!"

"Oh, I want the figs!"

"Oh, I want the marmalade!"

People kept leaving and returning, bringing new people with them.

"Hey, here's a fifth of whiskey in the cupboard! Do you drink, Henry?"

"Leave the whiskey."

The house was getting crowded. The toilet flushed. Somebody knocked a glass from the sink and broke it.

"You better save this vacuum cleaner, Henry. You can use it for your apartment."

"All right, I'll keep it."

"He had some garden tools in the garage. How about the garden tools?"

"No, I better keep those."

"I'll give you $15 for the garden tools."

"O.K."

He gave me the $15 and I gave him the key to the garage. Soon you could hear him rolling the lawn mower across the street to his place.

"You shouldn't have given him all that equipment for $15, Henry. It was worth much more than that."

I didn't answer.

"How about the car? It's four years old."

"I think I'll keep the car."

"I'll give you $50 for it."

"I think I'll keep the car."

Somebody rolled up the rug in the front room. After that people began to lose interest. Soon there were only three or four left, then they were all gone. They left me the garden hose, the bed, the refrigerator and stove, and a roll of toilet paper.

I walked outside and locked the garage door. Two small boys came by on roller skates. They stopped as I was locking the garage doors.

"See that man?"

"Yes."

"His father died."

They skated on. I picked up the hose, turned the faucet on and began to water the roses.

—*Hot Water Music*

The Genius of the Crowd

••

There is enough treachery, hatred,
                              violence,
Absurdity in the average human
                              being
To supply any given army on any given
    day.
AND The Best At Murder Are Those
    Who Preach Against It.
AND The Best At Hate Are Those
    Who Preach LOVE
AND THE BEST AT WAR
—FINALLY—ARE THOSE WHO
PREACH
                              PEACE

Those Who Preach GOD
    NEED God
Those Who Preach PEACE
    Do Not Have Peace.
THOSE WHO PREACH LOVE
    DO NOT HAVE LOVE
BEWARE THE PREACHERS
Beware The Knowers.

                Beware
                Those Who
                Are ALWAYS
                READING
                BOOKS

Beware Those Who Either Detest
    Poverty Or Are Proud Of It

BEWARE Those Quick To Praise
For They Need PRAISE In Return

BEWARE Those Quick To Censure:
They Are Afraid Of What They Do
Not Know

Beware Those Who Seek Constant
Crowds; They Are Nothing
Alone

      Beware
      The Average Man
      The Average Woman
      BEWARE Their Love

Their Love Is Average, Seeks
Average
But There Is Genius In Their Hatred
There Is Enough Genius In Their
Hatred To Kill You, To Kill
Anybody.

Not Wanting Solitude
Not Understanding Solitude
They Will Attempt To Destroy
Anything
That Differs
From Their Own

      Not Being Able
      To Create Art
      They Will Not
      Understand Art

They Will Consider Their Failure
As Creators
Only As A Failure
Of The World

Not Being Able To Love Fully
They Will BELIEVE Your Love
Incomplete
AND THEN THEY WILL HATE
YOU

And Their Hatred Will Be Perfect
Like A Shining Diamond
Like A Knife
Like A Mountain
LIKE A TIGER
LIKE Hemlock

      Their Finest
      ART

a free 25 page booklet

• •

dying for a beer dying
for and of life
on a windy afternoon in Hollywood
listening to symphony music from my little red radio
on the floor.

a friend said,
"all ya gotta do is go out on the sidewalk
and lay down
somebody will pick you up
somebody will take care of you."

I look out the window at the sidewalk
I see something walking on the sidewalk
she wouldn't lay down there,

only in special places for special people with special $$$$
and
special ways
while I am dying for a beer on a windy afternoon in
Hollywood,
nothing like a beautiful broad dragging it past you on the
sidewalk
moving it past your famished window
she's dressed in the finest cloth
she doesn't care what you say
how you look what you do
as long as you do not get in her
way, and it must be that she doesn't shit or
have blood
she must be a cloud, friend, the way she floats past us.

I am too sick to lay down
the sidewalks frighten me
the whole damned city frightens me,
what I will become
what I have become
frightens me.

ah, the bravado is gone
the big run through center is gone
on a windy afternoon in Hollywood
my radio cracks and spits its dirty music
through a floor full of empty beerbottles.

now I hear a siren
it comes closer
the music stops
the man on the radio says,
"we will send you a free 25-page booklet:
FACE THE FACTS ABOUT COLLEGE COSTS."

the siren fades into the cardboard mountains
and I look out the window again as the clasped fist of

boiling cloud comes down—
the wind shakes the plants outside
I wait for evening I wait for night I wait sitting in a chair
by the window—
the cook drops in the live
red-pink salty
rough-tit crab and
the game works
on

come get me.

funhouse

. . . .

I drive to the beach at night
in the winter
and sit and look at the burned-down amusement pier
wonder why they just let it sit there
in the water.
I want it out of there,
blown-up,
vanished,
erased;
that pier should no longer sit there
with madmen sleeping inside
the burned-out guts of the funhouse . . .
it's awful, I say, blow the damn thing up,
get it out of my eyes,
that tombstone in the sea.

the madmen can find other holes
to crawl into.
I used to walk that pier when I was 8
years old.

john dillinger and *le chasseur maudit*

it's unfortunate, and simply not the style, but I don't care:
girls remind me of hair in the sink, girls remind me of intestines
and bladders and excretory movements; it's unfortunate also that
ice-cream bells, babies, engine-valves, plagiostomes, palm trees,
footsteps in the hall . . . all excite me with the cold calmness
of the gravestone; nowhere, perhaps, is there sanctuary except
in hearing that there were other desperate men:
Dillinger, Rimbaud, Villon, Babyface Nelson, Seneca, Van Gogh,
or desperate women: lady wrestlers, nurses, waitresses, whores
poetesses . . . although,
I do suppose the breaking out of ice-cubes is important
or a mouse nosing an empty beercan—
two hollow emptinesses looking into each other,
or the nightsea stuck with soiled ships
that enter the chary web of your brain with their lights,
with their salty lights
that touch you and leave you
for the more solid love of some India;
or driving great distances without reason
sleep-drugged through open windows that
tear and flap your shirt like a frightened bird,
and always the stoplights, always red,
nightfire and defeat, defeat . . .
scorpions, scraps, fardels:
x-jobs, x-wives, x-faces, x-lives,
Beethoven in his grave as dead as a beet;
red wheel-barrows, yes, perhaps,
or a letter from Hell signed by the devil
or two good boys beating the guts out of each other
in some cheap stadium full of screaming smoke,
but mostly, I don't care, sitting here
with a mouthful of rotten teeth,
sitting here reading Herrick and Spenser and
Marvell and Hopkins and Bronte (Emily, today);
and listening to the Dvorak *Midday Witch*

or Franck's *Le Chasseur Maudit*,
actually I don't care, and it's unfortunate:
I have been getting letters from a young poet
(very young, it seems) telling me that some day
I will most surely be recognized as
one of the world's great poets. *Poet!*
a malversation: today I walked in the sun and streets
of this city: seeing nothing, learning nothing, being
nothing, and coming back to my room
I passed an old woman who smiled a horrible smile;
she was already dead, and everywhere I remembered wires:
telephone wires, electric wires, wires for electric faces
trapped like goldfish in the glass and smiling,
and the birds were gone, none of the birds wanted wire
or the smiling of wire
and I closed my door (at last)
but through the windows it was the same:
a horn honked, somebody laughed, a toilet flushed,
and oddly then
I thought of all the horses with numbers
that have gone by in the screaming,
gone by like Socrates, gone by like Lorca,
like Chatterton . . .
I'd rather imagine our death will not matter too much
except as a matter of disposal, a problem,
like dumping the garbage,
and although I have saved the young poet's letters,
I do not believe them
but like at the
diseased palm trees
and the end of the sun,
I sometimes look.

rain

• •

a symphony orchestra.
there is a thunderstorm,
they are playing a Wagner overture
and the people leave their seats under the trees
and run inside to the pavilion
the women giggling, the men pretending calm,
wet cigarettes being thrown away,
Wagner plays on, and then they are all under the
pavilion. the birds even come in from the trees
and enter the pavilion and then it is the Hungarian
Rhapsody #2 by Lizst, and it still rains, but look,
one man sits alone in the rain
listening. the audience notices him. they turn
and look. the orchestra goes about its
business. the man sits in the night in the rain,
listening. there is something wrong with him,
isn't there?
he came to hear the
music.

a radio with guts

• •

it was on the 2nd floor on Coronado Street
I used to get drunk
and throw the radio through the window
while it was playing, and, of course,
it would break the glass in the window
and the radio would sit out there on the roof
still playing
and I'd tell my woman,
"Ah, what a marvelous radio!"

the next morning I'd take the window
off the hinges
and carry it down the street
to the glass man
who would put in another pane.

I kept throwing that radio through the window
each time I got drunk
and it would sit out there on the roof
still playing—
a magic radio
a radio with guts,
and each morning I'd take the window
back to the glass man.

I don't remember how it ended exactly
though I do remember
we finally moved out.
there was a woman downstairs who worked in
the garden in her bathing suit
and her husband complained he couldn't sleep nights
because of me
so we moved out
and in the next place
I either forgot to throw the radio out the window
or I didn't feel like it
anymore.

I do remember missing the woman who worked in the
garden in her bathing suit,
she really dug with that trowel
and she put her behind up in the air
and I used to sit in the window
and watch the sun shine all over that thing

while the music played.

Layover

• •

Making love in the sun, in the morning sun
in a hotel room
above the alley
where poor men poke for bottles;
making love in the sun
making love by a carpet redder than our blood,
making love while the boys sell headlines
and Cadillacs,
making love by a photograph of Paris
and an open pack of Chesterfields,
making love while other men—poor fools—
work.

That moment—to this . . .
may be years in the way they measure,
but it's only one sentence back in my mind—
there are so many days
when living stops and pulls up and sits
and waits like a train on the rails.
I pass the hotel at 8
and at 5; there are cats in the alleys
and bottles and bums,
and I look up at the window and think,
I no longer know where you are,
and I walk on and wonder where
the living goes
when it stops.

3

· ·

get your name in lights
get it up there in
8½ × 11 mimeo

22,000 Dollars in 3 Months

night has come like something crawling
up the bannister, sticking out its tongue
of fire, and I remember the
missionaries up to their knees in muck
retreating across the beautiful blue river
and the machine gun slugs flicking spots of
fountain and Jones drunk on the shore
saying shit shit these Indians
where'd they get the fire power?
and I went in to see Maria
and she said, do you think they'll attack,
do you think they'll come across the river?
afraid to die? I asked her, and she said
who isn't?
and I went to the medicine cabinet
and poured a tall glassful, and I said
we've made 22,000 dollars in 3 months building roads
for Jones and you have to die a little
to make it that fast . . . Do you think the communists
started this? she asked, do you think it's the communists?
and I said, will you stop being a neurotic bitch.
these small countries rise because they are getting
their pockets filled from *both* sides . . . and she
looked at me with that beautiful schoolgirl idiocy
and she walked out, it was getting dark but I let her go,
you've got to know when to let a woman go if you want to keep her,
and if you don't want to keep her you let her go anyhow,
so it's always a process of letting go, one way or the other,
so I sat there and put the drink down and made another
and I thought, whoever thought an engineering course at Old Miss

would bring you where the lamps swing slowly
in the green of some far night?
and Jones came in with his arm around her blue waist
and she had been drinking too, and I walked up and said,
man and wife? and that made her angry for if a woman can't
get you by the nuts and squeeze, she's done,
and I poured another tall one, and
I said, you 2 may not realize it
but we're not going to get out of here alive.

we drank the rest of the night.
you could hear, if you were real still,
the water coming down between the god trees,
and the roads we had built
you could hear animals crossing them
and the Indians, savage fools with some savage cross to bear.
and finally there was the last look in the mirror
as the drunken lovers hugged
and I walked out and lifted a piece of straw
from the roof of the hut
then snapped the lighter, and I
watched the flames crawl, like hungry mice
up the thin brown stalks, it was slow but it was
real, and then not real, something like an opera,
and then I walked down toward the machine gun sounds,
the same river, and the moon looked across at me
and in the path I saw a small snake, just a small one,
looked like a rattler, but it couldn't be a rattler,
and it was scared seeing me, and I grabbed it behind the neck
before it could coil and I held it then
its little body curled around my wrist
like a finger of love and all the trees looked with eyes
and I put my mouth to its mouth
and love was lightning and remembrance,
dead communists, dead fascists, dead democrats, dead gods and
back in what was left of the hut Jones
had his dead black arm around her dead blue waist.

Maja Thurup

•••

It had gotten extensive press coverage and T.V. coverage and the lady was to write a book about it. The lady's name was Hester Adams, twice divorced, two children. She was 35 and one guessed that it was her last fling. The wrinkles were appearing, the breasts had been sagging for some time, the ankles and calves were thickening, there were signs of a belly. America had been taught that beauty only resided in youth, especially in the female. But Hester Adams had the dark beauty of frustration and upcoming loss; it crawled all over her, the upcoming loss, and it gave her a sexual something, like a desperate and fading woman sitting in a bar full of men. Hester had looked around, seen few signs of help from the American male, and had gotten onto a plane for South America. She had entered the jungle with her camera, her portable typewriter, her thickening ankles and her white skin and had gotten herself a cannibal, a black cannibal: Maja Thurup. Maja Thurup had a good look to his face. His face appeared to be written over with one thousand hangovers and one thousand tragedies. And it was true—he had had one thousand hangovers, but the tragedies all came from the same root: Maja Thurup was overhung, vastly overhung. No girl in the village would accept him. He had torn two girls to death with his instrument. One had been entered from the front, the other from the rear. No matter.

Maja was a lonely man and he drank and brooded over his loneliness until Hester Adams had come with guide and white skin and camera. After formal introductions and a few drinks by the fire, Hester had entered Maja's hut and taken all Maja Thurup could muster and had asked for more. It was a miracle for both of them and they were married in a three-day tribal ceremony, during which captured enemy tribesmen were roasted and consumed amid dancing, incantation, and drunkenness. It was after the ceremony, after the hangovers had cleared away that trouble began. The medicine man, having noted that Hester did not partake of the flesh of the roasted enemy tribesmen (garnished with pineapple, olives, and nuts) announced to one and all that this was not a white goddess, but one of the daughters of the evil god Ritikan. (Centuries ago Ritikan had been expelled from the tribal heaven for his refusal to eat anything but vegetables, fruits, and nuts.) This announcement caused dissension in the tribe and two friends of Maja Thurup were promptly murdered for suggesting that Hester's handling of Maja's overhang was a miracle in itself and the fact that she didn't ingest other forms of human meat could be forgiven—temporarily, at least.

Hester and Maja fled to America, to North Hollywood to be precise, where Hester began proceedings to have Maja Thurup become an American citizen. A former schoolteacher, Hester began instructing Maja in the use of clothing, the English language, California beer and wines, television, and foods purchased at the nearby Safeway market. Maja not only looked at television, he appeared on it along with Hester and they declared their love publicly. Then they went back to their North Hollywood apartment and made love. Afterwards Maja sat in the middle of the rug with his English grammar books, drinking beer and wine, and singing native chants and playing the bongo. Hester worked on her book about Maja and Hester. A major publisher was waiting. All Hester had to do was get it down.

One morning I was in bed about 8:00 a.m. The day before I had lost $40 at Santa Anita, my savings account at California Federal was getting dangerously low, and I hadn't written a decent story in a month. The phone rang. I woke up, gagged, coughed, picked it up.

"Chinaski?"

"Yeah?"

"This is Dan Hudson."

Dan ran the magazine *Flare* out of Chicago. He paid well. He was the editor and publisher.

"Hello, Dan, mother."

"Look, I've got just the thing for you."

"Sure, Dan. What is it?"

"I want you to interview this bitch who married the cannibal. Make the sex BIG. Mix love with horror, you know?"

"I know. I've been doing it all my life."

"There's $500 in it for you if you beat the March 27 deadline."

"Dan, for $500, I can make Burt Reynolds into a lesbian."

Dan gave me the address and phone number. I got up, threw water on my face, had two Alka-Seltzers, opened a bottle of beer and phoned Hester Adams. I told her that I wanted to publicize her relationship with Maja Thurup as one of the great love stories of the 20th century. For the readers of *Flare* magazine. I assured her that it would help

Maja obtain his American citizenship. She agreed to an interview at 1:00 p.m.

It was a walk-up apartment on the third floor. She opened the door. Maja was sitting on the floor with his bongo drinking a fifth of medium priced port from the bottle. He was barefooted, dressed in tight jeans, and in a white t-shirt with black zebra-stripes. Hester was dressed in an identical outfit. She brought me a bottle of beer, I picked up a cigarette from the pack on the coffee table and began the interview.

"You first met Maja when?"

Hester gave me a date. She also gave me the exact time and place.

"When did you first begin to have love feelings for Maja? What exactly were the circumstances which tripped them off?"

"Well," said Hester, "it was . . . "

"She love me when I give her the thing," said Maja from the rug.

"He has learned English quite quickly, hasn't he?"

"Yes, he's brilliant."

Maja picked up his bottle and drained off a good slug.

"I put this thing in her, she say, 'Oh my god oh my god oh my god!' Ha, ha, ha, ha!"

"Maja is marvelously built," she said.

"She eat too," said Maja, "she eat good. Deep throat, ha, ha, ha!"

"I loved Maja from the beginning," said Hester, "it was his eyes, his face . . . so tragic. And the way he walked. He walks, well, he walks something like a tiger."

"Fuck," said Maja, "we fuck we fucky fuck fuck fuck. I am getting tired."

Maja took another drink. He looked at me.

"You fuck her. I am tired. She big hungry tunnel."

"Maja has a genuine sense of humor," said Hester, "that's another thing that has endeared him to me."

"Only thing dear you to me," said Maja, "is my telephone pole piss-shooter."

"Maja has been drinking since this morning," said Hester, "you'll have to excuse him."

"Perhaps I'd better come back when he's feeling better."

"I think you should."

Hester gave me an appointment at 2:00 p.m. in the afternoon the next day.

* * *

It was just as well. I needed photographs. I knew a down-and-out photographer, one Sam Jacoby, who was good and would do the work cheap.
I took him back there with me. It was a sunny afternoon with only a thin
layer of smog. We walked up and I rang. There was no answer. I rang
again. Maja answered the door.

"Hester not in," he said, "she gone to grocery store."

"We had an appointment for two o'clock. I'd like to come in and
wait."

We walked in and sat down.

"I play drums for you," said Maja.

He played the drums and sang some jungle chants. He was quite
good. He was working on another bottle of port wine. He was still in his
zebra-striped t-shirt and jeans.

"Fuck fuck fuck," he said, "that's all she want. She make me mad."

"You miss the jungle, Maja?"

"You just ain't just shittin' upstream, daddy."

"But she loves you, Maja."

"Ha, ha, ha!"

Maja played us another drum solo. Even drunk he was good.

When Maja finished Sam said to me, "You think she might have a
beer in the refrigerator?"

"She might."

"My nerves are bad. I need a beer."

"Go ahead. Get two. I'll buy her some more. I should have brought
some."

Sam got up and walked into the kitchen. I heard the refrigerator
door open.

"I'm writing an article about you and Hester," I said to Maja.

"Big-hole woman. Never fill. Like volcano."

I heard Sam vomiting in the kitchen. He was a heavy drinker. I knew
he was hungover. But he was still one of the best photographers around.
Then it was quiet. Sam came walking out. He sat down. He didn't have a
beer with him.

"I play drums again," said Maja. He played the drums again. He was
still good. Though not as good as the preceding time. The wine was getting to him.

"Let's get out of here," Sam said to me.

"I have to wait for Hester," I said.

"Man, let's go," said Sam.

"You guys want some wine?" asked Maja.

I got up and walked into the kitchen for a beer. Sam followed me. I moved toward the refrigerator.

"*Please* don't open that door!" he said.

Sam walked over to the sink and vomited again. I looked at the refrigerator door. I didn't open it. When Sam finished, I said, "O.k., let's go."

We walked into the front room where Maja still sat by his bongo.

"I play drum once more," he said.

"No, thanks, Maja."

We walked out and down the stairway and out to the street. We got into my car. I drove off. I didn't know what to say. Sam didn't say anything. We were in the business district. I drove into a gas station and told the attendant to fill it up with regular. Sam got out of the car and walked to the telephone booth to call the police. I saw Sam come out of the phone booth. I paid for the gas. I hadn't gotten my interview. I was out $500. I waited as Sam walked toward the car.

—*SOUTH OF NO NORTH*

the trash men

• •

here they come
these guys
grey truck
radio playing

they are in a hurry

it's quite exciting:
shirt open
bellies hanging out

they run out the trash bins
roll them out to the fork lift
and then the truck grinds it upward
with far too much sound . . .

they had to fill out application forms
to get these jobs
they are paying for homes and
drive late model cars

they get drunk on Saturday night

now in the Los Angeles sunshine
they run back and forth with their trash bins

all that trash goes somewhere

and they shout to each other

then they are all up in the truck
driving west toward the sea

none of them know
that I am alive

REX DISPOSAL CO.

the strangest sight you ever did see—

I had this room in front on DeLongpre
and I used to sit for hours
in the daytime
looking out the front
window.

there were any number of girls who would
walk by
swaying;
it helped my afternoons,
added something to the beer and the
cigarettes.

one day I saw something
extra.
I heard the sound of it first.
"come on, push!" he said.
there was a long board
about 2½ feet wide and
8 feet long;
nailed to the ends and in the middle
were roller skates.
he was pulling in front
two long ropes attached to the board
and she was in back
guiding and also pushing.
all their possessions were tied to the
board:
pots, pans, bedquilts, and so forth
were roped to the board
tied down;
and the skatewheels were grinding.

he was white, red-necked, a
southerner—
thin, slumped, his pants about to
fall from his
ass—
his face pinked by the sun and
cheap wine,
and she was black
and walked upright
pushing;
she was simply beautiful

in turban
long green ear rings
yellow dress
from
neck to
ankle.
her face was gloriously
indifferent.

"don't worry!" he shouted, looking back
at her, "somebody will
rent us a place!"

she didn't answer.

then they were gone
although I still heard the
skatewheels.

they're going to make it,
I thought.

I'm sure they
did.

• •

It began as a mistake.

It was Christmas season and I learned from the drunk up the hill,
who did the trick every Christmas, that they would hire damned near
anybody, and so I went and the next thing I knew I had this leather sack
on my back and was hiking around at my leisure. What a job, I thought.
Soft! They only gave you a block or two and if you managed to finish, the
regular carrier would give you another block to carry, or maybe you'd go

back in and the soup would give you another, but you just took your time and shoved those Xmas cards in the slots.

I think it was my second day as a Christmas temp that this big woman came out and walked around with me as I delivered letters. What I mean by big was that her ass was big and her tits were big and that she was big in all the right places. She seemed a bit crazy but I kept looking at her body and I didn't care.

She talked and talked and talked. Then it came out. Her husband was an officer on an island far away and she got lonely, you know, and lived in this little house in back all by herself.

"What little house?" I asked.

She wrote the address on a piece of paper.

"I'm lonely too," I said, "I'll come by and we'll talk tonight."

I was shacked but the shackjob was gone half the time, off somewhere, and I was lonely all right. I was lonely for that big ass standing beside me.

"All right," she said, "see you tonight."

She was a good one all right, she was a good lay but like all lays after the third or fourth night I began to lose interest and didn't go back.

But I couldn't help thinking, god, all these mailmen do is drop in their letters and get laid. This is the job for me, oh yes yes yes.

So I took the exam, passed it, took the physical, passed it, and there I was—a substitute mail carrier. It began easy. I was sent to West Avon Station and it was just like Christmas except I didn't get laid. Every day I expected to get laid but I didn't. But the soup was easy and I strolled around doing a block here and there. I didn't even have a uniform, just a cap. I wore my regular clothes. The way my shackjob Betty and I drank there was hardly money for clothes.

Then I was transferred to Oakford Station.

The soup was a bullneck named Jonstone. Help was needed there and I understood why. Jonstone liked to wear dark-red shirts—that meant danger and blood. There were seven subs—Tom Moto, Nick Pelligrini, Herman Stratford, Rosey Anderson, Bobby Hansen, Harold Wiley and me, Henry Chinaski. Reporting time was 5 a.m. and I was the only drunk there. I always drank until past midnight, and there we'd sit, at 5 a.m. in the morning, waiting to get on the clock, waiting for some regular to call in sick. The regulars usually called in sick when it rained or during a heat-wave or the day after a holiday when the mail load was doubled.

There were 40 or 50 different routes, maybe more, each case was different, you were never able to learn any of them, you had to get your mail up and ready before 8 a.m. for the truck dispatches, and Jonstone would take no excuses. The subs routed their magazines on corners, went without lunch, and died in the streets. Jonstone would have us start casing the routes 30 minutes late—spinning in his chair in his red shirt—"Chinaski take route 539!" We'd start a halfhour short but were still expected to get the mail up and out and be back on time. And once or twice a week, already beaten, fagged and fucked we had to make the night pickups, and the schedule on the board was impossible—the truck wouldn't go that fast. You had to skip four or five boxes on the first run and the next time around they were stacked with mail and you stank, you ran with sweat jamming it into the sacks. I got laid all right. Jonstone saw to that.

The subs themselves made Jonstone possible by obeying his impossible orders. I couldn't see how a man of such obvious cruelty could be allowed to have his position. The regulars didn't care, the union man was worthless, so I filled out a 30 page report on one of my days off, mailed one copy to Jonstone and took the other down to the Federal Building. The clerk told me to wait. I waited and waited and waited. I waited an hour and 30 minutes, then was taken in to see a little grey-haired man with eyes like cigarette ash. He didn't even ask me to sit down. He began screaming at me as I entered the door.

"You're a wise son of a bitch, aren't you?"

"I'd rather you didn't curse me, sir!"

"Wise son of a bitch, you're one of those sons of bitches with a vocabulary and you like to lay it around!"

He waved my papers at me. And screamed: "MR. JONSTONE IS A FINE MAN!"

"Don't be silly. He's an obvious sadist," I said.

"How long have you been in the Post Office?"

"Three weeks."

"MR. JONSTONE HAS BEEN WITH THE POST OFFICE FOR 30 YEARS!"

"What does *that* have to do with it?"

"I said, MR. JONSTONE IS A FINE MAN!"

I believe the poor fellow actually wanted to kill me. He and Jonstone must have slept together.

"All right," I said, "Jonstone is a fine man. Forget the whole fucking thing." Then I walked out and took the next day off. Without pay, of course.

—Post Office

hot

• •

she was hot, she was so hot
I didn't want anybody else to have her,
and if I didn't get home on time
she'd be gone, and I couldn't bear that—
I'd go mad . . .
it was foolish I know, childish,
but I was caught in it, I was caught.

I delivered all the mail
and then Henderson put me on the night pickup run
in an old army truck,
the damn thing began to heat halfway through the run
and the night went on
me thinking about my hot Miriam
and jumping in and out of the truck
filling mailsacks
the engine continuing to heat up
the temperature needle was at the top
HOT HOT
like Miriam.

I leaped in and out
3 more pickups and into the station
I'd be, my car
waiting to get me to Miriam who sat on my blue couch
with scotch on the rocks
crossing her legs and swinging her ankles

like she did,
2 more stops . . .
the truck stalled at a traffic light, it was hell
kicking it over
again . . .
I had to be home by 8, 8 was the deadline for Miriam.

I made the last pickup and the truck stalled at a signal
½ block from the station . . .
it wouldn't start, it couldn't start . . .
I locked the doors, pulled the key and ran down to the
station . . .
I threw the keys down. . . . signed out . . .
your god damned truck is stalled at the signal,
I shouted,
Pico and Western . . .
. . . I ran down the hall, put the key into the door,
opened it. . . . her drinking glass was there, and a note:

> sun of a bitch:
> I wated until 5 after ate
> you don't love me
> you sun of a bitch
> somebody will love me
> I been wateing all day
>
>   Miriam

I poured a drink and let the water run into the tub
there were 5,000 bars in town
and I'd make 25 of them
looking for Miriam

her purple teddy bear held the note
as he leaned against a pillow

I gave the bear a drink, myself a drink
and got into the hot
water.

• •

"Chinaski! Take route 539!"

The toughest in the station. Apartment houses with boxes that had scrubbed-out names or no names at all, under tiny lightbulbs in dark halls. Old ladies standing in halls, up and down the streets, asking the same question as if they were one person with one voice:

"Mailman, you got any mail for me?"

And you felt like screaming, "Lady, how the *hell* do I know who *you* are or I am or anybody is?"

The sweat dripping, the hangover, the impossibility of the schedule, and Jonstone back there in his red shirt, knowing it, enjoying it, pretending he was doing it to keep costs down. But everybody knew why he was doing it. Oh, what a fine man he was!

The people. The people. And the dogs.

Let me tell you about the dogs. It was one of those 100 degree days and I was running along, sweating, sick, delirious, hungover. I stopped at a small apartment house with the box downstairs along the front pavement. I popped it open with my key. There wasn't a sound. Then I felt something jamming its way into my crotch. It moved way up there. I looked around and there was a German shepherd, full-grown, with his nose halfway up my ass. With one snap of his jaws he could rip off my balls. I decided that those people were not going to get their mail that day, and maybe never get any mail again. Man, I mean he worked that nose in there. SNUFF! SNUFF! SNUFF!

I put the mail back into the leather pouch, and then very slowly, very, I took a half step forward. The nose followed. I took another half step with the other foot. The nose followed. Then I took a slow, very slow full step. Then another. Then stood still. The nose was out. And he just stood there looking at me. Maybe he'd never smelled anything like it and didn't quite know what to do.

I walked quietly away.

—*Post Office*

the worst and the best

in the hospitals and jails
it's the worst
in madhouses
it's the worst
in penthouses
it's the worst
in skid row flophouses
it's the worst
at poetry readings
at rock concerts
at benefits for the disabled
it's the worst
at funerals
at weddings
it's the worst
at parades
at skating rinks
at sexual orgies
it's the worst
at midnight
at 3 a.m.
at 5:45 p.m.
it's the worst

falling through the sky
firing squads
that's the best

thinking of India
looking at popcorn stands
watching the bull get the matador
that's the best

boxed lightbulbs
an old dog scratching

peanuts in a celluloid bag
that's the best

spraying roaches
a clean pair of stockings
natural guts defeating natural talent
that's the best

in front of firing squads
throwing crusts to seagulls
slicing tomatoes
that's the best

rugs with cigarette burns
cracks in sidewalks
waitresses still sane
that's the best

my hands dead
my heart dead
silence
adagio of rocks
the world ablaze
that's the best
for me.

• •

The Stone's favorite carrier was Matthew Battles. Battles never came in with a wrinkled shirt on. In fact, everything he wore was new, looked new. The shoes, the shirts, the pants, the cap. His shoes really shined and none of his clothing appeared to have ever been laundered even once. Once a shirt or a pair of pants became the least bit soiled he threw them away.

The Stone often said to us as Matthew walked by:

"Now, *there* goes a carrier!"

And The Stone meant it. His eyes damn near shimmered with love.

And Matthew would stand at his case, erect and clean, scrubbed and well-slept, shoes gleaming victoriously, and he would fan those letters into the case with joy.

"You're a real carrier, Matthew!"

"Thank you, Mr. Jonstone!"

One 5 a.m. I walked in and sat down to wait behind The Stone. He looked a bit slumped under that red shirt.

Moto was next to me. He told me: "They picked up Matthew yesterday."

"Picked him up?"

"Yeah, for stealing from the mails. He'd been opening letters for the Nekalayla Temple and taking money out. After 15 years on the job."

"How'd they get him, how'd they find out?"

"The old ladies. The old ladies had been sending in letters to Nekalayla filled with money and they weren't getting any thank-you notes or response. Nekalayla told the P.O. and the P.O. put the Eye on Matthew. They found him opening letters down at the soak-box, taking money out."

"No shit?"

"No shit. They caught him in cold daylight."

I leaned back.

Nekalayla had built this large temple and painted it a sickening green, I guess it reminded him of money, and he had an office staff of 30 or 40 people who did nothing but open envelopes, take out checks and money, record the amount, the sender, date received and so on. Others were busy mailing out books and pamphlets written by Nekalayla, and his photo was on the wall, a large one of N. in priestly robes and beard, and a painting of N., very large too, looked over the office, watching.

Nekalayla claimed he had once been walking through the desert when he met Jesus Christ and Jesus Christ told him everything. They sat on a rock together and J.C. laid it on him. Now he was passing the secrets on to those who could afford it. He also held a service every Sunday. His help, who were also his followers, rang in and out on timeclocks.

Imagine Matthew Battles trying to outwit Nekalayla who had met Christ in the desert!

"Has anybody said anything to The Stone?" I asked.

"Are you *kidding?*"

We sat an hour or so. A sub was assigned to Matthew's case. The other subs were given other jobs. I sat alone behind The Stone. Then I got up and walked to his desk.

"Mr. Jonstone?"

"Yes, Chinaski?"

"Where's Matthew today? Sick?"

The Stone's head dropped. He looked at the paper in his hand and pretended to continue reading it. I walked back and sat down.

At 7 a.m. The Stone turned:

"There's nothing for you today, Chinaski."

I stood up and walked to the doorway. I stood in the doorway. "Good morning, Mr. Jonstone. Have a good day."

He didn't answer. I walked down to the liquor store and bought a half pint of Grandad for my breakfast.

The voices of the people were the same, no matter where you carried the mail you heard the same things over and over again.

"You're late, aren't you?"

"Where's the regular carrier?"

"Hello, Uncle Sam!"

"Mailman! Mailman! This doesn't go here!"

The streets were full of insane and dull people. Most of them lived in nice houses and didn't seem to work, and you wondered how they did it. There was one guy who wouldn't let you put the mail in his box. He'd stand in the driveway and watch you coming for two or three blocks and he'd stand there and hold his hand out.

I asked some of the others who had carried the route:

"What's wrong with that guy who stands there and holds his hand out?"

"What guy who stands there and holds his hand out?" they asked.

They all had the same voice too.

One day when I had the route, the man-who-holds-his-hand-out was a half a block up the street. He was talking to a neighbor, looked back at me more than a block away and knew he had time to walk back and meet me. When he turned his back to me, I began running. I don't believe I ever delivered mail that fast, all stride and motion, never stopping or pausing, I was going to kill him. I had the letter half in the slot of his box when he turned and saw me.

"OH NO NO NO!" he screamed, "DON'T PUT IT IN THE BOX!"

He ran down the street toward me. All I saw was the blur of his feet. He must have run a hundred yards in 9.2.

I put the letter in his hand. I watched him open it, walk across the porch, open the door and go into his house. What it meant somebody else will have to tell me.

Again I was on a new route. The Stone always put me on hard routes, but now and then, due to the circumstances of things, he was forced to place me on one less murderous. Route 511 was peeling off quite nicely, and there I was thinking about *lunch* again, the lunch that never came.

It was an average residential neighborhood. No apartment houses. Just house after house with well-kept lawns. But it was a *new* route and I walked along wondering where the trap was. Even the weather was nice.

By god, I thought, I'm going to make it! Lunch, and back in on schedule! Life, at last, was bearable.

These people didn't even own dogs. Nobody stood outside waiting for their mail. I hadn't heard a human voice in hours. Perhaps I had reached my postal maturity, whatever that was. I strolled along, efficient, almost dedicated.

I remembered one of the older carriers pointing to his heart and telling me, "Chinaski, someday it will get you, it will get you right *here!*"

"Heart attack?"

"Dedication to service. You'll see. You'll be proud of it."

"Balls!"

But the man had been sincere.

I thought about him as I walked along.

Then I had a registered letter with return attached.

I walked up and rang the doorbell. A little window opened in the door. I couldn't see the face.

"Registered letter!"

"Stand back!" said a woman's voice. "Stand back so I can see your face!"

Well, there it was, I thought, another nut.

"Look lady, you don't *have* to see my face. I'll just leave this slip in the mailbox and you can pick your letter up at the station. Bring proper identification."

I put the slip in the mailbox and began to walk off the porch.

The door opened and she ran out. She had on one of those see-through negligees and no brassiere. Just dark blue panties. Her hair was uncombed and stuck out as if it were trying to run away from her. There seemed to be some type of cream on her face, most of it under the eyes. The skin on her body was white as if it never saw sunlight and her face had an unhealthy look. Her mouth hung open. She had on a touch of lipstick, and she was *built* all the way . . .

I caught all this as she rushed at me. I was sliding the registered letter back into the pouch.

She screamed, "Give me my letter!"

I said, "Lady, you'll have to . . . "

She grabbed the letter and ran to the door, opened it and ran in.

God damn! You couldn't come back without either the registered letter or a signature! You even had to sign in and out with the things.

"HEY!"

I went after her and jammed my foot into the door just in time.

"HEY. GOD DAMN YOU!"

"Go away! Go away! You are an evil man!"

"Look, lady! Try to understand! You've got to sign for that letter! I can't let you have it that way! You are robbing the United States mails!"

"Go away, evil man!"

I put all my weight against the door and pushed into the room. It was dark in there. All the shades were down. All the shades in the house were down.

"YOU HAVE NO RIGHT IN MY HOUSE! GET OUT!"

"And you have no right to rob the mails! Either give me the letter back or sign for it. Then I'll leave."

"All right! All right! I'll sign."

I showed her where to sign and gave her a pen. I looked at her breasts and the rest of her and I thought, what a shame she's crazy, what a shame, what a shame.

She handed back the pen and her signature—it was just scrawled. She opened the letter, began to read it as I turned to leave.

Then she was in front of the door, arms spread across. The letter was on the floor.

"Evil evil evil man! You came here to rape me!"

"Look lady, let me by."

"THERE IS EVIL WRITTEN ALL OVER YOUR FACE!"

"Don't you think I know that? Now let me out of here!"

With one hand I tried to push her aside. She clawed one side of my face, good. I dropped my bag, my cap fell off, and as I held a handkerchief to the blood she came up and raked the other side.

"YOU CUNT! WHAT THE HELL'S WRONG WITH YOU!"

"See there? See there? You're evil!"

She was right up against me. I grabbed her by the ass and got my mouth on hers. Those breasts were against me, she was all up against me. She pulled her head back, away from me—"

"Rapist! Rapist! Evil rapist!"

I reached down with my mouth, got one of her tits, then switched to the other.

"Rape! Rape! I'm being raped!"

She was right. I got her pants down, unzipped my fly, got it in, then walked her backwards to the couch. We fell down on top of it.

She lifted her legs high.

"RAPE!" she screamed.

I finished her off, zipped my fly, picked up my mail pouch and walked out leaving her staring quietly at the ceiling . . .

I missed lunch but still couldn't make the schedule.

"You're 15 minutes late," said The Stone.

I didn't say anything.

The Stone looked at me. "God o mighty, what happened to your face?" he asked.

"What happened to yours?" I asked him.

"Whadda you mean?"

"Forget it."

—*Post Office*

a lovely couple

● ●

I had to take a shit
but instead I went
into this shop to
have a key made.
the woman was dressed
in gingham and smelled
like a muskrat.
"Ralph," she hollered
and an old swine in a
flowered shirt and
size 6 shoes, her
husband, came out and
she said, "this man
wants a key."
he started grinding
as if he really didn't
want to.
there were slinking
shadows and urine
in the air.
I moved along the
glass counter,
pointed and called
to her,
"here, I want this
one."
she handed it to
me: a switchblade
in a light purple
case.
$6.50 plus tax.
the key cost
practically
nothing.
I got my change and

walked out on
the street.
sometimes you need
people like that.

• •

After three years I made "regular." That meant holiday pay (subs didn't get paid for holidays) and a 40 hour week with two days off. The Stone was also forced to assign me as relief man to five different routes. That's all I had to carry—five different routes. In time, I would learn the cases well plus the shortcuts and traps on each route. Each day would be easier. I could begin to cultivate that comfortable look.

Somehow, I was not too happy. I was not a man to deliberately seek pain, the job was still different enough, but somehow it lacked the old glamour of my sub days—the not-knowing-what-the-hell was going to happen next.

A few of the regulars came around and shook my hand.

"Congratulations," they said.

"Yeh," I said.

Congratulations for what? I hadn't done anything. Now I was a member of the club. I was one of the boys. I could be there for years, eventually bid for my own route. Get Xmas presents from my people. And when I phoned in sick, they would say to some poor bastard sub, "Where's the *regular* man today? You're late. The regular man is never late."

So there I was. Then a bulletin came out that no caps or equipment were to be placed on top of the carrier's case. Most of the boys put their caps up there. It didn't hurt anything and saved a trip to the locker room. Now after three years of putting my cap up there I was ordered not to do so.

Well, I was still coming in hungover and I didn't have things like caps on my mind. So my cap was up there, the day after the order came out.

The Stone came running with his write-up. It said that it was against rules and regulations to have any equipment on top of the case. I put the write-up in my pocket and went on sticking letters. The Stone sat swiveled in his chair, watching me. All the other carriers had put their caps in their lockers. Except me and one other—one Marty. And The Stone had gone up to Marty and said, "Now, Marty, you read the order. Your cap isn't supposed to be on top of the case."

"Oh, I'm sorry, sir. Habit, you know. Sorry." Marty took his cap off the case and ran upstairs to his locker with it.

The next morning I forgot again. The Stone came with his write-up.

It said that it was against rules and regulations to have any equipment on top of the case.

I put the write-up in my pocket and went on sticking letters.

The next morning, as I walked in, I could see The Stone watching me. He was very deliberate about watching me. He was waiting to see what I would do with the cap. I let him wait awhile. Then I took the cap off my head and placed it on top of the case.

The Stone ran up with his write-up.

I didn't read it. I threw it in the wastebasket, left my cap up there and went on sticking mail.

I could hear The Stone at his typewriter. There was anger in the sound of the keys.

I wondered how he managed to learn how to type? I thought.

He came again. Handed me a 2nd write-up.

I looked at him.

"I don't have to read it. I know what it says. It says that I didn't read the first write-up."

I threw the 2nd write-up in the wastebasket.

The Stone ran back to his typewriter.

He handed me a 3rd write-up.

"Look," I said, "I know what all these things say. The first write-up was for having my cap on top of the case. The 2nd was for not reading the first. This 3rd one is for not reading the first or 2nd write-ups."

I looked at him, and then dropped the write-up into the wastebasket without reading it.

"Now I can throw these away as fast as you can type them. It can go on for hours, and soon one of us is going to begin looking ridiculous. It's up to you."

The Stone went back to his chair and sat down. He didn't type any-more. He just sat looking at me.

I didn't go in the next day. I slept until noon. I didn't phone. Then I went down to the Federal Building. I told them my mission. They put me in front of the desk of a thin old woman. Her hair was grey and she had a very thin neck that suddenly bent in the middle. It pushed her head forward and she looked up over the top of her glasses at me.

"Yes?"

"I want to resign."

"To *resign?*"

"Yes, resign."

"And you're a regular carrier?"

"Yes," I said.

"Tsk, tsk, tsk, tsk, tsk, tsk, tsk," she went, making this sound with her dry lips.

She gave me the proper papers and I sat there filling them out.

"How long have you been with the post office?"

"Three and one half years."

"Tsk, tsk, tsk, tsk, tsk, tsk, tsk, tsk," she went, "tsk, tsk, tsk, tsk."

And so there it was. I drove home to Betty and we uncapped the bottle.

Little did I know that in a couple of years I would be back as a clerk and that I would clerk, all hunched-up on a stool, for nearly 12 years.

—*Post Office*

The Day I Kicked Away a Bankroll

• •

and, I said, you can take your rich aunts and uncles
and grandfathers and fathers
and all their lousy oil
and their seven lakes
and their wild turkey

and buffalo
and the whole state of Texas,
meaning, your crow-blasts
and your Saturday night boardwalks,
and your 2-bit library
and your crooked councilmen
and your pansy artists—
you can take all these
and your weekly newspaper
and your famous tornadoes,
and your filthy floods
and all your yowling cats
and your subscription to *Time,*
and shove them, baby,
shove them.

I can handle a pick and ax again (I think)
and I can pick up
25 bucks for a 4-rounder (maybe);
sure, I'm 38
but a little dye can pinch the gray
out of my hair;
and I can still write a poem (sometimes),
don't forget *that,* and even if
they don't pay off,
it's better than waiting for death and oil,
and shooting wild turkey,
and waiting for the world
to begin.

all right, bum, she said,
get out.

what? I said.

get out. you've thrown your
last tantrum.
I'm tired of your damned tantrums:

you're always acting like a
character in an O'Neill play.

but I'm different, baby,
I can't help
it.

you're different, all right!
God, how different!
don't slam
the door
when you leave.

but, baby, I *love* your
money!

you never once said
you loved me!

what do you want
a liar or a
lover?

you're neither! out, bum,
out!

. . . but baby!

go back to O'Neill!

I went to the door,
softly closed it and walked away,
thinking: all they want
is a wooden Indian
to say yes and no
and stand over the fire and
not raise too much hell;
but you're getting to be

an old man, kiddo;
next time play it closer
to the
vest.

• •

On Christmas I had Betty over. She baked a turkey and we drank. Betty always liked huge Christmas trees. It must have been seven feet tall, and half as wide, covered with lights, bulbs, tinsel, various crap. We drank from a couple of fifths of whiskey, made love, ate our turkey, drank some more. The nail in the stand was loose and the stand was not big enough to hold the tree. I kept straightening it. Betty stretched out on the bed, passed out. I was drinking on the floor with my shorts on. Then I stretched out. Closed my eyes. Something awakened me. I opened my eyes. Just in time to see the huge tree covered with hot lights, lean slowly toward me, the pointed star coming down like a dagger. I didn't quite know what it was. It looked like the end of the world. I couldn't move. The arms of the tree enfolded me. I was under it. The light bulbs were red hot.

"Oh, OH JESUS CHRIST, MERCY! LORD HELP ME! JESUS! JESUS! HELP!"

The bulbs were burning me. I rolled to the left, couldn't get out, then I rolled to the right.

"YAWK!"

I finally rolled out from under. Betty was up, standing there.

"What happened? What is it?"

"CAN'T YOU SEE? THAT GOD DAMNED TREE TRIED TO MURDER ME!"

"What?"

"YES, LOOK AT ME!"

I had red spots all over my body.

"Oh, *poor* baby!"

I walked over and pulled the plug from the wall. The lights went out. The thing was dead.

"Oh, my poor tree!"

"Your poor tree?"

"Yes, it was *so* pretty!"

"I'll stand it up in the morning. I don't trust it now. I'm giving it the rest of the night off."

She didn't like that. I could see an argument coming, so I stood the thing up behind a chair and turned the lights back on. If the thing had burned her tits or ass, she would have thrown it out the window. I thought I was being very kind.

Several days after Christmas I stopped in to see Betty. She was sitting in her room, drunk, at 8:45 a.m. in the morning. She didn't look well but then neither did I. It seemed that almost every roomer had given her a fifth. There was wine, vodka, whiskey, scotch. The cheapest brands. The bottles filled her room.

"Those damn fools! Don't they *know* any better? If you drink all this stuff it will kill you!"

Betty just looked at me. I saw it all in that look.

She had two children who never came to see her, never wrote her. She was a scrubwoman in a cheap hotel. When I had first met her her clothes had been expensive, trim ankles fitting into expensive shoes. She had been firm-fleshed, almost beautiful. Wild-eyed. Laughing. Coming from a rich husband, divorced from him, and he was to die in a car wreck, drunk, burning to death in Connecticut. "You'll never tame her," they told me.

There she was. But I'd had some help.

"Listen," I said, "I ought to take that stuff. I mean, I'll just give you back a bottle now and then. I won't drink it."

"Leave the bottles," Betty said. She didn't look at me. Her room was on the top floor and she sat in a chair by the window watching the morning traffic.

I walked over. "Look, I'm beat. I've got to leave. But for Christ's sake, take it easy on that stuff!"

"Sure," she said.

I leaned over and kissed her goodbye.

About a week and a half later I came by again. There wasn't any answer to my knock.

"Betty! Betty! Are you all right?"

I turned the knob. The door was open. The bed was turned back. There was a large bloodspot on the sheet.

"Oh shit!" I said. I looked around. All the bottles were gone.

Then I looked around. There was a middle-aged Frenchwoman who owned the place. She stood in the doorway.

"She's at County General Hospital. She was very sick. I called the ambulance last night."

"Did she drink all that stuff?"

"She had some help."

I ran down the stairway and got into my car. Then I was there. I knew the place well. They told me the room number.

There were three or four beds in a tiny room. A woman was sitting up in hers across the way, chewing an apple and laughing with two female visitors. I pulled the drop sheet around Betty's bed, sat down on the stool and leaned over her.

"Betty! Betty!"

I touched her arm.

"Betty!"

Her eyes opened. They were beautiful again. Bright calm blue.

"I knew it would be you," she said.

Then she closed her eyes. Her lips were parched. Yellow spittle had caked at the left corner of her mouth. I took a cloth and washed it away. I cleaned her face, hands and throat. I took another cloth and squeezed a bit of water on her tongue. Then a little more. I wet her lips. I straightened her hair. I heard the women laughing through the sheets that separated us.

"Betty, Betty, Betty. Please, I want you to drink some water, just a sip of water, not too much, just a sip."

She didn't respond. I tried for ten minutes. Nothing.

More spittle formed at her mouth. I wiped it away.

Then I got up and pulled the drop sheet back. I stared at the three women.

I walked out and spoke to the nurse at the desk.

"Listen, why isn't anything being done for that woman in 45-c? Betty Williams."

"We're doing all we can, sir."

"But there's nobody there."

"We make our regular rounds."

"But where are the doctors? I don't see any doctors."

"The doctor has seen her, sir."

"Why do you just let her lay there?"

"We've done all we can, sir."

"SIR! SIR! SIR! FORGET THAT 'SIR' STUFF, WILL YOU? I'll bet if that were the president or governor or mayor or some rich son of a bitch, there would be doctors all over that room doing *something!* Why do you just let them die? What's the sin in being poor?"

"I've told you, sir, that we've done ALL we can."

"I'll be back in two hours."

"Are you her husband?"

"I used to be her common-law husband."

"May we have your name and phone number?"

I gave her that, then hurried out.

The funeral was to be at 10:30 a.m. but it was already hot. I had on a cheap black suit, bought and fitted in a rush. It was my first new suit in years. I had located the son. We drove along in his new Mercedes-Benz. I had traced him down with the help of a slip of paper with the address of his father-in-law on it. Two long distance calls and I had him. By the time he had driven in, his mother was dead. She died while I was making the phone calls. The kid, Larry, had never fit into the society thing. He had a habit of stealing cars from friends, but between the friends and the judge he managed to get off. Then the army got him, and somehow he got into a training program and when he got out he walked into a good-paying job. That's when he stopped seeing his mother, when he got that good job.

"Where's your sister?" I asked him.

"I don't know."

"This is a fine car. I can't even hear the engine."

Larry smiled. He liked that.

There were just three of us going to the funeral: son, lover and the subnormal sister of the owner of the hotel. Her name was Marcia. Marcia never said anything. She just sat around with this inane smile on her lips. Her skin was white as enamel. She had a mop of dead yellow hair and a hat that would not fit. Marcia had been sent by the owner in her place. The owner had to watch the hotel.

Of course, I had a very bad hangover. We stopped for coffee.

Already there had been trouble with the funeral. Larry had had an argument with the Catholic priest. There was some doubt that Betty was a true Catholic. The priest didn't want to do the service. Finally it was decided that he would do half a service. Well, half a service was better than none.

We even had trouble with the flowers. I had bought a wreath of roses, mixed roses, and they had been worked into a wreath. The flower shop spent an afternoon making it. The lady in the flower shop had known Betty. They had drank together a few years earlier when Betty and I had the house and dog. Delsie, her name was. I had always wanted to get into Delsie's pants but I never made it.

Delsie had phoned me. "Hank, what's the *matter* with those bastards?"

"Which bastards?"

"Those guys at the mortuary."

"What is it?"

"Well, I sent the boy in the truck to deliver your wreath and they didn't want to let him in. They said they were closed. You know, that's a long drive up there."

"Yeah, Delsie?"

"So finally they let the boy put the flowers inside the door but they wouldn't let him put them in the refrigerator. So the boy had to leave them inside the door. What the hell's wrong with those people?"

"I don't know. What the hell's wrong with people everywhere?"

"I won't be able to be at the funeral. Are you all right, Hank?"

"Why don't you come by and console me?"

"I'd have to bring Paul."

Paul was her husband.

"Forget it."

So there we were on our way to half a funeral.

Larry looked up from his coffee. "I'll write you about a headstone later. I don't have any more money now."

"All right," I said.

Larry paid for the coffees, then we went out and climbed into the Mercedes-Benz.

"Wait a minute," I said.

"What is it?" asked Larry.

"I think we forgot something."
I walked back into the cafe.
"Marcia."
She was still sitting at the table.
"We're leaving now, Marcia."
She got up and followed me out.

—*Post Office*

For Jane: With All the Love I Had, Which Was Not Enough:—

• •

I pick up the skirt,
I pick up the sparkling beads
in black,
this thing that moved once
around flesh,
and I call God a liar,
I say anything that moved
like that
or knew
my name
could never die
in the common verity of dying,
and I pick
up her lovely
dress,
all her loveliness gone,
and I speak
to all the gods,
Jewish gods, Christ-gods,
chips of blinking things,
idols, pills, bread,
fathoms, risks,
knowledgeable surrender,

rats in the gravy of 2 gone quite mad
without a chance,
hummingbird knowledge, hummingbird chance,
I lean upon this,
I lean on all of this
and I know:
her dress upon my arm:
but
they will not
give her back to me.

for Jane

225 days under grass
and you know more than I.

they have long taken your blood,
you are a dry stick in a basket.

is this how it works?

in this room
the hours of love
still make shadows.

when you left
you took almost
everything.

I kneel in the nights
before tigers
that will not let me be.

what you were
will not happen again.

the tigers have found me
and I do not care.

I Taste the Ashes of Your Death

the blossoms shake
sudden water
down my sleeve,
sudden water
cool and clean
as snow—
as the stem-sharp
swords
go in
against your breast
and the sweet wild
rocks
leap over
and
lock us in.

Then I developed a new system at the racetrack. I pulled in $3,000 in a month and a half while only going to the track two or three times a week. I began to dream. I saw a little house down by the sea. I saw myself in fine clothing, calm, getting up mornings, getting into my imported car, making the slow easy drive to the track. I saw leisurely steak dinners, preceded and followed by good chilled drinks in colored glasses. The big tip. The cigar. And women as you wanted them. It's easy to fall into this kind of thinking when men handed you large bills at the cashier's window. When in one six furlong race, say in a minute and nine seconds, you make a month's pay.

So I stood in the tour superintendent's office. There he was behind his desk. I had a cigar in my mouth and whiskey on my breath. I felt like money. I looked like money.

"Mr. Winters," I said, "the post office has treated me well. But I have outside business interests that simply must be taken care of. If you can't give me a leave of absence, I must resign."

"Didn't I give you a leave of absence earlier in the year, Chinaski?"

"No, Mr. Winters, you turned down my request for a leave of absence. This time there can't be any turndown. Or I will resign."

"All right, fill out the form and I'll sign it. But I can only give you 90 working days off."

"I'll take 'em," I said, exhaling a long trail of blue smoke from my expensive cigar.

—*Post Office*

no. 6

• •

I'll settle for the 6 horse
on a rainy afternoon
a paper cup of coffee
in my hand
a little way to go,
the wind twirling out
small wrens from
the upper grandstand roof,
the jocks coming out
for a middle race
silent
and the easy rain making

everything
at once
almost alike,
the horses at peace with
each other
before the drunken war
and I am under the grandstand
feeling for
cigarettes
settling for coffee,
then the horses walk by
taking their little men
away—
it is funereal and graceful
and glad
like the opening
of flowers.

• •

Somehow the money slipped away after that and soon I left the track and sat around in my apartment waiting for the 90 days' leave to run out. My nerves were raw from the drinking and the action. It's not a new story about how women descend upon a man. You think you have space to breathe, then you look up and there's another one. A few days after returning to work, there was another one. Fay. Fay had grey hair and always dressed in black. She said she was protesting the war. But if Fay wanted to protest the war, that was all right with me. She was a writer of some sort and went to a couple of writers' workshops. She had ideas about Saving the World. If she could Save it for me, that would be all right too. She had been living off alimony checks from a former husband—they had had three children—and her mother also sent money now and then. Fay had not had more than one or two jobs in her life.

Meanwhile Janko had a new load of bullshit. He sent me home each morning with my head aching. At the time I was getting numerous traffic citations. It seemed that every time I looked into the rear view mirror there were the red lights. A squad car or a bike.

I got to my place late one night. I was really beat. Getting that key out and into the door was about the last of me. I walked into the bedroom and there was Fay in bed reading *The New Yorker* and eating chocolates. She didn't even say hello.

I walked into the kitchen and looked for something to eat. There was nothing in the refrigerator. I decided to pour myself a glass of water. I walked to the sink. It was stopped-up with garbage. Fay liked to save empty jars and jar lids. The dirty dishes filled half the sink and on top of the water, along with a few paper plates, floated these jars and jar lids.

I walked back into the bedroom just as Fay was putting a chocolate in her mouth.

"Look, Fay," I said, "I know you want to save the world. But can't you start in the kitchen?"

"Kitchens aren't important," she said.

It was difficult to hit a woman with grey hair so I just went into the bathroom and let the water run into the tub. A burning bath might cool the nerves. When the tub was full I was afraid to get into it. My sore body had, by then, stiffened to such an extent that I was afraid I might drown in there.

I went into the front room and after an effort I managed to get out of my shirt, pants, shoes, stockings. I walked into the bedroom and climbed into bed next to Fay. I couldn't get settled. Every time I moved, it cost me.

The only time you are alone, Chinaski, I thought, is when you are driving to work or driving back.

I finally worked my way to a position on my stomach. I ached all over. Soon I'd be back on the job. If I could manage to sleep, it would help. Every now and then I could hear a page turn, the sound of chocolates being eaten. It had been one of her writers' workshop nights. If she would only turn out the lights.

"How was the workshop?" I asked from my belly.

"I'm worried about Robby."

"Oh," I asked, "what's wrong?"

Robby was a guy nearing 40 who had lived with his mother all his life. All he wrote, I was told, were terribly funny stories about the Catholic Church. Robby really laid it to the Catholics. The magazines just weren't ready for Robby, although he had been printed once in a Canadian journal. I had seen Robby once on one of my nights off. I drove Fay up to this mansion where they all read their stuff to each other. "Oh! There's Robby!" Fay had said, "he writes these very funny stories about the Catholic Church!"

She had pointed. Robby had his back to us. His ass was wide and big and soft; it hung in his slacks. Can't they see that? I thought.

"Won't you come in?" Fay had asked.

"Maybe next week . . . "

Fay put another chocolate into her mouth.

"Robby's worried. He lost his job on the delivery truck. He says he can't write without a job. He needs a feeling of security. He says he won't be able to write until he finds another job."

"Oh hell," I said, "I can get him another job."

"Where? How?"

"They are hiring down at the post office, right and left. The pay's not bad."

"THE POST OFFICE! ROBBY'S TOO SENSITIVE TO WORK AT THE POST OFFICE!"

"Sorry," I said, "thought it was worth a try. Good night."

Fay didn't answer me. She was angry.

—*Post Office*

His Wife, The Painter

• •

There are sketches on the walls of men and women and ducks,
and outside a large green bus swerves through traffic like
insanity sprung from a waving line; Turgenev, Turgenev,
says the radio, and Jane Austen, Jane Austen, too.

"I am going to do her portrait on the 28th, while you are
at work."

He is just this edge of fat and he walks constantly, he
fritters; they have him; they are eating him hollow like
a webbed fly, and his eyes are red-suckled with anger-fear.

He feels the hatred and discard of the world, sharper than
his razor, and his gut-feel hangs like a wet polyp; and he
self-decisions himself defeated trying to shake his
hung beard from razor in water (like life), not warm enough.

Daumier. Rue Transnonain, le 15 Avril, 1843. (Lithograph.)
Paris, Bibliotheque Nationale.

"She has a face unlike that of any woman I have ever known."

"What is it? A love affair?"

"Silly. I can't love a woman. Besides, she's pregnant."

I can paint—a flower eaten by a snake; that sunlight is a
lie; and that markets smell of shoes and naked boys clothed,
and under everything some river, some beat, some twist that
clambers along the edge of my temple and bites nip-dizzy . . .
men drive cars and paint their houses,
but they are mad; men sit in barber chairs; buy hats.

Corot. Recollection of Mortefontaine.
Paris, Louvre.

"I must write Kaiser, though I think he's a homosexual."

"Are you still reading Freud?"

"Page 299."

She made a little hat and he fastened two snaps under one
arm, reaching up from the bed like a long feeler from the
snail, and she went to church, and he thought now I h've
time and the dog.

About church: the trouble with a mask is it
never changes.

So rude the flowers that grow and do not grow beautiful.
So magic the chair on the patio that does not hold legs
and belly and arm and neck and mouth that bites into the
wind like the end of a tunnel.

He turned in bed and thought: I am searching for some
segment in the air. It floats about the people's heads.
When it rains on the trees it sits between the branches
warmer and more blood-real than the dove.

Orozco. Christ Destroying the Cross.
Hanover, Dartmouth College, Baker Library.

He burned away in sleep.

• •

Fay was pregnant. But it didn't change her and it didn't change the
post office either.

The same clerks did all the work while the miscellaneous crew stood
around and argued about sports. They were all big black dudes—built
like professional wrestlers. Whenever a new one came into the service
he was tossed into the miscellaneous crew. This kept them from murder-
ing the supervisors. If the miscellaneous crew had a supervisor you never
saw him. The crew brought in truckloads of mail that arrived via freight
elevator. This was a five minute on the hour job. Sometimes they count-
ed the mail, or pretended to. They looked very calm and intellectual,
making their counts with long pencils behind one ear. But most of the
time they argued the sports scene violently. They were all experts—they
read the same sports writers.

"All right, man, what's your all time outfield?"

"Well, Willie Mays, Ted Williams, Cobb."

"What? What?"

"That's right, baby!"

"What about the Babe? Whatta ya gonna do with the Babe?"

"O.K., O.K., who's your all star outfield?"

"All time, not all star!"

"O.K., O.K., you know what I mean, baby, you know what I mean!"

"Well, I'll take Mays, Ruth and Di Maj!"

"Both you guys are nuts! How about Hank Aaron, baby? How about Hank?"

At one time, all miscellaneous jobs were put on bid. Bids were filled mostly on a basis of seniority. The miscellaneous crew went about and ripped the bids out of the order books. Then they had nothing to do. Nobody filed a complaint. It was a long dark walk to the parking lot at night.

I began getting dizzy spells. I could feel them coming. The case would begin to whirl. The spells lasted about a minute. I couldn't understand it. Each letter was getting heavier and heavier. The clerks began to have that dead grey look. I began to slide off my stool. My legs would barely hold me up. The job was killing me.

I went to my doctor and told him about it. He took my blood pressure.

"No, no, your blood pressure is all right."

Then he put the stethoscope to me and weighed me.

"I can find nothing wrong."

Then he gave me a special blood test. He took blood from my arm three times at intervals, each time lapse longer than the last.

"Do you care to wait in the other room?"

"No, no, I'll go out and walk around and come back in time."

"All right but come back in time."

I was on time for the second blood extraction. Then there was a longer wait for the third one, 20 or 25 minutes. I walked out on the street. Nothing much was happening. I went into a drugstore and read a magazine. I put it down, looked at the clock and went outside. I saw this woman sitting at the bus stop. She was one of those rare ones. She was showing plenty of leg. I couldn't keep my eyes off her. I crossed the street and stood about 20 yards away.

Then she got up. I had to follow her. That big ass beckoned me. I was hypnotized. She walked into a post office and I walked in behind her. She stood in a long line and I stood behind her. She got two postcards. I bought 12 airmail postcards and two dollars worth of stamps.

When I came out she was getting on the bus. I saw the last of that delicious leg and ass get on the bus and the bus carried her away.

The doctor was waiting.

"What happened? You're five minutes late!"

"I don't know. The clock must have been wrong."

"THIS THING MUST BE EXACT!"

"Go ahead. Take the blood anyhow."

He stuck the needle into me . . .

A couple of days later, the tests said there was nothing wrong with me. I didn't know if it was the five minutes difference or what. But the dizzy spells got worse. I began to clock out after four hours work without filling out the proper forms.

I'd walk in around 11 p.m. and there would be Fay. Poor pregnant Fay.

"What happened?"

"I couldn't take any more," I'd say, "too sensitive . . . "

—POST OFFICE

A Shipping Clerk with a Red Nose
• •

When I first met Randall Harris he was 42 and lived with a grey haired woman, one Margie Thompson. Margie was 45 and not too handsome. I was editing the little magazine *Mad Fly* at the time and I had come over in an attempt to get some material from Randall.

Randall was known as an isolationist, a drunk, a crude and bitter man but his poems were raw, raw and honest, simple and savage. He was writing unlike anybody else at the time. He worked as a shipping clerk in an auto parts warehouse.

I sat across from both Randall and Margie. It was 7:15 p.m. and Harris was already drunk on beer. He set a bottle in front of me. I'd heard of Margie Thompson. She was an old-time communist, a world-saver, a do-gooder. One wondered what she was doing with Randall who cared for nothing and admitted it. "I like to photograph shit," he told me, "that's my art."

Randall had begun writing at the age of 38. At 42, after three small chapbooks (*Death Is a Dirtier Dog Than My Country, My Mother Fucked an Angel,* and *The Piss-Wild Horses of Madness*), he was getting what might be called critical acclaim. But he made nothing on his writing and he said, "I'm nothing but a shipping clerk with the deep blue blues." He lived in an old front court in Hollywood with Margie, and he was weird, truly. "I just don't like people," he said. "You know, Will Rogers once said, 'I never met a man I didn't like.' Me, I never met a man I liked."

But Randall had humor, an ability to laugh at pain and at himself. You liked him. He was an ugly man with a large head and a smashed-up face—only the nose seemed to have escaped the general smashup. "I don't have enough bone in my nose, it's like rubber," he explained. His nose was long and very red.

I had heard stories about Randall. He was given to smashing windows and breaking bottles against the wall. He was one nasty drunk. He also had periods where he wouldn't answer the door or the telephone. He didn't own a T.V., only a small radio and he only listened to symphony music—strange for a guy as crude as he was.

Randall also had periods when he took the bottom off the telephone and stuffed toilet paper around the bell so it wouldn't ring. It stayed that way for months. One wondered why he had a phone. His education was sparse but he'd evidently read most of the best writers.

"Well, fucker," he said to me, "I guess you wonder what I'm doing with her?" he pointed to Margie.

I didn't answer.

"She's a good lay," he said, "and she gives me some of the best sex west of St. Louis."

This was the same guy who had written four or five great love poems to a woman called Annie. You wondered how it worked.

Margie just sat there and grinned. She wrote poetry too but it wasn't very good. She attended two workshops a week which hardly helped.

"So you want some poems?" he asked me.

"Yes, I'd like to look some over."

Harris walked over to the closet, opened the door and picked some torn and crushed papers off the floor. He handed them to me. "I wrote these last night." Then he walked into the kitchen and came out with two more beers. Margie didn't drink.

I began to read the poems. They were all powerful. He typed with a very heavy hand and the words seemed chiseled in the paper. The force of his writing always astounded me. He seemed to be saying all the things we should have said but had never thought of saying.

"I'll take these poems," I said.

"O.k.," he said. "Drink up."

When you came to see Harris, drinking was a must. He smoked one cigarette after another. He dressed in loose brown chino pants two sizes too large and old shirts that were always ripped. He was around six feet and 220 pounds, much of it beerfat. He was round-shouldered, and peered out at you from behind slitted eyelids. We drank a good two hours and a half, the room heavy with smoke. Suddenly Harris stood up and said, "Get the hell out of here, fucker, you disgust me!"

"Easy now, Harris . . . "

"I said NOW!, fucker!"

I got up and left with the poems.

I returned to that front court two months later to deliver a couple of copies of *Mad Fly* to Harris. I had run all ten of his poems. Margie let me in. Randall wasn't there.

"He's in New Orleans," said Margie, "I think he's getting a break. Jack Teller wants to publish his next book but he wants to meet Randall first. Teller says he can't print anybody he doesn't like. He's paid the air fare both ways."

"Randall isn't exactly endearing," I said.

"We'll see," said Margie. "Teller's a drunk and an ex-con. They might make a lovely pair."

Teller put out the magazine *Rifraff* and had his own press. He did very fine work. The last issue of *Rifraff* had had Harris' ugly face on the cover sucking at a beer-bottle and had featured a number of his poems.

Rifraff was generally recognized as the number one lit mag of the time. Harris was beginning to get more and more notice. This would be a good chance for him if he didn't botch it with his mean tongue and his drunken manners. Before I left Margie told me she was pregnant—by Harris. As I said, she was 45.

"What'd he say when you told him?"

"He seemed indifferent."

I left.

The book did come out in an edition of 2,000, finely printed. The cover was made of cork imported from Ireland. The pages were vari-colored, of extremely good paper, set in rare type and interspersed with some of Harris' India ink sketches. The book received acclaim, both for itself and its contents. But Teller couldn't pay royalties. He and his wife lived on a very narrow margin. In ten years the book would go for $75 on the rare book market. Meanwhile Harris went back to his shipping clerk job at the auto parts warehouse.

When I called again four or five months later Margie was gone.

"She's been gone a long time," said Harris. "Have a beer."

"What happened?"

"Well, after I got back from New Orleans, I wrote a few short stories. While I was at work she got to poking around in my drawers. She read a couple of my stories and took exception to them."

"What were they about?"

"Oh, she read something about my climbing in and out of bed with some women in New Orleans."

"Were the stories true?" I asked.

"How's *Mad Fly* doing?" he asked.

The baby was born, a girl, Naomi Louise Harris. She and her mother lived in Santa Monica and Harris drove out once a week to see them. He paid child support and continued to drink his beer. Next I knew he had a weekly column in the underground newspaper *L.A. Lifeline*. He called his columns *Sketches of a First Class Maniac*. His prose was like his poetry—undisciplined, antisocial, and lazy.

Harris grew a goatee and grew his hair longer. The next time I saw him he was living with a 35-year-old girl, a pretty redhead called Susan. Susan worked in an art supply store, painted, and played fair guitar. She also drank an occasional beer with Randall which was more than Margie had done. The court seemed cleaner. When Harris finished a bottle he threw it into a paper bag instead of throwing it on the floor. He was still a nasty drunk, though.

"I'm writing a novel," he told me, "and I'm getting a poetry reading now and then at nearby universities. I also have one coming up in Michigan and one in New Mexico. The offers are pretty good. I don't like to read, but I'm a good reader. I give them a show and I give them some good poetry."

Harris was also beginning to paint. He didn't paint very well. He painted like a five-year-old drunk on vodka but he managed to sell one or two for $40 or $50. He told me that he was considering quitting his job. Three weeks later he did quit in order to make the Michigan reading. He'd already used his vacation for the New Orleans trip.

I remember once he had vowed to me, "I'll never read in front of those bloodsuckers, Chinaski. I'll go to my grave without ever giving a poetry reading. It's vanity, it's a sell-out." I didn't remind him of his statement.

His novel *Death in the Life of All the Eyes on Earth* was brought out by a small but prestige press which paid standard royalties. The reviews were good, including one in *The New York Review of Books.* But he was still a nasty drunk and had many fights with Susan over his drinking.

Finally, after one horrible drunk, when he had raved and cursed and screamed all night, Susan left him. I saw Randall several days after her departure. Harris was strangely quiet, hardly nasty at all.

"I loved her, Chinaski," he told me. "I'm not going to make it, baby."

"You'll make it, Randall. You'll see. You'll make it. The human being is much more durable than you think."

"Shit," he said. "I hope you're right. I've got this damned hole in my gut. Women have put many a good man under the bridge. They don't feel it like we do."

"They feel it. She just couldn't handle your drinking."

"Fuck, man, I write most of my stuff when I'm drunk."

"Is that the secret?"

"Shit, yes. Sober, I'm just a shipping clerk and not a very good one at that . . ."

I left him there hanging over his beer.

I made the rounds again three months later. Harris was still in his front court. He introduced me to Sandra, a nice-looking blonde of 27. Her father was a superior court judge and she was a graduate of U.S.C. Besides being well-shaped she had a cool sophistication that had been lacking in Randall's other women. They were drinking a bottle of good Italian wine.

Randall's goatee had turned into a beard and his hair was much longer. His clothes were new and in the latest style. He had on $40 shoes, a new wristwatch and his face seemed thinner, his fingernails clean . . . but his nose still reddened as he drank the wine.

"Randall and I are moving to West L.A. this weekend," she told me. "This place is filthy."

"I've done a lot of good writing here," he said.

"Randall, dear," she said, "it isn't the *place* that does the writing, it's *you*. I think we might get Randall a job teaching three days a week."

"I can't teach."

"Darling, you can teach them *everything*."

"Shit," he said.

"They're thinking of doing a movie of Randall's book. We've seen the script. It's a very fine script."

"A movie?" I asked.

"There's not much chance," said Harris.

"Darling, it's in the works. Have a little faith."

I had another glass of wine with them, then left. Sandra was a beautiful girl.

I wasn't given Randall's West L.A. address and didn't make any attempt to find him. It was over a year later when I read the review of the movie *Flower Up the Tail of Hell*. It had been taken from his novel. It was a fine review and Harris even had an acting bit in the film.

I went to see it. They'd done a good job on the book. Harris looked a little more austere than when I had last seen him. I decided to find him. After a bit of detective work I knocked on the door of his cabin in Malibu one night about 9:00 p.m. Randall answered the door.

"Chinaski, you old dog," he said. "Come on in."

A beautiful girl sat on the couch. She appeared to be about 19, she simply radiated natural beauty. "This is Karilla," he said. They were drinking a bottle of expensive French wine. I sat down with them and had a glass. I had several glasses. Another bottle came out and we talked quietly. Harris didn't get drunk and nasty and didn't appear to smoke as much.

"I'm working on a play for Broadway," he told me. "They say the theatre is dying but I have something for them. One of the leading producers is interested. I'm getting the last act in shape now. It's a good medium. I was always splendid on conversation, you know."

"Yes," I said.

I left about 11:30 that night. The conversation had been pleasant . . . Harris had begun to show a distinguished grey about the temples and he didn't say "shit" more than four or five times.

The play *Shoot Your Father, Shoot Your God, Shoot Away the Disentanglement* was a success. It had one of the longest runs in Broadway history. It had everything: something for the revolutionaries, something for the reactionaries, something for lovers of comedy, something for lovers of drama, even something for the intellectuals, and it still made sense. Randall Harris moved from Malibu to a large place high in the Hollywood Hills. You read about him now in the syndicated gossip columns.

I went to work and found the location of his Hollywood Hills place, a three-story mansion which overlooked the lights of Los Angeles and Hollywood.

I parked, got out of the car, and walked up the path to the front door. It was around 8:30 p.m., cool, almost cold; there was a full moon and the air was fresh and clear.

I rang the bell. It seemed a very long wait. Finally the door opened. It was the butler. "Yes, sir?" he asked me.

"Henry Chinaski to see Randall Harris," I said.

"Just a moment, sir." He closed the door quietly and I waited. Again a long time. Then the butler was back. "I'm sorry, sir, but Mr. Harris can't be disturbed at this time."

"Oh, all right."

"Would you care to leave a message, sir?"

"A message?"

"Yes, a message."

"Yes, tell him 'congratulations.'"

"'Congratulations'? Is that all?"

"Yes, that's all."

"Goodnight, sir."

"Goodnight."

I went back to my car, got in. It started and I began the long drive down out of the hills. I had that early copy of *Mad Fly* with me that I had wanted him to sign. It was the copy with ten of Randall Harris' poems in it. He probably was busy. Maybe, I thought, if I mail the magazine to him with a stamped return envelope, he'll sign.

It was only about 9:00 p.m. There was time for me to go somewhere else.

—SOUTH OF NO NORTH

girl in a miniskirt reading the bible outside my window

Sunday. I am eating a
grapefruit. church is over at the Russian
Orthodox to the
west.
she is dark
of Eastern descent,
large brown eyes look up from the Bible
then down. a small red and black
Bible, and as she reads
her legs keep moving, moving,
she is doing a slow rhythmic dance
reading the Bible . . .
long gold earrings;
2 gold bracelets on each arm,
and it's a mini-*suit*, I suppose,
the cloth hugs her body,
the lightest of tans is that cloth,
she twists this way and that,
long young legs warm in the sun . . .

there is no escaping her being
there is no desire to . . .
my radio is playing symphonic music
that she cannot hear
but her movements coincide *exactly*
to the rhythms of the
symphony . . .

she is dark, she is dark
she is reading about God.

I am God.

claws of paradise

••

wooden butterfly
baking soda smile
sawdust fly—
I love my belly
and the liquor store man
calls me,
"Mr. Schlitz."
the cashiers at the race track
scream,
"THE POET KNOWS!"
when I cash my tickets.
the ladies
in and out of bed
say they love me
as I walk by with wet
white feet.

albatross with drunken eyes
Popeye's dirt-stained shorts
bedbugs of Paris,
I have cleared the barricades
have mastered the
automobile
the hangover
the tears
but I know
the final doom

like any schoolboy viewing
the cat being crushed
by passing traffic.

my skull has an inch and a
half crack right at the
dome.
most of my teeth are
in front. I get
dizzy spells in supermarkets
spit blood when I drink
whiskey
and become saddened to
the point of
grief
when I think of all the
good women I have known
who have
dissolved
vanished
over trivialities:
trips to Pasadena,
children's picnics,
toothpaste caps down
the drain.

there is nothing to do
but drink
play the horse
bet on the poem

as the young girls
become women
and the machineguns
point toward me
crouched
behind walls thinner
than eyelids.

there's no defense
except all the errors
made.

meanwhile
I take showers
answer the phone
boil eggs
study motion and waste
and feel as good
as the next while
walking in the sun.

• •

Fay was all right with the pregnancy. For an old gal, she was all right.
We waited around at our place. Finally the time came.

"It won't be long," she said. "I don't want to get there too early."

I went out and checked the car. Came back.

"Oooh, oh," she said. "No, wait."

Maybe she *could* save the world. I was proud of her calm. I forgave
her for the dirty dishes and *The New Yorker* and her writers' workshop.
The old gal was only another lonely creature in a world that didn't care.

"We better go now," I said.

"No," said Fay, "I don't want to make you wait too long. I know you
haven't been feeling well."

"To hell with me. Let's make it."

"No, please, Hank."

She just sat there.

"What can I do for you?" I asked.

"Nothing."

She sat there ten minutes. I went into the kitchen for a glass of
water. When I came out she said, "You ready to drive?"

"Sure."

"You know where the hospital is?"

"Of course."

I helped her into the car. I had made two practice runs the week earlier. But when we got there I had no idea where to park. Fay pointed up a runway.

"Go in there. Park in there. We'll go in from there."

"Yes, ma'am," I said . . .

She was in bed in a back room overlooking the street. Her face grimaced. "Hold my hand," she said.

I did.

"Is it really going to happen?" I asked.

"Yes."

"You make it seem so easy," I said.

"You're so very nice. It helps."

"I'd like to *be* nice. It's that god damned post office . . . "

"I know. I know."

We were looking out the back window.

I said, "Look at those people down there. They have no idea what is going on up here. They just walk on the sidewalk. Yet, it's funny . . . they were once born themselves, each one of them."

"Yes, it is funny."

I could feel the movements of her body through her hand.

"Hold tighter," she said.

"Yes."

"I'll hate it when you go."

"Where's the doctor? Where is everybody? What the hell!"

"They'll be here."

Just then a nurse walked in. It was a Catholic hospital and she was a very handsome nurse, dark, Spanish or Portuguese.

"You . . . must go . . . now," she told me.

I gave Fay crossed fingers and a twisted smile. I don't think she saw. I took the elevator downstairs.

My German doctor walked up. The one who had given me the blood tests.

"Congratulations," he said, shaking my hand, "it's a girl. Nine pounds, three ounces."

"And the mother?"

"The mother will be all right. She was no trouble at all."

"When can I see them?"

"They'll let you know. Just sit there and they'll call you." Then he was gone.

I looked through the glass. The nurse pointed down at my child. The child's face was very red and it was screaming louder than any of the other children. The room was full of screaming babies. So many births! The nurse seemed very proud of my baby. At least, I hoped it was mine. She picked the girl up so I could see it better. I smiled through the glass, I didn't know how to act. The girl just screamed at me. Poor thing, I thought, poor little damned thing. I didn't know then that she would be a beautiful girl someday who would look just like me, hahaha.

I motioned the nurse to put the child down, then waved goodbye to both of them. She was a nice nurse. Good legs, good hips. Fair breasts.

Fay had a spot of blood on the left side of her mouth and I took a wet cloth and wiped it off. Women were meant to suffer; no wonder they asked for constant declarations of love.

"I wish they'd give me my baby," said Fay, "it's not right to separate us like this."

"I know. But I guess there's some medical reason."

"Yes, but it doesn't seem right."

"No, it doesn't. But the child looked fine. I'll do what I can to make them send up the child as soon as possible. There must have been 40 babies down there. They're making all the mothers wait. I guess it's to let them get their strength back. Our baby looked *very* strong, I assure you. Please don't worry."

"I'd be so happy with my baby."

"I know, I know. It won't be long."

"Sir," a fat Mexican nurse walked up, "I'll have to ask you to leave now."

"But I'm the father."

"We know. But your wife must rest."

I squeezed Fay's hand, kissed her on the forehead. She closed her eyes and seemed to sleep then. She was not a young woman. Maybe she hadn't saved the world but she had made a major improvement. Ring one up for Fay.

—*Post Office*

marina:

• •

majestic, magic
infinite
my little girl is
sun
on the carpet—
out the door
picking a
flower, ha!,
an old man,
battle-wrecked,
emerges from his
chair
and she looks at me
but only sees
love,
ha!, and I become
quick with the world
and love right back
just like I was meant
to do.

• •

The baby was crawling, discovering the world. Marina slept in bed with us at night. There was Marina, Fay, the cat and myself. The cat slept on the bed too. Look here, I thought, I have three mouths depending on me. How very strange. I sat there and watched them sleeping.

Then two nights in a row when I came home in the mornings, the early mornings, Fay was sitting up reading the classified sections.

"All these rooms are so damned expensive," she said.

"Sure," I said.

The next night I asked her as she read the paper:

"Are you moving out?"

"Yes."

"All right. I'll help you find a place tomorrow. I'll drive you around."

I agreed to pay her a sum each month. She said, "All right."

Fay got the girl. I got the cat.

We found a place eight or ten blocks away. I helped her move in, said goodbye to the girl and drove on back.

I went over to see Marina two or three or four times a week. I knew as long as I could see the girl I would be all right.

Fay was still wearing black to protest the war. She attended local peace demonstrations, love-ins, went to poetry readings, workshops, communist party meetings, and sat in a hippie coffee house. She took the child with her. If she wasn't out she was sitting in a chair smoking cigarette after cigarette and reading. She wore protest buttons on her black blouse. But she was usually off somewhere with the girl when I drove over to visit.

I finally found them in one day. Fay was eating sunflower seeds with yogurt. She baked her own bread but it wasn't very good.

"I met Andy, this truckdriver," she told me. "He paints on the side. That's one of his paintings." Fay pointed to the wall.

I was playing with the girl. I looked at the painting. I didn't say anything.

"He has a big cock," said Fay. "He was over the other night and he asked me, 'How would you like to be fucked with a big cock?' and I told him, 'I would rather be fucked with love!'"

"He sounds like a man of the world," I told her.

I played with the girl a little more, then left. I had a scheme test coming up.

Soon after, I got a letter from Fay. She and the child were living in a hippie commune in New Mexico. It was a nice place, she said. Marina would be able to breathe there. She enclosed a little drawing the girl had made for me.

—*Post Office*

notes upon the flaxen aspect:

• •

a John F. Kennedy flower knocks upon my door and is shot through the
neck;
the gladiolas gather by the dozens around the tip of
India
dripping into Ceylon;
dozens of oysters read Germaine Greer.

meanwhile, I itch from the slush of the Philippines
to the eye of the minnow
the minnow being eaten by the cumulative dreams of
Simon Bolivar. O,
freedom from the limitation of angular distance would be
delicious.
war is perfect,
the solid way drips and leaks,
Schopenhauer laughed for 72 years,
and I was told by a very small man in a New York City
pawnshop
one afternoon:
"Christ got more attention than I did
but I went further on less . . ."

well, the distance between 5 points is the same as the
distance between 3 points is the same as the distance
between one point:

it is all as cordial as a bonbon:
all this that we are wrapped
in:

eunuchs are more exact than sleep

the postage stamp is mad, Indiana is ridiculous

the chameleon is the last walking flower.

No Way to Paradise

• •

I was sitting in a bar on Western Ave. It was around midnight and I was in my usual confused state. I mean, you know, nothing works right: the women, the jobs, the no jobs, the weather, the dogs. Finally you just sit in a kind of stricken state and wait like you're on the bus stop bench waiting for death.

Well, I was sitting there and here comes this one with long dark hair, a good body, sad brown eyes. I didn't turn on for her. I ignored her even though she had taken the stool next to mine when there were a dozen other empty seats. In fact, we were the only ones in the bar except for the bartender. She ordered a dry wine. Then she asked me what I was drinking.

"Scotch and water."

"Give him a scotch and water," she told the barkeep.

Well, that was unusual.

She opened her purse, removed a small wire cage and took some little people out and sat them on the bar. They were all around three inches tall and they were alive and properly dressed. There were four of them, two men and two women.

"They make these now," she said, "they're very expensive. They cost around $2,000 apiece when I got them. They go for around $2,400 now. I don't know the manufacturing process but it's probably against the law."

The little people were walking around on the top of the bar. Suddenly one of the little guys slapped one of the little women across the face.

"You bitch," he said, "I've had it with you!"

"No, George, you can't," she cried, "I love you! I'll kill myself! I've got to have you!"

"I don't care," said the little guy, and he took out a tiny cigarette and lit it. "I've got a right to live."

"If you don't want her," said the other little guy, "I'll take her. I love her."

"But I don't want you, Marty. I'm in love with George."

"But he's a bastard, Anna, a real bastard!"

"I know, but I love him anyhow."

The little bastard then walked over and kissed the other little woman.

"I've got a triangle going," said the lady who had bought me the drink. "That's Marty and George and Anna and Ruthie. George goes down, he goes down good. Marty's kind of square."

"Isn't it sad to watch all that? Er, what's your name?"

"Dawn. It's a terrible name. But that's what mothers do to their children sometimes."

"I'm Hank. But isn't it sad . . . "

"No, it isn't sad to watch it. I haven't had much luck with my own loves, terrible luck really . . . "

"We all have terrible luck."

"I suppose. Anyhow, I bought these little people and now I watch them, and it's like having it and not having any of the problems. But I get awfully hot when they start making love. That's when it gets difficult."

"Are they sexy?"

"Very, very sexy. My god, it makes me hot!"

"Why don't you make them do it? I mean, right now. We'll watch them together."

"Oh, you can't make them do it. They've got to do it on their own."

"How often do they do it?"

"Oh, they're pretty good. They go four or five times a week."

They were walking around on the bar. "Listen," said Marty, "give me a chance. Just give me a chance, Anna."

"No," said Anna, "my love belongs to George. There's no other way it can be."

George was kissing Ruthie, feeling her breasts. Ruthie was getting hot.

"Ruthie's getting hot," I told Dawn.

"She is. She really is."

I was getting hot too. I grabbed Dawn and kissed her.

"Listen," she said, "I don't like them to make love in public. I'll take them home and have them do it."

"But then I can't watch."

"Well, you'll just have to come with me."

"All right," I said, "let's go."

I finished my drink and we walked out together. She carried the little people in the small wire cage. We got into her car and put the people in between us on the front seat. I looked at Dawn. She was really young and beautiful. She seemed to have good insides too. How could she have gone wrong with her men? There were so many ways those things could miss. The four little people had cost her $8,000. Just *that* to get away from relationships and *not* to get away from relationships.

Her house was near the hills, a pleasant looking place. We got out and walked up to the door. I held the little people in the cage while Dawn opened the door.

"I heard Randy Newman last week at The Troubador. Isn't he great?" she asked.

"Yes, he is."

We walked into the front room and Dawn took the little people out and placed them on the coffeetable. Then she walked into the kitchen and opened the refrigerator and got out a bottle of wine. She brought in two glasses.

"Pardon me," she said, "but you seem a little bit crazy. What do you do?"

"I'm a writer."

"Are you going to write about this?"

"They'll never believe it, but I'll write it."

"Look," said Dawn, "George has got Ruthie's panties off. He's fingering her. Ice?"

"Yes, he is. No, no ice. Straight's fine."

"I don't know," said Dawn, "it really gets me hot to watch them. Maybe it's because they're so small. It really heats me up."

"I know what you mean."

"Look, George is going down on her now."

"He is, isn't he?"

"Look at them!"

"God o mighty!"

I grabbed Dawn. We stood there kissing. As we did her eyes went from mine to them and then back to mine again.

Little Marty and little Anna were watching too.

"Look," said Marty, "they're going to make it. We might as well make it. Even the big folks are going to make it. Look at them!"

"Did you hear that?" I asked Dawn. "They said we're going to make it. Is that true?"

"I hope it's true," said Dawn.

I got her over to the couch and worked her dress up around her hips. I kissed her along the throat. "I love you," I said.

"Do you? Do you?"

"Yes, somehow, yes . . . "

"All right," said little Anna to little Marty, "we might as well do it too, even though I don't love you."

They embraced in the middle of the coffeetable. I had worked Dawn's panties off. Dawn groaned. Little Ruthie groaned. Marty closed in on Anna. It was happening everywhere. I got the idea that everybody in the world was doing it. Then I forgot about the rest of the world. We somehow walked into the bedroom. Then I got into Dawn for the long slow ride. . . .

When she came out of the bathroom I was reading a dull dull story in *Playboy*.

"It was so good," she said.

"My pleasure," I answered.

She got back into bed with me. I put the magazine down.

"Do you think we can make it together?" she asked.

"What do you mean?"

"I mean, do you think we can make it together for any length of time?"

"I don't know. Things happen. The beginning is always easiest."

Then there was a scream from the front room. "Oh-oh," said Dawn. She leaped up and ran out of the room. I followed. When I got there she was holding George in her hands.

"Oh, my god!"

"What happened?"

"Anna did it to him!"

"Did what?"

"She cut off his balls! George is a eunuch!"

"Wow!"

"Get me some toilet paper, quickly! He might bleed to death!"

"That son of a bitch," said little Anna from the coffeetable, "if I can't have George, nobody can have him!"

"Now both of you belong to me!" said Marty.

"No, you've got to choose between us," said Anna.

"Which one of us is it?" asked Ruthie.

"I love you both," said Marty.

"He's stopped bleeding," said Dawn. "He's out cold." She wrapped George in a handkerchief and put him on the mantel.

"I mean," Dawn said to me, "if you don't think we can make it, I don't want to go into it anymore."

"I think I love you, Dawn."

"Look," she said, "Marty's embracing Ruthie!"

"Are they going to make it?"

"I don't know. They seem excited."

Dawn picked Anna up and put her in the wire cage.

"Let me out of here! I'll kill both of them! Let me out of here!"

George moaned from inside his handkerchief upon the mantel. Marty had Ruthie's panties off. I pulled Dawn to me. She was beautiful and young and had insides. I could be in love again. It was possible. We kissed. I fell down inside her eyes. Then I got up and began running. I knew where I was. A cockroach and an eagle made love. Time was a fool with a banjo. I kept running. Her long hair fell across my face.

"I'll kill everybody!" screamed little Anna. She rattled about in her wire cage at 3 a.m. in the morning.

—*SOUTH OF NO NORTH*

Dow Jones: Down

• •

how can we endure?
how can we talk about roses
or Verlaine?
this is a hungry band
that likes to work and count
and knows the special laws,
that likes to sit in parks
thinking of nothing valuable.

this is where the stricken bagpipes blow
upon the chalky cliffs
where faces go mad as sunburned violets
where brooms and ropes and torches fail,
squeezing shadows . . .
where walls come down en masse.

tomorrow the bankers set the time
to close the gates against our flood
and prevaricate the waters;
bang, bang the time,
remember now
  the flowers are opening in the wind
  and it doesn't matter finally
  except as a twitch in the back of the head
when back in our broad land
dead again
we walk among the dead.

the world's greatest loser

he used to sell papers in front:
"Get your winners! Get rich on a dime!"
and about the 3rd or 4th race
you'd see him rolling in on his rotten board
with roller skates underneath.
he'd propel himself along on his hands;
he just had small stumps for legs
and the rims of the skate wheels were worn off.
you could see inside the wheels and they would wobble
something awful
shooting and flashing
imperialistic sparks!
he moved faster than anybody, rolled cigarette dangling,
you could hear him coming
"god o mighty, what was that?" the new ones asked.

he was the world's greatest loser
but he never gave up
wheeling toward the 2 dollar window screaming:
"IT'S THE 4 HORSE, YOU FOOLS! HOW THE HELL YA
GONNA BEAT THE

4?"
up on the board the 4 would be reading
60 to one.
I never heard him pick a winner.

they say he slept in the bushes. I guess that's where he
died. he's not around any
more.

there was the big fat blond whore
who kept touching him for luck, and
laughing.

nobody had any luck. the whore is gone
too.

I guess nothing ever works for us. we're fools, of course—
bucking the inside plus a 15 percent take,
but how are you going to tell a dreamer
there's a 15 percent take on the
dream? he'll just laugh and say,
is that all?

I miss those
sparks.

a wild, fresh wind blowing . . .

I should not have blamed only my father, but,
he was the first to introduce me to
raw and stupid hatred.
he was really best at it: anything and everything made him
mad—things of the slightest consequence brought his hatred quickly
to the surface

and I seemed to be the main source of his
irritation.
I did not fear him
but his rages made me ill at heart
for he was most of my world then
and it was a world of horror but I should not have blamed only
my father
for when I left that . . . home . . . I found his counterparts
everywhere: my father was only a small part of the
whole, though he was the best at hatred
I was ever to meet.
but others were very good at it too: some of the
foremen, some of the street bums, some of the women
I was to live with,
most of the women, were gifted at
hating—blaming my voice, my actions, my presence
blaming me
for what *they*, in retrospect, had failed
at.
I was simply the target of their discontent
and in some real sense
they blamed me
for not being able to rouse them
out of a failed past; what they didn't consider was
that I had my troubles too—most of them caused by
simply living with them.

I am a dolt of a man, easily made happy or even
stupidly happy almost without cause
and left alone I am mostly content.

but I've lived so often and so long with this hatred
that
my only freedom, my only peace is when I am away from
them, when I am anywhere else, no matter where—
some fat old waitress bringing me a cup of coffee
is in comparison
like a fresh wild wind blowing.

A Working Day

• •

Joe Mayer was a freelance writer. He had a hangover and the telephone awakened him at 9 a.m. He got up and answered it. "Hello?"

"Hi, Joe. How's it going?"

"Oh, beautiful."

"Beautiful, eh?"

"Yes?"

"Vicki and I just moved into our new house. We don't have a phone yet. But I can give you the address. You got a pen there?"

"Just a minute."

Joe took down the address.

"I didn't like that last story of yours I saw in *Hot Angel*."

"O.K." said Joe.

"I don't mean I didn't like it, I mean I don't like it compared to most of your stuff. By the way, do you know where Buddy Edwards is? Griff Martin who used to edit *Hot Tales* is looking for him. I thought you might know."

"I don't know where he is."

"I think he might be in Mexico."

"He might be."

"Well, listen, we'll be around to see you soon."

"Sure." Joe hung up. He put a couple of eggs in a pan of water, set some coffee water on and took an Alka Seltzer. Then he went back to bed.

The phone rang again. He got up and answered it.

"Joe?"

"Yes?"

"This is Eddie Greer."

"Oh yes."

"We want you to read for a benefit . . . "

"What is it?"

"For the I.R.A."

"Listen, Eddie, I don't go for politics or religion or whatever. I really don't know what's going on over there. I don't have a tv, read the papers . . . any of that. I don't know who's right or who's wrong, if there is such a thing."

"England's wrong, man."

"I can't read for the I.R.A., Eddie."

"All right, then . . . "

The eggs were done. He sat down, peeled them, put on some toast and mixed the Sanka in with the hot water. He got down the eggs and toast and had two coffees. Then he went back to bed.

He was just about asleep when the phone rang again. He got up and answered it.

"Mr. Mayer?"

"Yes?"

"I'm Mike Haven, I'm a friend of Stuart Irving's. We once appeared in *Stone Mule* together when *Stone Mule* was edited in Salt Lake City."

"Yes?"

"I'm down from Montana for a week. I'm staying at the Hotel Sheraton here in town. I'd like to come see you and talk to you."

"Today's a bad day, Mike."

"Well, maybe I can come over later in the week?"

"Yes, why don't you call me later on?"

"You know, Joe, I write just like you do, both in poetry and prose. I want to bring some of my stuff over and read it to you. You'll be surprised. My stuff is really powerful."

"Oh yes?"

"You'll see."

The mailman was next. One letter. Joe opened it:

Dear Mr. Mayer:

I got your address from Sylvia who you used to write to in Paris many years ago. Sylvia is still alive in San Francisco today and still writing her wild and prophetic and angelic and mad poems. I'm living in Los Angeles now and would just love to come and visit you! Please tell me when it would be all right with you.

love, Diane

Joe got out of his robe and got dressed. The phone rang again. He walked over to it, looked at it and didn't answer it. He walked out, got into his car and drove it toward Santa Anita. He drove slowly. He turned the radio on and got some symphony music. It wasn't too smoggy. He drove down Sunset, took his favorite cutoff, drove over the hill toward Chinatown, past the Annex, up past Little Joe's, past Chinatown and took the slow easy ride past the railroad yards, looking down at the old brown boxcars. If he were any damned good at painting he'd like to get that one down. Maybe he'd paint them anyhow. He drove in up Broadway and over Huntington Drive to the track. He got a corned beef sandwich and a coffee, split the Form and sat down. It looked like a fair card.

He caught Rosalena in the first at $10.80, Wife's Objection in the second at $9.20 and hooked them in the daily double for $48.40. He'd had $2 win on Rosalena and $5 win on Wife's Objection, so he was $73.20 up. He ran out on Sweetott, was second with Harbor Point, second with Pitch Out, second with Brannan, all win bets, and he was sitting $48.20 ahead when he hit $20 win on Southern Cream, which brought him back to $73.20 again.

It wasn't bad at the track. He only met three people he knew. Factory workers. Black. From the old days.

The eighth race was the problem. Cougar who was packing 128 was in against Unconscious packing 123. Joe didn't consider the others in the race. He couldn't make up his mind. Cougar was 3-to-5 and Unconscious was 7-to-2. Being $73.20 ahead he felt he could afford the luxury of betting the 3-to-5 shot. He laid $30 win. Cougar broke sluggishly, acting as if he were running in a ditch. By the time he was halfway around the first turn he was 17 lengths back of the lead horse. Joe knew he had a loser. At the finish his 3-to-5 was five lengths back and the race was over.

He went $10 and $10 on Barbizon, Jr. and Lost at Sea in the ninth, failed, and walked out with $23.20. It was easier picking tomatoes. He got into his old car and drove slowly back . . .

Just as he got into the tub the doorbell rang. He toweled and got into his shirt and pants. It was Max Billinghouse. Max was in his early twenties, toothless, red-haired. He worked as a janitor and always wore bluejeans and a dirty white t-shirt. He sat down in a chair and crossed his legs.

"Well, Mayer, what's happening?"

"What do you mean?"

"I mean, are you surviving on your writing?"

"At the moment."

"Is there anything new?"

"Not since you were here last week."

"How did your poetry reading come out?"

"It was all right."

"The crowd that goes to poetry readings is a very phoney crowd."

"Most crowds are."

"You got any candy?" Max asked.

"Candy?"

"Yeah, I got a sweet tooth. I've got this sweet tooth."

"I don't have any candy."

Max got up and walked into the kitchen. He came out with a tomato and two slices of bread. He sat down.

"Jesus, you don't have anything to eat around here."

"I'm going to have to go to the store."

"You know," said Max, "if I had to read in front of a crowd, I'd really insult them, I'd hurt their feelings."

"You might."

"But I can't write. I think I'm going to carry around a tape recorder. I talk to myself sometimes when I'm working. Then I can write down what I say and I'll have a story."

Max was an hour-and-a-half man. He was good for an hour-and-a-half. He never listened, he just talked. After an hour-and-a-half, Max stood up.

"Well, I gotta go."

"O.K., Max."

Max left. He always talked about the same things. How he had insulted some people on a bus. How once he had met Charles Manson. How a man was better off with a whore than with a decent woman. Sex was in the head. He didn't need new clothes, a new car. He was a loner. He didn't need people.

Joe went into the kitchen and found a can of tuna and made three sandwiches. He took out the pint of scotch he had been saving and poured a good scotch and water. He flicked the radio to the classical station. "The Blue Danube Waltz." He flicked it off. He finished the sandwiches. The doorbell rang. Joe walked to the door and opened it. It was Hymie. Hymie had a soft job somewhere in some city government near L.A. He was a poet.

"Listen," he said, "that book I had an idea for, *An Anthology of L.A. Poets,* let's forget it."

"All right."

Hymie sat down. "We need a new title. I think I have it. *Mercy for the Warmongers*. Think about it."

"I kind of like it," said Joe.

"And we can say, 'This book is for Franco, and for Lee Harvey Oswald and Adolf Hitler.' Now I'm Jewish, so that takes some guts. What do you think?"

"Sounds good."

Hymie got up and did his imitation of a typical old-time Jewish fat man, a very Jewish fat man. He spit on himself and sat down. Hymie was very funny. Hymie was the funniest man Joe knew. Hymie was good for an hour. After an hour, Hymie stood up and left. He always talked about the same things. How most of the poets were very bad. That it was tragic, it was so tragic it was laughable. What could a guy do?

Joe had another good scotch and water and walked over to the typewriter. He typed two lines, then the phone rang. It was Dunning at the hospital. Dunning liked to drink a lot of beer. He'd done his 20 in the army. Dunning's father had been the editor of a famous little magazine. Dunning's father had died in June. Dunning's wife was ambitious. She had pushed him to be a doctor, hard. He'd made it to chiropractor. And was working as a male nurse while trying to save up for an eight or ten thousand dollar x-ray machine.

"How about coming over and drinking some beer with you?" asked Dunning.

"Listen, can we put it off?" asked Joe.

"What'sa matter? You writing?"

"Just started."

"All right. I'll take a rain check."

"Thanks, Dunning."

Joe sat down at the machine again. It wasn't bad. He got halfway down the page when he heard footsteps. Then a knock. Joe opened the door.

It was two young kids. One with a black beard, the other smooth-shaven.

The kid with the beard said, "I saw you at your last reading."

"Come in," said Joe.

They came in. They had six bottles of imported beer, green bottles.

"I'll get an opener," said Joe.

They sat there sucking at the beer.

"It was a good reading," said the kid with the beard.

"Who was your major influence?" asked the one without the beard.

"Jeffers. Longer poems. *Tamar. Roan Stallion.* So forth."

"Any new writing that interests you?"

"No."

"They say you're coming out of the underground, that you're part of the Establishment. What do you think of that?"

"Nothing."

There were some more questions of the same order. The boys were only good for one beer apiece. Joe took care of the other four. They left in 45 minutes. But the one without the beard said, just as they left, "We'll be back."

Joe sat down to the machine again with a new drink. He couldn't type. He got up and walked to the phone. He dialed. And waited. She was there. She answered.

"Listen," said Joe, "let me get out of here. Let me come down there and lay up."

"You mean you want to stay tonight?"

"Yes."

"Again?"

"Yes, again."

"All right."

Joe walked around the corner of the porch and right down the driveway. She lived three or four courts down. He knocked. Lu let him in. The lights were out. She just had on panties and led him to the bed.

"God," he moaned.

"What is it?"

"Well, it's all unexplainable in a way or *almost* unexplainable."

"Just take off your clothes and come to bed."

Joe did. He crawled in. He didn't know at first if it would work again. So many nights in a row. But her body was there and it was a young body. And the lips were open and real. Joe floated in. It was good being in the dark. He worked her over good. He even got down there again and tongued that cunt. Then as he mounted, after four or five strokes he heard a voice . . .

"Mayer . . . I'm looking for a Joe Mayer . . . "

He heard his landlord's voice. His landlord was drunk.

"Well, if he ain't in that front apartment, you check this one back here. He's either in one or the other."

Joe got in four or five more strokes before the knocking began at the door. Joe slid out and, naked, went to the door. He opened a side window.

"Yeah?"

"Hey, Joe! Hi, Joe, what you doin', Joe?"

"Nothing."

"Well, how about some beer, Joe?"

"No," said Joe. He slammed the side window and walked back to the bed, got in.

"Who was it?" she asked.

"I don't know. I didn't recognize the face."

"Kiss me, Joe. Just don't lay there."

He kissed her as the Southern California moon came through the Southern California curtains. He was Joe Mayer. Freelance writer.

He had it made.

—*Hot Water Music*

the happy life of the tired

· ·

neatly in tune with
the song of a fish
I stand in the kitchen
halfway to madness
dreaming of Hemingway's
Spain.
it's muggy, like they say,
I can't breathe,
have crapped and
read the sports pages,
opened the refrigerator
looked at a piece of purple

meat,
tossed it back
in.

the place to find the center
is at the edge
that pounding in the sky
is just a water pipe
vibrating.

terrible things inch in the
walls; cancer flowers grow
on the porch; my white cat has
one eye torn
away and there are only 7 days
of racing left in the
summer meet.

the dancer never arrived from the
Club Normandy
and Jimmy didn't bring the
hooker,
but there's a postcard from
Arkansas
and a throwaway from Food King:
10 free vacations to Hawaii,
all I got to do is
fill out the form.
but I don't want to go to
Hawaii.

I want the hooker with the pelican eyes
brass belly-button
and
ivory heart.

I take out the piece of purple
meat

drop it into the
pan.

then the phone rings.

I fall to one knee and roll under the
table. I remain there
until it
stops.

then I get up and
turn on the
radio.
no wonder Hemingway was a
drunk, Spain be damned,
I can't stand it
either.

it's so
muggy.

the poetry reading

at high noon
at a small college near the beach
sober
the sweat running down my arms
a spot of sweat on the table
I flatten it with my finger
blood money blood money
my god they must think I love this like the others
but it's for bread and beer and rent

blood money
I'm tense lousy feel bad
poor people I'm failing I'm failing

a woman gets up
walks out
slams the door

a dirty poem
somebody told me not to read dirty poems
here

it's too late.

my eyes can't see some lines
I read it
out—
desperate trembling
lousy

they can't hear my voice
and I say,
I quit, that's it, I'm
finished.

and later in my room
there's scotch and beer:
the blood of a coward.

this then
will be my destiny:
scrabbling for pennies in dark tiny halls
reading poems I have long since become tired
of.

and I used to think
that men who drove buses
or cleaned out latrines

or murdered men in alleys were
fools.

short order

• •

I took my girlfriend to your last poetry reading,
she said.
yes, yes? I asked.
she's young and pretty, she said.
and? I asked.
she hated your
guts.

then she stretched out on the couch
and pulled off her
boots.

I don't have very good legs,
she said.

all right, I thought, I don't have very good
poetry; she doesn't have very good
legs.

scramble two.

A Man

• •

George was lying in his trailer, flat on his back, watching a small
portable T.V. His dinner dishes were undone, his breakfast dishes were
undone, he needed a shave, and ash from his rolled cigarette dropped

onto his undershirt. Some of the ash was still burning. Sometimes the burning ash missed the undershirt and hit his skin, then he cursed, brushing it away.

There was a knock on the trailer door. He got slowly to his feet and answered the door. It was Constance. She had a fifth of unopened whiskey in a bag.

"George, I left that son of a bitch, I couldn't stand that son of a bitch anymore."

"Sit down."

George opened the fifth, got two glasses, filled each a third with whiskey, two thirds with water. He sat down on the bed with Constance. She took a cigarette out of her purse and lit it. She was drunk and her hands trembled.

"I took his damn money too. I took his damn money and split while he was at work. You don't know how I've suffered with that son of a bitch."

"Lemme have a smoke," said George.

She handed it to him and as she leaned near, George put his arm around her, pulled her over and kissed her.

"You son of a bitch," she said, "I missed you."

"I missed those good legs of yours, Connie. I've really missed those good legs."

"You still like 'em?"

"I get hot just looking."

"I never could make it with a college guy," said Connie. "They're too soft, they're milktoast. And he kept his house clean. George, it was like having a maid. He did it all. The place was spotless. You could eat beef stew right out of the crapper. He was *antiseptic*, that's what he was."

"Drink up. You'll feel better."

"And he couldn't make love."

"You mean he couldn't get it up?"

"Oh, he got it up. He got it up all the time. But he didn't know how to make a woman happy, you know. He didn't know what to do. All that money, all that education—he was useless."

"I wish I had a college education."

"You don't need one. You've got everything you need, George."

"I'm just a flunky. All the shit jobs."

"I said you've got everything you need, George. You know how to make a woman happy."

"Yeh?"

"Yes. And you know what else? His *mother* came around! His *mother!* Two or three times a week. And she'd sit there looking at me, pretending to like me but all the time treating me like I was a whore. Like I was a big bad whore stealing her son away from her! Her precious Walter! Christ! What a mess!"

"Drink up, Connie."

George was finished. He waited for Connie to empty her glass, then took it, refilled both glasses.

"He claimed he loved me. And I'd say, 'Look at my pussy, Walter!' And he wouldn't look at my pussy. He said, 'I don't want to look at that thing.' That *thing!* That's what he called it! You're not afraid of my pussy, are you, George?"

"It's never bit me yet."

"But you've bit it, you've nibbled on it, haven't you, George?"

"I suppose I have."

"And you've licked it, sucked it?"

"I suppose so."

"You know damn well, George, what you've done."

"How much money did you get?"

"Six hundred dollars."

"I don't like people who rob other people, Connie."

"That's why you're a fucking dishwasher. You're honest. But he's such an ass, George. And he can afford the money, and I've earned it . . . him and his *mother* and his *love,* his *mother-love,* his clean little washbowls and toilets and disposal bags and new cars and breath chasers and after-shave lotions and his little hard-ons and his precious love-making. All for *himself,* you understand, all for *himself!* You know what a woman wants, George . . . "

"Thanks for the whiskey, Connie. Lemme have another cigarette."

George filled them up again. "I've missed your legs, Connie. I've really missed those legs. I like the way you wear those high heels. They drive me crazy. These modern women don't know what they're missing. The high heel shapes the calf, the thigh, the ass; it puts rhythm into the walk. It really turns me on!"

"You talk like a poet, George. Sometimes you do talk like that. You are one hell of a dishwasher."

"You know what I'd really like to do?"

"What?"

"I'd like to whip you with my belt on the legs, the ass, the thighs. I'd like to make you quiver and cry and then when you're quivering and crying I'd slam it into you in pure love."

"I don't want that, George. You've never talked that way before. You've always done right with me."

"Pull your dress up higher."

"What?"

"Pull your dress up higher, I want to see more of your legs."

"You do like my legs, don't you, George?"

"Let the light shine on them!"

Constance hiked her dress.

"God Christ shit," said George.

"You like my legs?"

"I love your legs!"

Then George reached across the bed and slapped Constance hard across the face. Her cigarette flipped out of her mouth.

"What'd you do that for?"

"You fucked Walter! You fucked Walter!"

"So what the hell?"

"So pull your dress higher!"

"No!"

"Do what I say!"

George slapped her again, harder. Constance hiked her skirt.

"Just up to the panties!" shouted George. "I don't quite want to see the panties!"

"Christ, George, what's gone wrong with you?"

"You fucked Walter!"

"George, I swear, you've gone crazy. I want to leave. Let me out of here, George!"

"Don't move or I'll kill you!"

"You'd kill me?"

"I swear it!"

George got up and poured himself a full glass of straight whiskey, drank it, and sat down next to Constance. He took his cigarette and held it against her wrist. She screamed. He held it there, firmly, then pulled it away.

"I'm a man, baby, understand that?"

"I know you're a man, George."

"Here, look at my muscles!" George stood up and flexed both of his arms. "Beautiful, eh, baby? Look at that muscle! Feel it! Feel it!"

Constance felt one of his arms. Then the other.

"Yes, you have a beautiful body, George."

"I'm a man. I'm a dishwasher but I'm a man, a real man."

"I know it, George."

"I'm not like that milkshit you left."

"I know it."

"And I can sing too. You ought to hear my voice."

Constance sat there. George began to sing. He sang "Old Man River." Then he sang "Nobody Knows the Trouble I've Seen." He sang "The St. Louis Blues." He sang "God Bless America," stopping several times and laughing. Then he sat down next to Constance. He said, "Connie, you have beautiful legs." He asked for another cigarette. He smoked it, drank two more drinks, then put his head down on Connie's legs, against the stockings, in her lap, and he said, "Connie, I guess I'm no good, I guess I'm crazy, I'm sorry I hit you, I'm sorry I burned you with that cigarette."

Constance sat there. She ran her fingers through George's hair, stroking him, soothing him. Soon he was asleep. She waited a while longer. Then she lifted his head and placed it on the pillow, lifted his legs and straightened them out on the bed. She stood up, walked to the fifth, poured a good jolt of whiskey into her glass, added a touch of water and drank it down. She walked to the trailer door, pulled it open, stepped out, closed it. She walked through the backyard, opened the fence gate, walked up the alley under the one o'clock moon. The sky was clear of clouds. The same skyful of stars was up there. She got on the boulevard and walked east and reached the entrance of The Blue Mirror. She walked in, looked around and there was Walter sitting alone and drunk at the end of the bar. She walked up and sat down next to him.

"Missed me, baby?" she asked.

Walter looked up. He recognized her. He didn't answer. He looked

at the bartender and the bartender walked toward them. They all knew
each other.

—*SOUTH OF NO NORTH*

on going out to get the mail

the droll noon
where squadrons of worms creep up like
stripteasers
to be raped by blackbirds.

I go outside
and all up and down the street
the green armies shoot color
like an everlasting 4th of July,
and I too seem to swell inside,
a kind of unknown bursting, a
feeling, perhaps, that there isn't any
enemy
anywhere.

and I reach down into the box
and there is
nothing—not even a
letter from the gas co. saying they will
shut it off
again.

not even a short note from my x-wife
bragging about her present
happiness.

my hand searches the mailbox in a kind of
disbelief long after the mind has
given up.

there's not even a dead fly
down in there.

I am a fool, I think, I should have known it
works like this.

I go inside as all the flowers leap to
please me.

anything? the woman
asks.

nothing, I answer, what's for
breakfast?

somebody

god I got the sad blue blues,
this woman sat there and she
said
are you really Charles
                        Bukowski?
and I said
            forget that
I do not feel good
I've got the sad sads
all I want to do is
fuck you

and she laughed
she thought I was being
clever
and O I just looked up her long slim legs of heaven
I saw her liver and her quivering intestine
I saw Christ in there
jumping to a folk-rock

all the long lines of starvation within me
rose
and I walked over
and grabbed her on the couch
ripped her dress up around her face

and I didn't care
rape or the end of the earth
one more time
to be there
anywhere
real

yes
her panties were on the
floor
and my cock went in
my cock my god my cock went in

I was Charles
Somebody.

Scream When You Burn

• •

Henry poured a drink and looked out the window at the hot and bare Hollywood street. Jesus Christ, it had been a long haul and he was still up against the wall. Death was next, death was always there. He'd made a dumb mistake and bought an underground newspaper and they were still idolizing Lenny Bruce. There was a photo of him, dead, right after the bad fix. All right, Lenny had been funny at times: "I can't come!"—that bit had been a masterpiece but Lenny really hadn't been all that good. Persecuted, all right, sure, physically and spiritually. Well, we all ended up dead, that was just mathematics. Nothing new. It was waiting around that was the problem. The phone rang. It was his girl-friend.

"Listen, you son of a bitch, I'm tired of your drinking. I had enough of that with my father . . . "

"Oh hell, it's not all that bad."

"It is, and I'm not going through it again."

"I tell you, you're making too much of it."

"No, I've had it, I tell you, I've had it. I saw you at the party, sending out for more whiskey, that's when I left. I've had it, I'm not going to take any more . . . "

She hung up. He walked over and poured a scotch and water. He walked into the bedroom with it, took off his shirt, pants, shoes, stock-ings. In his shorts he went to bed with the drink. It was 15 minutes to noon. No ambition, no talent, no chance. What kept him off the row was raw luck and luck never lasted. Well, it was too bad about Lu, but Lu wanted a winner. He emptied the glass and stretched out. He picked up Camus' *Resistance, Rebellion and Death* . . . read some pages. Camus talked about anguish and terror and the miserable condition of Man but he talked about it in such a comfortable and flowery way . . . his language . . . that one got the feeling that things neither affected him *nor* his writ-ing. In other words, things might as well have been fine. Camus wrote like a man who had just finished a large dinner of steak and french fries, salad, and had topped it with a bottle of good French wine. Humanity may have been suffering but not him. A wise man, perhaps, but Henry preferred somebody who screamed when they burned. He dropped the book to the floor and tried to sleep. Sleep was always difficult. If he could sleep three hours in 24 he was satisfied. Well, he thought, the walls are still here, give a man four walls and he had a chance. Out on the streets, nothing could be done.

The doorbell rang. "Hank!" somebody screamed. "Hey, Hank!"

What the shit? he thought. Now what?

"Yeah?" he asked, lying there in his shorts.

"Hey! What are you doing?"

"Wait a minute . . . "

He got up, picked up his shirt and pants and walked into the front room.

"What are you doing?"

"Getting dressed . . . "

"Getting dressed?"

"Yeah."

It was ten minutes after 12. He opened the door. It was the professor from Pasadena who taught English lit. He had a looker with him. The prof introduced the looker. She was an editor in one of the large New York publishing houses.

"Oh you sweet thing," he said, and walked up and squeezed her right thigh. "I love you."

"You're fast," she said.

"Well, you know writers have always had to kiss the asses of publishers."

"I thought it was the other way around."

"It isn't. It's the writer who's starving."

"She wants to see your novel."

"All I have is a hardcover. I can't give her a hardcover."

"Let her have one. They might buy it," said the prof.

They were talking about his novel, *Nightmare.* He figured she just wanted a free copy of the novel.

"We were going to Del Mar but Pat wanted to see you in the flesh."

"How nice."

"Hank read his poems to my class. We gave him $50. He was frightened and crying. I had to push him out in front of my class."

"I was indignant. Only $50. Auden used to get $2,000. I don't think he's that much better than I am. In fact . . . "

"Yes, we know what you think."

Henry gathered up the old Racing Forms from around the editor's feet.

"People owe me $1100. I can't collect. The sex mags have become impossible. I've gotten to know the girl in the front office. One Clara. 'Hello, Clara,' I phone her, 'did you have a nice breakfast?' 'Oh yes, Hank, did you?' 'Sure,' I tell her, 'two hard-boiled eggs.' 'I know what you're phoning about,' she answers. 'Sure,' I tell her, 'the same thing.'

'Well, we have it right here, our p.o. 984765 for $85.' 'And there's another one, Clara, your p.o. 973895 for five stories, $570.' 'Oh yes, well I'll try to get these signed by Mr. Masters.' 'Thank you, Clara,' I tell her. 'Oh that's all right,' she says, 'you fellows deserve your money.' 'Sure,' I say. And then she says, 'And if you don't get your money you'll phone again, won't you? Ha, ha, ha.' 'Yes, Clara,' I tell her, 'I'll phone again.'"

The professor and the editor laughed.

"I can't make it, god damn it, anybody want a drink?"

They didn't answer so Henry poured himself one. "I even tried to make it playing the horses. I started well but I hit a slump. I had to stop. I can only afford to win."

The professor started to explain his system for beating twenty-one at Vegas. Henry walked over to the editor.

"Let's go to bed," he said.

"You're funny," she said.

"Yeah," he said, "like Lenny Bruce. Almost. He's dead and I'm dying."

"You're still funny."

"Yeah, I'm the hero. The myth. I'm the unspoiled one, the one who hasn't sold out. My letters are auctioning for $250 back east. I can't buy a bag of farts."

"All you writers are always hollering 'wolf.'"

"Maybe the wolf has finally arrived. You can't live off your soul. You can't pay the rent with your soul. Try it some time."

"Maybe I ought to go to bed with you," she said.

"Come on, Pat," said the prof, standing up, "we've got to make Del Mar."

They walked to the door. "It was good to see you."

"Sure," Henry said.

"You'll make it."

"Sure," he said, "goodbye."

He walked back to the bedroom, took off his clothing and got back into bed. Maybe he could sleep. Sleep was something like death. Then he was asleep. He was at the track. The man at the window was giving him money and he was putting it into his wallet. It was a lot of money.

"You ought to get a new wallet," said the man, "that one's torn."

"No," he said, "I don't want people to know I'm rich."

The doorbell rang. "Hey Hank! Hank!"

"All right, all right . . . wait a minute . . . "

He put his clothes back on and opened the door. It was Harry Stobbs. Stobbs was another writer. He knew too many writers.

Stobbs walked in.

"You got any money, Stobbs?"

"Hell no."

"All right, I'll buy the beer. I thought you were rich."

"No, I was living with this gal in Malibu. She dressed me well, fed me. She booted me out. I'm living in a shower now."

"A shower?"

"Yes, it's nice. Real glass sliding doors."

"All right, let's go. You got a car?"

"No."

"We'll take mine."

They got into his '62 Comet and drove up toward Hollywood and Normandy.

"I sold an article to *Time*. Man, I thought I was in the big money. I got their check today. I haven't cashed it yet. Guess what it reads?" asked Stobbs.

"$800?"

"No, $165."

"What? *Time* magazine? $165?"

"That's right."

They parked and went into a small liquor store for the beer. "My woman dumped me," Henry told Stobbs. "She claims I drink too much. A bareass lie." He reached into the cooler for two six-packs. "I'm tapering off. Bad party last night. Nothing but starving writers, and professors who were about to lose their jobs. Shop talk. Very wearing."

"Writers are whores," said Stobbs, "writers are the whores of the universe."

"The whores of the universe do much better, my friend."

They walked to the counter.

"'Wings of Song,'" said the owner of the liquor store.

"'Wings of Song,'" Henry answered.

The owner had read an article in the *L.A. Times* a year ago about Henry's poetry and had never forgotten. It was their Wings of Song routine. At first he had hated it, and now he found it amusing. Wings of Song, by god.

They got into the car and drove back. The mailman had been by. There was something in the box.

"Maybe it's a check," Henry said.

He took the letter inside, opened two beers and opened the letter. It said,

"Dear Mr. Chinaski, I just finished reading your novel, *Nightmare*, and your book of poems, *Photographs From Hell*, and I think you're a great writer. I am a married woman, 52 years old, and my children are grown. I would very much like to hear from you. Respectfully, Doris Anderson."

The letter was from a small town in Maine.

"I didn't know that people still lived in Maine," he told Stobbs.

"I don't think they do," Stobbs said.

"They do. This one does."

Henry threw the letter in the trash sack. The beer was good. The nurses were coming home to the highrise apartment across the street. Many nurses lived there. Most of them wore see-through uniforms and the afternoon sun did the rest. He stood there with Stobbs watching them get out of their cars and walk through the glass entrance, to vanish to their showers and their tv sets and their closed doors.

"Look at that one," said Stobbs.

"Uh huh."

"There's another one."

"Oh my!"

We're acting like 15-year-olds, Henry thought. We don't deserve to live. I'll bet Camus never peeked out of windows.

"How are you going to make it, Stobbs?"

"Well, as long as I've got that shower, I've got it made."

"Why don't you get a job?"

"A job? Don't talk like a crazy man."

"I guess you're right."

"Look at that one! Look at the ass on that one!"

"Yes, indeed."

They sat down and worked at the beer.

"Mason," he told Stobbs, mentioning a young unpublished poet, "has gone to Mexico to live. He hunts meat with his bow and arrow, catches fish. He's got his wife and a servant girl. He's got four books out looking. Even wrote a Western. The problem is that when you're out of the country it's almost impossible to collect your money. The only way to collect your money is to threaten them with death. I'm good at those letters. But if you're a thousand miles away they know you'll cool off before you get to their door. I like hunting your own meat, though. It beats going to the A & P. You pretend those animals are editors and publishers. It's great."

Stobbs stayed around until 5 p.m. They bitched about writing, about how the top guys really stank. Guys like Mailer, guys like Capote. Then Stobbs left, and Henry took off his shirt, his pants, his shoes and stockings and went back to bed. The phone rang. It was on the floor near the bed. He reached down and picked it up. It was Lu.

"What are you doing? Writing?"

"I seldom write."

"Are you drinking?"

"Tapering off."

"I think you need a nurse."

"Let's go to the track tonight."

"All right. When will you be by?"

"6:30 O.K.?"

"6:30's O.K."

"Goodbye, then."

He stretched out in bed. Well, it was good to be back with Lu. She was good for him. She was right, he drank too much. If Lu drank like he did, he wouldn't want her. Be fair, man, be fair. Look what happened to Hemingway, always sitting with a drink in his hand. Look at Faulkner, look at them all. Well, shit.

The phone rang again. He picked it up.

"Chinaski?"

"Yeah?"

It was the poetess, Janessa Teel. She had a nice body but he'd never been to bed with her.

"I'd like you to come to dinner tomorrow night."

"I'm going steady with Lu," he said. God, he thought, I'm loyal. God, he thought, I'm a nice guy. God.

"Bring her with you."

"Do you think that would be wise?"

"It'll be all right with me."

"Listen, let me phone you tomorow. I'll let you know."

He hung up and stretched out again. For 30 years, he thought, I wanted to be a writer and now I'm a writer and what does it mean?

The phone rang again. It was Doug Eshlesham, the poet.

"Hank, baby . . ."

"Yeah, Doug?"

"I'm tapped, baby, I need a five, baby. Lemme have a fiver."

"Doug, the horses have smashed me. I'm flat, absolutely."

"Oh," said Doug.

"Sorry, baby."

"Well, all right."

Doug hung up. Doug owed him 15 right then. But he did have the fiver. He should have given Doug the fiver. Doug was probably eating dog food. I'm not a very nice guy, he thought. God, I'm not a very nice guy after all.

He stretched out in bed, full, in his unglory.

—*Hot Water Music*

the shoelace

• •

a woman, a
tire that's flat, a
disease, a
desire; fears in front of you,
fears that hold so still
you can study them
like pieces on a
chessboard . . .
it's not the large things that
send a man to the
madhouse. death he's ready for, or
murder, incest, robbery, fire, flood . . .
no, it's the continuing series of *small* tragedies

that send a man to the
madhouse . . .
not the death of his love
but a shoelace that snaps
with no time left . . .
the dread of life
is that swarm of trivialities
that can kill quicker than cancer
and which are always there—
license plates or taxes
or expired driver's license,
or hiring or firing,
doing it or having it done to you, or
constipation
speeding tickets
rickets or crickets or mice or termites or
roaches or flies or a
broken hook on a
screen, or out of gas
or too much gas,
the sink's stopped-up, the landlord's drunk,
the president doesn't care and the governor's
crazy.
lightswitch broken, mattress like a
porcupine;
$105 for a tune-up, carburetor and fuel pump at
Sears Roebuck;
and the phone bill's up and the market's
down
and the toilet chain is
broken,
and the light has burned out—
the hall light, the front light, the back light,
the inner light; it's
darker than hell
and twice as
expensive.
then there's always crabs and ingrown toenails

and people who insist they're
your friends;
there's always that and worse;
leaky faucet, Christ and Christmas;
blue salami, 9 day rains,
50 cent avocados
and purple
liverwurst.

or making it
as a waitress at Norm's on the split shift,
or as an emptier of
bedpans,
or as a carwash or a busboy
or a stealer of old lady's purses
leaving them screaming on the sidewalks
with broken arms at the age of
80.

suddenly
2 red lights in your rear view mirror
and blood in your
underwear;
toothache, and $979 for a bridge
$300 for a gold
tooth,
and China and Russia and America, and
long hair and short hair and no
hair, and beards and no
faces, and plenty of *zigzag* but no
pot, except maybe one to piss in and
the other one around your
gut.

with each broken shoelace
out of one hundred broken shoelaces,
one man, one woman, one
thing

enters a
madhouse.

so be careful
when you
bend over.

if we take—

if we take what we can see—
the engines driving us mad,
lovers finally hating;
this fish in the market
staring upward into our minds;
flowers rotting, flies web-caught;
riots, roars of caged lions,
clowns in love with dollar bills,
nations moving people like pawns;
daylight thieves with beautiful
nighttime wives and wines;
the crowded jails,
the commonplace unemployed,
dying grass, 2-bit fires;
men old enough to love the grave.

These things, and others, in content
show life swinging on a rotten axis.

But they've left us a bit of music
and a spiked show in the corner,
a jigger of scotch, a blue necktie,
a small volume of poems by Rimbaud,
a horse running as if the devil were
twisting his tail

over bluegrass and screaming, and then,
love again
like a streetcar turning the corner
on time,
the city waiting,
the wine and the flowers,
the water walking across the lake
and summer and winter and summer and summer
and winter again.

4

· ·

one more creature
dizzy with love

the strongest of the strange

you won't see them often
for wherever the crowd is
they
are not.

these odd ones, not
many
but from them
come
the few
good paintings
the few
good symphonies
the few
good books
and other
works.

and from the
best of the
strange ones
perhaps
nothing.

they are
their own
paintings
their own
books

their own
music
their own
work.

sometimes I think
I see
them—say
a certain old
man
sitting on a
certain bench
in a certain
way

or
a quick face
going the other
way
in a passing
automobile

or
there's a certain motion
of the hands
of a bag-boy or a bag-
girl
while packing
supermarket
groceries.

sometimes
it is even somebody
you have been
living with
for some
time—
you will notice

a
lightning quick
glance
never seen
from them
before.

sometimes
you will only note
their
existence
suddenly
in
vivid
recall
some months
some years
after they are
gone.

I remember
such a
one—
he was about
20 years old
drunk at
10 a.m.
staring into
a cracked
New Orleans
mirror

face dreaming
against the
walls of
the world

where
did I
go?

the last days of the suicide kid

I can see myself now
after all these suicide days and nights,
being wheeled out of one of those sterile rest homes
(of course, this is only if I get famous and lucky)
by a subnormal and bored nurse . . .
there I am sitting upright in my wheelchair . . .
almost blind, eyes rolling backward into the dark part of my skull
looking
for the mercy of death . . .

"Isn't it a lovely day, Mr. Bukowski?"

"O, yeah, yeah . . . "

the children walk past and I don't even exist
and lovely women walk by
with big hot hips
and warm buttocks and tight hot everything
praying to be loved
and I don't even
exist . . .

"It's the first sunlight we've had in 3 days,
Mr. Bukowski."

"Oh, yeah, yeah."

there I am sitting upright in my wheelchair,
myself whiter than this sheet of paper,

bloodless,
brain gone, gamble gone, me, Bukowski,
gone . . .

"Isn't it a lovely day, Mr. Bukowski?"

"O, yeah, yeah . . . " pissing in my pajamas, slop drooling out of
my mouth.

2 young schoolboys run by—

"Hey, did you see that old guy?"

"Christ, yes, he made me sick!"

after all the threats to do so
somebody else has committed suicide for me
at last.

the nurse stops the wheelchair, breaks a rose from a nearby bush,
puts it in my hand.

I don't even know
what it is. it might as well be my pecker
for all the good
it does.

Loneliness

Edna was walking down the street with her bag of groceries when
she passed the automobile. There was a sign in the side window:

WOMAN WANTED.

She stopped. There was a large piece of cardboard in the window with some material pasted on it. Most of it was typewritten. Edna couldn't read it from where she stood on the sidewalk. She could only see the large letters:

WOMAN WANTED.

It was an expensive new car. Edna stepped forward on the grass to read the typewritten portion:

Man age 49. Divorced. Wants to meet woman for marriage. Should be 35 to 44. Like television and motion pictures. Good food. I am a cost accountant, reliably employed. Money in bank. I like women to be on the fat side.

Edna was 37 and on the fat side. There was a phone number. There were also three photos of the gentleman in search of a woman. He looked quite staid in a suit and necktie. Also he looked dull and a little cruel. And made of wood, thought Edna, made of wood.

Edna walked off, smiling a bit. She also had a feeling of repulsion. By the time she reached her apartment she had forgotten about him. It was some hours later, sitting in the bathtub, that she thought about him again and this time she thought how truly lonely he must be to do such a thing:

WOMAN WANTED.

She thought of him coming home, finding the gas and phone bills in the mailbox, undressing, taking a bath, the T.V. on. Then the evening paper. Then into the kitchen to cook. Standing there in his shorts, staring down at the frying pan. Taking his food and walking to a table, eating it. Drinking his coffee. Then more T.V. And maybe a lonely can of beer before bed. There were millions of men like that all over America.

Edna got out of the tub, toweled, dressed and left her apartment. The car was still there. She took down the man's name, Joe Lighthill, and the phone number. She read the typewritten section again. "Motion pictures." What an odd term to use. People said "movies" now. WOMAN WANTED. The sign was very bold. He was original there.

When Edna got home she had three cups of coffee before dialing the number. The phone rang four times. "Hello?" he answered.

"Mr. Lighthill?"

"Yes?"

"I saw your ad. Your ad on the car."

"Oh, yes."

"My name's Edna."

"How you doing, Edna?"

"Oh, I'm all right. It's been so hot. This weather's too much."

"Yes, it makes it difficult to live."

"Well, Mr. Lighthill . . . "

"Just call me Joe."

"Well, Joe, hahaha, I feel like a fool. You know what I'm calling about?"

"You saw my sign?"

"I mean, hahaha, what's wrong with you? Can't you get a woman?"

"I guess not, Edna. Tell me, where are they?"

"Women?"

"Yes."

"Oh, everywhere, you know."

"Where? Tell me. Where?"

"Well, church, you know. There are women in church."

"I don't like church."

"Oh."

"Listen, why don't you come over, Edna?"

"You mean over there?"

"Yes. I have a nice place. We can have a drink, talk. No pressure."

"It's late."

"It's not that late. Listen, you saw my sign. You must be interested."

"Well . . . "

"You're scared, that's all. You're just scared."

"No, I'm not scared."

"Then come on over, Edna."

"Well . . . "

"Come on."

"All right. I'll see you in fifteen minutes."

It was on the top floor of a modern apartment complex. Apt. 17. The swimming pool below threw back the lights. Edna knocked. The door opened and there was Mr. Lighthill. Balding in front; hawknosed with the nostril hairs sticking out; the shirt open at the neck.

"Come on in, Edna . . . "

She walked in and the door closed behind her. She had on her blue knit dress. She was stockingless, in sandals, and smoking a cigarette.

"Sit down. I'll get you a drink."

It was a nice place. Everything in blue and green and *very* clean. She heard Mr. Lighthill humming as he mixed the drinks, hmmmmmmmm, hmmmmmmmmm, hmmmmmmmmmm . . . He seemed relaxed and it helped her.

Mr. Lighthill—Joe—came out with the drinks. He handed Edna hers and then sat in a chair across the room from her.

"Yes," he said, "it's been hot, hot as hell. I've got air-conditioning, though."

"I noticed. It's very nice."

"Drink your drink."

"Oh, yes."

Edna had a sip. It was a good drink, a bit strong but it tasted nice. She watched Joe tilt his head as he drank. He appeared to have heavy wrinkles around his neck. And his pants were much too loose. They appeared sizes too large. It gave his legs a funny look.

"That's a nice dress, Edna."

"You like it?"

"Oh yes. You're plump too. It fits you snug, real snug."

Edna didn't say anything. Neither did Joe. They just sat looking at each other and sipping their drinks.

Why doesn't he talk? thought Edna. It's up to him to talk. There *is* something wooden about him. She finished her drink.

"Let me get you another," said Joe.

"No, I really should be going."

"Oh, come on," he said, "let me get you another drink. We need something to loosen us up."

"All right, but after this one, I'm going."

Joe went into the kitchen with the glasses. He wasn't humming anymore. He came out, handed Edna her drink and sat back down in his chair across the room from her. This drink was stronger.

"You know," he said, "I do well on the sex quizzes."

Edna sipped at her drink and didn't answer.

"How do you do on the sex quizzes?" Joe asked.

"I've never taken any."

"You should, you know, so you'll find out who you are and what you are."

"Do you think those things are valid? I've seen them in the newspaper. I haven't taken them but I've seen them," said Edna.

"Of course they're valid."

"Maybe I'm no good at sex," said Edna, "maybe that's why I'm alone." She took a long drink from her glass.

"Each of us is, finally, alone," said Joe.

"What do you mean?"

"I mean, no matter how well it's going sexually or love-wise or both, the day arrives when it's over."

"That's sad," said Edna.

"Of course. So the day arrives when it's over. Either there is a split or the whole thing resolves into a truce: two people living together without feeling anything. I believe that being alone is better."

"Did you divorce your wife, Joe?"

"No, she divorced me."

"What went wrong?"

"Sexual orgies."

"Sexual orgies?"

"You know, a sexual orgy is the loneliest place in the world. Those orgies—I felt a sense of desperation—those cocks sliding in and out—excuse me . . . "

"It's all right."

"Those cocks sliding in and out, legs locked, fingers working, mouths, everybody clutching and sweating and determined to do it—somehow."

"I don't know much about those things, Joe," Edna said.

"I believe that without love, sex is nothing. Things can only be meaningful when some feeling exists between the participants."

"You mean people have to like each other?"

"It helps."

"Suppose they get tired of each other? Suppose they *have* to stay together? Economics? Children? All that?"

"Orgies won't do it."

"What does it?"

"Well, I don't know. Maybe the swap."

"The swap?"

"You know, when two couples know each other *quite* well and switch partners. Feelings, at least, have a chance. For example, say I've always liked Mike's wife. I've liked her for months. I've watched her walk across the room. I like her movements. Her movements have made me curious. I wonder, you know, what goes with those movements. I've seen her angry, I've seen her drunk, I've seen her sober. And then, the swap. You're in the bedroom with her, at last you're knowing her. There's a chance for something real. Of course, Mike has your wife in the other room. Good luck, Mike, you think, and I hope you're as good a lover as I am."

"And it works all right?"

"Well, I dunno . . . Swaps can cause difficulties . . . afterwards. It all has to be talked out . . . very well talked out ahead of time. And then maybe people don't know enough, no matter how much they talk . . . "

"Do you know enough, Joe?"

"Well, these swaps . . . I think it might be good for some . . . maybe good for many. I guess it wouldn't work for me. I'm too much of a prude."

Joe finished his drink. Edna set the remainder of hers down and stood up.

"Listen Joe, I have to be going . . . "

Joe walked across the room toward her. He looked like an elephant in those pants. She saw his big ears. Then he grabbed her and was kissing her. His bad breath came through all the drinks. He had a very sour smell. Part of his mouth was not making contact. He was strong but his strength was not pure, it begged. She pulled her head away and still he held her.

WOMAN WANTED.

"Joe, let me go! You're moving too fast, Joe! Let go!"

"Why did you come here, bitch?"

He tried to kiss her again and succeeded. It was horrible. Edna brought her knee up. She got him good. He grabbed and fell to the rug.

"God, god . . . why'd you have to do that? You tried to kill me . . . "

He rolled on the floor.

His behind, she thought, he had such an *ugly* behind.

She left him rolling on the rug and ran down the stairway. The air was clean outside. She heard people talking, she heard their T.V. sets. It wasn't a long walk to her apartment. She felt the need of another bath, got out of her blue knit dress and scrubbed herself. Then she got out of the tub, toweled herself dry and set her hair in pink curlers. She decided not to see him again.

—SOUTH OF NO NORTH

alone with everybody

the flesh covers the bone
and they put a mind
in there and
sometimes a soul,
and the women break
vases against the walls
and the men drink too
much
and nobody finds the
one
but they keep
looking
crawling in and out
of beds.
flesh covers
the bone and the
flesh searches
for more than
flesh.

there's no chance
at all:
we are all trapped

by a singular
fate.

nobody ever finds
the one.

the city dumps fill
the junkyards fill
the madhouses fill
the hospitals fill
the graveyards fill

nothing else
fills.

• •

    I was 50 years old and hadn't been to bed with a woman for 4 years.
I had no women friends. I looked at them as I passed them on the streets
or wherever I saw them, but I looked at them without yearning and with
a sense of futility. I masturbated regularly, but the idea of having a relationship with a woman—even on non-sexual terms—was beyond my
imagination. I had a six-year-old daughter born out of wedlock. She lived
with her mother and I paid child support. I had been married years
before at the age of 35. That marriage lasted two and one half years. My
wife divorced me. I had been in love only once. She had died of acute
alcoholism. She died at 48 when I was 38. My wife had been 12 years
younger than I. I believe that she too is dead now, although I'm not sure.
She wrote me a long letter each Christmas for 6 years after the divorce. I
never responded. . . .

I'm not sure when I first saw Lydia Vance. It was about 6 years ago and I
had just quit a twelve year job as a postal clerk and was trying to be a
writer. I was terrified and drank more than ever. I was attempting my
first novel. I drank a pint of whiskey and two six packs of beer each night

while writing. I smoked cheap cigars and typed and drank and listened to classical music on the radio until dawn. I set a goal of ten pages a night but I never knew until the next day how many pages I had written. I'd get up in the morning, vomit, then walk to the front room and look on the couch to see how many pages were there. I always exceeded my ten. Sometimes there were 17, 18, 23, 25 pages. Of course, the work of each night had to be cleaned up or thrown away. It took me 21 nights to write my first novel.

The owners of the court where I then lived, who lived in the back, thought I was crazy. Each morning when I awakened there would be a large brown paper bag on the porch. The contents varied but mostly the bags contained tomatoes, radishes, oranges, green onions, cans of soup, red onions. I drank beer with them every other night until 4 or 5 AM. The old man would pass out and the old lady and I would hold hands and I'd kiss her now and then. I always gave her a big one at the door. She was terribly wrinkled but she couldn't help that. She was Catholic and looked cute when she put on her pink hat and went to church on Sunday morning.

I think I met Lydia Vance at my first poetry reading. It was at a bookstore on Kenmore Ave., The Drawbridge. Again, I was terrified. Superior yet terrified. When I walked in there was standing room only. Peter, who ran the store and was living with a black girl, had a pile of cash in front of him. "Shit," he said to me, "if I could always pack them in like this I'd have enough money to take another trip to India!" I walked in and they began applauding. As far as poetry readings were concerned, I was about to bust my cherry.

I read 30 minutes then called a break. I was still sober and I could feel the eyes staring at me from out of the dark. A few people came up and talked to me. Then during a lull Lydia Vance walked up. I was sitting at a table drinking beer. She put both hands on the edge of the table, bent over and looked at me. She had long brown hair, quite long, a prominent nose, and one eye didn't quite match the other. But she projected vitality—you knew that she was there. I could feel vibrations running between us. Some of the vibrations were confused and were not good but they were there. She looked at me and I looked back. Lydia Vance had on a suede cowgirl jacket with a fringe around the neck. Her breasts were good. I told her, "I'd like to rip that fringe off your jacket—

we could begin there!" Lydia walked off. It hadn't worked. I never knew what to say to the ladies. But she had a behind. I watched that beautiful behind as she walked away. The seat of her bluejeans cradled it and I watched it as she walked away.

I finished the second half of the reading and forgot about Lydia just as I forgot about the women I passed on the sidewalks. I took my money, signed some napkins, some pieces of paper, then left, and drove back home.

—*Women*

a horse with greenblue eyes

what you see is what you see:
madhouses are rarely
on display.

that we still walk about and
scratch ourselves and light
cigarettes

is more the miracle

than bathing beauties
than roses and the moth.

to sit in a small room
and drink a can of beer
and roll a cigarette
while listening to Brahms
on a small red radio

is to have come back
from a dozen wars
alive

listening to the sound
of the refrigerator

as bathing beauties rot

and the oranges and apples
roll away.

• •

A day or so later I got a poem in the mail from Lydia. It was a long poem and it began:

Come out, old troll,
Come out of your dark hole, old troll,
Come out into the sunlight with us and
Let us put daisies in your hair . . .

The poem went on to tell me how good it would feel to dance in the fields with female fawn creatures who would bring me joy and true knowledge. I put the letter in a dresser drawer.

I was awakened the next morning by a knocking on the glass panes of my front door. It was 10:30 AM.

"Go away," I said.

"It's Lydia."

"All right. Wait a minute."

I put on a shirt and some pants and opened the door. Then I ran to the bathroom and vomited. I tried to brush my teeth but only vomited again—the sweetness of the toothpaste turned my stomach. I came out.

"You're sick," Lydia said. "Do you want me to leave?"

"Oh no, I'm all right. I always wake up like this."

Lydia looked good. The light came through the curtains and shone on her. She had an orange in her hand and was tossing it into the air. The orange spun through the sunlit morning.

"I can't stay," she said, "but I want to ask you something."

"Sure."

"I'm a sculptress. I want to sculpt your head."

"All right."

"You'll have to come to my place. I don't have a studio. We'll have to do it at my place. That won't make you nervous, will it?"

"No."

I wrote down her address, and instructions how to get there.

"Try to show up by eleven in the morning. The kids come home from school in mid-afternoon and it's distracting."

"I'll be there at eleven," I told her.

I sat across from Lydia in her breakfast nook. Between us was a large mound of clay. She began asking questions.

"Are your parents still alive?"

"No."

"You like L.A.?"

"It's my favorite city."

"Why do you write about women the way you do?"

"Like what?"

"You know."

"No, I don't."

"Well, I think it's a damned shame that a man who writes as well as you do just doesn't know anything about women."

I didn't answer.

"Damn it! What did Lisa do with . . . ?" She began searching the room. "Oh, little girls who run off with their mother's tools!"

Lydia found another one. "I'll make this one do. Hold still now, relax but hold still."

I was facing her. She worked at the mound of clay with a wooden tool tipped with a loop of wire. She waved the tool at me over the mound of clay. I watched her. Her eyes looked at me. They were large, dark brown. Even her bad eye, the one that didn't quite match the other, looked good. I looked back. Lydia worked. Time passed. I was in a trance. Then she said, "How about a break? Care for a beer?"

"Fine. Yes."

When she got up to go to the refrigerator I followed her. She got the bottle out and closed the door. As she turned I grabbed her around the waist and pulled her to me. I put my mouth and body against hers. She held the beer bottle out at arm's length with one hand. I kissed her. I kissed her again. Lydia pushed me away.

"All right," she said, "enough. We have work to do."

—WOMEN

my groupie

I read last Saturday in the
redwoods outside of Santa Cruz
and I was about ¾'s finished
when I heard a long high scream
and a quite attractive
young girl came running toward me
long gown & divine eyes of fire
and she leaped up on the stage
and screamed: "I WANT YOU!
I WANT YOU! TAKE ME! TAKE
ME!"
I told her, "look, get the hell
away from me."
but she kept tearing at my
clothing and throwing herself
at me.
"where were you," I
asked her, "when I was living
on one candy bar a day and
sending short stories to the
Atlantic Monthly?"
she grabbed my balls and almost
twisted them off. her kisses
tasted like shitsoup.
2 women jumped up on the stage
and

carried her off into the
woods.
I could still hear her screams
as I began the next poem.

maybe, I thought, I should have
taken her on the stage in front
of all those eyes.
but one can never be sure
whether it's good poetry or
bad acid.

· ·

I didn't see Lydia for a couple of days, although I did manage to phone her six or seven times during that period. Then the weekend arrived. Her ex-husband, Gerald, always took the children over the weekend.

I drove up to her court about 11 AM that Saturday morning and knocked. She was in tight bluejeans, boots, orange blouse. Her eyes seemed a darker brown than ever and in the sunlight, as she opened the door, I noticed a natural red in her dark hair. It was startling. She allowed me to kiss her, then she locked the door behind us and we went to my car. We had decided on the beach—not for bathing—it was mid-winter—but for something to do.

We drove along. It felt good having Lydia in the car with me.

"That was *some* party," she said. "You call that a collating party? That was a copulating party, that's what that was. A copulating party!"

I drove with one hand and rested the other on her inner thigh. I couldn't help myself. Lydia didn't seem to notice. As I drove along the hand slid down between her legs. She went on talking. Suddenly she said, "Take your hand off. That's my pussy!"

"Sorry," I said.

Neither of us said anything until we reached the parking lot at Venice beach. "You want a sandwich and a Coke or something?" I asked.

"All right," she said.

We went into the small Jewish delicatessen to get the things and we took them to a knoll of grass that overlooked the sea. We had sandwiches, pickles, chips and soft drinks. The beach was almost deserted and the food tasted fine. Lydia was not talking. I was amazed at how quickly she ate. She ripped into her sandwich with a savagery, took large swallows of Coke, ate half a pickle in one bite and reached for a handful of potato chips. I am, on the contrary, a very slow eater.

Passion, I thought, she has passion.

"How's that sandwich?" I asked.

"Pretty good. I was hungry."

"They make good sandwiches. Do you want anything else?"

"Yes, I'd like a candy bar."

"What kind?"

"Oh, any kind. Something good."

I took a bite of my sandwich, a swallow of Coke, put them down and walked over to the store. I bought two candy bars so that she might have a choice. As I walked back a tall black man was moving toward the knoll. It was a chilly day but he had his shirt off and he had a very muscular body. He appeared to be in his early twenties. He walked very slowly and erect. He had a long slim neck and a gold earring hung from the left ear. He passed in front of Lydia, along the sand on the ocean side of the knoll. I came up and sat down beside Lydia.

"Did you see that guy?" she asked.

"Yes."

"Jesus Christ, here I am with you, you're 20 years older than I am. I could have something like that. What the hell's wrong with me?"

"Look. Here are a couple of candy bars. Take one."

She took one, ripped the paper off, took a bite and watched the young black man as he walked away along the shore.

"I'm tired of the beach," she said, "let's go back to my place."

We remained apart a week. Then one afternoon I was over at Lydia's place and we were on her bed, kissing. Lydia pulled away.

"You don't know anything about women, do you?"

"What do you mean?"

"I mean, I can tell by reading your poems and stories that you just don't know anything about women."

"Tell me more."

"Well, I mean for a man to interest me he's got to eat my pussy. Have you ever eaten pussy?"

"No."

"You're over 50 years old and you've never eaten pussy?"

"No."

"It's too late."

"Why?"

"You can't teach an old dog new tricks."

"Sure you can."

"No, it's too late for you."

"I've always been a slow starter."

Lydia got up and walked into the other room. She came back with a pencil and a piece of paper. "Now, look, I want to show you something." She began to draw on the paper. "Now, this is a cunt, and here is something you probably don't know about—the clit. That's where the feeling is. The clit hides, you see, it comes out now and then, it's pink and very *sensitive*. Sometimes it will hide from you and you have to find it, you just *touch* it with the tip of your tongue. . . ."

"O.K.," I said, "I've got it."

"I don't think you can do it. I tell you, you can't teach an old dog new tricks."

"Let's take our clothes off and lay down."

We undressed and stretched out. I began kissing Lydia. I dropped from the lips to the neck, then down to the breasts. Then I was down at the bellybutton. I moved lower.

"No you *can't*," she said. "Blood and pee come out of there, think of it, blood and pee. . . ."

I got down there and began licking. She had drawn an accurate picture for me. Everything was where it was supposed to be. I heard her breathing heavily, then moaning. It excited me. I got a hard-on. The clit came out but it wasn't exactly pink, it was purplish-pink. I teased the clit. Juices appeared and mixed with the cunt hairs. Lydia moaned and moaned. Then I heard the front door open and close. I heard footsteps. I looked up. A small black boy about five years old stood beside the bed.

"What the hell do you want?" I asked him.

"You got any empty bottles?" he asked me.

"No, I don't have any empty bottles," I told him.

He walked out of the bedroom, into the front room, out the front door and was gone.

"God," said Lydia, "I thought the front door was locked. That was Bonnie's little boy."

Lydia got up and locked the front door. She came back and stretched out. It was about 4 PM on a Saturday afternoon.

I ducked back down.

—WOMEN

the shower

• •

we like to shower afterwards
(I like the water hotter than she)
and her face is always soft and peaceful
and she'll wash me first
spread the soap over my balls
lift the balls
squeeze them,
then wash the cock:
"hey, this thing is still hard!"
then get all the hair down there,—
the belly, the back, the neck, the legs,
I grin grin grin,
and then I wash her . . .
first the cunt, I
stand behind her, my cock in the cheeks of her ass
I gently soap up the cunt hairs,
wash there with a soothing motion,
I linger perhaps longer than necessary,
then I get the backs of the legs, the ass,
the back, the neck, I turn her, kiss her,
soap up the breasts, get them and the belly, the neck,
the fronts of the legs, the ankles, the feet,
and then the cunt, once more, for luck . . .

another kiss, and she gets out first,
toweling, sometimes singing while I stay in
turn the water on hotter
feeling the good times of love's miracle
I then get out . . .
it is usually mid-afternoon and quiet,
and getting dressed we talk about what else
there might be to do,
but being together solves most of it,
in fact, solves all of it
for as long as those things stay solved
in the history of woman and
man, it's different for each
better and worse for each—
for me, it's splendid enough to remember
past the marching of armies
and the horses that walk the streets outside
past the memories of pain and defeat and unhappiness:
Linda, you brought it to me,
when you take it away
do it slowly and easily
make it as if I were dying in my sleep instead of in
my life, amen.

• •

Dee Dee had a place in the Hollywood Hills. Dee Dee shared the place with a friend, another lady executive, Bianca. Bianca took the top floor and Dee Dee the bottom. I rang the bell. It was 8:30 PM when Dee Dee opened the door. Dee Dee was about 40, had black, cropped hair, was Jewish, hip, freaky. She was New York City oriented, knew all the names: the right publishers, the best poets, the most talented cartoon-ists, the right revolutionaries, anybody, everybody. She smoked grass continually and acted like it was the early 1960's and Love-In Time, when she had been mildly famous and much more beautiful.

A long series of bad love affairs had finally done her in. Now I was standing at her door. There was a good deal left of her body. She was small but buxom and many a young girl would have loved to have her figure.

I followed her in. "So Lydia split?" Dee Dee asked.

"I think she went to Utah. The 4th of July dance in Muleshead is coming up. She never misses it."

I sat down in the breakfast nook while Dee Dee uncorked a red wine. "Do you miss her?"

"Christ, yes. I feel like crying. My whole gut is chewed up. I might not make it."

"You'll make it. We'll get you over Lydia. We'll pull you through."

"Then you know how I feel?"

"It has happened to most of us a few times."

"That bitch never cared to begin with."

"Yes, she did. She still does."

I decided it was better to be there in Dee Dee's large home in the Hollywood Hills than to be sitting all alone back in my apartment and brooding.

"It must be that I'm just not good with the ladies," I said.

"You're good enough with the ladies," Dee Dee said. "And you're a helluva writer."

"I'd rather be good with the ladies."

Dee Dee was lighting a cigarette. I waited until she was finished, then I leaned across the table and gave her a kiss. "You make me feel good. Lydia was always on the attack."

"That doesn't mean what you think it means."

"But it can get to be unpleasant."

"It sure as hell can."

"Have you found a boyfriend yet?"

"Not yet."

"I like this place. But how do you keep it so neat and clean?"

"We have a maid."

"Oh?"

"You'll like her. She's big and black and she finishes her work as fast as she can after I leave. Then she goes to bed and eats cookies and watches t.v. I find cookie crumbs in my bed every night. I'll have her fix you breakfast after I leave tomorrow morning."

"All right."

"No, wait. Tomorrow's Sunday. I don't work Sundays. We'll eat out. I know a place. You'll like it."

"All right."

"You know, I think I've always been in love with you."

"What?"

"For years. You know, when I used to come and see you, first with Bernie and later with Jack, I would want you. But you never noticed me. You were always sucking on a can of beer or you were obsessed with something."

"Crazy, I guess, near crazy. Postal Service madness. I'm sorry I didn't notice you."

"You can notice me now."

Dee Dee poured another glass of wine. It was good wine. I liked her. It was good to have a place to go when things went bad. I remembered the early days when things would go bad and there wasn't anywhere to go. Maybe that had been good for me. Then. But now I wasn't interested in what was good for me. I was interested in how I felt and how to stop feeling bad when things went wrong. How to start feeling good again.

"I don't want to fuck you over, Dee Dee," I said. "I'm not always good to women."

"I told you I love you."

"Don't do it. Don't love me."

"All right," she said, "I won't love you, I'll *almost* love you. Will that be all right?"

"It's much better than the other."

We finished our wine and went to bed. . . .

—Women

I'm in love

• •

she's young, she said,
but look at me,
I have pretty ankles,
and look at my wrists, I have pretty

wrists
o my god,
I thought it was all working,
and now it's her again,
every time she phones you go crazy,
you told me it was over
you told me it was finished,
listen, I've lived long enough to become a
good woman,
why do you need a bad woman?
you need to be tortured, don't you?
you think life is rotten if somebody treats you
rotten it all fits,
doesn't it?
tell me, is that it? do you want to be treated like a
piece of shit?
and my son, my son was going to meet you.
I told my son
and I dropped all my lovers.
I stood up in a cafe and screamed
I'M IN LOVE,
and now you've made a fool of me . . .

I'm sorry, I said, I'm really sorry.

hold me, she said, will you please hold me?

I've never been in one of these things before, I said,
these triangles . . .

she got up and lit a cigarette, she was trembling all
over. she paced up and down, wild and crazy. she had
a small body. her arms were thin, very thin and when
she screamed and started beating me I held her
wrists and then I got it through the eyes: hatred,
centuries deep and true. I was wrong and graceless and
sick. all the things I had learned had been wasted.

there was no living creature as foul as I
and all my poems were
false.

White Dog Hunch

• •

Henry took the pillow and bunched it behind his back and waited.
Louise came in with toast, marmalade and coffee. The toast was but-
tered.

"Are you sure you don't want a couple of soft-boiled eggs?" she
asked.

"No, it's O.K. This is fine."

"You should have a couple of eggs."

"All right, then."

Louise left the bedroom. He'd been up earlier to go to the bathroom
and noticed his clothes had been hung up. Something Lita would never
do. And Louise was an excellent fuck. No children. He loved the way she
did things, softly, carefully. Lita was always on the attack—all hard edges.
When Louise came back with the eggs he asked her, "What was it?"

"What was what?"

"You even peeled the eggs. I mean, why did your husband divorce
you?"

"Oh, wait," she said, "the coffee is boiling!" and she ran from the
room.

He could listen to classical music with her. She played the piano.
She had books: *The Savage God* by Alvarez; *The Life of Picasso;* E. B.
White; e. e. cummings; T. S. Eliot; Pound; Ibsen, and on and on. She
even had nine of his *own* books. Maybe that was the best part.

Louise returned and got into bed, put her plate on her lap. "What
went wrong with *your* marriage?"

"Which one? There've been five!"

"The last. Lita."

"Oh. Well, unless Lita was in *motion* she didn't think anything was
happening. She liked dancing and parties, her whole life revolved
around dancing and parties. She liked what she called 'getting high.'

That meant men. She claimed I restricted her 'highs.' She said I was jealous."

"Did you restrict her?"

"I suppose so, but I tried not to. During the last party I went into the backyard with my beer and let her carry on. There was a houseful of men, I could hear her in there squealing, *'Yeehooo! Yee Hoo! Yee Hoo!'* I suppose she was just a natural country girl."

"You could have danced too."

"I suppose so. Sometimes I did. But they turn the stereo up so high that you can't think. I went out into the yard. I went back for some beer and there was a guy kissing her under the stairway. I walked out until they were finished, then went back again for the beer. It was dark but I thought it had been a friend and later I asked him what he was doing under the stairway there."

"Did she love you?"

"She said she did."

"You know, kissing and dancing isn't so bad."

"I suppose not. But you'd have to see her. She had a way of dancing as if she were offering herself as a sacrifice. For rape. It was very effective. The men loved it. She was 33 years old with two children."

"She didn't realize you were a solitary. Men have different natures."

"She never considered my nature. Like I say, unless she was in motion, or turning on, she didn't think anything was happening. Otherwise she was bored. 'Oh, this bores me or that bores me. Eating breakfast with you bores me. Watching you write bores me. I need challenges.'"

"That doesn't seem completely wrong."

"I suppose not. But you know, only boring people get bored. They have to prod themselves continually in order to feel alive."

"Like your drinking, for instance?"

"Yes, like my drinking. I can't face life straight on either."

"Was that all there was to the problem?"

"No, she was a nymphomaniac but didn't know it. She claimed I satisfied her sexually but I doubt if I satisfied her spiritual nymphomania. She was the second nymph I had lived with. She had fine qualities aside from that, but her nymphomania was embarrassing. Both to me and to my friends. They'd take me aside and say, 'What the hell's the matter with her?' And I'd say, 'Nothing, she's just a country girl.'"

"Was she?"

"Yes. But the other part was embarrassing."

"More toast?"

"No, this is fine."

"What was embarrassing?"

"Her behavior. If there was another man in the room she'd sit as close to him as possible. He would duck down to put out a cigarette in an ashtray on the floor, she'd duck down too. Then he'd turn his head to look at something and she'd do the same thing."

"Was it a coincidence?"

"I used to think so. But it happened too often. The man would get up to walk across the room and she'd get up and walk right alongside of him. Then when he walked back across the room she'd follow right by his side. The incidents were continuous and numerous, and like I say, embarrassing to both me and my friends. And yet I'm sure she didn't know what she was doing, it all came from the subconscious."

"When I was a girl there was a woman in the neighborhood with this 15-year-old daughter. The daughter was uncontrollable. The mother would send her out for a loaf of bread and she'd come back eight hours later with the bread but meanwhile she would have fucked six men."

"I guess the mother should have baked her own bread."

"I suppose so. The girl couldn't help herself. Whenever she saw a man she'd start to jiggle all over. The mother finally had her spayed."

"Can they do that?"

"Yes, but you have to go through all kinds of legal procedures. There was nothing else to do with her. She'd have been pregnant all her life.

"Do you have anything against dancing?" Louise continued.

"Most people dance for joy, out of good feeling. She crossed over into dirty areas. One of her favorite dances was The White Dog Hunch. A guy would wrap both his legs around her leg and hump her like a male dog in heat. Another of her favorites was The Drunk Dance. She and her partner would end up on the floor rolling over on top of each other."

"She said you were jealous of her dancing?"

"That was the word she used most often: jealous."

"I used to dance in high school."

"Yeah? Listen, thanks for breakfast."

"It's all right. I had a partner in high school. We were the best dancers in school. He had three balls; I thought it was a sign of masculinity."

"Three balls?"

"Yes, three balls. Anyhow, we really knew how to dance. I'd signal by touching him on the wrist, then we'd both leap and turn in the air, very high, and land on our feet. One time we were dancing, I touched his wrist and I made my leap and turn, but I didn't land on my feet. I landed on my ass. He put his hand over his mouth and stared down at me and said, 'Oh, good heavens!' and he walked off. He didn't pick me up. He was a homosexual. We never danced again."

"Do you have something against three-balled homosexuals?"

"No, but we never danced again."

"Lita, she was really dance-obsessed. She'd go into strange bars and ask men to dance with her. Of course, they would. They thought she was an easy fuck. I don't know if she did or didn't. I suppose that sometimes she did. The trouble with men who dance or hang out in bars is that their perception is on a parallel with the tape worm."

"How did you know that?"

"They're caught in the ritual."

"What ritual?"

"The ritual of misdirected energy."

Henry got up and began to dress. "Kid, I got to get going."

"What is it?"

"I just have to get some work done. I'm supposed to be a writer."

"There's a play by Ibsen on tv tonight. 8:30. Will you come over?"

"Sure. I left that pint of scotch. Don't drink it all."

Henry got into his clothes and went down the stairway and got into his car and drove to his place and his typewriter. Second floor rear. Every day as he typed, the woman downstairs would beat on her ceiling with the broom. He wrote the hard way, it had always been the hard way: *The White Dog Hunch* . . .

Louise phoned at 5:30 p.m. She'd been at the scotch. She was drunk. She slurred her words. She rambled. The reader of Thomas Chatterton and D. H. Lawrence. The reader of nine of his books.

"Henry?"

"Yes?"

"Oh, something marvelous has happened!"

"Yes?"

"This black boy came to see me. He's *beautiful!* He's more beautiful than you . . . "

"Of course."

". . . more beautiful than you and I."

"Yes."

"He got me so excited! I'm about to go out of my mind!"

"Yes."

"You don't mind?"

"No."

"You know how we spent the afternoon?"

"No."

"Reading *your poems!*"

"Oh?"

"And you know what he said?"

"No."

"He said your poems were *great!*"

"That's O.K."

"Listen, he got me so *excited.* I don't know how to handle it. Won't you come over? Now? I want to see you now . . . "

"Louise, I'm working . . . "

"Listen, you don't have anything against black men?"

"No."

"I've known this boy for ten years. He used to work for me when I was rich."

"You mean when you were still with your rich husband."

"Will I see you later? Ibsen is on at 8:30."

"I'll let you know."

"Why did that bastard come around? I was all right and then he came around. Christ. I'm so excited, I've got to see you. I'm about to go crazy. He was so *beautiful.*"

"I'm working, Louise. The word around here is 'Rent.' Try to understand."

Louise hung up. She called again at 8:20 about Ibsen. Henry said he was still working. He was. Then he began to drink and just sat in a chair, he just sat in a chair. At 9:50 there was a knock on the door. It was Booboo Meltzer, the number one rock star of 1970, currently unemployed, still living off royalties. "Hello, kid," said Henry.

Meltzer walked in and sat down.

"Man," he said, "you're a beautiful old cat. I can't get over you."

"Lay off, kid, cats are out of style, dogs are in now."

"I got a hunch you need help, old man."

"Kid, it's never been different."

Henry walked into the kitchen, found two beers, cracked them and walked out.

"I'm out of cunt, kid, which to me is like being out of love. I can't separate them. I'm not that clever."

"None of us are clever, Pops. We all need help."

"Yeh."

Meltzer had a small celluloid tube. Carefully he tapped out two little white spots on the coffee table.

"This is cocaine, Pops, *cocaine . . .* "

"Ah, hah."

Meltzer reached into his pocket, pulled out a $50 bill, rolled the fifty tightly, then worked it up one nostril. Pressing a finger on the other nostril he bent over one of the white spots on the coffee table and inhaled it. Then he took the $50 bill, worked it up the other nostril and sniffed the second white spot.

"Snow," said Meltzer.

"It's Christmas. Appropriate," said Henry.

Meltzer tapped out two more white spots and passed the fifty. Henry said, "Hold it, I'll use my own," and he found a one dollar bill and sniffed up. Once for each nostril.

"What do you think of *The White Dog Hunch?*" asked Henry.

"This is 'The White Dog Hunch,'" said Meltzer, tapping out two more spots.

"God," said Henry, "I don't think I'll ever be bored again. You're not bored with me, are you?"

"No way," said Meltzer, sniffing it up through the fifty with all his might. "Pops, there's just no way . . . "

—HOT WATER MUSIC

Sandra

is the slim tall
ear-ringed
bedroom damsel
dressed in a long
gown

she's always high
in heels
spirit
pills
booze

Sandra leans out of
her chair
leans toward
Glendale

I wait for her head
to hit the closet
doorknob
as she attempts to
light
a new cigarette on an
almost burnt-out
one

at 32 she likes
young neat
unscratched boys
with faces like the bottoms
of new saucers

she has proclaimed as much
to me
has brought her prizes

over for me to view:
silent blonde zeros of young
flesh
who
a) sit
b) stand
c) talk
at her command

sometimes she brings one
sometimes two
sometimes three
for me to
view

Sandra looks very good in
long gowns
Sandra could probably break
a man's heart

I hope she finds
one.

•••

    I began receiving letters from a girl in New York City. Her name was Mindy. She had run across a couple of my books, but the best thing about her letters was that she seldom mentioned writing except to say that she was not a writer. She wrote about things in general and men and sex in particular. Mindy was 25, wrote in longhand, and the handwriting was stable, sensible, yet humorous. I answered her letters and was always glad to find one of hers in my mailbox. Most people are much better at saying things in letters than in conversation, and some people can write artistic, inventive letters, but when they try a poem or story or novel they become pretentious.

Then Mindy sent some photographs. If they were faithful she was quite beautiful. We wrote for several more weeks and then she mentioned that she had a two week vacation coming up.

Why don't you fly out? I suggested.

All right, she replied.

We began to phone one another. Finally she gave me her arrival date at L.A. International.

I'll be there, I told her, nothing will stop me.

I sat in the airport and waited. You never knew about photos. You could never tell. I was nervous. I felt like vomiting. I lit a cigarette and gagged. Why did I do these things? I didn't want her now. And Mindy was flying all the way from New York City. I knew plenty of women. Why always more women? What was I trying to do? New affairs were exciting but they were also hard work. The first kiss, the first fuck had some drama. People were interesting at first. Then later, slowly but surely, all the flaws and madness would manifest themselves. I would become less and less to them; they would mean less and less to me.

I was old and I was ugly. Maybe that's why it felt so good to stick it into young girls. I was King Kong and they were lithe and tender. Was I trying to screw my way past death? By being with young girls did I hope I wouldn't grow old, feel old? I just didn't want to age badly, simply quit, be dead before death itself arrived.

Mindy's plane landed and taxied in. I felt I was in danger. Women knew me beforehand because they had read my books. I had exposed myself. On the other hand, I knew nothing of them. I was the real gambler. I could get killed, I could get my balls cut off. Chinaski without balls. *Love Poems of a Eunuch.*

I stood waiting for Mindy. The passengers came out of the gate.

Oh, I hope *she's* not the one.

Or her.

Or especially her.

Now that one would be fine! Look at those legs, that behind, those eyes. . . .

One of them moved towards me. I hoped it was her. She was the best of the whole damned lot. I couldn't be that lucky. She walked up to me and smiled. "I'm Mindy."

"I'm glad you're Mindy."

"I'm glad you're Chinaski."

"Do you have to wait for your baggage?"

"Yes, I brought enough for a long stay!"

"Let's wait in the bar."

We walked in and found a table. Mindy ordered a vodka and tonic. I ordered a vodka-7. Ah, almost in tune. I lit her cigarette. She looked fine. Almost virginal. It was difficult to believe. She was small, blond and perfectly put together. She was more natural than sophisticated. I found it easy to look at her eyes—blue-green. She wore two tiny earrings. And she wore high heels. I had told Mindy that high heels excited me.

"Well," she said, "are you frightened?"

"Not so much anymore. I like you."

"You look much better than your photos," she said. "I don't think you're ugly at all."

"Thanks."

"Oh, I don't mean you're handsome, not the way people think of handsome. Your face seems kind. But your eyes—they're beautiful. They're wild, crazy, like some animal peering out of a forest on fire. God, something like that. I'm not very good with words."

"I think that you're beautiful," I said. "And very nice. I feel good around you. I think it's good that we're together. Drink up. We need another. You're like your letters."

We had the second drink and went down for the luggage. I was proud to be with Mindy. She walked with style. So many women with good bodies just slouched along like overloaded creatures. Mindy flowed.

I kept thinking, this is too good. This is simply not possible.

—*Women*

who in the hell is Tom Jones?

● ●

I was shacked with a
24 year old girl from
New York City for
two weeks—about

the time of the garbage
strike out there, and
one night my 34 year
old woman arrived and
she said, "I want to see
my rival." she did
and then she said, "o,
you're a cute little thing!"
next I knew there was a
screech of wildcats—
such screaming and scratching, wounded animal moans,
blood and piss . . .

I was drunk and in my
shorts. I tried to
separate them and fell,
wrenched my knee. then
they were through the screen
door and down the walk
and out in the street.

squadcars full of cops
arrived. a police heli-
copter circled overhead.

I stood in the bathroom
and grinned in the mirror.
it's not often at the age
of 55 that such splendid
things occur.
better than the Watts
riots.

the 34 year old
came back in. she had
pissed all over her-
self and her clothing

was torn and she was
followed by 2 cops who
wanted to know why.

pulling up my shorts
I tried to explain.

You Can't Write a Love Story

Margie was going to go out with this guy but on the way over this
guy met another guy in a leather coat and the guy in the leather coat
opened the leather coat and showed the other guy his tits and the other
guy went over to Margie's and said he couldn't keep his date because this
guy in the leather coat had showed him his tits and he was going to fuck
this guy. So Margie went to see Carl. Carl was in, and she sat down and
said to Carl, "This guy was going to take me to a café with tables outside
and we were going to drink wine and talk, just drink wine and talk, that's
all, nothing else, but on the way over this guy met another guy in a
leather coat and the guy in the leather coat showed the other guy his tits
and now this guy is going to fuck the guy in the leather coat, so I don't
get my table and my wine and my talk."

"I can't write," said Carl. "It's gone."

Then he got up and went to the bathroom, closed the door, and took
a shit. Carl took four or five shits a day. There was nothing else to do. He
took five or six baths a day. There was nothing else to do. He got drunk
for the same reason.

Margie heard the toilet flush. Then Carl came out.

"A man simply can't write eight hours a day. He can't even write
every day or every week. It's a wicked fix. There's nothing to do but
wait."

Carl went to the refrigerator and came out with a six-pack of Michelob. He opened a bottle.

"I'm the world's greatest writer," he said. "Do you know how difficult
that is?"

Margie didn't answer.

"I can feel pain crawling all over me. It's like a second skin. I wish I could shed that skin like a snake."

"Well, why don't you get down on the rug and give it a try?"

"Listen," he asked, "where did I meet you?"

"Barney's Beanery."

"Well, that explains some of it. Have a beer."

Carl opened a bottle and passed it over.

"Yeah," said Margie, "I know. You need your solitude. You need to be alone. Except when you want some, or except when we split, then you're on the phone. You say you need me. You say you're dying of a hangover. You get weak fast."

"I get weak fast."

"And you're so *dull* around me, you never turn on. You writers are so . . . *precious* . . . you can't stand people. Humanity stinks, right?"

"Right."

"But every time we split you start throwing giant four-day parties. And suddenly you get *witty*, you start to TALK! Suddenly you're full of life, talking, dancing, singing. You dance on the coffeetable, you throw bottles through the window, you act parts from Shakespeare. Suddenly you're alive—when I'm gone. Oh, I hear about it!"

"I don't like parties. I especially dislike people at parties."

"For a guy who doesn't like parties you certainly throw enough of them."

"Listen, Margie, you don't understand. I can't write anymore. I'm finished. Somewhere I made a wrong turn. Somewhere I died in the night."

"The only way you're going to die is from one of your giant hangovers."

"Jeffers said that even the strongest men get trapped."

"Who was Jeffers?"

"He was the guy who turned Big Sur into a tourist trap."

"What were you going to do tonight?"

"I was going to listen to the songs of Rachmaninoff."

"Who's that?"

"A dead Russian."

"Look at you. You just sit there."

"I'm waiting. Some guys wait for two years. Sometimes it never comes back."

"Suppose it never comes back?"

"I'll just put on my shoes and walk down to Main Street."

"Why don't you get a decent job?"

"There aren't any decent jobs. If a writer doesn't make it through creation, he's dead."

"Oh, come on, Carl! There are billions of people in the world who don't make it through creation. Do you mean to tell me they're dead?"

"Yes."

"And you have soul? You are one of the few with a soul?"

"It would appear so."

"It would *appear* so! You and your little typewriter! You and your tiny checks! My grandmother makes more money than you do!"

Carl opened another bottle of beer.

"Beer! Beer! You and your goddamned beer! It's in your stories too. 'Marty lifted his beer. As he looked up, this big blonde walked into the bar and sat down beside him . . .' You're right. You're finished. Your material is limited, very limited. You can't write a love story, you can't write a decent love story."

"You're right, Margie."

"If a man can't write a love story, he's useless."

"How many have you written?"

"I don't claim to be a writer."

"But," said Carl, "you appear to pose as one hell of a literary critic."

Margie left soon after that. Carl sat and drank the remaining beers. It was true, the writing had left him. It would make his few underground enemies happy. They could step one notch up. Death pleased them, underground or overground. He remembered Endicott, Endicott sitting there saying, "Well, Hemingway's gone, Dos Passos is gone, Patchen is gone, Pound is gone, Berryman jumped off the bridge . . . things are looking better and better and better."

The phone rang. Carl picked it up. "Mr. Gantling?"

"Yes?" he answered.

"We wondered if you'd like to read at Fairmount College?"

"Well, yes, what date?"

"The thirtieth of next month."

"I don't think I'm doing anything then."

"Our usual payment is one hundred dollars."

"I usually get a hundred and a half. Ginsberg gets a thousand."

"But that's Ginsberg. We can only offer a hundred."

"All right."

"Fine, Mr. Gantling. We'll send you the details."

"How about travel? That's a hell of a drive."

"O.k., twenty-five dollars for travel."

"O.k."

"Would you like to talk to some of the students in their classes?"

"No."

"There's a free lunch."

"I'll take that."

"Fine, Mr. Gantling, we'll be looking forward to seeing you on campus."

"Goodbye."

Carl walked about the room. He looked at the typewriter. He put a sheet of paper in there, then watched a girl in an amazingly short mini skirt walk past the window. Then he started to type:

"Margie was going to go out with this guy but on the way over this guy met another guy in a leather coat and the guy in the leather coat opened the leather coat and showed the other guy his tits and the other guy went over to Margie's and said he couldn't keep his date because this guy in the leather coat had showed him his tits . . . "

Carl lifted his beer. It felt good to be writing again.

—*South of No North*

Friendly Advice to a Lot of Young Men
• •

Go to Tibet.

Ride a camel.

Read the bible.

Dye your shoes blue.

Grow a beard.

Circle the world in a paper canoe.

Subscribe to *The Saturday Evening Post*.

Chew on the left side of your mouth only.

Marry a woman with one leg and shave with a straight razor.
And carve your name in her arm.

Brush your teeth with gasoline.
Sleep all day and climb trees at night.
Be a monk and drink buckshot and beer.
Hold your head under water and play the violin.
Do a belly dance before pink candles.
Kill your dog.
Run for Mayor.
Live in a barrel.
Break your head with a hatchet.
Plant tulips in the rain.

But don't write poetry.

• •

To pacify Lydia I agreed to go to Muleshead, Utah. Her sister was camping in the mountains. The sisters actually owned much of the land. It had been inherited from their father. Glendoline, one of the sisters, had a tent pitched in the woods. She was writing a novel, *The Wild Woman of the Mountains.* The other sisters were to arrive any day. Lydia and I arrived first. We had a pup tent. We squeezed in there the first night and the mosquitoes squeezed in with us. It was terrible.

The next morning we sat around the campfire. Glendoline and Lydia cooked breakfast. I had purchased $40 worth of groceries which included several six packs of beer. I had them cooling in a mountain spring. We finished breakfast. I helped with the dishes and then Glendoline brought out her novel and read to us. It wasn't really bad, but it was very unprofessional and needed a lot of polishing. Glendoline presumed that the reader was as fascinated by her life as she was—which was a deadly mistake. The other deadly mistakes she had made were too numerous to mention.

• • •

I walked to the spring and came back with three bottles of beer. The girls said no, they didn't want any. They were very anti-beer. We discussed Glendoline's novel. I figured that anybody who would read their novel aloud to others had to be suspect. If that wasn't the old kiss of death, nothing was.

The conversation shifted and the girls started chatting about men, parties, dancing, and sex. Glendoline had a high, excited voice, and laughed nervously, laughed constantly. She was in her mid-forties, quite fat and very sloppy. Besides that, just like me, she was simply ugly.

Glendoline must have talked non-stop for over an hour, entirely about sex. I began to get dizzy. She waved her arms over her head, "I'M THE WILD WOMAN OF THE MOUNTAINS! O WHERE O WHERE IS THE MAN, THE REAL MAN WITH THE COURAGE TO TAKE ME?"

Well, he's certainly not here, I thought.

I looked at Lydia. "Let's go for a walk."

"No," she said, "I want to read this book." It was called *Love and Orgasm: A Revolutionary Guide to Sexual Fulfillment.*

"All right," I said, "I'll take a walk then."

I walked up to the mountain spring. I reached in for another beer, opened it and sat there drinking. I was trapped in the mountains and woods with two crazy women. They took all the joy out of fucking by talking about it all the time. I liked to fuck too, but it wasn't my religion. There were too many ridiculous and tragic things about it. People didn't seem to know how to handle it. So they made a toy out of it. A toy that destroyed people.

The main thing, I decided, was to find the right woman. But how? I had a red notebook and a pen with me. I scribbled a meditative poem into it. Then I walked up to the lake. Vance Pastures, the place was called. The sisters owned most of it. I had to take a shit. I took off my pants and squatted in the brush with the flies and the mosquitoes. I'd take the conveniences of the city any time. I had to wipe with leaves. I walked over to the lake and stuck one foot in the water. It was ice cold.

Be a man, old man. Enter.

My skin was ivory white. I felt very old, very soft. I moved out into the ice water. I went in up to my waist, then I took a deep breath and leaped forward. I was all the way in! The mud swirled up from the bottom and got into my ears, my mouth, my hair. I stood there in the muddy water, my teeth chattering.

I waited a long time for the water to settle and clear. Then I walked back out. I got dressed and made my way along the edge of the lake. When I got to the end of the lake I heard a sound like that of a waterfall. I went into a forest, moving toward the sound. I had to climb around some rocks across a gully. The sound came closer and closer. The flies and mosquitoes swarmed all over me. The flies were large and angry and hungry, much larger than city flies, and they knew a meal when they saw one.

I pushed my way through some thick brush and there it was: my first real honest-to-Christ waterfall. The water just poured down the mountain and over a rocky ledge. It was beautiful. It kept coming and coming. The water was coming from somewhere. And it was running off somewhere. There were three or four streams that probably led to the lake.

Finally I got tired of watching it and decided to go back. I also decided to take a different route back, a shortcut. I worked my way down to the opposite side of the lake and cut off toward camp. I knew about where it was. I still had my red notebook. I stopped and wrote another poem, less meditative, then I went on. I kept walking. The camp didn't appear. I walked some more. I looked around for the lake. I couldn't find the lake, I didn't know where it was. Suddenly it hit me: I was LOST. Those horny sex bitches had driven me out of my mind and now I was LOST. I looked around. There was the backdrop of mountains and all around me were trees and brush. There was no center, no starting point, no connection between anything. I felt fear, real fear. Why had I let them take me out of my city, my Los Angeles? A man could call a cab there, he could telephone. There were reasonable solutions to reasonable problems.

Vance Pastures stretched out around me for miles and miles. I threw away my red notebook. What a way for a writer to die! I could see it in the newspaper:

HENRY CHINASKI, MINOR POET, FOUND DEAD IN UTAH WOODS

Henry Chinaski, former post office clerk turned writer, was found in a decomposed state yesterday afternoon by forest ranger W.K. Brooks Jr.

Also found near the remains was a small red notebook which evidently contained Mr. Chinaski's last written work.

I walked on. Soon I was in a soggy area full of water. Every now and then one of my legs would sink to the knee in the bog and I'd have to haul myself out.

I came to a barbed wire fence. I knew immediately that I shouldn't climb the fence. I knew that it was the wrong thing to do, but there seemed no alternative. I climbed over the fence and stood there, cupped both hands around my mouth and screamed: "LYDIA!"

There was no answer.

I tried it again: "LYDIA!"

My voice sounded very mournful. The voice of a coward.

I moved on. It would be nice, I thought, to be back with the sisters, hearing them laugh about sex and men and dancing and parties. It would be so nice to hear Glendoline's voice. It would be nice to run my hand through Lydia's long hair. I'd faithfully take her to every party in town. I'd even dance with all the women and make brilliant jokes about everything. I'd endure all that subnormal driveling shit with a smile. I could almost hear myself. "Hey, that's a *great* dance tune! Who wants to really *go*? Who wants to *boogie* on out?"

I kept walking through the bog. Finally I reached dry land. I got to a road. It was just an old dirt road, but it looked good. I could see tire marks, hoof prints. There were even wires overhead that carried electricity somewhere. All I had to do was follow those wires. I walked along the road. The sun was high in the sky, it must have been noon. I walked along feeling foolish.

I came to a locked gate across the road. What did that mean? There was a small entry at one side of the gate. Evidently the gate was a cattle guard. But where were the cattle? Where was the owner of the cattle? Maybe he only came around every six months.

The top of my head began to ache. I reached up and felt where I had been blackjacked in a Philadelphia bar 30 years before. Some scar tissue remained. Now the scar tissue, baked by the sun, was swollen. It stood up like a small horn. I broke a piece off and threw it in the road.

I walked another hour, then decided to turn back. It meant having to walk all the way back yet I felt it was the thing to do. I took my shirt off and draped it over my head. I stopped once or twice and screamed, "LYDIA!" There was no reply.

Some time later I got back to the gate. All I had to do was walk around it but there was something in the way. It stood in front of the gate, about 15 feet from me. It was a small doe, a fawn, a something.

I moved slowly toward it. It didn't budge. Was it going to let me by? It didn't seem to fear me. I guessed it sensed my confusion, my cowardice. I approached closer and closer. It wouldn't get out of the way. It had large beautiful brown eyes, more beautiful than the eyes of any woman I had ever seen. I couldn't believe it. I was within three feet of it, ready to back off, when it bolted. It ran off the road and into the woods. It was in excellent shape; it could really run.

As I walked further along the road I heard the sound of running water. I needed water. You couldn't live very long without water. I left the road and moved toward the sound of rushing water. There was a little hill covered with grass and as I topped the hill there it was: water spilling out of several cement pipes in the face of a dam and into some kind of reservoir. I sat down at the edge of the reservoir and took off my shoes and stockings, pulled up my pants, and stuck my legs into the water. Then I poured water over my head. Then I drank—but not too much or too fast—just like I'd seen it done in the movies.

After recovering a bit I noticed a pier that went out over the reservoir. I walked out on the pier and came to a large metal box bolted to the side of the pier. It was locked with a padlock. There was probably a telephone in there! I could phone for help!

I went and found a large rock and started smashing it against the lock. It wouldn't give. What the hell would Jack London do? What would Hemingway do? Jean Genet?

I kept smashing the rock against the lock. Sometimes I missed and my hand hit the lock or the metal box itself. Skin ripped, blood flowed. I gathered myself and gave the lock one final blow. It opened. I took it off and opened the metal box. There was no telephone. There were a series of switches and some heavy cables. I reached in, touched a wire, and got a terrible shock. Then I pulled a switch. I heard the roar of water. Out of three or four of the holes in the concrete face of the dam shot giant white jets of water. I pulled another switch. Three or four other holes opened up, releasing tons of water. I pulled a third switch and the whole dam let loose. I stood and watched the water pouring forth. Maybe I could start a flood and cowboys would come on horses or in rugged little pickup trucks to rescue me. I could see the headline:

HENRY CHINASKI, MINOR POET, FLOODS UTAH COUNTRYSIDE IN ORDER TO SAVE HIS SOFT LOS ANGELES ASS.

I decided against it. I threw all the switches back to normal, closed the metal box, and hung the broken lock back on it.

I left the reservoir, found another road up the way, and began following it. This road seemed more used than the other. I walked along. I had never been so tired. I could hardly see. Suddenly there was a little girl about five years old walking toward me. She wore a little blue dress and white shoes. She looked frightened when she saw me. I tried to look pleasant and friendly as I edged toward her.

"Little girl, don't go away. I won't hurt you. I'M LOST! Where are your *parents?* Little girl, take me to your *parents!*"

The little girl pointed. I saw a trailer and a car parked up ahead. "HEY, I'm LOST!" I shouted. "CHRIST, AM I GLAD TO SEE YOU."

Lydia stepped around the side of the trailer. Her hair was done up in red curlers. "Come on, city boy," she said. "Follow me home."

"I'm so glad to see you, baby, kiss me!"

"No. Follow me."

Lydia took off running about 20 feet in front of me. It was hard keeping up.

"I asked those people if they had seen a city boy around," she called back over her shoulder. "They said, No."

"Lydia, I *love* you!"

"Come on! You're slow!"

"Wait, Lydia, *wait!*"

She vaulted over a barbed wire fence. I couldn't make it. I got tangled in the wire. I couldn't move. I was like a trapped cow. "LYDIA!"

She came back with her red curlers and started helping me get loose from the barbs. "I tracked you. I found your red notebook. You got lost deliberately because you were pissed."

"No, I got lost out of ignorance and fear. I am not a complete person—I'm a stunted city person. I am more or less a failed drizzling shit with absolutely nothing to offer."

"Christ," she said, "don't you think *I* know that?"

She freed me from the last barb. I lurched after her. I was back with Lydia again.

—*Women*

the night I was going to die

• •

the night I was going to die
I was sweating on the bed
and I could hear the crickets
and there was a cat fight outside
and I could feel my soul dropping down through the
mattress
and just before it hit the floor I jumped up
I was almost too weak to walk
but I walked around and turned on all the lights
then made it back to the bed
and again my soul dropped down through the mattress
and I leaped up
just before it hit the floor
I walked around and I turned on all the lights
and then I went back to bed
and down it dropped again and
I was up
turning on all the lights

I had a 7-year-old daughter
and I felt sure she didn't want me dead
otherwise it wouldn't have
mattered

but all that night
nobody phoned

nobody came by with a beer
my girlfriend didn't phone
all I could hear were the crickets and it was
hot
and I kept working at it
getting up and down
until the first of the sun came through the window
through the bushes
and then I got on the bed
and the soul stayed
inside at last and
I slept.
now people come by
beating on the doors and windows
the phone rings
the phone rings again and again
I get great letters in the mail
hate letters and love letters.
everything is the same again.

• •

Two mornings later, at 4 AM, somebody beat on the door.
"Who is it?"
"It's a redheaded floozie."
I let Tammie in. She sat down and I opened a couple of beers.
"I've got bad breath, I have these two bad teeth. You can't kiss me."
"All right."
We talked. Well, I listened. Tammie was on speed. I listened and looked at her long red hair and when she was preoccupied I looked and looked at that body. It was bursting out of her clothing, begging to get out. She talked on and on. I didn't touch her.
At 6 AM Tammie gave me her address and phone number.

"I've got to go," she said.

"I'll walk you to your car."

It was a bright red Camaro, completely wrecked. The front was smashed in, one side was ripped open and the windows were gone. Inside were rags and shirts and Kleenex boxes and newspapers and milk cartons and Coke bottles and wire and rope and paper napkins and magazines and paper cups and shoes and bent colored drinking straws. This mass of stuff was piled above seat level and covered the seats. Only the driver's area had a little clear space.

Tammie stuck her head out the window and we kissed.

Then she tore away from the curb and by the time she reached the corner she was doing 45. She did hit the brakes and the Camaro bobbed up and down, up and down. I walked back inside.

I went to bed and thought about her hair. I'd never known a real redhead. It was fire.

Like lightning from heaven, I thought.

Somehow her face didn't seem to be as hard anymore. . . .

Tammie came by that night. She appeared to be high on uppers.

"I want some champagne," she said.

"All right," I said.

I handed her a twenty.

"Be right back," she said, walking out the door.

Then the phone rang. It was Lydia. "I just wondered how you were doing. . . ."

"Things are all right."

"Not here. I'm pregnant."

"What?"

"And I don't know who the father is."

"Oh?"

"You know Dutch, the guy who hangs around the bar where I'm working now?"

"Yes, old Baldy."

"Well, he's really a nice guy. He's in love with me. He brings me flowers and candy. He wants to marry me. He's been real nice. And one night I went home with him. We did it."

"All right."

"Then there's Barney, he's married but I like him. Of all the guys in the bar he's the only one who never tried to put the make on me. It fascinated me. Well, you know, I'm trying to sell my house. So he came over one afternoon. He just came by. He said he wanted to look the house over for a friend of his. I let him in. Well, he came at just the right time. The kids were in school so I let him go ahead. . . . Then one night this stranger came into the bar late. He asked me to go home with him. I told him no. Then he said he just wanted to sit in my car with me, talk to me. I said all right. We sat in the car and talked. Then we shared a joint. Then he kissed me. That kiss did it. If he hadn't kissed me I wouldn't have done it. Now I'm pregnant and I don't know who. I'll have to wait and see who the child looks like."

"All right, Lydia, lots of luck."

"Thanks."

I hung up. A minute passed and then the phone rang again. It was Lydia. "Oh," she said, "I wondered how *you* were doing?"

"About the same, horses and booze."

"Then everything's all right with you?"

"Not quite."

"What is it?"

"Well, I sent this woman out for champagne. . . ."

"Woman?"

"Well, girl, really . . . "

"A girl?"

"I sent her out with $20 for champagne and she hasn't come back. I think I've been taken."

"Chinaski, I don't want to *hear* about your women. Do you understand that?"

"All right."

Lydia hung up. There was a knock on the door. It was Tammie. She'd come back with the champagne and the change.

It was noon the next day when the phone rang. It was Lydia again.

"Well, did she come back with the champagne?"

"Who?"

"Your whore."

"Yes, she came back. . . ."

"Then what happened?"

"We drank the champagne. It was good stuff."

"Then what happened?"

"Well, you know, shit . . . "

I heard a long insane wail like a wolverine shot in the arctic snow and left to bleed and die alone. . . .

She hung up.

I slept most of the afternoon and that night I drove out to the harness races.

I lost $32, got into the Volks and drove back. I parked, walked up on the porch and put the key into the door. All the lights were on. I looked around. Drawers were ripped out and overturned on the floor, the bed covers were on the floor. All my books were missing from the bookcase, including the books I had written, 20 or so. And my typewriter was gone and my toaster was gone and my radio was gone and my paintings were gone.

Lydia, I thought.

All she'd left me was my t.v. because she knew I never looked at it.

I walked outside and there was Lydia's car, but she wasn't in it. "Lydia," I said. "Hey, baby!"

I walked up and down the street and then I saw her feet, both of them, sticking out from behind a small tree up against an apartment house wall. I walked up to the tree and said, "Look, what the hell's the matter with you?"

Lydia just stood there. She had two shopping bags full of my books and a portfolio of my paintings.

"Look, I've got to have my books and paintings back. They belong to me."

Lydia came out from behind the tree—screaming. She took the paintings out and started tearing them. She threw the pieces in the air and when they fell to the ground she stomped on them. She was wearing her cowgirl boots.

Then she took my books out of the shopping bags and started throwing them around, out into the street, out on the lawn, everywhere.

"Here are your paintings! Here are your books! AND DON'T TELL ME ABOUT YOUR WOMEN! DON'T TELL ME ABOUT YOUR WOMEN!"

Then Lydia ran down to my court with a book in her hand, my latest, *The Selected Works of Henry Chinaski.* She screamed, "So you want your books back? So you want your books back? Here are your god-damned books! AND DON'T TELL ME ABOUT YOUR WOMEN!"

She started smashing the glass panes in my front door. She took *The Selected Works of Henry Chinaski* and smashed pane after pane, screaming, "You want your books back? Here are your goddamned books! AND DON'T TELL ME ABOUT YOUR WOMEN! I DON'T WANT TO HEAR ABOUT YOUR WOMEN!"

I stood there as she screamed and broke glass.

Where are the police? I thought. Where?

Then Lydia ran down the court walk, took a quick left at the trash bin and ran down the driveway of the apartment house next door. Behind a small bush was my typewriter, my radio and my toaster.

Lydia picked up the typewriter and ran out into the center of the street with it. It was a heavy old-fashioned standard machine. Lydia lifted the typer high over her head with both hands and smashed it in the street. The platen and several other parts flew off. She picked the typer up again, raised it over her head and screamed, "DON'T TELL ME ABOUT YOUR WOMEN!" and smashed it into the street again.

Then Lydia jumped into her car and drove off.

Fifteen seconds later the police cruiser drove up.

"It's an orange Volks. It's called the Thing, looks like a tank. I don't remember the license number, but the letters are HZY, like HAZY, got it?"

"Address?"

I gave them her address. . . .

Sure enough, they brought her back. I heard her in the back seat, wailing, as they drove up.

"STAND BACK!" said one cop as he jumped out. He followed me up to my place. He walked inside and stepped on some broken glass. For some reason he shone his flashlight on the ceiling and the ceiling mouldings.

"You want to press charges?" the cop asked me.

"No. She has children. I don't want her to lose her kids. Her ex-husband is trying to get them from her. But *please* tell her that people aren't supposed to go around doing this sort of thing."

"O.K.," he said, "now sign this."

He wrote it down in hand in a little notebook with lined paper. It said that I, Henry Chinaski, would not press charges against one Lydia Vance.

I signed it and he left.

I locked what was left of the door and went to bed and tried to sleep. In an hour or so the phone rang. It was Lydia. She was back home.

"YOU-SON-OF-A-BITCH, YOU EVER TELL ME ABOUT YOUR WOMEN AGAIN AND I'LL DO THE SAME THING ALL OVER AGAIN!"

She hung up.

Two nights later I went over to Tammie's place on Rustic Court. I knocked. The lights weren't on. It seemed empty. I looked in her mailbox. There were letters in there. I wrote a note, "Tammie, I have been trying to phone you. I came over and you weren't in. Are you all right? Phone me. . . . Hank."

I drove over at 11 AM the next morning. Her car wasn't out front. My note was still stuck in the door. I rang anyhow. The letters were still in the mailbox. I left a note in the mailbox: "Tammie, where the hell are you? Contact me. . . . Hank."

I drove all over the neighborhood looking for that smashed red Camaro.

I returned that night. It was raining. My notes were wet. There was more mail in the box. I left her a book of my poems, inscribed. Then I went back to my Volks. I had a Maltese cross hanging from my rearview mirror. I cut the cross down, took it back to her place and tied it around her doorknob.

I didn't know where any of her friends lived, where her mother lived, where her lovers lived.

I went back to my court and wrote some love poems.

—*Women*

like a flower in the rain

I cut the middle fingernail of the middle
finger
right hand
real short
and I began rubbing along her cunt
as she sat upright in bed
spreading lotion over her arms
face
and breasts
after bathing.
then she lit a cigarette:
"don't let this put you off,"
and smoked and continued to rub the
lotion on.
I continued to rub the cunt.
"you want an apple?" I asked.
"sure," she said, "you got one?"
but I got to her—
she began to twist
then she rolled on her side,
she was getting wet and open
like a flower in the rain.
then she rolled on her stomach
and her most beautiful ass
looked up at me
and I reached under and got the
cunt again.
she reached around and got my
cock, she rolled and twisted,
I mounted
my face falling into the mass
of red hair that overflowed
from her head
and my fattened cock entered

into the miracle.
later we joked about the lotion
and the cigarette and the apple.
then I went out and got some chicken
and shrimp and french fries and buns
and mashed potatoes and gravy and
cole slaw, and we ate. she told me
how good she felt and I told her
how good I felt and we ate
the chicken and the shrimp and the
french fries and the buns and the
mashed potatoes and the gravy and
the cole slaw too.

• •

I drove home. The apartment looked the way it always had—bottles and trash everywhere. I'd have to clean it up a bit. If anybody saw it that way they'd have me committed.

There was a knock. I opened the door. It was Tammie. "Hi!" she said.

"Hello."

"You must have been in an awful hurry when you left. All the doors were unlocked. The back door was wide open. Listen, promise you won't tell if I tell you something?"

"All right."

"Arlene went in and used your phone, long distance."

"All right."

"I tried to stop her but I couldn't. She was on pills."

"All right."

"Where've you been?"

"Galveston."

"Why did you go flying off like that? You're crazy."

"I've got to leave again Saturday."

"Saturday? What's today?"

"Thursday."

"Where are you going?"

"New York City."

"Why?"

"A reading. They sent the tickets two weeks ago. And I get a percentage of the gate."

"Oh, take me *with* you! I'll leave Dancy with Mother. I want to go!"

"I can't afford to take you. It'll eat up my profits. I've had some heavy expenses lately."

"I'll be *good!* I'll be *so* good! I'll never leave your side! I really missed you."

"I can't do it, Tammie."

She went to the refrigerator and got a beer. "You just don't give a fuck. All those love poems, you didn't mean it."

"I meant it when I wrote them."

The phone rang. It was my editor. "Where've you been?"

"Galveston. Research."

"I hear you're reading in New York City this Saturday."

"Yes, Tammie wants to go, my girl."

"Are you taking her?"

"No, I can't afford it."

"How much is it?"

"$316 round trip."

"Do you really want to take her?"

"Yes, I think so."

"All right, go ahead. I'll mail you a check."

"Do you mean it?"

"Yes."

"I don't know what to say. . . ."

"Forget it. Just remember Dylan Thomas."

"They won't kill *me.*"

We said goodbye. Tammie was sucking on her beer.

"All right," I told her, "you've got two or three days to pack."

"You mean, I'm *going?*"

"Yes, my editor is paying your way."

Tammie leaped up and grabbed me. She kissed me, grabbed my balls, pulled at my cock. "You're the sweetest old fuck!"

New York City. Outside of Dallas, Houston, Charleston, and Atlanta, it was the worst place I had ever been. Tammie pushed up against me and my cock rose. Joanna Dover hadn't gotten it all. . . .

We had a 3:30 PM flight out of Los Angeles that Saturday. At 2 PM I went up and knocked on Tammie's door. She wasn't there. I went back to my place and sat down. The phone rang. It was Tammie. "Look," I said, "we have to think about leaving. I have people meeting me at Kennedy airport. Where are you?"

"I'm six dollars short on a prescription. I'm getting some Quaaludes."

"Where are you?"

"I'm just below Santa Monica Boulevard and Western, about a block. It's an Owl drugstore. You can't miss it."

I hung up, got into the Volks and drove over. I parked a block below Santa Monica and Western, got out and looked around. There was no pharmacy.

I got back in the Volks and drove along looking for her red Camaro. Then I saw it, five blocks further down. I parked and walked in. Tammie was sitting in a chair. Dancy ran up and made a face at me.

"We can't take the kid."

"I know. We'll drop her off over at my mother's."

"Your mother's? That's three miles the other way."

"It's on the way to the airport."

"No, it's in the other direction."

"Do you have the six bucks?"

I gave Tammie the six.

"I'll see you back at your place. You packed?"

"Yes, I'm ready."

I drove back and waited. Then I heard them.

"Mommy!" Dancy said, "I want a Ding-Dong!"

They went up the stairs. I waited for them to come down. They didn't come down. I went up. Tammie was packed, but she was down on her knees zipping and unzipping her baggage.

"Look," I said, "I'll carry your other stuff down to the car."

She had two large paper shopping bags, stuffed, and three dresses on hangers. All this besides her luggage.

I took the shopping bags and the dresses down to the Volks. When I came back she was still zipping and unzipping her luggage.

"Tammie, let's go."

"Wait a minute."

She knelt there running the zipper back and forth, up and down. She didn't look into the baggage. She just ran the zipper up and down.

"Mommy," said Dancy, "I want a Ding-Dong."

"Come on, Tammie, let's go."

"Oh, all right."

I picked up the zipper bag and they followed me out.

I followed her battered red Camaro to her mother's place. We went in. Tammie stood at her mother's dresser and started pulling drawers out, in and out. Each time she pulled a drawer out she reached in and mixed everything up. Then she'd slam the drawer and go to the next. Same thing.

"Tammie, the plane is ready to take off."

"Oh no, we've got plenty of time. I *hate* hanging around airports."

"What are you going to do about Dancy?"

"I'm going to leave her here until Mother gets home from work."

Dancy let out a wail. Finally she knew, and she wailed, and the tears ran, and then she stopped, balled her fists and screamed, "I WANT A DING-DONG!"

"Listen, Tammie, I'll be waiting in the car."

I went out and waited. I waited five minutes then went back in. Tammie was still sliding the drawers in and out.

"Please, Tammie, let's leave!"

"All right."

She turned to Dancy. "Look, you stay here until Grandma gets home. Keep the door locked and don't let *anybody* in but Grandma!"

Dancy wailed again. Then she screamed, "I HATE YOU!"

Tammie followed me and we got into the Volks. I started the engine. She opened the door and was gone. "I HAVE TO GET SOMETHING OUT OF MY CAR!"

Tammie ran over to the Camaro. "Oh shit, I locked it and I don't have the key for the door! Do you have a coat hanger?"

"No," I screamed, "I *don't* have a coat hanger!"

"Be *right* back!"

Tammie ran back to her mother's apartment. I heard the door open. Dancy wailed and shouted. Then I heard the door slam and Tammie returned with a coat hanger. She went to the Camaro and jimmied the door.

I walked over to her car. Tammie had climbed into the back seat and was going through that incredible mess—clothing, paper bags, paper cups, newspapers, beer bottles, empty cartons—piled in there. Then she found it: her camera, the Polaroid I had given her for her birthday.

As I drove along, racing the Volks like I was out to win the 500, Tammie leaned over.

"You really love me, don't you?"

"Yes."

"When we get to New York I'm going to fuck you like you've *never* been fucked before!"

"You mean it?"

"Yes."

She grabbed my cock and leaned against me.

My first and only redhead. I was lucky. . . .

We ran up the long ramp. I was carrying her dresses and the shopping bags.

At the escalator Tammie saw the flight insurance machine.

"Please," I said, "we only have five minutes until take-off."

"I want Dancy to have the money."

"All right."

"Do you have two quarters?"

I gave her two quarters. She inserted them and a card jumped out of the machine.

"You got a pen?"

Tammie filled out the card and then there was an envelope. She put the card in the envelope. Then she tried to insert it in the slot in the machine.

"This thing won't go in!"

"We're going to miss the plane."

She kept trying to jam the envelope in the slot. She couldn't get it in.

She stood there and kept jamming the envelope at the slot. Now the envelope was completely bent in half and all the edges were bent.

"I'm going mad," I told her. "I can't *stand* it."

She jammed a few more times. It wouldn't go. She looked at me. "O.K., let's go."

We went up the escalator with her dresses and shopping bags.

We found the boarding gate. We got two seats near the back. We strapped in. "You see," she said, "I told you we had plenty of time."

I looked at my watch. The plane started to roll. . . .

We were in the air 20 minutes when she took a mirror out of her purse and began to make up her face, mostly the eyes. She worked at her eyes with a small brush, concentrating on the eyelashes. While she was doing this she opened her eyes very wide and she held her mouth open. I watched her and began to get a hard-on.

Her mouth was so very full and round and open and she kept working on her eyelashes. I ordered two drinks.

Tammie stopped to drink, then she continued.

A young fellow in the seat to the right of us began playing with himself. Tammie kept looking at her face in the mirror, holding her mouth open. It looked like she could really suck with that mouth.

She continued for an hour. Then she put the mirror and the brush away, leaned against me and went to sleep.

There was a woman in the seat to our left. She was in her mid-forties. Tammie was sleeping next to me.

The woman looked at me.

"How old is she?" she asked me.

It was suddenly very quiet on that jet. Everyone nearby was listening.

"23."

"She looks 17."

"She's 23."

"She spends two hours making up her face and then goes to sleep."

"It was about an hour."

"Are you going to New York?" the lady asked me.

"Yes."

"Is she your daughter?"

"No, I'm not her father *or* her grandfather. I'm not related to her in any way. She's my girlfriend and we're going to New York." I could see the headline in her eyes:

MONSTER FROM EAST HOLLYWOOD DRUGS 17-YEAR-OLD GIRL, TAKES HER TO NEW YORK CITY WHERE HE SEXUALLY ABUSES HER, THEN SELLS HER BODY TO NUMEROUS BUMS

The lady questioner gave up. She stretched back in her seat and closed her eyes. Her head slipped down toward me. It was almost in my lap, it seemed. Holding Tammie, I watched that head. I wondered if she would mind if I crushed her lips with a crazy kiss. I got another hard-on.

We were ready to land. Tammie seemed very limp. It worried me. I strapped her in.

"Tammie, it's *New York City!* We're getting ready to *land!* Tammie, *wake up!*"

No response.

An o.d.?

I felt her pulse. I couldn't feel anything.

I looked at her enormous breasts. I watched for some sign of breathing. They didn't move. I got up and found a stewardess.

"Please take your seat, sir. We are preparing to land."

"Look, I'm worried. My girlfriend won't wake up."

"Do you think she's dead?" she whispered.

"I don't know," I whispered back.

"All right, sir. As soon as we land I'll come back there."

The plane was starting to drop. I went into the crapper and wet some paper towels. I came back, sat next to Tammie and rubbed them over her face. All that makeup, wasted. Tammie didn't respond.

"You whore, wake up!"

I ran the towels down between her breasts. Nothing. No movement. I gave up.

I'd have to ship her body back somehow. I'd have to explain to her mother. Her mother would hate me.

We landed. The people got up and stood in line, waiting to get out. I sat there. I shook Tammie and pinched her. "It's New York City, Red. The rotten apple. Come around. Cut out the shit."

The stewardess came back and shook Tammie.

"Honey, what's the matter?"

Tammie started responding. She moved. Then her eyes opened. It was only the matter of a *new* voice. Nobody listened to an old voice anymore. Old voices became a part of one's self, like a fingernail.

Tammie got out her mirror and started combing her hair. The stewardess was patting her shoulder. I got up and got the dresses out of the overhead compartment. The shopping bags were up there too. Tammie continued to look into the mirror and comb her hair.

"Tammie, we're in New York. Let's get off."

She moved quickly. I had the two shopping bags and the dresses. She went through the exit wiggling the cheeks of her ass. I followed her.

—WOMEN

liberty

she was sitting in the window
of room 1010 at the Chelsea
in New York,
Janis Joplin's old room.
it was 104 degrees
and she was on speed
and had one leg over
the sill,
and she leaned out and said,
"God, this is great!"
and then she slipped
and almost went out,
just catching herself.
it was very close.
she pulled herself in
walked over and stretched
on the bed.

I've lost a lot of women
in a lot of different ways
but that would have been

the first time
that way.

then she rolled off the bed
landed on her back
and when I walked over
she was asleep.

all day she had been wanting
to see the Statue of Liberty.
now she wouldn't worry me about that
for a while.

prayer in bad weather

by God, I don't know what to
do.
they're so nice to have around.
they have a way of playing with
the balls
and looking at the cock very
seriously
turning it
tweeking it
examining each part
as their long hair falls on
your belly.

it's not the fucking and sucking
alone that reaches into a man
and softens him, it's the extras,
it's all the extras.

now it's raining tonight
and there's nobody
they are elsewhere
examining things
in new bedrooms
in new moods
or maybe in old
bedrooms.

anyhow, it's raining tonight,
one hell of a dashing, pouring
rain. . . .

very little to do.
I've read the newspaper
paid the gas bill
the electric co.
the phone bill.

it keeps raining.

they soften a man
and then let him swim
in his own juice.

I need an old-fashioned whore
at the door tonight
closing her green umbrella,
drops of moonlit rain on her
purse, saying, "shit, man,
can't you get better music
than *that* on your radio?
and turn up the heat . . . "

it's always when a man's swollen
with love and everything
else
that it keeps raining

splattering
flooding
rain
good for the trees and the
grass and the air . . .
good for things that
live alone.

I would give anything
for a fcmalc's hand on me
tonight.
they soften a man and
then leave him
listening to the rain.

eat your heart out

I've come by, she says, to tell you
that this is it. I'm not kidding, it's
over. this is it.

I sit on the couch watching her arrange
her long red hair before my bedroom
mirror.
she pulls her hair up and
piles it on top of her head—
she lets her eyes look at
my eyes—
then she drops the hair and
lets it fall down in front of her face.

we go to bed and I hold her
speechlessly from the back
my arm around her neck

I touch her wrists and hands
feel up to
her elbows
no further.

she gets up.

this is it, she says,
eat your heart out. you
got any rubber bands?

I don't know.

here's one, she says,
this will do. well,
I'm going.

I get up and walk her
to the door
just as she leaves
she says,
I want you to buy me
some high-heeled shoes
with tall thin spikes,
black high-heeled shoes.
no, I want them
red.

I watch her walk down the cement walk
under the trees
she walks all right and
as the poinsettias drip in the sun
I close the door.

I made a mistake

• •

I reached up into the top of the closet
and took out a pair of blue panties
and showed them to her and
asked "are these yours?"

and she looked and said,
"no, those belong to a dog."

she left after that and I haven't seen
her since. she's not at her place.
I keep going there, leaving notes stuck
into the door. I go back and the notes
are still there. I take the Maltese cross
cut it down from my car mirror, tie it
to her doorknob with a shoelace, leave
a book of poems.
when I go back the next night everything
is still there.

I keep searching the streets for that
blood-wine battleship she drives
with a weak battery, and the doors
hanging from broken hinges.

I drive around the streets
an inch away from weeping,
ashamed of my sentimentality and
possible love.

a confused old man driving in the rain
wondering where the good luck
went.

the most

here comes the fishhead singing
here comes the baked potato in drag

here comes nothing to do all day long
here comes another night of no sleep

here comes the phone ringing the wrong tone

here comes a termite with a banjo
here comes a flagpole with blank eyes
here comes a cat and a dog wearing nylons

here comes a machinegun singing
here comes bacon burning in the pan
here comes a voice saying something dull

here comes a newspaper stuffed with small red birds
with flat brown beaks

here comes a cunt carrying a torch
a grenade
a deathly love

here comes victory carrying
one bucket of blood
and stumbling over the berrybush

and the sheets hang out the windows

and the bombers head east west north south
get lost
get tossed like salad

as all the fish in the sea line up and form
one line

one long line
one very long thin line
the longest line you could ever imagine

and we get lost
walking past purple mountains

we walk lost
bare at last like the knife

having given
having spit it out like an unexpected olive seed

as the girl at the call service
screams over the phone:
"don't call back! you sound like a jerk!"

one for old snaggle-tooth

I know a woman
who keeps buying puzzles
chinese
puzzles
blocks
wires
pieces that finally fit
into some order.
she works it out
mathematically
she solves all her

puzzles
lives down by the sea
puts sugar out for the ants
and believes
ultimately
in a better world.
her hair is white
she seldom combs it
her teeth are snaggled
and she wears loose shapeless
coveralls over a body most
women would wish they had.
for many years she irritated me
with what I considered her
eccentricities—
like soaking eggshells in water
(to feed the plants so that
they'd get calcium).
but finally when I think of her
life
and compare it to other lives
more dazzling, original
and beautiful
I realize that she has hurt fewer
people than anybody I know
(and by hurt I simply mean hurt).
she has had some terrible times,
times when maybe I should have
helped her more
for she is the mother of my only
child
and we were once great lovers,
but she has come through
like I said
she has hurt fewer people than
anybody I know,
and if you look at it like that,
well,

she has created a better world.
she has won.

Frances, this poem is for
you.

● ●

I saw Sara every three or four days, at her place or at mine. We slept together but there was no sex. We came close but we never quite got to it. Drayer Baba's precepts held strong.

We decided to spend the holidays together at my place, Christmas and New Year's.

Sara arrived about noon on the 24th in her Volks van. I watched her park, then went out to meet her. She had lumber tied to the roof of the van. It was to be my Christmas present: she was going to build me a bed. My bed was a mockery: a simple box spring with the innards sticking out of the mattress. Sara had also brought an organic turkey plus the trimmings. I was to pay for that and the white wine. And there were some small gifts for each of us.

We carried in the lumber and the turkey and the sundry bits and pieces. I placed the box spring, mattress and headboard outside and put a sign on them: "Free." The headboard went first, the box spring second, and finally somebody took the mattress. It was a poor neighborhood.

I had seen Sara's bed at her place, slept in it, and had liked it. I had always disliked the average mattress, at least the ones I was able to buy. I had spent over half my life in beds which were better suited for somebody shaped like an angleworm.

Sara had built her own bed, and she was to build me another like it. A solid wood platform supported by 7 four-by-four legs (the seventh directly in the middle) topped by a layer of firm four-inch foam. Sara had some good ideas. I held the boards and Sara drove home the nails. She was good with a hammer. She only weighed 105 pounds but she could drive a nail. It was going to be a fine bed.

It didn't take Sara long.

Then we tested it—non-sexually—as Drayer Baba smiled over us.

• • •

We drove around looking for a Christmas tree. I wasn't too anxious to get a tree (Christmas had always been an unhappy time in my childhood) and when we found all the lots empty, the lack of a tree didn't bother me. Sara was unhappy as we drove back. But after we got in and had a few glasses of white wine she regained her spirits and went about hanging Christmas ornaments, lights, and tinsel everywhere, some of the tinsel in my hair.

I had read that more people committed suicide on Christmas Eve and on Christmas Day than at any other time. The holiday had little or nothing to do with the Birth of Christ, apparently.

All the radio music was sickening and the t.v. was worse, so we turned it off and she phoned her mother in Maine. I spoke to Mama too and Mama was not all that bad.

"At first," said Sara, "I was thinking about fixing you up with Mama but she's older than you are."

"Forget it."

"She had nice legs."

"Forget it."

"Are you prejudiced against old age?"

"Yes, everybody's old age but mine."

"You act like a movie star. Have you always had women 20 or 30 years younger than you?"

"Not when I was in my twenties."

"All right then. Have you ever had a woman older than you, I mean lived with her?"

"Yeah, when I was 25 I lived with a woman 35."

"How'd it go?"

"It was terrible. I fell in love."

"What was terrible?"

"She made me go to college."

"And that's terrible?"

"It wasn't the kind of college you're thinking of. She was the faculty, and I was the student body."

"What happened to her?"

"I buried her."

"With honors? Did you kill her?"

"Booze killed her."

"Merry Christmas."

"Sure. Tell me about yours."

"I pass."

"Too many?"

"Too many, yet too few."

Thirty or forty minutes later there was a knock on the door. Sara got up and opened it. A sex symbol walked in. On Christmas Eve. I didn't know who she was. She was in a tight black outfit and her huge breasts looked as if they would burst out of the top of her dress. It was magnificent. I had never seen breasts like that, showcased in just that way, except in the movies.

"Hi, Hank!"

She knew me.

"I'm Edie. You met me at Bobby's one night."

"Oh?"

"Were you too drunk to remember?"

"Hello, Edie. This is Sara."

"I was looking for Bobby. I thought Bobby might be down here."

"Sit down and have a drink."

Edie sat in a chair to my right, very near to me. She was about 25. She lit a cigarette and sipped at her drink. Each time she leaned forward over the coffee table I was sure that it would happen, I was sure that those breasts would spring out. And I was afraid of what I might do if they did. I just didn't know. I had never been a breast man, I had always been a leg man. But Edie really knew how to *do* it. I was afraid and I peeked sideways at her breasts not knowing whether I wanted them to fall out or to stay in.

"You met Manny," she said to me, "down at Bobby's?"

"Yeh."

"I had to kick his ass out. He was too fucking jealous. He even hired a private dick to follow me! Imagine that! That simple sack of shit!"

"Yeh."

"I hate men who are beggars! I hate little toadies!"

"'A good man nowadays is hard to find,'" I said. "That's a song. Out of World War Two. They also had, 'Don't sit under the apple tree with anybody else but me.'"

"Hank, you're babbling. . . ." said Sara.

"Have another drink, Edie," I said and I poured her one.

"Men are such *shits!*" she continued. "I walked into a bar the other day. I was with four guys, close friends. We sat around chugalugging pitchers of beer, we're *laughing,* you know, just having a *good time,* we weren't bothering anybody. Then I got the idea that I would like to shoot a game of pool. I like to shoot pool. I think that when a lady shoots pool it shows her class."

"I can't shoot pool," I said. "I always rip up the green. And I'm not even a lady."

"Anyway, I go up to the table and there's this guy shooting pool all by himself. I go up to him and I say, 'Look, you've had this table a long time. My friends and myself want to shoot a little pool. Do you mind letting us have the table for a while?' He turned and looked at me. He waited. Then he *sneered,* and he said, 'All right.'"

Edie became animated and bounced around as she spoke and I peeked at her things.

"I went back and told my friends, 'We got the table.' Finally this guy shooting is down to his last ball when a buddy of his walks up and says, 'Hey, Ernie, I hear you're giving up the table.' And you know what he *tells* this guy? He says, 'Yeah, I'm giving it up to that bitch!' I heard it and I saw RED! This guy is bent over the table to cue in on his last ball. I grabbed a pool stick and while he was bent over I hit him over the head as hard as I could. The guy dropped on the table like he was dead. He was known in the bar and so a bunch of his friends rush over but meanwhile my four buddies rush over too. Boy, *what a brawl!* Bottles smashing, broken mirrors. . . . I don't know how we got out of there but we did. You got some shit?"

"Yeah but I don't roll too good."

"I'll take care of it."

Edie rolled a tight thin joint, just like a pro. She sucked it up, hissing, then passed it to me.

"So I went back the next night, alone. The owner who is the bartender, he recognizes me. His name is Claude. 'Claude,' I told him, 'I'm sorry about yesterday but that guy at the table was a real bastard. He called me a bitch.'"

I poured more drinks all around. In another minute her breasts would be out.

"The owner said, 'It's O.K., forget it.' He seemed like a nice guy. 'What do you drink?' he asked me. I hung around the bar and had two or three free drinks and he said, 'You know, I can use another waitress.'"

Edie took a hit on the joint and continued. "He told me about the other waitress. 'She pulled the men in but she made a lot of trouble. She played one guy against the other. She was always on stage. Then I found out she was tricking on the side. She was using MY place to peddle her pussy!'"

"Really?" Sara asked.

"That's what he said. Anyhow, he offered me a position as a waitress. And he said, 'No tricking on the job!' I told him to cut the shit, I wasn't one of those. I thought maybe now I'll be able to save some money and go to U.C.L.A., to become a chemist and to study French, that's what I've always wanted to do. Then he said, 'Come on back here, I want to show you where we store our excess stock and also I've got an outfit I'd like you to try on. It's never been worn and I think it's your size.' So I went into this dark little room with him and he tried to grab me. I pushed him off. Then he said, 'Just give me a little kiss.' 'Fuck off!' I told him. He was bald and fat and very short and had false teeth and black warts with hairs growing out of them on his cheeks. He rushed me and grabbed a hunk of my ass with one hand and some titty with the other and he tried to kiss me. I pushed him off again. 'I got a wife,' he said, 'I love my wife, don't worry!' He rushed me again and I gave him a knee *you-know-where*. I guess he didn't have anything there, he didn't even flinch. 'I'll give you *money*,' he said, 'I'll be *nice* to you!' I told him to eat shit and die. And so I lost another job."

"That is a sad story," I said.

"Listen," said Edie, "I gotta go. Merry Christmas. Thanks for the drinks."

She got up and I walked her to the door, opened it. She walked off through the court. I came back and sat down.

"You son-of-a-bitch," said Sara.

"What is it?"

"If I hadn't been here you would have fucked her."

"I hardly know the lady."

"All that tit! You were terrified! You were afraid to even *look* at her!"

"What's she doing wandering around on Christmas Eve?"

"Why didn't you ask her?"

"She said she was looking for Bobby."

"If I hadn't been here you would have fucked her."

"I don't know. I have no way of knowing. . . ."

Then Sara stood up and screamed. She began to sob and then she ran into the other room. I poured a drink. The colored lights on the walls blinked off and on.

Sara was preparing the turkey dressing and I sat in the kitchen talking to her. We were both sipping white wine.

The phone rang. I went and got it. It was Debra. "I just wanted to wish you a Merry Christmas, wet noodle."

"Thank you, Debra. And a happy Santa Claus to you."

We talked awhile, then I went back and sat down.

"Who was that?"

"Debra."

"How is she?"

"All right, I guess."

"What did she want?"

"She sent Christmas greetings."

"You'll like this organic turkey, and the stuffing is good too. People eat poison, pure poison. America is one of the few countries where cancer of the colon is prevalent."

"Yeah, my ass itches a lot, but it's just my hemorrhoids. I had them cut out once. Before they operate they run this snake up your intestine with a little light attached and they peek into you looking for cancer. That snake is pretty long. They just run it up you!"

The phone rang again. I went and got it. It was Cassie. "How are you doing?"

"Sara and I are preparing a turkey."

"I miss you."

"Merry Christmas to you too. How's the job going?"

"All right. I'm off until January second."

"Happy New Year, Cassie!"

"What the hell's the matter with you?"

"I'm a little airy. I'm not used to white wine so early in the day."

"Give me a call some time."

"Sure."

I walked back into the kitchen. "It was Cassie. People phone on Christmas. Maybe Drayer Baba will call."

"He won't."

"Why?"

"He never spoke aloud. He never spoke and he never touched money."

"That's pretty good. Let me eat some of that raw dressing."

"O.K."

"Say—not bad!"

Then the phone rang again. It worked like that. Once it started ringing it kept ringing. I walked into the bedroom and answered it.

"Hello," I said. "Who's this?"

"You son-of-a-bitch. Don't you know?"

"No, not really." It was a drunken female.

"Guess."

"Wait. I know! It's *Iris!*"

"Yes, *Iris*. And I'm pregnant!"

"Do you know who the father is?"

"What difference does it make?"

"I guess you're right. How are things in Vancouver?"

"All right. Goodbye."

"Goodbye."

I walked back into the kitchen again.

"It was the Canadian belly dancer," I told Sara.

"How's she doing?"

"She's just full of Christmas cheer."

Sara put the turkey in the oven and we went into the front room. We talked small talk for some time. Then the phone rang again. "Hello," I said.

"Are you Henry Chinaski?" It was a young male voice.

"Yes."

"Are you Henry Chinaski, the writer?"

"Yeah."

"Really?"

"Yeah."

"Well, we're a gang of guys from Bel Air and we really dig your stuff, man! We dig it so much that we're going to *reward* you, man!"

"Oh?"

"Yeah, we're coming over with some six packs of beer."

"Stick that beer up your ass."

"What?"

"I said, 'Stick it up your ass!'"

I hung up.

"Who was that?" asked Sara.

"I just lost three or four readers from Bel Air. But it was worth it."

The turkey was done and I pulled it out of the oven, put it on a platter, moved the typer and all my papers off the kitchen table, and placed the turkey there. I began carving as Sara came in with the vegetables. We sat down. I filled my plate, Sara filled hers. It looked good.

"I hope that one with the tits doesn't come by again," said Sara. She looked very upset at the thought.

"If she does I'll give her a piece."

"*What?*"

I pointed to the turkey. "I said, 'I'll give her a piece.' You can watch."

Sara screamed. She stood up. She was trembling. Then she ran into the bedroom. I looked at my turkey. I couldn't eat it. I had pushed the wrong button again. I walked into the front room with my drink and sat down. I waited 15 minutes and then I put the turkey and the vegetables in the refrigerator.

Sara went back to her place the next day and I had a cold turkey sandwich about 3 PM. About 5 PM there was a terrific pounding on the door. I opened it up. It was Tammie and Arlene. They were cruising on speed. They walked in and jumped around, both of them talking at once.

"Got anything to *drink?*"

"Shit, Hank, ya got *anything* to drink?"

"How was your *fucking* Christmas?"

"Yeah. How was your fucking *Christmas,* man?"

"There's some beer and wine in the icebox," I told them.

(You can always tell an old-timer: he calls a refrigerator an icebox.)

They danced into the kitchen and opened the icebox.

"Hey, here's a *turkey!*"

"We're hungry, Hank! Can we have some turkey?"

"Sure."

Tammie came out with a leg and bit into it. "Hey, this is an awful turkey! It needs spices!"

Arlene came out with slices of meat in her hands. "Yeah, this needs spices. It's too mellow! You got any spices?"

"In the cupboard," I said.

They jumped back into the kitchen and began sprinkling on the spices.

"There! That's better!"

"Yeah, it *tastes* like something now!"

"Organic turkey, shit!"

"Yeah, it's shit!"

"I want some *more!*"

"Me too. But it needs *spices.*"

Tammie came out and sat down. She had just about finished the leg. Then she took the leg bone, bit and broke it in half, and started chewing the bone. I was astonished. She was eating the leg bone, spitting splinters out on the rug.

"Hey, you're eating the bone!"

"Yeah, it's *good!*"

Tammie ran back into the kitchen for some more.

Soon they both came out, each of them with a bottle of beer.

"Thanks, Hank."

"Yeah, thanks, man."

They sat there sucking at the beers.

"Well," said Tammie, "we gotta get going."

"Yeah, we're going out to rape some junior high school boys!"

"Yeah!"

The both jumped up and they were gone out the door. I walked into the kitchen and looked into the refrig. That turkey looked like it had been mauled by a tiger—the carcass had simply been ripped apart. It looked obscene.

Sara drove over the next evening.

"How's the turkey?" she asked.

"O.K."

She walked in and opened the refrigerator door. She screamed. Then she ran out.

"My god, what *happened?*"

"Tammie and Arlene came by. I don't think they had eaten for a week."

"Oh, it's sickening. It hurts my heart!"

"I'm sorry. I should have stopped them. They were on uppers."

"Well, there's just one thing I can do."

"What's that?"

"I can make you a nice turkey soup. I'll go get some vegetables."

"All right." I gave her a twenty.

Sara prepared the soup that night. It was delicious. When she left in the morning she gave me instructions on how to heat it up.

Tammie knocked on the door around 4 PM. I let her in and she walked straight to the kitchen. The refrigerator door opened.

"Hey, soup, huh?"

"Yeah."

"Is it any good?"

"Yeah."

"Mind if I try some?"

"O.K."

I heard her put it on the stove. Then I heard her dipping in there.

"God! This stuff is *mild!* It needs *spices!*"

I heard her spooning the spices in. Then she tried it.

"That's *better!* But it needs more! I'm *Italian,* you know. Now . . . there . . . that's better! Now I'll let it heat up. Can I have a beer?"

"All right."

She came in with her bottle and sat down.

"Do you miss me?" she asked.

"You'll never know."

"I think I'm going to get my job back at the Play Pen."

"Great."

"Some good tippers come in that place. One guy he tipped me five bucks each night. He was in love with me. But he never asked me out. He just ogled me. He was strange. He was a rectal surgeon and sometimes he masturbated as he watched me walking around. I could smell the stuff on him, you know."

"Well, you got him off. . . ."

"I think the soup is ready. Want some?"

"No thanks."

Tammie went in and I heard her spooning it out of the pot. She was in there a long time. Then she came out.

"Could you lend me a five until Friday?"

"No."

"Then lend me a couple of bucks."

"No."

"Just give me a dollar then."

I gave Tammie a pocketful of change. It came to a dollar and 37 cents.

"Thanks," she said.

"It's all right."

Then she was gone out of the door.

Sara came by the next evening. She seldom came by this often, it was something about the holiday season, everybody was lost, half-crazy, afraid. I had the white wine ready and poured us both a drink.

"How's the Inn going?" I asked her.

"Business is crappy. It hardly pays to stay open."

"Where are your customers?"

"They've all left town; they've all gone somewhere."

"All our schemes have holes in them."

"Not all of them. Some people just keep making it and making it."

"True."

"How's the soup?"

"Just about finished."

"Did you like it?"

"I didn't have too much."

Sara walked into the kitchen and opened the refrigerator door.

"What happened to the soup? It looks strange."

I heard her tasting it. Then she ran to the sink and spit it out.

"Jesus, it's been poisoned! What happened? Did Tammie and Arlene come back and eat *soup* too?"

"Just Tammie."

Sara didn't scream. She just poured the remainder of the soup into the sink and ran the garbage disposal. I could hear her sobbing, trying not to make any sound. That poor organic turkey had had a rough Christmas.

—*Women*

metamorphosis

• •

a girlfriend came in
built me a bed
scrubbed and waxed the kitchen floor
scrubbed the walls
vacuumed
cleaned the toilet
the bathtub
scrubbed the bathroom floor
and cut my toenails and
my hair.

then
all on the same day
the plumber came and fixed the kitchen faucet
and the toilet
and the gas man fixed the heater
and the phone man fixed the phone.
now I sit here in all this perfection.
it is quiet.
I have broken off with all 3 of my girlfriends.

I felt better when everything was in
disorder.
it will take me some months to get back to
normal:
I can't even find a roach to commune with.

I have lost my rhythm.
I can't sleep.
I can't eat.

I have been robbed of
my filth.

Dr. Nazi

• •

Now, I'm a man of many problems and I suppose that most of them are self-created. I mean with the female, and gambling, and feeling hostile toward groups of people, and the larger the group, the greater the hostility. I'm called negative and gloomy, sullen.

I keep remembering the female who screamed at me: "You're so goddamned negative! Life can be beautiful!"

I suppose it can, and especially with a little less screaming. But I want to tell you about my doctor. I don't go to shrinks. Shrinks are worthless and too contented. But a good doctor is often disgusted and/or mad, and therefore far more entertaining.

I went to Dr. Kiepenheuer's office because it was closest. My hands were breaking out with little white blisters—a sign, I felt, either of my actual anxiety or possible cancer. I wore workingman's gloves so people wouldn't stare. And I burned through the gloves while smoking two packs of cigarettes a day.

I walked into the doctor's place. I had the first appointment. Being a man of anxiety I was 30 minutes early, musing about cancer. I walked across the sitting room and looked into the office. Here was the nurse-receptionist squatted on the floor in her tight white uniform, her dress pulled almost up to her hips, gross and thunderous thighs showing through tightly-pulled nylon. I forgot all about the cancer. She hadn't heard me and I stared at her unveiled legs and thighs, measured the delicious rump with my eyes. She was wiping water from the floor, the toilet had overrun and she was cursing, she was passionate, she was pink and brown and living and unveiled and I stared.

She looked up. "Yes?"

"Go ahead," I said, "don't let me disturb you."

"It's the toilet," she said, "it keeps running over."

She kept wiping and I kept looking over the top of *Life* magazine. She finally stood up. I walked to the couch and sat down. She went through her appointment book.

"Are you Mr. Chinaski?"

"Yes."

"Why don't you take your gloves off? It's warm in here."

"I'd rather not, if you don't mind."

"Dr. Kiepenheuer will be in soon."

"It's all right. I can wait."

"What's your problem?"

"Cancer."

"Cancer?"

"Yes."

The nurse vanished and I read *Life* and then I read another copy of *Life* and then I read *Sports Illustrated* and then I sat staring at paintings of seascapes and landscapes and piped-in music came from somewhere. Then, suddenly, all the lights blinked off, then on again, and I wondered if there would be any way to rape the nurse and get away with it when the doctor walked in. I ignored him and he ignored me, so that went off even.

He called me into his office. He was sitting on a stool and he looked at me. He had a yellow face and yellow hair and his eyes were lusterless. He was dying. He was about 42. I eyed him and gave him six months.

"What's with the gloves?" he asked.

"I'm a sensitive man, Doctor."

"You are?"

"Yes."

"Then I should tell you that I was once a Nazi."

"That's all right."

"You don't mind that I was once a Nazi?"

"No, I don't mind."

"I was captured. They rode us through France in a boxcar with the doors open and the people stood along the way and threw stink bombs and rocks and all sorts of rubbish at us—fishbones, dead plants, excreta, everything imaginable."

Then the doctor sat and told me about his wife. She was trying to skin him. A real bitch. Trying to get all his money. The house. The garden. The garden house. The gardener too, probably, if she hadn't already. And the car. And alimony. Plus a large chunk of cash. Horrible woman. He'd worked so hard. Fifty patients a day at ten dollars a head. Almost impossible to survive. And that woman. Women. Yes, women. He broke down the word for me. I forget if it was woman or female or what it was, but he broke it down into Latin and he broke it down from there to show what the root was—in Latin: women were basically insane.

As he talked about the insanity of women I began to feel pleased with the doctor. My head nodded in agreement.

Suddenly he ordered me to the scales, weighed me, then he listened to my heart and to my chest. He roughly removed my gloves, washed my hands in some kind of shit and opened the blisters with a razor, still talking about the rancor and vengeance that all women carried in their hearts. It was glandular. Women were directed by their glands, men by their hearts. That's why only the men suffered.

He told me to bathe my hands regularly and to throw the goddamned gloves away. He talked a little more about women and his wife and then I left.

My next problem was dizzy spells. But I only got them when I was standing in line. I began to get very terrified of standing in line. It was unbearable.

I realized that in America and probably everyplace else it came down to standing in line. We did it everywhere. Driver's license: three or four lines. The racetrack: lines. The movies: lines. The market: lines. I hated lines. I felt there should be a way to avoid them. Then the answer came to me. Have more *clerks*. Yes, that was the answer. Two clerks for every person. *Three* clerks. Let the clerks stand in line.

I knew that lines were killing me. I couldn't accept them, but everybody else did. Everybody else was normal. Life was beautiful for them. They could stand in line without feeling pain. They could stand in line forever. They even *liked* to stand in line. They chatted and grinned and smiled and flirted with each other. They had nothing else to do. They could think of nothing else to do. And I had to look at their ears and mouths and necks and legs and asses and nostrils, all that. I could feel death-rays oozing from their bodies like smog, and listening to their conversations I felt like screaming *"Jesus Christ, somebody help me! Do I have to suffer like this just to buy a pound of hamburger and a loaf of rye bread?"*

The dizziness would come, and I'd spread my legs to keep from falling down; the supermarket would whirl, and the faces of the supermarket clerks with their gold and brown mustaches and their clever happy eyes, all of them going to be supermarket managers someday, with their white scrubbed contented faces, buying homes in Arcadia and nightly mounting their pale blond grateful wives.

• • •

I made an appointment with the doctor again. I was given the first appointment. I arrived half an hour early and the toilet was fixed. The nurse was dusting in the office. She bent and straightened and bent halfway and then bent right and then bent left, and she turned her ass toward me and bent over. That white uniform twitched and hiked, climbed, lifted; here was dimpled knee, there was thigh, here was haunch, there was the whole body. I sat down and opened a copy of *Life*.

She stopped dusting and stuck her head out at me, smiling. "You got rid of your gloves, Mr. Chinaski."

"Yes."

The doctor came in looking a bit closer to death and he nodded and I got up and followed him in.

He sat down on his stool.

"Chinaski: how goes it?"

"Well, Doctor . . . "

"Trouble with women?"

"Well, of course, but . . . "

He wouldn't let me finish. He had lost more hair. His fingers twitched. He seemed short of breath. Thinner. He was a desperate man.

His wife was skinning him. They'd gone to court. She slapped him in court. He'd liked that. It helped the case. They saw through that bitch. Anyhow, it hadn't come off too badly. She'd left him something. Of course, you know lawyer's fees. Bastards. You ever noticed a lawyer? Almost always fat. Especially around the face. "Anyhow, shit, she nailed me. But I got a little left. You wanna know what a scissors like this costs? Look at it. Tin with a screw. $18.50. My God, and they hated the Nazis. What is a Nazi compared to this?"

"I don't know, Doctor. I've told you that I'm a confused man."

"You ever tried a shrink?"

"It's no use. They're dull, no imagination. I don't need the shrinks. I hear they end up sexually molesting their female patients. I'd like to be a shrink if I could fuck all the women; outside of that, their trade is useless."

My doctor hunched up on his stool. He yellowed and greyed a bit more. A giant twitch ran through his body. He was almost through. A nice fellow though.

"Well, I got rid of my wife," he said, "that's over."

"Fine," I said, "tell me about when you were a Nazi."

"Well, we didn't have much choice. They just took us in. I was young. I mean, hell, what are you going to do? You can only live in one country at a time. You go to war, and if you don't end up dead you end up in an open boxcar with people throwing shit at you . . . "

I asked him if he'd fucked his nice nurse. He smiled gently. The smile said yes. Then he told me that since the divorce, well, he'd dated one of his patients, and he knew it wasn't ethical to get that way with patients . . .

"No, I think it's all right, Doctor."

"She's a very intelligent woman. I married her."

"All right."

"Now I'm happy . . . but . . . "

Then he spread his hands apart and opened his palms upward . . .

I told him about my fear of lines. He gave me a standing prescription for Librium.

Then I got a nest of boils on my ass. I was in agony. They tied me with leather straps, these fellows can do anything they want with you, they gave me a local and strapped my ass. I turned my head and looked at my Doctor and said, "Is there any chance of me changing my mind?"

There were three faces looking down at me. His and two others. Him to cut. Her to supply cloths. The third to stick needles.

"You can't change your mind," said the doctor, and he rubbed his hands and grinned and began . . .

The last time I saw him it had something to do with wax in my ears. I could see his lips moving, I tried to understand, but I couldn't hear. I could tell by his eyes and his face that it was hard times for him all over again, and I nodded.

It was warm. I was a bit dizzy and I thought, well, yes, he's a fine fellow but why doesn't he let me tell him about my problems, this isn't fair, I have problems too, and I have to pay him.

Eventually my doctor realized I was deaf. He got something that looked like a fire extinguisher and jammed it into my ears. Later he showed me huge pieces of wax . . . it was the wax, he said. And he pointed down into a bucket. It looked, really, like refried beans.

I got up from the table and paid him and I left. I still couldn't hear anything. I didn't feel particularly bad or good and I wondered what ailment I would bring him next, what he would do about it, what he would do about his 17-year-old daughter who was in love with another woman and who was going to marry the woman, and it occurred to me that *everybody* suffered continually, including those who pretended they didn't. It seemed to me that this was quite a discovery. I looked at the newsboy and I thought, hmmmm, hmmmm, and I looked at the next person to pass and I thought hmmmm, hmmmm, hmmmmmmm, and at the traffic signal by the hospital a new black car turned the corner and knocked down a pretty young girl in a blue mini dress, and she was blond and had blue ribbons in her hair, and she sat up in the street in the sun and the scarlet ran from her nose.

—*SOUTH OF NO NORTH*

one for the shoeshine man

the balance is preserved by the snails climbing the
Santa Monica cliffs;
the luck is in walking down Western Avenue
and having the girls in a massage
parlor holler at you, "Hello, Sweetie!"
the miracle is having 5 women in love
with you at the age of 55,
and the goodness is that you are only able
to love one of them.
the gift is having a daughter more gentle
than you are, whose laughter is finer
than yours.
the peace comes from driving a
blue 67 Volks through the streets like a
teenager, radio tuned to The Host Who Loves You
Most, feeling the sun, feeling the solid hum
of the rebuilt motor
as you needle through traffic.

the grace is being able to like rock music,
symphony music, jazz . . .
anything that contains the original energy of
joy.

and the probability that returns
is the deep blue low
yourself flat upon yourself
within the guillotine walls
angry at the sound of the phone
or anybody's footsteps passing;
but the other probability—
the lilting high that always follows—
makes the girl at the checkstand in the
supermarket look like   .
Marilyn
like Jackie before they got her Harvard lover
like the girl in high school that we
all followed home.

there is that which helps you believe
in something else besides death:
somebody in a car approaching
on a street too narrow,
and he or she pulls aside to let you
by, or the old fighter Beau Jack
shining shoes
after blowing the entire bankroll
on parties
on women
on parasites,
humming, breathing on the leather,
working the rag
looking up and saying:
"what the hell, I had it for a
while. that beats the
other."

I am bitter sometimes
but the taste has often been
sweet. it's only that I've
feared to say it. it's like
when your woman says,
"tell me you love me," and
you can't.

if you see me grinning from
my blue Volks
running a yellow light
driving straight into the sun
I will be locked in the
arms of a
crazy life
thinking of trapeze artists
of midgets with big cigars
of a Russian winter in the early 40's
of Chopin with his bag of Polish soil
of an old waitress bringing me an extra
cup of coffee and laughing
as she does so.

the best of you
I like more than you think.
the others don't count
except that they have fingers and heads
and some of them eyes
and most of them legs
and all of them
good and bad dreams
and a way to go.

justice is everywhere and it's working
and the machine guns and the frogs
and the hedges will tell you
so.

5

....

my wrists are rivers
my fingers are words

the mockingbird
••

the mockingbird had been following the cat
all summer
mocking mocking mocking
teasing and cocksure;
the cat crawled under rockers on porches
tail flashing
and said something angry to the mockingbird
which I didn't understand.

yesterday the cat walked calmly up the driveway
with the mockingbird alive in its mouth,
wings fanned, beautiful wings fanned and flopping,
feathers parted like a woman's legs,
and the bird was no longer mocking,
it was asking, it was praying
but the cat
striding down through centuries
would not listen.

I saw it crawl under a yellow car
with the bird
to bargain it to another place.

summer was over.

Less Delicate Than the Locust

• •

"Balls," he said, "I'm tired of painting. Let's go out. I'm tired of the stink of oils, I'm tired of being great. I'm tired of waiting to die. Let's go out."

"Go out where?" she asked.

"Anywhere. Eat, drink, see."

"Jorg," she said, "what will I do when you die?"

"You will eat, sleep, fuck, piss, shit, clothe yourself, walk around and bitch."

"I need security."

"We all do."

"I mean, we're not married. I won't even be able to collect your insurance."

"That's all right, don't worry about it. Besides, you don't believe in marriage, Arlene."

Arlene was sitting in the pink chair reading the afternoon newspaper. "You say five thousand women want to sleep with you. Where does that leave me?"

"Five thousand and one."

"You think I can't get another man?"

"No, there's no problem for you. You can get another man in three minutes."

"You think I need a great painter?"

"No, you don't. A good plumber would do."

"Yes, as long as he loved me."

"Of course. Put on your coat. Let's go out."

They came down the stairway from the top loft. All around were cheap, roach-filled rooms, but nobody seemed to be starving: they always seemed to be cooking things in large pots and sitting around, smoking, cleaning their fingernails, drinking cans of beer or sharing a tall blue bottle of white wine, screaming at each other or laughing, or farting, belching, scratching or asleep in front of the tv. Not many people in the world had very much money but the less money they had the better they seemed to live. Sleep, clean sheets, food, drink and hemorrhoid ointment were their only needs. And they always left their doors a bit open.

"Fools," said Jorg as they walked down the stairway, "they twaddle away their lives and clutter up mine."

"Oh, Jorg," Arlene sighed. "You just don't *like* people, do you?"

Jorg arched an eyebrow at her, didn't answer. Arlene's response to his feelings for the masses was always the same—as if not loving the people revealed an unforgivable shortcoming of soul. But she was an excellent fuck and pleasant to have around—most of the time.

They reached the boulevard and walked along, Jorg with his red and white beard and broken yellow teeth and bad breath, purple ears, frightened eyes, stinking torn overcoat and white ivory cane. When he felt worst he felt best. "Shit," he said, "everything shits until it dies."

Arlene bobbled her ass, making no secret of it, and Jorg pounded the pavement with his cane, and even the sun looked down and said, Ho ho. Finally they reached the old dingy building where Serge lived. Jorg and Serge had both been painting for many years but it was not until recently that their work sold for more than pig farts. They had starved together, now they were getting famous separately. Jorg and Arlene entered the hotel and began climbing the stairway. The smell of iodine and frying chicken was in the halls. In one room somebody was getting fucked and making no secret of it. They climbed to the top loft and Arlene knocked. The door popped open and there was Serge. "Peek-a-boo!" he said. Then he blushed. "Oh, sorry . . . come in."

"What the hell's the matter with you?" asked Jorg.

"Sit down. I thought it was Lila . . . "

"You play peek-a-boo with Lila?"

"It's nothing."

"Serge, you've got to get rid of that girl, she's destroying your mind."

"She sharpens my pencils."

"Serge, she's too young for you."

"She's 30."

"And you're 60. That's 30 years."

"Thirty years is too much?"

"Of course."

"How about 20?" asked Serge, looking at Arlene.

"Twenty years is acceptable. Thirty years is obscene."

"Why don't you both get women your own age?" asked Arlene.

They both looked at her. "She likes to make little jokes," said Jorg. "Yes," said Serge, "she is funny. Come on, look, I'll show you what I'm doing . . . "

They followed him into the bedroom. He took off his shoes and lay flat on the bed. "See? Like this? All the comforts." Serge had his paint brushes on long handles and he painted on a canvas fastened to the ceiling. "It's my back. Can't paint ten minutes without stopping. This way I go on for hours."

"Who mixes your colors?"

"Lila. I tell her, 'Stick it in the blue. Now a bit of green.' She's quite good. Eventually I might even let her work the brushes, too, and I'll just lay around and read magazines."

Then they heard Lila coming up the stairway. She opened the door, came across the front room and entered the bedroom. "Hey," she said, "I see the old fuck's painting."

"Yeah," said Jorg, "he claims you hurt his back."

"I said no such thing."

"Let's go out and eat," said Arlene. Serge moaned and got up.

"Honest to Christ," said Lila. "He just lays around like a sick frog most of the time."

"I need a drink," said Serge. "I'll snap back."

They went down to the street together and moved toward The Sheep's Tick. Two young men in their mid-20's ran up. They had on turtleneck sweaters. "Hey, you guys are the painters, Jorg Swenson and Serge Maro!"

"Get the hell out of the way!" said Serge.

Jorg swung his ivory cane. He got the shorter of the young men right on the knee. "Shit," the young man said, "you've broken my leg!"

"I hope so," said Jorg. "Maybe you'll learn some damned civility!"

They moved on toward The Sheep's Tick. As they entered a buzzing arose from the diners. The headwaiter immediately rushed up, bowing and waving menus and speaking endearments in Italian, French and Russian.

"Look at that long, black hair in his nostrils," said Serge. "Truly sickening!"

"Yes," said Jorg, and then he shouted at the waiter, "HIDE YOUR NOSE!"

"Five bottles of your best wine!" screamed Serge, as they sat down at the best table.

The headwaiter vanished. "You two are real assholes," said Lila.

Jorg ran his hand up her leg. "Two living immortals are allowed certain indiscretions."

"Get your hand off my pussy, Jorg."

"It's not your pussy. It's Serge's pussy."

"Get your hand off Serge's pussy or I'll scream."

"My will is weak."

She screamed. Jorg removed his hand. The headwaiter came toward them with the wagon and bucket of chilled wine. He rolled it up, bowed and pulled one cork. He filled Jorg's glass. Jorg drained it. "It's shit, but O.K. Open the bottles!"

"All the bottles?"

"All the bottles, asshole, and be *quick* about it!"

"He's clumsy," said Serge. "Look at him. Shall we dine?"

"Dine?" said Arlene. "All you guys do is drink. I don't think I've seen either of you eat more than a soft-boiled egg."

"Get out of my sight, coward," Serge said to the waiter.

The headwaiter vanished.

"You guys shouldn't talk to people that way," said Lila.

"We've paid our dues," said Serge.

"You've got no right," said Arlene.

"I suppose not," said Jorg, "but it's interesting."

"People don't have to take that crap," said Lila.

"People accept what they accept," said Jorg. "They accept far worse."

"It's your paintings they want, that's all," said Arlene.

"*We* are our paintings," said Serge.

"Women are stupid," said Jorg.

"Be careful," said Serge. "They also are capable of terrible acts of vengeance . . ."

They sat for a couple of hours drinking the wine.

"Man is less delicate than the locust," said Jorg finally.

"Man is the sewer of the universe," said Serge.

"You guys are really assholes," said Lila.

"Sure are," said Arlene.

"Let's switch tonight," said Jorg. "I'll fuck your pussy and you fuck mine."

"Oh no," said Arlene, "none of that."

"Right," said Lila.

"I feel like painting now," said Jorg. "I'm bored with drinking."

"I feel like painting, too," said Serge.

"Let's get out of here," said Jorg.

"Listen," said Lila, "you guys haven't paid the bill yet."

"*Bill?*" screamed Serge. "*You don't think we are going to pay money for this rotgut?*"

"Let's go," said Jorg.

As they rose, the headwaiter came up with the bill.

"*This rotgut stinks,*" screamed Serge, jumping up and down. "*I would never ask anyone to pay for stuff like this! I want you to know the proof is in the piss!*"

Serge grabbed a half-full bottle of the wine, ripped open the waiter's shirt and poured the wine over his chest. Jorg held his ivory cane like a sword. The headwaiter looked confused. He was a beautiful young man with long fingernails and an expensive apartment. He was studying chemistry and had once won second prize in an opera competition. Jorg swung his cane and caught the waiter, hard, just below the left ear. The waiter turned very white and swayed. Jorg hit him three more times in the same spot and he dropped.

They walked out together, Serge, Jorg, Lila and Arlene. They were all drunk but there was a certain stature about them, something unique. They got out the door and went down the street.

A young couple seated at a table near the door had watched the entire proceedings. The young man looked intelligent, only a rather large mole near the end of his nose marred the effect. His girl was fat but lovable in a dark blue dress. She had once wanted to be a nun.

"Weren't they magnificent?" asked the young man.

"They were assholes," said the girl.

The young man waved for a third bottle of wine. It was going to be another difficult night.

—*Hot Water Music*

junk

• •

sitting in a dark bedroom with 3 junkies,
female.
brown paper bags filled with trash are
everywhere.
it is one-thirty in the afternoon.
they talk about madhouses,
hospitals.
they are waiting for a fix.
none of them work.
it's relief and foodstamps and
Medi-Cal.

men are usable objects
toward the fix.

it is one-thirty in the afternoon
and outside small plants grow.
their children are still in school.
the females smoke cigarettes
and suck listlessly on beer and
tequila
which I have purchased.

I sit with them.
I wait on my fix:
I am a poetry junkie.

they pulled Ezra through the streets
in a wooden cage.
Blake was sure of God.
Villon was a mugger.
Lorca sucked cock.
T.S. Eliot worked a teller's cage.

most poets are swans,
egrets.

I sit with 3 junkies
at one-thirty in the afternoon.

the smoke pisses upward.

I wait.

death is a nothing jumbo.

one of the females says that she likes
my yellow shirt.

I believe in a simple violence.

this is
some of it.

hug the dark

●●

turmoil is the god
madness is the god

permanent living peace is
permanent living death.

agony can kill
or
agony can sustain life
but peace is always horrifying
peace is the worst thing
walking

talking
smiling,
seeming to be.

don't forget the sidewalks
the whores,
betrayal,
the worm in the apple,
the bars, the jails,
the suicides of lovers.

here in America
we have assassinated a president and his brother,
another president has quit office.

people who believe in politics
are like people who believe in god:
they are sucking wind through bent
straws.

there is no god
there are no politics
there is no peace
there is no love
there is no control
there is no plan

stay away from god
remain disturbed

slide.

• •

I was leaning against the bar in Musso's. Sarah had gone to the lady's room. I liked the bar at Musso's, bar just as bar, but I didn't like the room it was in. It was known as the "New Room." The "Old Room" was on the other side and I preferred to eat there. It was darker and quieter. In the old days I used to go to the Old Room to eat but I never actually ate. I just looked at the menu and told them, "Not yet," and kept ordering drinks. Some of the ladies I brought there were of ill-repute and as we drank on and on, often loud arguments began, replete with cursing and spilling of drinks, calls for more to drink. I usually gave the ladies cab fare and told them to get the hell out and I went on drinking alone. I doubt they ever used the cab fare for cab fare. But one of the nicest things about Musso's was that when I returned again, after fucking up, I was always greeted with warm smiles. So strange.

Anyhow, I was leaning against the bar and the New Room was full, mostly with tourists, they were chatting and they were twisting their necks and they were giving off rays of death. I ordered a new drink and then there was a tap on my shoulder.

"Chinaski, how are you?"

I turned and looked. I never knew who anybody was. I could meet you the night before and not remember you the next day. If they dug my mother out of her grave I wouldn't know who she was.

"I'm all right," I said. "Can I buy you a drink?"

"No, thanks. We haven't met. I'm Harold Pheasant."

"Oh yeah. Jon told me you were thinking of . . . "

"Yes. I want to finance your screenplay. I've read your work. You've got a marvelous sense of dialogue. I've read your work: *very* filmatic!"

"Sure you won't have a drink?"

"No, I have to get back to my table."

"Yeah. What ya been doing lately, Pheasant?"

"Just finished producing a film about the life of Mack Derouac."

"Yeah? What's it called?"

"*The Heart's Song.*"

I took a drink.

"Hey, wait a minute! You're *joking!* You're not going to call it *The Heart's Song?*"

"Oh yes, that's what it's going to be called."

He was smiling.

"You can't fool me, Pheasant. You're a real joker! *The Heart's Song!* Jesus Christ!"

"No," he said, "I'm serious."

He suddenly turned and walked off . . .

Just then Sarah came back. She looked at me.

What are you grinning about?"

"Let me order you a drink and I'll tell you."

I got the barkeep over and also ordered another for myself.

"Guess who I saw in the Old Room," she said.

"Who?"

"Jonathan Winters."

"Yeah. Guess who I talked to while you were gone."

"One of your x-sluts."

"No, no. Worse."

"There's nothing worse than those."

"I talked to Harold Pheasant."

"The producer?"

"Yes, he's over at that corner table."

"Oh, I *see!*"

"No, don't *look.* Don't wave. Drink your drink. I'll drink mine."

"What the hell's wrong with you?"

"You see, he was the producer who was going to produce the screenplay that I haven't written."

"I know."

"While you were gone he came over to talk to me."

"You already said."

"He didn't even want a drink."

"So you screwed it up and you're not even drunk."

"Wait. He wanted to talk about a movie he had just produced."

"How'd you screw it up?"

"I didn't screw it up. *He* screwed it up."

"Sure. Tell me."

I looked in the mirror. I liked myself but I didn't like myself in the mirror. I didn't look like that. I finished my drink.

"Finish your drink," I said.

She did.

"Tell me."

"That's twice you've said, 'Tell me.'"

"Remarkable memory and you're not even drunk yet."

I motioned the barkeep in, ordered again.

"Well, Pheasant came over and he told me about this movie he produced. It's about a writer who couldn't write but who got famous because he looked like a rodeo rider."

"Who?"

"Mack Derouac."

"And that upset you?"

"No, that didn't matter. It was fine until he told me the title of the movie."

"Which was?"

"Please. I am trying to drive it out of my mind. It's utterly stupid."

"Tell me."

"All right . . . "

The mirror was still there.

"Tell me, tell me, tell me . . . "

"All right: *The Furry Flotsam Flies.*"

"I like that."

"I didn't. I told him so. He walked off. We lost our only backer."

"You ought to go over there and apologize."

"No way. Horrendous title."

"You just wanted his movie to be about *you.*"

"*That's it!* I'll write a screenplay about myself!"

"Got the title?"

"Yeah: *Flies in the Furry Flotsam.*"

"Let's get out of here."

With that, we did.

—HOLLYWOOD

the proud
thin
dying

I see old people on pensions in the
supermarkets and they are thin and they are
proud and they are dying
they are starving on their feet and saying
nothing. long ago, among other lies,
they were taught that silence was
bravery. now, having worked a lifetime,
inflation has trapped them. they look around
steal a grape
chew on it. finally they make a tiny
purchase, a day's worth.
another lie they were taught:
thou shalt not steal.
they'd rather starve than steal
(one grape won't save them)
and in tiny rooms
while reading the market ads
they'll starve
they'll die without a sound
pulled out of roominghouses
by young blond boys with long hair
who'll slide them in
and pull away from the curb, these
boys
handsome of eye
thinking of Vegas and pussy and
victory.
it's the order of things: each one
gets a taste of honey
then the knife.

• •

Vin Marbad came highly recommended by Michael Huntington, my official photographer. Michael snapped me constantly, but so far there had been no large call for these efforts.

Marbad was a tax consultant. He arrived one night with his brief-case, a dark little man. I had been drinking quietly for some hours, sitting with Sarah while watching a movie on my old black-and-white tv.

He knocked with a rapid dignity and I let him in, introduced him to Sarah, poured him a wine.

"Thank you," he said, taking a sip. "You know, that here in America, if you don't spend money they are going to take it away."

"Yeah? What you want me to do?"

"Put a payment down on a house."

"Huh?"

"Mortgage payments are tax deductible."

"Yeah, what else?"

"Buy a car. Tax deductible."

"All of it?"

"No, just some. Let me handle that. What we have to do is build you some tax shelters. Look here—"

Vin Marbad opened his briefcase and slipped out many sheets of paper. He stood up and came toward me with the papers.

"Real estate. Here, I've bought some land in Oregon. This is a tax write-off. There are some acres still available. You can get in now. We look for a 23% appreciation each year. In other words, after four years your money is doubled . . . "

"No, no, please sit back down."

"What's the matter?"

"I don't want to buy anything that I can't see, I don't want to buy anything that I can't reach out and touch."

"You mean, you don't trust me?"

"I just met you."

"I have world-wide recommendations!"

"I always go by my instincts."

Vin Marbad spun back toward the couch where he had left his coat; he slipped into it and then with briefcase he rushed to the door, opened it, was out, closed it.

"You've hurt his feelings," said Sarah. "He's just trying to show you some ways to save money."

"I have two rules. One is, never trust a man who smokes a pipe. The other is, never trust a man with shiny shoes."

"He wasn't smoking a pipe."

"Well, he looks like a pipe smoker."

"You hurt his feelings."

"Don't worry, he'll be back . . . "

The door flung open and there was Vin Marbad. He rushed across the room to his original place on the couch, took off his coat again, placed the briefcase at his feet. He looked at me.

"Michael tells me you play the horses."

"Well, yeah . . . "

"My first job when I came here from India was at Hollywood Park. I was a janitor there. You know the brooms they use to sweep up the discarded tickets?"

"Yeah."

"Ever notice how wide they are?"

"Yeah."

"Well, that was *my* idea. Those brooms used to be regular size. I designed the new broom. I went to Operations with it and they put it to use. I moved up into Operations and I've been moving up ever since."

I poured him another wine. He took a sip.

"Listen, do you drink when you write?"

"Yes, quite a bit."

"That's part of your inspiration. I'll make that tax deductible."

"Can you do that?"

"Of course. You know, I was the one who began making deductions for gasoline use in the automobile. That was my idea."

"Son of a bitch," I said.

"Very interesting," said Sarah.

"I'll fix it so you won't have to pay any taxes at all and it will all be legal."

"Sounds nice."

"Michael Huntington doesn't pay taxes. Ask him."

"I believe you. Let's not pay taxes."

"All right, but you must do what I tell you. First, you put a down payment on a house, then on a car. Get started. Get a good car. Get a new BMW."

"All right."

"What do you type on? A manual?"

"Yes."

"Get an electric. It's tax deductible."

"I don't know if I can write on an electric."

"You can pick it up in a couple of days."

"I mean, I don't know if I can *create* on an electric."

"You mean, you're afraid to change?"

"Yes, he is," said Sarah. "Take the writers of past centuries, they used quill pens. Back then, he would have held on to that quill pen, he would have fought any change."

"I worry too much about my god damned soul."

"You change your brands of booze, don't you?" asked Vin.

"Yeah . . . "

"O.K., then . . . "

Vin lifted his glass, drained it.

I poured the wine around.

"What we want to do is to make you a Corporation, so you get all the tax breaks."

"It sounds awful."

"I told you, if you don't want to pay taxes you must do as I say."

"All I want to do is type, I don't want to carry around a big load."

"All you do is to appoint a Board of Directors, a Secretary, Treasurer, so forth . . . It's easy."

"It sounds horrible. Listen, all this sounds like pure shit. Maybe I'd be better off just paying taxes. I just don't want anybody bothering me. I don't want a tax man knocking on my door at midnight. I'll even pay extra just to make sure they leave me alone."

"That's stupid," said Vin, "nobody should *ever* pay taxes."

"Why don't you give Vin a chance? He's just trying to help you," said Sarah.

"Look, I'll mail you the Corporation papers. Just read them over and then sign them. You'll see that there's nothing to fear."

"All this stuff, you see, it gets in the way. I'm working on this screenplay and I need a clear mind."

"A screenplay, huh? What's it about?"

"A drunk."

"Ah, you, huh?"

"Well, there are others."

"I've got him drinking wine now," said Sarah. "He was about dead when I met him. Scotch, beer, vodka, gin, ale . . . "

"I've been a consultant for Darby Evans for some years now. You heard of him, he's a screenwriter."

"I don't go to movies."

"He wrote *The Bunny That Hopped into Heaven; Waffles with Lulu; Terror in the Zoo.* He's easily into six figures. And, he's a Corporation."

I didn't answer.

"He hasn't paid a dime in taxes. And, it's all legal . . . "

"Give Vin a chance," said Sarah.

I lifted my glass.

"All right. Shit. Here's to it!"

"Atta boy," said Vin.

I drained my glass and got up and found another bottle. I got the cork out and poured all around.

I let my mind go along with it: you're a wheeler dealer. You're slick. Why pay for bombs that mangle helpless children? Drive a BMW. Have a view of the harbor. Vote Republican.

Then another thought came to my mind:

Are you becoming what you've always hated?

And then the answer came:

Shit, you don't have any real money anyhow. Why not play around with this thing for laughs?

We went on drinking, celebrating something.

—HOLLYWOOD

3:16 and one half . . .

• •

here I'm supposed to be a great poet
and I'm sleepy in the afternoon
here I am aware of death like a giant bull
charging at me
and I'm sleepy in the afternoon

here I'm aware of wars and men fighting in the ring
and I'm aware of good food and wine and good women
and I'm sleepy in the afternoon
I'm aware of a woman's love
and I'm sleepy in the afternoon,
I lean into the sunlight behind a yellow curtain
I wonder where the summer flies have gone
I remember the most bloody death of Hemingway
and I'm sleepy in the afternoon.

some day I won't be sleepy in the afternoon
some day I'll write a poem that will bring volcanoes
to the hills out there
but right now I'm sleepy in the afternoon
and somebody asks me, "Bukowski, what time is it?"
and I say, "3:16 and a half."
I feel very guilty, I feel obnoxious, useless,
demented, I feel
sleepy in the afternoon,
they are bombing churches, o.k., that's o.k.,
the children ride ponies in the park, o.k., that's o.k.,
the libraries are filled with thousands of books of knowledge,
great music sits inside the nearby radio
and I am sleepy in the afternoon,
I have this tomb within myself that says,
ah, let the others do it, let them win,
let me sleep,
wisdom is in the dark
sweeping through the dark like brooms,
I'm going where the summer flies have gone,
try to catch me.

• •

So, there I was over 65 years old, looking for my first house. I remembered how my father had virtually mortgaged his whole life to buy a house. He had told me, "Look, I'll pay for one house in my lifetime and when I die you'll get that house and then in your lifetime you'll pay for a house and when you die you'll leave those houses to your son. That'll make two houses. Then your son will . . . "

The whole process seemed terribly slow to me: house by house, death by death. Ten generations, ten houses. Then it would take just one person to gamble all those houses away, or burn them down with a match and then run down the street with his balls in a fruit-picker's pail.

Now I was looking for a house I really didn't want and I was going to write a screenplay I really didn't want to write. I was beginning to lose control and I realized it but I seemed unable to reverse the process.

The first realtor we stopped at was in Santa Monica. It was called TwentySecond Century Housing. Now, that was modern.

Sarah and I got out of the car and walked in. There was a young fellow at the desk, bow tie, nice striped shirt, red suspenders. He looked hip. He was shuffling papers at his desk. He stopped and looked up.

"Can I help you?"

"We want to buy a house," I said.

The young fellow just turned his head to one side and kept looking away. A minute went past. Two minutes.

"Let's go," I said to Sarah.

We got back into the car and I started the engine.

"What was all that about?" Sarah asked.

"He didn't want to do business with us. He took a reading and he thought we were indigent, worthless. He thought we would waste his time."

"But it's not true."

"Maybe not, but the whole thing made me feel as if I was covered with slime."

I drove the car along, hardly knowing where I was going.

Somehow, that had hurt. Of course, I was hungover and I needed a shave and I always wore clothing that somehow didn't seem to fit me quite right and maybe all the years of poverty had just given me a certain look. But I didn't think it was wise to judge a man from the outside like that. I would much rather judge a man on the way he acted and spoke.

"Christ," I laughed, "maybe nobody will sell us a house!"

"The man was a fool," said Sarah.

"TwentySecond Century Housing is one of the largest real estate chains in the state."

"The man was a fool," Sarah repeated.

I still felt diminished. Maybe I *was* a jerk-off of some kind. All I knew how to do was to type—sometimes.

Then we were in a hilly area driving along.

"Where are we?" I asked.

"Topanga Canyon," Sarah answered.

"This place looks fucked."

"It's all right except for floods and fires and burned-out-neohippy types."

Then I saw the sign: APES HAVEN. It was a bar. I pulled up along-side and we got out. There was a cluster of bikes outside. Sometimes called hogs.

We went in. It was damn near full. Fellows in leather jackets. Fellows wearing dirty scarfs. Some of the fellows had scabs on their faces. Others had beards that didn't grow quite right. Most of the eyes were pale blue and round and listless. They sat very still as if they had been there for weeks.

We found a couple of stools.

"Two beers," I said, "anything in a bottle."

The barkeep trotted off.

The beers came back and Sarah and I had a hit.

Then I noticed a face thrust forward along the bar looking at us. It was a very fat round face, a touch imbecilic. It was a young man and his hair and his beard were a dirty red, but his eyebrows were pure white. His lower lip hung down as if an invisible weight were pulling at it, the lip was twisted and you saw the inner lip and it was wet and it shimmered.

"Chinaski," he said, "son of a bitch, it's CHINASKI!"

I gave a small wave, then looked straight ahead.

"One of my readers," I said to Sarah.

"Oh oh," she said.

"Chinaski," I heard a voice to my right.

"Chinaski," I heard another voice.

A whiskey appeared before me. I lifted it, "Thank you, fellows!" and I knocked it off.

"Go easy," said Sarah, "you know how you are. We'll never get out of here."

The bartender brought another whiskey. He was a little guy with dark red blotches all over his face. He looked meaner than anybody in there. He just stood there, staring at me.

"Chinaski," he said, "the world's greatest writer."

"If you insist," I said and raised the glass of whiskey. Then I passed it to Sarah who knocked it off.

She gave a little cough and set the glass down.

"I only drank that to help save you."

Then there was a little group gathering slowly behind us.

"Chinaski. Chinaski . . . Motherfuck . . . I've read all your books, ALL YOUR BOOKS! . . . I can kick your ass, Chinaski . . . Hey, Chinaski, can you still get it up? . . . Chinaski, Chinaski, can I read you one of my poems?"

I paid the barkeep and we backed off our stools and moved toward the door. Again I noticed the leather jackets and the *blandness* of the faces and the feeling that there wasn't much joy or daring in any of them. There was something totally missing in the poor fellows and something in me wrenched, for just a moment, and I felt like throwing my arms around them, consoling and embracing them like some Dostoevsky, but I knew that would finally lead nowhere except to ridicule and humiliation, for myself and for them. The world had somehow gone too far, and spontaneous kindness could never be so easy. It was something we would all have to work for once again.

And they followed us out. "Chinaski, Chinaski . . . Who's your beautiful lady? You don't deserve her, man! . . . Chinaski, come on, stay and drink with us! Be a good guy! Be like your writing, Chinaski! Don't be a prick!"

They were right, of course. We got in the car and I started the engine and we drove slowly through them as they crowded around us, slowly giving way, some of them blowing kisses, some of them giving me the finger, a few beating on the windows. We got through.

We made it to the road and drove along.

"So," said Sarah, "those are your readers?"

"That's most of them, I think."

"Don't any intelligent people read you?"

"I hope so."

We kept driving along not saying anything. Then Sarah asked, "What are you thinking about?"

"Dennis Body."

"Dennis Body? Who's that?"

"He was my only friend in grammar school. I wonder whatever happened to him."

—*Hollywood*

helping the old

• •

I was standing in line at the bank today
when the old fellow in front of me
dropped his glasses (luckily, within the
case)
and as he bent over
I saw how difficult it was for
him
and I said, "wait, let me get
them . . ."
but as I picked them up
he dropped his cane
a beautiful, black polished
cane
and I got the glasses back to him
then went for the cane
steadying the old boy
as I handed him his cane.
he didn't speak,
he just smiled at me.
then he turned
forward.

I stood behind him waiting
my turn.

• •

The place I was living in at that time did have some qualities. One of the finest was the bedroom which was painted a dark, dark blue. That dark dark blue had provided a haven for many a hangover, some of them brutal enough to almost kill a man, especially at a time when I was popping pills which people would give me without my bothering to ask what they were. Some nights I knew that if I slept I would die. I would walk around alone all night, from the bedroom to the bathroom and from the bathroom through the front room and into the kitchen. I opened and closed the refrigerator, time and time again. I turned the faucets on and off. Then I went to the bathroom and turned the faucets on and off. I flushed the toilet. I pulled at my ears. I inhaled and exhaled. Then, when the sun came up, I knew I was safe. Then I would sleep with the dark dark blue walls, healing.

Another feature of that place were the knocks of unsavory women at 3 or 4 a.m. They certainly weren't ladies of great charm, but having a foolish turn of mind, I felt that somehow they brought me adventure. The real fact of the matter was that many of them had no place else to go. And they liked the fact that there was drink and that I didn't work too hard trying to bed down with them.

Of course, after I met Sarah, this part of my lifestyle changed quite a bit.

That neighborhood around Carlton Way near Western Avenue was changing too. It had been almost all lower-class white, but political troubles in Central America and other parts of the world had brought a new type of individual to the neighborhood. The male usually was small, a dark or light brown, usually young. There were wives, children, brothers, cousins, friends. They began filling up the apartments and courts. They lived many to an apartment and I was one of the few whites left in the court complex.

The children ran up and down, up and down the court walkway.

They all seemed to be between two and seven years old. They had no bikes or toys. The wives were seldom seen. They remained inside, hidden. Many of the men also remained inside. It was not wise to let the landlord know how many people were living in a single unit. The few men seen outside were the legal renters. At least they paid the rent. How they survived was unknown. The men were small, thin, silent, unsmiling. Most sat on the porch steps in their undershirts, slumped forward a bit, occasionally smoking a cigarette. They sat on the porch steps for hours, motionless. Sometimes they purchased very old junk automobiles and the men drove them *slowly* about the neighborhood. They had no auto insurance or driver's licenses and they drove with expired license plates. Most of the cars had defective brakes. The men almost never stopped at the corner stop sign and often failed to heed red lights, but there were few accidents. Something was watching over them.

After a while the cars would break down but my new neighbors wouldn't leave them on the street. They would drive them up the walkways and park them directly outside their door. First they would work on the engine. They would take off the hood and the engine would rust in the rain. Then they would put the car on blocks and remove the wheels. They took the wheels inside and kept them there so they wouldn't be stolen at night.

While I was living there, there were two rows of cars lined up in the court, just sitting there on blocks. The men sat motionless on their porches in their undershirts. Sometimes I would nod or wave to them. They never responded. Apparently they couldn't understand or read the eviction notices and they tore them up, but I did see them studying the daily L.A. papers. They were stoic and durable because compared to where they had come from, things were now easy.

Well, no matter. My tax consultant had suggested I purchase a house, and so for me it wasn't really a matter of "white flight." Although, who knows? I had noticed that each time I had moved in Los Angeles over the years, each move had always been to the North and to the West.

Finally, after a few weeks of house hunting, we found the one. After the down payment the monthly payments came to $789.81. There was a huge hedge in front on the street and the yard was also in front so the house sat way back on the lot. It looked like a damned good place to hide. There was even a stairway, an *upstairs* with a bedroom, bathroom and what was to become my typing room. And there was an old desk left in there, a huge ugly old thing. Now, after decades, I was a writer with a desk. Yes, I felt the fear, the fear of becoming like *them*. Worse, I had an assignment to write a screenplay. Was I doomed and damned, was I about to be sucked dry? I didn't feel it would be that way. But does anybody, ever?

Sarah and I moved our few possessions in.

The big moment came. I sat the typewriter down on the desk and I put a piece of paper in there and I hit the keys. The typewriter still worked. And there was plenty of room for an ashtray, the radio and the bottle. Don't let anybody tell you different. Life begins at 65.

—*Hollywood*

air and light and time and space

"—you know, I've either had a family, a job, something
has always been in the
way
but now
I've sold my house, I've found this
place, a large studio, you should see the *space* and
the *light*.
for the first time in my life I'm going to have a place and the time to
create."

no baby, if you're going to create
you're going to create whether you work
16 hours a day in a coal mine
or
you're going to create in a small room with 3 children
while you're on
welfare,
you're going to create with part of your mind and your
body blown
away,

you're going to create blind
crippled
demented,
you're going to create with a cat crawling up your
back while
the whole city trembles in earthquake, bombardment,
flood and fire.

baby, air and light and time and space
have nothing to do with it
and don't create anything
except maybe a longer life to find
new excuses
for.

• •

That night without Jon listening downstairs, the screenplay began to move. I was writing about a young man who wanted to write and drink but most of his success was with the bottle. The young man had been me. While the time had not been an unhappy time, it had been mostly a time of void and waiting. As I typed along, the characters in a certain bar returned to me. I saw each face again, the bodies, heard the voices, the conversations. There was one particular bar that had a certain deathly charm. I focused on that, relived the barroom fights with the bartender. I had not been a good fighter. To begin with my hands were too small and I was underfed, grossly underfed. But I had a certain amount of guts and I took a punch very well. My main problem during a fight was that I couldn't truly get angry, even when it seemed my life was at stake. It was all play-acting with me. It mattered and it didn't. Fighting the bartender was something to do and it pleased the patrons who were a clubby little group. I was the outsider. There is something to be said for drinking—all those fights would have killed me had I been sober but being drunk it was as if the body turned to rubber and the head to cement. Sprained wrists, puffed lips and battered kneecaps were about all I came up with the next day. Also, knots on the head from falling. How all this could become a screenplay, I didn't know. I only knew that it was the only part of my life I hadn't written much about. I believe that I was sane at that time, as sane as anybody. And I knew that there was a whole civilization of lost souls that lived in and off bars, daily, nightly and forever, until they died. I had never read about this civilization so I decided to write about it, the way I remembered it. The good old typer clicked along.

The next day about noon the phone rang. It was Jon.

"I have found a place. François is with me. It's beautiful, it has *two* kitchens and the rent is nothing, really nothing . . . "

"Where are you located?"

"We're in the ghetto in Venice. Brooks Avenue. All blacks. The streets are war and destruction. It's beautiful!"

"Oh?"

"You must come see the place!"

"When?"

"Today!"

"I don't know."

"Oh, you wouldn't want to miss this! There are people living under our house. We can hear them under there, talking and playing their radio! There are gangs everywhere! There's a large hotel somebody built down here. But nobody paid their rent. They boarded the place up, cut off the electricity, the water, the gas. But people still live there. THIS IS A WAR ZONE! The police do not come in here, it's like a separate state with its own rules. I love it! You must visit us!"

"How do I get there?"

Jon gave me the instructions, then hung up.

I found Sarah.

"Listen, I've got to go see Jon and François."

"Hey, I'm coming too!"

"No, you can't. It's in the ghetto in Venice."

"Oh, the ghetto! I wouldn't miss that for anything!"

"Look, do me a favor: please *don't* come along!"

"What? Do you think I would let you go down there all by *yourself*?"

I got my blade, put my money in my shoes. "O.K.," I said. . . .

• • •

We drove slowly into the Venice ghetto. It was not true that it was all black. There were some Latinos on the outskirts. I noted a group of 7 or 8 young Mexican men standing around and leaning against an old car. Most of the men were in their undershirts or had their shirts off. I drove slowly past, not staring, just taking it in. They didn't seem to be doing much. Just waiting. Ready and waiting. Actually, they were probably just bored. They looked like fine fellows. And they didn't look worried worth a shit.

Then we got to black turf. Right away, the streets were cluttered: a left shoe, an orange shirt, an old purse . . . a rotted grapefruit . . . another left shoe . . . a pair of bluejeans . . . a rubber tire . . .

I had to steer through the stuff. Two young blacks about 11 years old stared at us from bicycles. It was pure, perfect hate. I could feel it. Poor blacks hated. Poor whites hated. It was only when blacks got money and whites got money that they mixed. Some whites loved blacks. Very few, if any, blacks loved whites. They were still getting even. Maybe they never would. In a capitalistic society the losers slaved for the winners and you have to have more losers than winners. What did I think? I knew politics would never solve it and there wasn't enough time left to get lucky.

We drove on until we found the address, parked the car, got out, knocked.

A little window slid open and there was an eye looking at us.

"Ah, Hank and Sarah!"

The door opened, shut, and we were inside.

I walked to the window and looked out.

"What are you doing?" asked Jon.

"Just want to check the car now and then . . . "

"Oh, yes, come look, I'll show you the two kitchens!"

Sure enough there were two kitchens, a stove in each, a refrigerator in each, a sink in each.

"This used to be two places. It's been turned into one."

"Nice," said Sarah, "you can cook in one kitchen and François can cook in the other . . . "

"Right now we are living mostly on eggs. We have chickens, they lay many eggs . . . "

"Christ, Jon, is it that bad?"

"No, not really. We figure we are here for a long stand. We need most of our money for wine and cigars. How's the screenplay coming?"

"I'm happy to say that there are quite a few pages. Only sometimes I don't know about CAMERA, ZOOM IN, PAN IN . . . all that crap . . . "

"Don't worry, I'll take care of that."

"Where's François?" asked Sarah.

"Ah, he's in the other room . . . come . . . "

We went in and there was François spinning his little roulette wheel. When he drank his nose became very red, like a cartoon drunk. Also, the more he drank the more depressed he became. He was sucking on a wet half-finished cigar. He managed a few sad puffs. There was an almost empty bottle of wine nearby.

"Shit," he said, "I am now sixty thousand dollars in the hole and I am drinking this cheap wine of Jon's which he claims is good stuff but it is pure crap. He pays a dollar and thirty-five cents a bottle. My stomach is like a balloon full of piss! I am sixty thousand dollars in the hole and I have no visible means of employment I must . . . kill . . . myself. . . "

"Come on, François," said Jon, "let's show our friends the chickens . . . "

"The chickens! HEGGS! All the time we eat HEGGS! Nothing but HEGGS! Poop, poop, poop! The chickens poop HEGGS! All day, all night long my job is to save the chickens from the young black boys! All the time the young black boys climb the fence and run at the chicken coop! I hit them with a long stick, I say, 'You muthafuckas you stay away from my chickens which poop the HEGGS!' I cannot think, I cannot think of my own life or my own death, I am always chasing these young black boys with the long stick! Jon, I need more wine, another cigar!"

He gave the wheel another spin.

It was more bad news. The system was failing.

"You see, in France they only have one zero for the house! Here in America they have a zero and a double zero for the house! THEY TAKE BOTH YOUR BALLS! WHY? Come on, I'll show you the chickens. . . ."

We walked into the yard and there were the chickens and the chicken coop. François had built it himself. He was good that way. He had a real talent for that. Only he hadn't used chicken wire. There were bars. And locks on each door.

"I give roll call each night. 'Cecile, you there?' 'Cluck, cluck,' she answers. 'Bernadette, you there?' 'Cluck, cluck,' she answers. And so on. 'Nicole?' I asked one night. She did not cluck. Can you believe it, through all the bars and all the locks they got Nicole! They have taken her out already! Nicole is gone, gone forever! Jon, Jon, I need more wine!"

We went back in and sat down and the new wine poured. Jon gave François a new cigar.

"If I can have my cigar when I want it," said François, "I can live."

We drank a while, then Sarah asked, "Listen, Jon is your landlord black?"

"Oh, yes . . . "

"Didn't he ask why you were renting here?"

"Yes . . . "

"And what did you tell him?"

"I told him that we were filmmakers and actors from France."

"And he said?"

"He said, 'oh.'"

"Anything else?"

"Yes, he said, 'well it's *your* ass!'"

We drank for some time making small talk.

Now and then I got up and went to the window to see if the car was still there.

As we drank on I began to feel guilty about the whole thing.

"Listen, Jon, let me give you the screenplay money back. I've driven you to the wall. This is terrible. . . ."

"No, I want you to do this screenplay. It *will* become a movie, I promise you . . . "

"All right, god damn it . . . "

We drank a bit more.

Then Jon said, "Look . . . "

Through a hole in the wall where we were sitting could be seen a hand, a black hand. It was wriggling through the broken plaster, fingers gripping, moving. It was like a small dark animal.

"GO AWAY," yelled François. "GO AWAY MURDERER OF NICOLE! YOU HAVE LEFT A HOLE IN MY HEART FOREVER! GO AWAY!"

The hand did not go away.

François walked over to the wall and the hand.

"I tell you now, go away. I only wish to smoke my cigar and drink my wine in peace. You disturb my sight! I cannot feel right with you grabbing and looking at me through your poor black fingers!"

The hand did not go away.

"ALL RIGHT THEN!"

The stick was right there. With one demonic move François picked up the long stick and began whacking it against the wall, again and again and again . . .

"CHICKEN KILLER, YOU HAVE WOUNDED MY HEART FOREVER!"

The sound was deafening. Then François stopped.

The hand was gone.

François sat back down.

"Shit, Jon, my cigar is out! Why don't you buy better cigars, Jon?"

"Listen, Jon," I said, "we've got to be going now . . . "

"Oh, come now . . . please . . . the night is just *beginning!* You've seen nothing yet . . . "

"We've got to be going . . . I have more work to do on the screenplay . . . "

"Oh . . . in that case . . . "

Back at the house I went upstairs and did work on the screenplay but strangely or maybe not so strangely my past life hardly seemed as strange or wild or as mad as what was occurring now.

—*HOLLYWOOD*

car wash

• •

got out, fellow said, "hey!" walked toward
me, we shook hands, he slipped me 2 red
tickets for free car washes, "find you later,"
I told him, walked on through to waiting
area with wife, we sat on outside bench.
black fellow with a limp came up, said,
"hey, man, how's it going?"
I answered, "fine, bro, you makin' it?"

"no problem," he said, then walked off to
dry down a Caddy.
"these people know you?" my wife asked.
"no."
"how come they talk to you?"
"they like me, people have always liked me,
it's my cross."
then our car was finished, fellow flipped
his rag at me, we got up, got to the
car, I slipped him a buck, we got in, I
started the engine, the foreman walked
up, big guy with dark shades, huge guy,
he smiled a big one, "good to see you,
man!"
I smiled back, "thanks, but it's your party,
man!"
I pulled out into traffic, "they know you,"
said my wife.
"sure," I said, "I've been there."

confession

● ●

waiting for death
like a cat
that will jump on the
bed

I am so very sorry for
my wife

she will see this
stiff
white
body

shake it once, then
maybe
again:

"Hank!"

Hank won't
answer.

it's not my death that
worries me, it's my wife
left with this
pile of
nothing.

I want to
let her know
though
that all the nights
sleeping
beside her

even the useless
arguments
were things
ever splendid

and the hard
words
I ever feared to
say
can now be
said:

I love
you.

• •

We were a little late for the party but there still weren't very many people there. Victor Norman was seated a few tables away from ours. After Sarah and I were seated the waiter came with our wine. White wine. Well, it was free.

I drained my glass and nodded the waiter over for a refill.

I noticed Victor peering at me.

People were gradually arriving. I saw the famous actor with the perpetual tan. I'd heard that he went to almost every Hollywood party, everywhere.

Then Sarah gave me the elbow. It was Jim Serry, the old drug guru of the 60's. He too went to many of the parties. He looked tired, sad, drained. I felt sorry for him. He went from table to table. Then he was at ours. Sarah gave a delighted laugh. She was a child of the 60's. I shook hands with him.

"Hi, baby," I said.

Quickly it began to get crowded. I didn't know most of the people. I kept waving the waiter in for more wine. He then brought a full bottle, plopped it down.

"When you finish that, I'll bring another."

"Thank you, buster . . . "

Sarah had wrapped a little present for Harry Friedman. I had it in my lap.

Jon arrived and sat at our table.

"I'm glad you and Sarah could make it," he said. "Look, it's filling up, this place is full of gangsters and killers, the worst!"

Jon loved it. He had some imagination. It helped get him through the days and the nights.

Then a very important looking man walked in. I heard some applause.

I leaped up with the birthday gift. I moved toward him.

"Mr. Friedman, happy . . . "

Jon rushed up and grabbed me from behind. He pulled me back to the table.

"No! No! That isn't Friedman! That's Fischman!"

"Oh . . . "

I sat back down.

I noticed Victor Norman staring at me. I figured he would let up in a while. When I looked again, Victor was still staring. He was looking at me as if he couldn't believe his eyes.

"All right, Victor," I said loudly, "so I shit my pants! Want to make a World War out of it?"

He glanced away.

I got up and looked for the men's room.

Coming out I got lost and went into the kitchen. There was a busboy there smoking a cigarette. I reached into my wallet and got a ten. I gave him the ten. I put it in his shirt pocket.

"I can't take this, sir."

"Why not?"

"I just can't."

"Everybody else gets tipped. Why not the busboy? I always wanted to be a busboy."

I walked off, found the main room again and the table.

When I sat down Sarah leaned over and whispered, "Victor Norman came over while you were gone. He says that it's very nice of you that you haven't said anything about his writing."

"I've been good, haven't I, Sarah?"

"Yes."

"Haven't I been a good boy?"

"Yes."

I looked over at Victor Norman, got his attention. I gave a little nod, winked.

Just then the real Harry Friedman walked in. Some rose to their feet and applauded. Others looked bored.

Friedman sat down at his table and the food was served. Pasta. The pasta came around. Harry Friedman got his and went right in. He looked like an eater. He was wide, yes. He was in an old suit, his shoes were scuffed. He had a large head, big cheeks. He shoved that pasta into those cheeks. He had large round eyes and the eyes were sad and full of suspicion. Alas, to live in the world! There was a button missing from his wrinkled white shirt, near his belly, and the belly pushed out. He looked like a big baby who had some-how gotten loose, grown real fast, and almost turned into a man. There was charm there but it could be dangerous to believe in it—it would be used against you. No necktie. Happy birthday, Harry Friedman!

A young lady came in dressed as a cop. She walked right up to Fried-man's table.

"YOU ARE UNDER ARREST!" she screamed.

Harry Friedman stopped eating and smiled. His lips were wet from the pasta.

Then the lady cop took off her coat and then her blouse. She had huge breasts. She shook her breasts under Harry Friedman's nose.

"YOU ARE UNDER ARREST!" she screamed.

Everybody applauded. I don't know why they applauded.

Then Friedman motioned the lady cop to bend over. She bent close and he whispered something into her ear. Nobody knew what it was.

You take me to your place. We'll see what happens?

You forgot your club. I'll take care of that?

You come see me. I'll get you in the movies?

The lady cop put her blouse back on, her coat back on, and then she was gone.

People came up to Friedman's table and said little things to him. He looked at them as if he didn't know who they were. Soon he was finished eating and was drinking wine. He did well with the wine. I liked that.

He really went for the wine. After a while he went around from table to table, bending over, talking to people.

"Christ," I said to Sarah, "look at that!"

"What?"

"He's got a little piece of pasta hanging out of one side of his mouth and nobody is telling him about it. It's just *hanging* there!"

"I see it! I see it!" said Jon.

Harry Friedman kept walking from table to table, bending over, talk-ing. Nobody told him.

Finally, he got closer. He was a table or so away from ours when I stood up and walked over to him.

"Mr. Friedman," I said.

He looked at me from that big monster baby face.

"Yes?"

"Hold still!"

I reached out, got hold of the end of the pasta and yanked. It came away.

"You been walkin' around with that danglin'. I couldn't stand it any-more."

"Thank you," he said.

I went back to our table.

"Well, well," asked Jon, "what do you think of him?"

"I think he's delightful."

"I told you. I haven't met anybody like him since Lido Mamin."

"Anyhow," said Sarah, "it was nice of you to clean that pasta off his face since nobody else had the nerve to. It was very nice of you."

"Thank you, I am a very nice guy, really."

"Oh yes? What else have you done that is nice lately?"

Our wine bottle was empty. I got the attention of the waiter. He scowled at me and moved forward with another bottle.

And I couldn't think of anything nice that I had done. Lately.

—HOLLYWOOD

fan letter

• •

I been readin' you for a long time now,
I just put Billy Boy to bed,
he got 7 mean ticks from somewhere,
I got 2,
my husband, Benny, he got 3.
some of us love bugs, others hate
them.
Benny writes poems.
he was in the same magazine as you
once.
Benny is the world's greatest writer
but he got this temper.
he gave a readin' once and somebody
laughed at one of his serious poems
and Benny took his thing out right
there
and pissed on stage.
he says you write good but that you

couldn't carry his balls in a paper
bag.
anyhow, I made a BIG POT OF MARMALADE
tonight,
we all just LOVE marmalade here.
Benny lost his job yesterday, he told his
boss to stick it up his ass
but I still got my job down at the
manicure shop.
you know fags come in to get their nails
done?
you aren't a fag, are you, Mr.
Chinaski?
anyhow, I just felt like writing you.
your books are read and read around
here.
Benny says you're an old fart, you
write pretty good but that you
couldn't carry his balls in a
paper sack.
do you like bugs, Mr. Chinaski?
I think the marmalade is cool enough to
eat now.
so goodbye.

    Dora

be kind

· ·

we are always asked
to understand the other person's
viewpoint
no matter how

out-dated
foolish or
obnoxious.

one is asked
to view
their total error
their life-waste
with
kindliness,
especially if they are
aged.

but age is the total of
our doing.
they have aged
badly
because they have
lived
out of focus,
they have refused to
see.

not their fault?

whose fault?
mine?

I am asked to hide
my viewpoint
from them
for fear of their
fear.

age is no crime

but the shame
of a deliberately

wasted
life

among so many
deliberately
wasted
lives

is.

● ●

I was there at 8:50 a.m. I parked and waited for Jon. He rolled up at 8:55 a.m. I got out and walked over to Jon's car.

"Good morning, Jon . . . "

"Hello, Hank . . . How are you?"

"Fine. Listen, what happened to the hunger strike?"

"Oh, I am still on that. But more important is the cutting off of the parts."

Jon had the Black and Decker with him. It was wrapped in a dark green towel. We walked into the Firepower building together. The elevator took us up to the lawyer's office. Neeli Zutnick. The receptionist was expecting our arrival. "Please go right in," she said.

Neeli Zutnick was waiting. He rose from behind his desk and shook hands with us. Then he returned, sat down behind his desk. "Would you gentleman care for some coffee?" he asked.

"No," said Jon.

"I'll have some," I said.

Zutnick hit the intercom button. "Rose? Rose, my dear . . . one coffee, please . . . " He looked at me, "Cream and sugar?"

"Black."

"Black. Thank you, Rose . . . Now, gentlemen . . . "

"Where's Friedman?" Jon asked.

"Mr. Friedman has given me full instructions. Now . . . "

"Where's your plug?" Jon asked.

"Plug?"

"For this . . . " Jon pulled the towel away revealing the Black and Decker.

"Please, Mr. Pinchot . . . "

"Where's the plug? Never mind, I see it . . . "

Jon walked over and plugged the Black and Decker into the wall.

"You must understand," said Zutnick, "that if I had known you were going to bring that instrument I would have arranged to turn off the electricity."

"That's all right," said Jon.

"There's no need for that instrument," said Zutnick.

"I hope not. It's just . . . in case . . . "

Rose entered with my coffee. Jon pressed the button on the Black and Decker. The blade sprang into action and began to hum.

Rose nervously tilted the coffee cup just a bit . . . just enough to spill a touch of it on her dress. It was a nice red dress and Rose, a heavy girl, filled it nicely.

"Wow! That *scared* me!"

"I'm sorry," Jon said, "I was just . . . testing . . . "

"Who gets the coffee?"

"I do," I told her, "thank you."

Rose brought the coffee over to me. I needed it.

Rose exited, giving us a worried look over her shoulder.

"Both Mr. Friedman and Mr. Fischman have expressed dismay at your present state of mind . . . "

"Cut the shit, Zutnick! Either I get the release or the first piece of my flesh will be deposited . . . *there!*"

Jon tapped the center of Zutnick's desk with the end of the Black and Decker.

"Now, Mr. Pinchot, there is no need . . . "

"THERE IS A NEED! AND YOU'RE RUNNING OUT OF TIME! I WANT THAT RELEASE! NOW!"

Zutnick looked at me. "How is your coffee, Mr. Chinaski?"

Jon squeezed the trigger of the Black and Decker and held up his left hand, little finger extended. He waved the Black and Decker about as the blade furiously worked away.

"NOW!"

"VERY WELL!" yelled Zutnick.

Jon took his finger off the trigger.

Zutnick opened the top drawer of his desk and pulled out two legal-sized sheets of paper. He slid them toward Jon. Jon walked over, picked them up, sat back down, began reading.

"Mr. Zutnick," I asked, "can I have another cup of coffee?"

Zutnick glared at me, hit the intercom.

"Another cup of coffee, Rose. Black . . . "

"Like in Black and Decker," I said.

"Mr. Chinaski, that isn't funny."

Jon continued to read.

My coffee arrived.

"Thank you, Rose . . . "

Jon continued to read as we waited. The Black and Decker lay across his lap.

Then Jon said, "No, this won't do . . . "

"WHAT?" said Zutnick. "THAT IS A COMPLETE RELEASE!"

"All of clause 'e' must be deleted. It contains too many ambiguities."

"May I see those papers?" asked Zutnick.

"Certainly . . . "

Jon placed them on the blade of the Black and Decker and passed them over to Zutnick. Zutnick took them off the blade with some disgust. He began reading clause 'e.'

"I see nothing wrong here . . . "

"Delete it . . . "

"Do you really intend to cut off one of your fingers?"

"Yes. I may even cut off one of yours."

"Is that a threat? Are you threatening me?"

"Consider this: I have nothing to lose here. Only you have."

"A contract signed under these conditions can be considered invalid."

"You are making me sick, Zutnick! Eliminate clause 'e' or my finger goes! NOW!"

Jon hit the button. The Black and Decker sprang into action again. Jon Pinchot stuck out his little finger, left hand.

"STOP!" screamed Zutnick.

Jon stopped.

Zutnick was on the intercom. "ROSE! I need you . . . "

Rose entered. "More coffee for the gentleman?"

"No, Rose. I want this entire contract revised and run out again, but eliminate clause 'e,' then return it to me."

"Yes, Mr. Zutnick."

We all just sat a while then.

Then Zutnick said, "You can unplug that thing now."

"Not yet," said Jon. "Not until everything is finalized . . . "

"Do you really have another producer for this thing?"

"Of course . . . "

"Do you mind telling me who?"

"Of course not. Hal Edleman. Friedman knows that."

Zutnick blinked. Edleman was money. He knew the name.

"I've read the screenplay. It seems very . . . crude . . . to me."

"Have you read any other of Mr. Chinaski's works?" Jon asked.

"No. But my daughter has. She read his book of stories, *Cesspool Dreams.*"

"And?"

"She hated it."

Rose was back with the new contract. She handed it to Zutnick. Zutnick gave it a glance, stood up and walked it over to Jon.

Jon reread the whole thing.

"Very well."

He walked it over to the desk, bent over, signed it. Zutnick signed for Friedman and Fischman. It was done. One copy each.

Then Zutnick laughed. He looked relieved.

"The practice of law gets stranger all the time . . . ."

Jon unplugged the Black and Decker. Zutnick walked to a small cabinet on the wall, opened it, pulled out a bottle, 3 glasses. He sat them on his desk, poured around.

"To the deal, gentlemen . . . "

"To the deal . . . " said Jon.

"To the deal," the writer chimed in.

We drank them down. It was brandy. And we had the movie again.

I walked Jon to his car. He threw the Black and Decker into the back seat, then climbed into the front.

"Jon," I asked from the sidewalk, "can I try you with the big question?"

"Sure."

"You can tell me the truth about the Black and Decker. It will never get further than this. Were you really going to do it?"

"Of course . . . "

"But the other parts to follow? The other pieces. Were you going to do that?"

"Of course. Once you begin such a thing there is no stopping."

"You've got guts, my man . . . "

"It is nothing. Now I am hungry."

"Can I buy you breakfast?"

"Well, all right . . . I know just the place . . . Get into your car and follow me . . . "

"All right."

I followed Jon through Hollywood, the light and the shadows of Alfred Hitchcock, Laurel and Hardy, Clark Gable, Gloria Swanson, Mickey Mouse and Humphrey Bogart, falling all around us.

—*HOLLYWOOD*

trashcan lives

• •

the wind blows hard tonight
and it's a cold wind
and I think about
the boys on the row.
I hope some of them have a bottle
of red.

it's when you're on the row
that you notice that
everything
is owned
and that there are locks on
everything.
this is the way a democracy
works:

you get what you can,
try to keep that
and add to it
if possible.

this is the way a dictatorship
works too
only they either enslave or
destroy their
derelicts.

we just forget
ours.

in either case
it's a hard
cold
wind.

• •

The shooting was to start in Culver City. The bar was there and the hotel with my room. The next part of the shooting was to be done in the Alvarado Street district, where the apartment of the female lead was located.

Then there was a bar to be used near 6th Street and Vermont. But the first shots were to be in Culver City.

Jon took us up to see the hotel. It looked authentic. The barflies lived there. The bar was downstairs. We stood and looked at it.

"How do you like it?" Jon asked.

"It's great. But I've lived in worse places."

"I know," said Sarah, "I've seen them."

Then we walked up to the room.

"Here it is. Look familiar?"

It was painted grey as so many of those places were. The torn shades. The table and the chair. The refrigerator thick with coats of dirt. And the poor sagging bed.

"It's perfect, Jon. It's *the* room."

I was a little sad that I wasn't young and doing it all over again, drinking and fighting and playing with words. When you're young you can really take a battering. Food didn't matter. What mattered was drinking and sitting at the machine. I must have been crazy but there are many kinds of crazy and some are quite delightful. I starved so that I could have time to write. That just isn't done much anymore. Looking at that table I saw myself sitting there again. I'd been crazy and I knew it and I didn't care.

"Let's go down and check the bar again . . . "

We went down. The barflies who were to be in the movie were sitting there. They were drinking.

"Come on, Sarah, let's grab a stool. See you later, Jon . . . "

The bartender introduced us to the barflies. There was Big Monster and Little Monster, The Creeper, Buffo, Doghead, Lady Lila, Freestroke, Clara and others.

Sarah asked The Creeper what he was drinking. "It looks good," she said.

"This is a Cape Cod, cranberry juice and vodka."

"I'll have a Cape Cod," Sarah told the barkeep, Cowboy Cal.

"Vodka seven," I told the Cowboy.

We had a few. Big Monster told me a story about how they had all got in a fight with the cops. Quite interesting. And I knew by the way he told it that it was the truth.

Then there was lunch call for the actors and crew. The barflies just stayed in there.

"We'd better eat," said Sarah.

We went out behind and to the east of the hotel. A large bench was set up. The extras, technicians, hands and so forth were already eating. The food looked good. Jon met us out there. We got our servings at the wagon and followed Jon down to the end of the table. As we walked along, Jon paused. There was a man eating by himself. Jon introduced us.

"This is Lance Edwards . . . "

Edwards gave a slight nod and went back to his steak.

We sat down at the end of the table. Edwards was one of the co-producers.

"This Edwards acts like a prick," I said.

"Oh," said Jon, "he's very bashful. He's one of the guys that Friedman was trying to get rid of."

"Maybe Friedman was right."

"Hank," said Sarah, "you don't even know the man."

I was working at my beer.

"Eat your food," said Sarah.

Sarah was going to add ten years to my life, for better or worse.

"We are going to shoot a scene with Jack in the room. You ought to come watch it."

"After we finish eating we're going back to the bar. When you're ready to shoot, have somebody come get us."

"All right," said Jon.

After we ate we walked around the other side of the hotel, checking it out. Jon was with us. There were several trailers parked along the street. We saw Jack's Rolls-Royce. And next to it was a large silver trailer. There was a sign on the door: JACK BLEDSOE.

"Look," said Jon, "he has a periscope sticking out of the roof so he can see who's coming . . ."

"Jesus . . ."

"Listen, I've got to set things up . . ."

"All right . . . See you . . ."

Funny thing about Jon. His French accent was slipping away as he spoke only English here in America. It was a little sad.

Then the door of Jack's trailer opened. It was Jack.

"Hey, come on in!"

We went up the steps. There was a tv on. A young girl was lying in a bunk watching the tv.

"This is Cleo. I bought her a bike. We ride together."

There was a fellow sitting at the end.

"This is my brother, Doug . . ."

I moved toward Doug, did a little shadow boxing in front of him. He didn't say anything. He just stared. Cool number. Good. I liked cool numbers.

"Got anything to drink?" I asked Jack.

"Sure . . ."

Jack found some whiskey, poured me a whiskey and water.

"Thanks . . . "

"You care for some?" he asked Sarah.

"Thanks," she said, "I don't like to mix drinks."

"She's on Cape Cods," I said.

"Oh . . . "

Sarah and I sat down. The whiskey was good.

"I like this place," I said.

"Stay as long as you like," said Jack.

"Maybe we'll stay forever . . . "

Jack gave me his famous smile.

"Your brother doesn't say much, does he?"

"No, he doesn't."

"A cool number."

"Yeah."

"Well, Jack, you memorized your lines?"

"I never look at my lines until right before the shooting."

"Great. Well, listen, we've got to be going."

"I know you can do it, Jack," said Sarah, "we're glad you got the lead."

"Thanks . . . "

Back at the bar the barflies were still there and they didn't look any drunker. It took a lot to buzz a pro.

Sarah had another Cape Cod. I went back to the Vodka seven.

We drank and there were more stories. I even told one. Maybe an hour went by. Then I looked up and there was Jack standing looking over the swinging doors in the entrance. I could just see his head.

"Hey, Jack," I yelled, "come on in and have a drink!"

"No, Hank, we're going to shoot now. Why don't you come up and watch?"

"Be right there, baby . . . "

We ordered up another pair of drinks. We were working on them when Jon walked in.

"We're going to shoot now," he said.

"All right," said Sarah.

"All right," I said.

We finished our drinks and I got a couple of bottles of beer to take with us.

We followed Jon up the stairway and into the room. Cables everywhere. Technicians were moving about.

"I'll bet they could shoot a movie with about one-third of these fucking people."

"That's what Friedman says."

"Friedman is sometimes right."

"All right," said Jon, "we're just about ready. We've had a few dry runs. Now we shoot. You," he said to me, "stand in this corner. You can watch from here and not be in the scene."

Sarah moved back there with me.

"SILENCE!" screamed Jon's assistant director, "WE'RE GETTING READY TO ROLL!"

It became very quiet.

Then from Jon: "CAMERA! ACTION!"

The door to the room opened and Jack Bledsoe weaved in. Shit, it was the young Chinaski! It was me! I felt a tender aching within me. Youth, you son of a bitch, where did you go?

I wanted to be the young drunk again. I wanted to be Jack Bledsoe. But I was just the old guy in the corner, sucking on a beer.

Bledsoe weaved to the window by the table. He pulled up the tattered shade. He did a little shadow boxing, a smile on his face. Then he sat down at the table, found a pencil and a piece of paper. He sat there a while, then pulled the cork from a wine bottle, had a hit, lit a cigarette. He turned on the radio and lucked into Mozart.

He began writing on that piece of paper with the pencil as the scene faded . . .

He had it. He had it the way it was, whether it meant anything or not, he had it the way it was.

I walked up to Jack, shook his hand.

"Did I get it?" he asked.

"You got it," I said . . .

Down at the bar, the barflies were still at it and they looked about the same.

Sarah went back to her Cape Cods and I went the Vodka seven route. We heard more stories which were very very good. But there was a sadness in the air because after the movie was shot the bar and hotel were going to be torn down to further some commercial purpose. Some of the regulars had lived in the hotel for decades. Others lived in a deserted train station nearby and action was being taken to remove them from there. So it was heavy sad drinking.

Sarah said finally, "We've got to get home and feed the cats."

Drinking could wait.

Hollywood could wait.

The cats could not wait.

I agreed.

We said our goodbyes to the barflies and made it to the car. I wasn't worried about driving. Something about seeing young Chinaski in that old hotel room had steadied me. Son of a bitch, I had been a hell of a young bull. Really a top-notch fuck-up.

Sarah was worried about the future of the barflies. I didn't like it either. On the other hand I couldn't see them sitting around our front room, drinking and telling their stories. Sometimes charm lessens when it gets too close to reality. And how many brothers can you keep?

I drove on in. We got there.

The cats were waiting.

Sarah got down and cleaned their bowls and I opened the cans.

Simplicity, that's what was needed.

We went upstairs, washed, changed, made ready for bed.

"What are those poor people going to do?" asked Sarah.

"I know. I know . . . "

Then it was time for sleep. I went downstairs for a last look, came back up. Sarah was asleep. I turned out the light. We slept. Having seen the movie made that afternoon we were now somehow different, we would never think or talk quite the same. We now knew something more but what it was seemed very vague and even perhaps a bit disagreeable.

—*HOLLYWOOD*

poetry contest

• •

send as many poems as you wish, only
keep each to a maximum of ten lines.
no limit as to style or content
although we prefer poems of
affirmation.
double space
with your name and address in the
upper left hand
corner.
editors not responsible for
manuscripts
without an s.a.s.e.
every effort
will be made to
judge all works within 90
days.
after careful screening
the final choices will be made by
Elly May Moody,
general editor in charge.
please enclose ten dollars for
each poem
submitted.
a final grand prize of
seventy-five dollars will
be awarded the winner
of the
Elly May Moody Golden Poetry
Award,
along with a scroll
signed by
Elly May Moody.
there will also be 2nd, 3rd and
4th prize scrolls
also signed by

Elly May Moody.
all decisions will be
final.
the prize winners will
appear in the Spring issue of
The Heart of Heaven.
prize winners will also receive
one copy of the magazine
along with
Elly May Moody's
latest collection of
poetry,
*The Place Where Winter
Died.*

• •

The bathtub scene was a simple one. Francine was to sit in the tub and Jack Bledsoe was to sit with his back against it, there on the floor, while Francine sat in the water talking about various things, mainly about a killer who lived there in her building, now on parole. He was shacked up with an old woman and beat her continually. One could hear the killer and his lady ranting and cursing through the walls.

Jon Pinchot had asked me to write the sound of people cursing through the walls and I had given him several pages of dialog. Basically, that had been the most enjoyable part of writing the screenplay.

Oftentimes in those roominghouses and cheap apartments there was nothing to do when you were broke and starving and down to the last bottle. There was nothing to do but listen to those wild arguments. It made you realize that you weren't the only one who was more than discouraged with the world, you weren't the only one moving toward madness.

We couldn't watch the bathtub scene because there just wasn't space enough in there, so Sarah and I waited in the front room of the apartment with its kitchen off to the side. Actually, over 30 years ago I had briefly lived in that same building on Alvarado Street with the lady I was writing the screenplay about. Strange and chilling indeed. "Everything that goes around comes around." In one way or another. And after 30 years the place looked just about the same. Only the people I'd known had all died. And the lady had died 3 decades ago and there I was sitting drinking a beer in that same building full of cameras and sound and crew. Well, I'd die too, soon enough. Pour one for me.

They were cooking food in the little kitchen and the refrigerator was full of beers. I made a few trips in there. Sarah found people to talk to. She was lucky. Every time somebody spoke to me I felt like diving out a window or taking the elevator down. People just weren't interesting. Maybe they weren't supposed to be. But animals, birds, even insects were. I couldn't understand it.

Jon Pinchot was still one day ahead of the shooting schedule and I was damned glad for that. It kept Firepower off our backs. The big boys didn't come around. They had their spies, of course. I could pick them out.

Some of the crew had books of mine. They asked for autographs. The books they had were curious ones. That is, I didn't consider them my best. (My best book is always the last one that I have written.) Some of them had a book of my early dirty stories, *Jacking-Off the Devil*. A few had books of poems, *Mozart In the Fig Tree* and *Would You Let This Man Babysit Your 4-Year-Old Daughter?* Also, *The Bar Latrine Is My Chapel*.

The day wafted on, peacefully but listlessly.

Some bathtub scene, I thought. Francine must be fully cleansed by now.

Then Jon Pinchot just about ran into the room. He looked undone. Even his zipper was only halfway up. He was uncombed. His eyes looked wild and drained at the same time.

"My god!" he said, "here you are!"

"How's it going?"

He leaned over and whispered into my ear. "It's awful, it's maddening! Francine is worried that her tits might show above the water! She keeps asking 'Do my tits show?'"

"What's a little titty?"

Jon leaned closer. "She's not as young as she'd like to be . . . And Hyans hates the lighting . . . He can't abide the lighting and he's drinking more than ever . . . "

Hyans was the cameraman. He'd won damn near every award and prize in the business, one of the best cameramen alive, but like most good souls he liked a drink now and then.

Jon went on, whispering frantically: "And Jack, he can't get this one line right. We have to cut again and again. There is something about the line that bothers him and he gets this silly smile on his face when he says it."

"What's the line?"

"The line is, 'He must masturbate his parole officer when he comes around.'"

"All right, try, 'He must jack-off his parole officer when he comes around.'"

"Good, thank you! THIS IS GOING TO BE THE NINETEENTH TAKE!"

"My god," I said.

"Wish me luck . . . "

"Luck. . . ."

Jon was out of the room then. Sarah walked over.

"What's wrong?"

"Nineteenth take. Francine is afraid to show her tits, Jack can't say his line and Hyans doesn't like the lighting . . . "

"Francine needs a drink," she said, "it will loosen her up."

"Hyans doesn't need a drink."

"I know. And Jack will be able to say his line when Francine loosens up."

"Maybe."

Just then Francine walked into the room. She looked totally lost, completely out of it. She was in a bathrobe, had a towel around her head.

"I'm going to tell her," Sarah said.

She walked over to Francine and spoke quietly to her. Francine listened. She gave a little nod, then walked into the bedroom off to the left. In a moment Sarah came out of the kitchen with a coffeecup. Well, there was scotch, vodka, whiskey, gin in that kitchen. Sarah had mixed something. The door opened, closed and the coffeecup was gone.

Sarah came over. "She'll be all right now . . . "

Two or three minutes passed, then the bedroom door flung open. Francine came out, headed for the bathroom and the camera. As she went past, her eyes found Sarah: "Thank you!"

Well, there was nothing to do but sit about and indulge in more small talk.

I couldn't help but look back into the past. This was the very building I had been thrown out of for having 3 women in my room one night. In those days there was no such thing as Tenants' Rights.

"Mr. Chinaski," the landlady had said, "we have religious people living here, working people, people with children. Never have I heard such complaints from the other tenants. And I heard you too—all that singing, all that cursing . . . things breaking . . . coarse language and laughter . . . In all my days, never have I heard anything like what went on in your room last night!"

"All right, I'll leave . . . "

"Thank you."

I must have been mad. Unshaven. Undershirt full of cigarette holes. My only desire was to have more than one bottle on the dresser. I was not fit for the world and the world was not fit for me and I had found some others like myself, and most of them were women, women most men would never want to be in the same room with, but I adored them, they inspired me, I play-acted, swore, pranced about in my underwear telling them how great I was, but only *I* believed that. They just hollered, "Fuck off! Pour some more booze!" Those ladies from hell, those ladies in hell with me.

Jon Pinchot walked briskly into the room.

"It worked!" he told me. "Everything worked! What a day! Now, tomorrow we start again!"

"Give Sarah the credit," I said. "She knows how to mix a magic drink."

"What?"

"She loosened up Francine with something in a coffeecup."

Jon turned to Sarah.

"Thank you very much . . . "

"Any time," Sarah answered.

"God," said Jon, "I've been in this business a long time and never *nineteen* takes!"

"I've heard," I answered, "that Chaplin sometimes took a hundred takes before he got it right."

"That was Chaplin," said Jon. "A hundred takes and our whole budget would be used up."

And that was about all for that day. Except Sarah said, "Hell, let's go to Musso's."

Which we did. And we got a table in the Old Room and ordered a couple of drinks while we looked at the menu.

"Remember?" I asked, "remember in the old days when we used to come here to look at the people at the tables and try to spot the types, the actor types, the producer or director types, the porno types, the agents, the pretenders? And we used to think, 'Look at them, talking about their half-assed movie deals or their contracts or their last films.' What moles, what misfits . . . better to look away when the swordfish and the sand dabs arrive."

"We thought they were shit," said Sarah, "and now we are."

"What goes around comes around . . . "

"Right! I think I'll have the sand dabs . . . "

The waiter stood above us, shuffling his feet, scowling, the hairs of his eyebrows falling down into his eyes. Musso's had been there since 1919 and everything was a pain in the ass to him: us, and everybody else in the place. I agreed. Decided on the swordfish. With french fries.

—*HOLLYWOOD*

the genius

• •

this man sometimes forgets who
he is.
sometimes he thinks he's the
Pope.

other times he thinks he's a
hunted rabbit

and hides under the
bed.

then
all at once
he'll recapture total
clarity
and begin creating
works of
art.

then he'll be all right
for some
time.

then, say,
he'll be sitting with his
wife
and 3 or 4 other
people
discussing various
matters

he will be charming,
incisive,
original.

then he'll do
something
strange.
like once
he stood up
unzipped
and began
pissing
on the
rug.

another time
he ate a paper
napkin.

and there was
the time
he got into his
car
and drove it
backwards
all the way to
the
grocery store
and back
again
backwards
the other motorists
screaming at
him
but he
made it
there and
back
without
incident
and without
being
stopped
by a patrol
car.

but he's best
as the
Pope
and his
Latin
is very
good.

his works of
art
aren't that
exceptional
but they allow him
to
survive
and to live with
a series of
19-year-old
wives
who
cut his hair
his toenails
bib
tuck and
feed
him.

he wears everybody
out
but
himself.

• •

It was 10 a.m. when the phone rang. It was Jon Pinchot.

"The film has been cancelled . . . "

"Jon, I no longer believe such stories. It's just their way of getting more leverage."

"No, it's true, the film has been cancelled."

"How can they? They've invested too much, they'd take a huge loss on the project . . . "

"Hank, Firepower just doesn't have any more money. Not only has our film been cancelled, *all* films have been cancelled. I went to their office building this morning. There are only the security guards. There is NOBODY in the building! I walked all through it, screaming, 'Hello! Hello! Is anybody here?' There was no answer. The whole building is empty."

"But, Jon, how about Jack Bledsoe's 'Play or Pay' clause?"

"They can't pay *or* play him. All the people at Firepower, including us, are without any more income. Some of them have been working for two weeks now without pay. Now there's no more money for anybody . . ."

"What are you going to do?"

"I don't know, Hank, this looks like the end . . ."

"Don't make any hasty moves, Jon. Maybe some other company will take over the film?"

"They won't. Nobody likes the screenplay."

"Oh, yeah, that's right . . ."

"What are you going to do?"

"Me? I'm going to the track. But if you want to come over for some drinks this evening, I'd be glad to see you."

"Thanks, Hank, but I've got a date with a couple of lesbians."

"Good luck."

"Good luck to you too . . ."

I drove north up the Harbor Freeway toward Hollywood Park. I'd been playing the horses over 30 years. It started after my near fatal hemorrhage at the L.A. County Hospital. They told me that if I took another drink that I was dead.

"What'll I do?" I had asked Jane.

"About what?"

"What'll I use as a substitute for drink?"

"Well, there are the horses."

"Horses? What do you do?"

"Bet on them."

"Bet on them? Sounds stupid."

We went and I won handsomely. I began to go on a daily basis. Then, slowly, I began to drink a little again. Then I drank more. And I didn't die. So then I had both drinking *and* the horses. I was hooked all around. In those days there was no Sunday racing, so I would nurse the old car all the way to Agua Caliente and back on Sunday, a few times staying for the dog races after the horses were through, and then hitting the

Caliente bars. I was never robbed or rolled and was treated rather kindly by both the Mexican bartenders and the patrons even though sometimes I was the only gringo. The late night drive back was nice and when I got home I didn't care whether Jane was there or not. I had told her that Mexico was simply too dangerous for a lady. She usually wasn't home when I got in. She was in a much more dangerous place: Alvarado Street. But as long as there were 3 or 4 beers waiting for me, it was all right. If she drank those and left the refrigerator empty, then she was in *real* trouble.

As for horses, I became a real student of the game. I had about 2 dozen systems. They all worked only you couldn't apply them all at one time because they were based on varying factors. My systems had only one common factor: that the Public must always lose. You had to determine what the Public play was and then try to do the opposite.

One of my systems was based on index numbers and post positions. There are certain numbers that the public is reluctant to call. When these numbers get a certain amount of play on the board in relation to their post position you have a high percentage winner. By studying many years of result charts from tracks in Canada, the USA and Mexico I came up with a winning play based solely upon these index numbers. (The index number indicates the track and race where the horse made its last appearance.) The *Racing Form* used to put out big, fat, red result books for $10. I read them over for hours, for weeks. All results have a pattern. If you can find the pattern, you're in. And you can tell your boss to jam it up his ass. I had told this to several bosses, only to have to find new ones. Mostly because I altered or cheated on my own systems. The weakness of human nature is one more thing you must defeat at the track.

I pulled into Hollywood Park and drove through the "Sticker Lane." A horse trainer I knew had given me an "Owner/Trainer" parking sticker and also a pass to the clubhouse. He was a good man and the best thing about him was that he wasn't a writer or an actor.

I walked into the clubhouse, found a table and worked at my figures. I always did that first, then paid a buck to go over to the Cary Grant Pavilion. There weren't many people there and you could think better. About Cary Grant, they have a huge photo of him hanging in the pavilion. He's got on old-fashioned glasses and that smile. Cool. But what a horseplayer he was. He was a $2 bettor. And when he lost he would run out toward the track screaming, waving his arms and yelling, "YOU

CAN'T DO THIS TO ME!" If you're only going to bet $2 you might as well stay home and take your money and move it from one pocket to the other.

On the other hand, *my* biggest bet was $20 win. Excessive greed can create errors because very heavy outlays affect your thinking processes. Two more things. Never bet the horse with the highest speed rating off his last race and never bet a big closer.

My day out there was pleasant enough but as always I resented that 30 minute wait between races. It was too long. You can feel your life being pounded to a pulp by the useless waste of time. I mean, you just sit in your chair and hear all the voices talking about who should win and why. It's really sickening. Sometimes you think that you're in a mad-house. And in a way, you are. Each of those jerk-offs thinks he knows more than the other jerk-offs and there they were all together in one place. And there I was, sitting there with them.

I liked the actual action, that time when all your calculations came out correctly at the wire and life had some sense, some rhythm and meaning. But the wait between races was a real horror: sitting with a mumbling, bumbling humanity that would never learn or get better, would only get worse with time. I often threatened my good wife Sarah that I would stay home from the track during the days and write dozens and dozens of immortal poems.

So I managed to get through the afternoon out there and headed back home, winner of a little over $100. Drove back with the working crowd. What a gang they were. Pissed and vicious and broke. In a hurry to get home to fuck if possible, to look at tv, to get to sleep early in order to do the same thing next day all over again.

I pulled into the driveway and Sarah was watering the garden. She was a great gardener. And she put up with my insanities. She fed me healthy food, cut my hair and toenails and generally kept me going in many ways.

I parked the car and went out to the garden, gave her a hello kiss.

"Did you win?" she asked.

"Yeah. Sure. A little."

"No phone calls," she said.

"Too bad, all this . . . " I said. "You know, after Jon threatened to cut off his finger and all that. I really feel sorry for him."

"Maybe you should have asked him over tonight."

"I did, but he was tied up."

"S & M?"

"I don't know. A couple of lesbians. Some sort of relief for him."

"Did you notice the roses?"

"Yes, they look great. Those reds and whites and yellows. Yellow is my favorite color. I feel like eating yellow."

Sarah walked with the hose over to the faucet, shut off the water and we walked into the house together. Life was not too bad, sometimes.

—*HOLLYWOOD*

this

self-congratulatory nonsense as the
famous gather to applaud their seeming
greatness

you
wonder where
the real ones are

what
giant cave
hides them

as
the deathly talentless
bow to
accolades

as
the fools are
fooled
again

you
wonder where
the real ones are

if there are
real ones.

this
self-congratulatory nonsense
has lasted
decades
and
with some exceptions

centuries.

this
is so dreary
is so absolutely pitiless

it
churns the gut to
powder
shackles hope

it
makes little things
like
pulling up a shade
or
putting on your shoes
or
walking out on the street

more difficult
near
damnable

as
the famous gather to
applaud their
seeming
greatness

as
the fools are
fooled
again

humanity
you sick
motherfucker.

• •

Then, just like that, the movie was on again. Like most of the news it came over the phone via Jon.

"Yes," he told me, "we begin production again tomorrow."

"I don't understand. I thought the movie was dead."

"Firepower sold some assets. A film library and some hotels they owned in Europe. On top of that they managed to swing a big loan from an Italian group. It's said that this Italian money is a bit tainted but . . . it's money. Anyhow, I'd like you and Sarah to come to the shooting tomorrow."

"I don't know . . . "

"It's tomorrow night . . . "

"O.K., fine . . . When and where?"

Sarah and I sat in a booth. It was Friday night and there was a good feel in the air. We were sitting there when Rick Talbot walked in and sat down with us. There he was in our booth. He only wanted a coffee. I had seen him many times on tv reviewing movies with his counterpart, Kirby Hudson. They were very good at what they did and often got emotional about it all. They gave entertaining evaluations and although others had attempted to copy their format, they were far superior to their competitors.

Rick Talbot looked much younger than he did on tv. Also, he appeared to be more withdrawn, almost shy.

"We watch you often," Sarah said.

"Thank you . . . "

"Listen," I asked him, "what bothers you most about Kirby Hudson?"

"It's his finger . . . When he points his finger."

Then Francine Bowers walked in. She slid into the booth. We greeted her. She knew Rick Talbot. Francine had a little note pad.

"Listen, Hank, I want to know some more about Jane. Indian, right?"

"Half-Indian, half-Irish."

"Why did she drink?"

"It was a place to hide and also a slow form of suicide."

"Did you ever take her any place besides a bar?"

"I took her to a baseball game once. To Wrigley Field, back when the L.A. Angels played in the Pacific Coast League."

"What happened?"

"We both got quite drunk. She got mad at me and ran out of the park. I drove for hours looking for her. When I got back to the room, there she was passed out on the bed."

"How did she speak? Was she loud?"

"She would be quiet for hours. Then all at once she would go crazy and start yelling, cursing and throwing things. I wouldn't react at first. Then she'd get to me. I'd walk up and down, up and down, yelling and cursing back. This would go on for maybe about twenty minutes, then we'd quiet down, drink some more and begin again. We were continually being evicted. We were thrown out of so many places that we couldn't remember them all. Once, looking for a new place, we knocked on a door. It opened and there stood a landlady who had just gotten rid of us. She saw us, turned white, screamed and slammed the door . . . "

"Is Jane dead now?" asked Rick Talbot.

"Long time dead. They're all dead. All those I drank with."

"What keeps *you* going?"

"I like to type. It gives me a thrill."

"And I've got him on vitamins and a low-fat, non-red-meat diet," Sarah told her.

"Do you still drink?" Rick asked.

"Mostly when I type or when people come around. I'm not happy around people and after I drink enough they seem to vanish."

"Tell me some more about Jane," Francine asked.

"Well, she slept with a rosary under her pillow . . . "

"Did she go to church?"

"At strange times she went to what she called 'the alka seltzer mass.' I believe it began at 8:30 a.m. and ran about an hour. She hated the ten o'clock mass which often ran over two hours."

"Did she go to Confession?"

"I didn't ask . . . "

"Can you tell me anything about her which would explain her character?"

"Only that in spite of all the seemingly terrible things she did, the cursing, the madness, the love of the bottle, she always did things with a certain style. I'd like to think that I learned a few things about style from her . . . "

"I want to thank you for these things, I think they might help."

"You're welcome."

Then Francine and her note pad were gone.

"I don't think I've ever had such a good time on a set," said Rick Talbot.

"What do you mean, Rick?" Sarah asked.

"It's a feel in the air. Sometimes with low budget films you get that feel, that carnival feel. It's here. But I feel it more here than I ever have . . . "

He meant it. His eyes sparkled, he smiled with real joy.

I called for another round of drinks.

"Just coffee for me," he said.

The new round came and then Rick said, "Look! There's Sesteenov!"

"Who?" I asked.

"He did that marvelous film on pet cemeteries! Hey, Sesteenov!"

Sesteenov came over.

"Please sit down," I asked.

Sesteenov slid into the booth.

"Care for anything to drink?" I asked.

"Oh, no . . . "

"Look," said Rick Talbot, "there's Illiantovitch!"

I knew Illiantovitch. He had made some crazy dark movies, the main theme being the violence in life overcome by the courage of people. But he did it well, roaring out of the blackness.

He was a very tall man with a crooked neck and crazy eyes. The crazy eyes kept looking at you, looking at you. It was a bit embarrassing.

We slid over to let him in. The booth was full.

"Care for a drink?" I asked him.

"Double vodka," he said.

I liked that, waved to the barkeep.

"Double vodka," he told the barkeep while fixing him with his crazy eyes. The barkeep ran off to do his duty.

"This is a great night," said Rick.

I loved Rick's lack of sophistication. That took guts, when you were on top, to say that you enjoyed what you did, that you were having fun while you did it.

Illiantovitch got his double vodka, slammed it down.

Rick Talbot was asking questions of everybody, including Sarah. There was no feeling of competition or envy in that booth. I felt totally comfortable.

Then Jon Pinchot walked in. He came up to the booth, gave a little bow, grinning, "We're going to shoot soon, I hope. I will come get everybody then . . . "

"Thank you, Jon . . . "

Then he moved off.

"He's a good director," said Rick Talbot, "but I'd like to know why you chose him."

"He chose me . . . "

"Really?"

"Yes . . . and I can tell you a story about him that will explain why he is a good director and why I like him. But it's off the record. . . "

"Let me hear it," said Rick.

"Off the record?"

"Of course . . . "

I leaned forward into the booth and told the story about Jon and the electric chainsaw and his little finger.

"That really happen?" Rick asked.

"Yes. Off the record."

"Of course . . ."

(I knew: nothing is off the record once you tell it.)

Meanwhile, Illiantovitch had finished 2 double vodkas and was sitting looking at another. He kept staring at me. Then he took out his wallet and pulled out a greasy business card. He handed it to me. All 4 corners were worn away and it was limp and dark with grime. It had given up being a business card. Illiantovitch looked like a soiled genius. I admired him for it. He was hardly weighed down by pretense. He grabbed the double vodka and tossed it down his throat.

Then he looked at me, heavily. I stared back. But his dark eyes were entirely too much. I had to look away. I motioned in the barkeep for a refill. Then I looked back at Illiantovitch.

"You're the best man," I said. "After you there is nothing."

"No, not so," he said, "YOU are the best! I give you my card! On card is time of SCREENING OF MY NEW MOVIE! YOU MUST BE THERE!"

"Sure, baby," I said and I took out my wallet and carefully placed the card in there.

"This is a hell of a night," said Rick Talbot.

There was some more small talk, then Jon Pinchot walked in.

"We're about ready to shoot. Will you please come outside now so that we can find places for you?"

We all got up to follow Jon, except Illiantovitch. He sank into the booth.

"Fuck it! I am going to have more double vodkas! You people go!"

That bastard had stolen a page or two from me. He waved to the barkeep, took out a bent cigarette, stuck it between his lips, flicked his lighter and burnt part of his nose.

That bastard.

We walked out into the night.

—HOLLYWOOD

art

• •

as the
spirit
wanes
the
form
appears.

• •

Then, just like that, the 32 days of shooting were over and it was time for the wrap party.

On the first floor was a long bar, some tables and a large dance floor. There was a stairway that led to an upper floor. Essentially it was the film crew and cast, although all of them weren't there and there were other people that I didn't recognize. There was no live band and most of the music coming over the speakers was disco but the drinks at the bar were real. Sarah and I pushed in. There were 2 lady bartenders. I had a vodka and Sarah had red wine.

One of the lady bartenders recognized me and brought out one of my books. I signed it.

It was crowded and hot in there, a summer night, no air conditioning.

"Let's get another drink and go upstairs," I suggested to Sarah. "It's too hot down here."

"O.K.," she said.

We made our way up the stairway. It was cooler up there and not so many people. A few people were dancing. As a party it seemed to lack a center but most parties were that way. I started getting depressed. I finished my drink.

"I'm going to get another drink," I told Sarah. "You want one?"

"No, you go ahead . . ."

I walked down the stairway but before I could get to the bar a fat round fellow, lots of hair, dark shades, grabbed my hand and started shaking it.

"Chinaski, I've read everything you've ever written, everything!"

"Is that right?" I asked.

He kept shaking my hand.

"I got drunk with you one night at Barney's Beanery! Remember me?"

"No."

"You mean you don't remember getting drunk with me at Barney's Beanery?"

"No."

He lifted his shades and perched them on top of his head.

"Now do you remember me?"

"No," I said, pulled my hand away and walked toward the bar.

"Double vodka," I told the lady bartender.

She brought it to me. "I have a girlfriend named Lola," she said. "Do you know a Lola?"

"No."

"She said she was married to you for two years."

"Not true," I said.

I moved from the bar, made my way toward the stairway. Here was another heavy fellow, no hair on his head but a big beard.

"Chinaski," he said.

"Yes?"

"Andre Wells . . . I had a bit part in the movie . . . I'm also a writer . . . I have a novel finished and ready to go. I'd like you to read it. Can I mail you a copy?"

"All right . . . " I gave him my p.o. box number.

"But don't you have a street address?"

"Of course, but mail it to the box number."

I walked to the stairway. I drank half my drink walking up the stairs. Sarah was talking to a female extra. Then I saw Jon Pinchot. He was standing alone with his drink. I walked over.

"Hank," he said, "I'm surprised to see you here . . . "

"And I'm surprised that Firepower put up the money for this . . . "

"They are charging it . . . "

"Oh . . . Well, what's next?"

"We're in the cutting room now, working on it . . . After that, we mix in the music . . . Why don't you come up and see how it's done?"

"When?"

"Anytime. We're working twelve to fourteen hours every day."

"All right . . . Listen, whatever happened to Poppy?"

"Who?"

"The one who put up the ten grand while you were living down at the beach."

"Oh, she's in Brazil now. We'll take care of her."

I finished my drink.

"Aren't you going to go down and dance?" I asked Jon.

"Oh no, that's nonsense . . . "

Then somebody called Jon's name.

"Excuse me," he said, "and don't forget to come to the cutting room!"

"Sure."

Then Jon was off across the room.

I walked over to the railing and looked down at the bar. While I had been talking to Jon, Jack Bledsoe and his motorcycle buddies had walked in. His buddies leaned against the bar, backs to the bar, facing the crowd. They each held a beerbottle, except for Jack who had a 7-Up. They were dressed in leather jackets, scarves, leather pants, boots.

I walked over to Sarah. "I'm going to go down and see Jack Bledsoe and his gang . . . You coming?"

"Sure . . . "

We went on down and Jack introduced us to each of his buddies.

"This is Blackjack Harry . . . "

"Hi, man . . . "

"This is The Scourge . . . "

"Hello there . . . "

"This is The Nightworm . . . "

"Hey, hey!"

"This is Dogcatcher . . . "

"Too much!"

"This is Three-Ball Eddie . . . "

"God damn . . . "

"This is FastFart . . . "

"Pleased to meet ya . . . "

"And Pussykiller . . . "

"Yeah. . . ."

That was it. They all seemed to be fine fellows but they looked a little on-stage, leaning back against the bar and holding their beerbottles.

"Jack," I said, "you did a great job of acting."

"And how!" said Sarah.

"Thank you . . . " he flashed his beautiful smile.

"Well," I said, "we're going back upstairs, it's too damned hot down here . . . Why don't you come up?"

I motioned to the barmaid for refills.

"You going to write another movie script?" Jack asked.

"I don't think so . . . Too much loss of privacy . . . I just like to sit around and stare at walls . . . "

"If you write one, let me see it."

"Sure. Listen, why are your boys facing away from the bar like that? They looking for girls?"

"Naw, they've had too many girls. They are just easing up . . . "

"All right, see you, Jack . . . "

"Keep doing your good work," Sarah said.

We went back upstairs. Soon Jack and his gang were gone.

It wasn't much of a night. I kept going up and down the stairway for drinks. After 3 hours, almost everybody was gone. Sarah and I were leaning over the balcony. Then I saw Jon. I had noticed him dancing earlier. I waved him over.

"Hey, whatever happened to Francine? She didn't make the wrap party."

"No, there's no media here tonight . . . "

"Got it."

"I've got to go now," said Jon. "Have to get up early and go to the cutting room."

"All right . . . "

Then Jon was gone.

It was empty downstairs and it was cooler and so we went down to the bar. Sarah and I were the last ones there. Now there was only one lady bartender.

"We'll have one for the road," I told her.

"I'm supposed to charge you for drinks now," she said.

"How come?"

"Firepower only rented this place until midnight . . . It's ten after twelve . . . But I'll slip you some drinks anyhow because I like your writing so much, but please don't tell anybody that I did it."

"My dear, nobody will ever know."

She poured the drinks. The late disco crowd was beginning to come in. It was time to go. Yes, it was. Our 5 cats were waiting for us. Somehow, I felt sad that the shooting was over. There was something explorative about it. There had been some gamble. We finished our drinks and walked out into the street. The car was still there. I helped Sarah in and got in on the other side. We belted up. I started the car and soon we were on the Harbor Freeway going south. We were moving back toward everyday normalcy and in a way I liked it and in another way I didn't.

Sarah lit a cigarette. "We'll feed the cats and then we'll go to sleep."

"And maybe a drink?" I suggested.

"All right," said Sarah.

Sarah and I got along all right, sometimes.

—HOLLYWOOD

the creative act

• •

for the broken egg on the floor
for the 5th of July
for the fish in the tank
for the old man in room 9
for the cat on the fence

for yourself

not for fame
not for money

you've got to keep chopping

as you get older
the glamour recedes

it's easier when you're young

anybody can rise to the
heights now and then

the buzzword is
consistency

anything that keeps it
going

this life dancing in front of
Mrs. Death.

• •

There it was. The film was rolling. I was being beaten up in the alley by the bartender. As I've explained before I had small hands which are a terrible disadvantage in a fist fight. This particular bartender had huge hands. To make matters worse, I took a punch very well which allowed me to absorb much more punishment. I had some luck on my side: I didn't have much fear. The fights with the bartender were a way to pass the time. After all, you just couldn't sit on your barstool all day and all night. And there wasn't much pain in the fight. The pain came the next morning and it wasn't so bad if you had made it back to your room.

And by fighting 2 or 3 times a week I was getting better at it. Or the bartender was getting worse.

But that had been over 4 decades before. Now I was sitting in a Hollywood screening room.

No need to recall the film here. Perhaps it's better to tell about a part left out. Later in the film this lady wants to take care of me. She thinks I'm a genius and wants to shield me from the streets. In the film I don't stay in the lady's house but overnight. But in actual life I stayed about 6 weeks.

The lady, Tully, lived in this large house in the Hollywood Hills. She shared it with another lady, Nadine. Both Tully and Nadine were high-powered executives. They were into the entertainment scene: music, publishing, whatever. They seemed to know everybody and there were 2 or 3 parties a week, lots of New York types. I didn't like Tully's parties and entertained myself by getting totally drunk and insulting as many people as I could.

And living with Nadine was a fellow a bit younger than I. He was a composer or a director or something, temporarily out of work. I didn't like him at first. I kept running into him around the house or out on the patio in the morning when we were both hungover. He always wore this damned scarf.

One morning about 11 a.m. we were both out on the patio sucking on beers, trying to recover from our hangovers. His name was Rich. He looked at me.

"You need another beer?"

"Sure . . . Thank you . . . "

He went into the kitchen, came back out, handed me my beer, then sat down.

Rich took a good swallow. Then he sighed heavily.

"I don't know how much longer I can fool her . . . "

"What?"

"I mean, I don't have any talent of any kind. It's all just bullshit."

"Beautiful," I said, "that's really beautiful. I admire you."

"Thank you. How about you?" he asked.

"I type. But that's not the problem."

"What is it?"

"My dick is rubbed raw from fucking. She can't get enough."

"I have to eat Nadine every night."

"Jesus . . . "

"Hank, we're just a couple of kept men."

"Rich, these liberated women have our balls in a sack."

"I think we should start in on the vodka now," he said.

"Fine," I said.

• • •

That evening when our ladies arrived neither of us were able to perform our duties.

Rich lasted another week, then was gone.

After that I often ran into Nadine walking about the house naked, usually when Tully was gone.

"What the hell are you doing?" I finally asked.

"This is my house and if I want to run around with my ass in the wind, that's my business."

"Come on, Nadine, what is it really? You want some turkeyneck?"

"Not if you were the last man on earth."

"If I were the last man on earth you'd have to stand in line."

"You just be glad I don't tell Tully."

"Well, just stop running around with your pussy dangling."

"You pig!"

She ran up the stairway, plop, plop, plop. Big ass. A door slammed somewhere. I didn't follow it up. A totally over-rated commodity.

That night when Tully came home she packed me off to Catalina for a week. I think she knew Nadine was in heat.

That wasn't in the film. You can't put everything in a film.

And then back in the screening room, the film was over. There was applause. We all walked around shaking each other's hands, hugging. We were all great, hell yes.

Then Harry Friedman found me. We hugged, then shook hands.

"Harry," I said, "you've got a winner."

"Yes, yes, a great screenplay! Listen, I heard you've done a novel about prostitutes!"

"Yes."

"I want you to write me a screenplay about that. I want to do it!"

"Sure, Harry, sure . . . "

Then he saw Francine Bowers and rushed toward her. "Francine, honey doll, you were magnificent!"

Gradually things wound down and the room was almost empty. Sarah and I walked outside.

Lance Edwards and his car were gone. We had the long walk back to our car. It was all right. The night was cool and clear. The movie was fin-ished and would soon be showing. The critics would have their say. I knew that too many movies were made, one after the other after the other. The public saw so many movies that they no longer knew what a movie was and the critics were in the same fix

Then we were in the car driving back.

"I liked it," said Sarah, "only there were parts . . . "

"I know. It's not an immortal movie but it's a good one."

"Yes, it is . . . "

Then we were on the freeway.

"I'll be glad to see the cats," said Sarah.

"Me too . . . "

"You going to write another screenplay?"

"I hope not . . . "

"Harry Friedman wants us to come to Cannes, Hank."

"What? And leave the cats?"

"He said to bring the cats."

"No way!"

"That's what I told him."

It had been a good night and there would be others. I cut into the fast lane and went for it.

—*HOLLYWOOD*

the orderly

● ●

I am sitting on a tin chair outside the x-ray lab as
death, on stinking wings, wafts through the
halls forevermore.
I remember the hospital stenches from when
I was a boy and when I was a man and now
as an old man
I sit in my tin chair waiting.

then an orderly
a young man of 23 or 24
pushes in a piece of equipment.

it looks like a hamper of
freshly done laundry
but I can't be sure.

the orderly is awkward.
he is not deformed
but his legs work
in an unruly fashion
as if disassociated from the
motor workings of the brain.

he is in blue, dressed all in blue,
pushing,
pushing his load.

ungainly little boy blue.

then he turns his head and yells at
the receptionist at the x-ray window:
"anybody wants me, I'll be in 76
for about 20 minutes!"

his face reddens as he yells,
his mouth forms a down
turned crescent like a
pumpkin's halloween mouth.

then he's gone into some doorway,
probably 76.

not a very *prepossessing* chap.
lost as a human,
long gone down some
numbing road.

but
he's healthy

he's healthy.

HE'S HEALTHY!

are you drinking?

washed-up, on shore, the old yellow notebook
out again
I write from the bed
as I did last
year.

will see the doctor,
Monday.

"yes, doctor, weak legs, vertigo, head-
aches and my back
hurts."

"are you drinking?" he will ask.
"are you getting your
exercise, your
vitamins?"

I think that I am just ill
with life, the same stale yet
fluctuating
factors.

even at the track
I watch the horses run by
and it seems
meaningless.

I leave early after buying tickets on the
remaining races.

"taking off?" asks the mutuel
clerk.

"yes, it's boring,"
I tell him.

"if you think it's boring
out there," he tells me, "you oughta be
back here."

so here I am
propped against my pillows
again

just an old guy
just an old writer
with a yellow
notebook.

something is
walking across the
floor
toward
me.

oh, it's just
my cat

this
time.

ill

• •

being very ill and very weak is a very strange
thing.
when it takes all your strength to get from the
bedroom to the bathroom and back, it seems like
a joke but
you don't laugh.

back in bed you consider death again and find
the same thing: the closer you get to it
the less forbidding it
becomes.

you have much time to examine the walls
and outside
birds on a telephone wire take on much
importance.
and there's the tv: men playing baseball
day after day.

no appetite.
food tastes like cardboard, it makes you
ill, more than
ill.

the good wife keeps insisting that you
eat.
"the doctor said . . . "

poor dear.

and the cats.
the cats jump up on the bed and look at me.
they stare, then jump
off.

what a world, you think: eat, work, fuck,
die.

luckily I have a contagious disease: no
visitors.

the scale reads 155, down from
217.

I look like a man in a death camp.
I
am.

still, I'm lucky: I feast on solitude, I
will never miss the crowd.

I could read the great books but the great books don't
interest me.

I sit in bed and wait for the whole thing to go
one way or the
other.

just like everybody
else.

8 count

· ·

from my bed
I watch
3 birds
on a telephone
wire.

one flies
off.
then
another.

one is left,
then
it too
is gone.

my typewriter is
tombstone
still.

and I am
reduced to bird
watching.

just thought I'd
let you
know,
fucker.

Bring Me Your Love

Harry walked down the steps and into the garden. Many of the
patients were out there. He had been told that his wife, Gloria, was out
there. He saw her sitting alone at a table. He approached her obliquely,
from one side and a bit from the rear. He circled the table and sat down
across from her. Gloria sat very straight, she was very pale. She looked at
him but didn't see him. Then she saw him.

"Are you the conductor?" she asked.

"The conductor of what?"

"The conductor of verisimilitude?"

"No, I'm not."

She was pale, her eyes were pale, pale blue.

"How do you feel, Gloria?"

It was an iron table, painted white, a table that would last for centuries. There was a small bowl of flowers in the center, wilted dead flowers hanging from sad, limp stems.

"You are a whore-fucker, Harry. You fuck whores."

"That's not true, Gloria."

"Do they suck you too? Do they suck your dick?"

"I was going to bring your mother, Gloria, but she was down with the flu."

"That old bat is always down with something. . . . Are you the conductor?"

The other patients sat at tables or stood up against the trees or were stretched out on the lawn. They were motionless and silent.

"How's the food here, Gloria? Do you have any friends?"

"Terrible. And no. Whore-fucker."

"Do you want something to read? What can I bring you to read?"

Gloria didn't answer. Then she brought her right hand up, looked at it, clenched it into a fist and punched herself squarely in the nose, hard. Harry reached across and held both of her hands. "Gloria, *please!*"

She began to cry. "Why didn't you bring me any *chocolates?*"

"Gloria, you told me you *hated* chocolates."

Her tears rolled down profusely. "I *don't* hate chocolates! I *love* chocolates!"

"Don't cry, Gloria, please . . . I'll bring you chocolates, anything you want. . . . Listen, I've rented a motel room a couple blocks away, just to be near you."

Her pale eyes widened. "A *motel* room? You're there with some fucking whore! You watch x-rated movies together, there's a full-length mirror on the ceiling!"

"I'll be nearby for a couple of days, Gloria," Harry said soothingly. "I'll bring you anything you want."

"*Bring me your love, then,*" she screamed. "*Why the hell don't you bring me your love?*"

A few of the patients turned and looked.

"Gloria, I'm sure that there is nobody who cares for you more than I do."

"You want to bring me chocolates? Well, jam those chocolates up your ass!"

Harry took a card out of his wallet. It was from the motel. He handed it to her.

"I just want to give you this before I forget. Are you allowed to phone out? Just phone me if you want anything at all."

Gloria didn't answer. She took the card and folded it into a small square. Then she bent down, took off one of her shoes, put the card in the shoe and put the shoe back on.

Then Harry saw Dr. Jensen approaching across the lawn. Dr. Jensen walked up smiling and saying, "Well, well, well. . . ."

"Hello, Dr. Jensen." Gloria spoke without emotion.

"May I sit down?" the doctor asked.

"Surely," said Gloria.

The doctor was a heavy man. He reeked of weight and responsibility and authority. His eyebrows looked thick and heavy, they *were* thick and heavy. They wanted to slide down into his wet circular mouth and vanish but life wouldn't let them.

The doctor looked at Gloria. The doctor looked at Harry. "Well, well, well," he said. "I'm really *pleased* with the progress we've made so far. . . ."

"Yes, Dr. Jensen, I was just telling Harry how much more *stable* I felt, how much the consultations and the group sessions have helped. I've lost so much of my unreasonable anger, my useless frustration and much of my destructive self-pity. . . ."

Gloria sat with her hands folded in her lap, smiling.

The doctor smiled at Harry. "Gloria has made a *remarkable* recovery!"

"Yes," Harry said, "I've noticed."

"I think it will only be a matter of a *little* more time and then Gloria will be home with you again, Harry."

"Doctor?" Gloria asked. "May I have a cigarette?"

"Why, of course," the doctor said pulling out a pack of exotic cigarettes and tapping one out. Gloria took it and the doctor extended his gold-plated lighter, flicked it into life. Gloria inhaled, exhaled. . . .

"You have beautiful hands, Dr. Jensen," she said.

"Why, thank you, my dear."

"And a kindness that saves, a kindness that cures. . . ."

"Well, we do the best we can around the old place . . . " Dr. Jensen said gently. "Now, if you'll both excuse me, I have to talk to some of the other patients."

He lifted his bulk easily from the chair and made his way toward a table where another woman was visiting another man.

Gloria stared at Harry. "That fat fuck! He eats the nurses' shit for lunch. . . ."

"Gloria, it's been wonderful seeing you but it was a long drive and I need some rest. And I think the doctor is correct. I've noticed some progress."

She laughed. But it wasn't a joyful laugh, it was a stage laugh, like a part memorized. "I haven't made any progress at all, in fact, I've *retrograded*. . . . "

"That's not true, Gloria. . . ."

"*I'm* the patient, Fishhead. I can make a better diagnosis than anybody."

"What's this 'Fishhead'?"

"Hasn't anybody ever told you that you have a head like a fish?"

"No."

"Next time you shave, take a look. And be careful not to cut off your gills."

"I'm going to leave now . . . but I'll visit you again, tomorrow. . . ."

"Next time bring the conductor."

"You sure I can't bring you anything?"

"You're just going back to that motel room to fuck some whore!"

"Suppose I bring you a copy of *New York*? You used to like that magazine. . . ."

"Jam *New York* up your ass, Fishhead! And follow it with *TIME!*"

Harry reached across and squeezed the hand she had hit herself in the nose with. "Keep it together, keep trying. You're going to be well soon. . . ."

Gloria gave no sign she had heard him. Harry got up slowly, turned and walked toward the stairway. When he got halfway up the stairs he turned and gave Gloria a little wave. She sat, motionless.

They were in the dark, going good, when the phone rang.

Harry kept going but the phone kept going. It was very disturbing. Soon, his cock went soft.

"Shit," he said and rolled off. He switched on the lamp and picked up the phone.

"Hello?"

It was Gloria. "You're fucking some whore!"

"Gloria, do they let you phone out this late? Don't they give you a sleeping pill or something?"

"What took you so long to answer the phone?"

"Don't you ever take a crap? I was in the middle of a good one, you get me in the middle of a good one."

"I'll bet I did. . . . You going to finish it after you get me off the phone?"

"Gloria, it's your god-damned extreme paranoia that has put you where you are."

"Fishhead, *my* paranoia has often been the forerunner of an approaching truth."

"Listen, you're not making any sense at all. Get yourself some *sleep*. I'll come see you tomorrow."

"O.K., Fishhead, finish your FUCK!"

Gloria hung up.

Nan was in her dressing gown, sitting on the edge of the bed with a whiskey and water on the night table. She lit a cigarette and crossed her legs.

"Well," she asked, "how's the little wifey?"

Harry poured a drink and sat down beside her.

"I'm sorry, Nan. . . ."

"Sorry for what, for who? For her or me or what?"

Harry drained his shot of whiskey. "Let's not make a god-damned soap opera out of this thing."

"Oh yeah? Well, what do you want to make out of it? A simple roll in the hay? You want to try to finish? Or would you rather go into the bathroom and beat it off?"

Harry looked at Nan. "God damn it, don't get smart. You knew the situation as well as I did. *You* were the one who wanted to come along!"

"That's because I knew if you didn't take me you'd bring some whore!"

"Oh shit," said Harry, "there's *that* word again."

"What word? What word?" Nan drained her glass, threw it against the wall.

Harry walked over, picked up her glass, refilled it, handed it to Nan, then filled his own.

Nan looked down into her glass, took a hit, put it down on the night-stand. "I'm going to phone her, I'm going to tell her everything!"

"Like hell you will! That's a *sick* woman."

"And *you're* a sick son-of-a-bitch!"

Just then the phone rang again. It was sitting on the floor in the center of the room where Harry had left it. They both leaped from the bed toward the phone. On the second ring they both landed, each grabbing a piece of the receiver. They rolled over and over on the rug, breathing heavily, all legs and arms and bodies in a desperate juxtaposition, and reflected that way in the full-length mirror overhead.

—*SEPTUAGENARIAN STEW*

putrefaction

• •

of late
I've had this thought
that this country
has gone backwards
4 or 5 decades
and that all the
social advancement
the good feeling of
person toward
person
has been washed
away
and replaced by the same
old
bigotries.

we have
more than ever
the selfish wants of power
the disregard for the
weak
the old
the impoverished
the
helpless.

we are replacing want with
war
salvation with
slavery.

we have wasted the
gains
we have become
rapidly
less.

we have our Bomb
it is our fear
our damnation
and our
shame.

now
something so sad
has hold of us
that
the breath
leaves
and we can't even
cry.

face of a political candidate on a street billboard

· ·

there he is:
not too many hangovers
not too many fights with women
not too many flat tires
never a thought of suicide

not more than three toothaches
never missed a meal
never in jail
never in love

7 pairs of shoes

a son in college

a car one year old

insurance policies

a very green lawn

garbage cans with tight lids

he'll be elected.

peace

· ·

near the corner table in the
cafe
a middle-aged couple
sit.

they have finished their
meal
and they are each drinking a
beer.
it is 9 in the evening.
she is smoking a
cigarette.
then he says something.
she nods.
then she speaks.
he grins, moves his
hand.
then they are
quiet.
through the blinds next to
their table
flashing red neon
blinks on and
off.

there is no war.
there is no hell.

then he raises his beer
bottle.
it is green.
he lifts it to his lips,
tilts it.

it is a coronet.

her right elbow is
on the table
and in her hand
she holds the
cigarette
between her thumb and
forefinger

and
as she watches
him
the streets outside
flower
in the
night.

Fooling Marie

• •

It was a warm night at the quarterhorse races. Ted had arrived carrying $200 and now going into the third race he was carrying $530. He knew his horses. Maybe he wasn't much good at anything else but he knew his horses. Ted stood watching the toteboard and looking at the people. They lacked any ability to rate a horse. But they still brought their money and their dreams to the track. The track ran a $2 exacta almost every race to lure them in. That and the Pick-6. Ted never touched the Pick-6 or the exactas or the doubles. Just straight win on the best horse, which wasn't necessarily the favorite.

Marie bitched so much about his going to the track that he only went two or three times a week. He had sold his company and retired early from the construction business. There really wasn't much else for him to do.

The four horse looked good at six-to-one but there was still 18 minutes to post. He felt a tug at his coat sleeve.

"Pardon me, sir, but I've lost the first two races. I saw you cashing in your tickets. You look like a guy who knows what he's doing. Who do you like in this next race?"

She was a strawberry blonde, about 24, slender hips, surprisingly big breasts; long legs, a cute turned-up nose, flower mouth; dressed in a pale blue dress, wearing white high-heeled shoes. Her blue eyes looked up at him.

"Well," Ted smiled at her, "I've usually got the winner."

"I'm used to betting on thoroughbreds," said the strawberry blonde. "These quarterhorse races are so *fast!*"

"Yeah. Most of them are run in under 18 seconds. You find out pretty quick whether you're right or wrong."

"If my mother knew I was out here losing my money she'd belt-whip me."

"I'd like to belt-whip you myself," said Ted.

"You're not one of those, are you?" she asked.

"Just joking," said Ted. "Come on, let's go to the bar. Maybe we can pick you a winner."

"All right, Mr.—?"

"Just call me Ted. What's your name?"

"Victoria."

They walked into the bar. "What'll you have?" Ted asked.

"Whatever you're having," said Victoria.

Ted ordered two Jack Danielses. He stood and knocked his off and she sipped at hers, looking straight ahead. Ted checked her ass: perfect. She was better than some god damned movie starlet, and she didn't look spoiled.

"Now," said Ted, pointing to his program, "in the next race the four horse figures best and they are giving six-to-one odds . . ."

Victoria let out a very sexy, "Oooh . . . ?" She leaned over to look at his program, touching him with her arm. Then he felt her leg press against his.

"People just don't know how to rate a horse," he told her. "Show me a man who can rate a horse and I'll show you a man who can win all the money he can carry."

She smiled at him. "I wish I had going what you've got going."

"You've got plenty going, baby. Want another drink?"

"Oh no, thank you . . ."

"Well, listen," said Ted, "we better bet."

"All right, I'll bet $2 to win. Which is it, the number four horse?"

"Yeah, baby, it's the four . . ."

They placed their bets and went out to watch the race. The four didn't break well, got bumped on both sides, righted himself, was running fifth in a nine horse field, but then began to accelerate and came down to the wire bobbing heads with the two-to-one favorite. Photo.

God damn, thought Ted, I've *got* to have this one. Please give me *this* one!

"Oh," said Victoria, "I'm so *excited!*"

The toteboard flashed the number. *Four.*

Victoria screamed and jumped up and down gleefully. "We won, we won, we WON!"

She grabbed Ted and he felt the kiss on his cheek.

"Take it easy, baby, the best horse won, that's all."

They waited for the official sign and then the tote flashed the payoff. $14.60.

"How much did you bet?" Victoria asked.

"$40 win," said Ted.

"How much do you get back?"

"$292. Let's collect."

They began walking toward the windows. Then Ted felt Victoria's hand in his. She pulled him to a stop.

"Bend over," she said, "I want to whisper something in your ear."

Ted leaned over, felt her cool pink lips up against his ear. "You're a . . . magic man . . . I want to . . . fuck you . . . "

Ted stood there grinning weakly at her. "My god," he said.

"What's the matter? Are you afraid?"

"No, no, it's not that . . . "

"What is the matter then?"

"It's Marie . . . my wife . . . I'm married . . . and she has me timed down to the minute. She knows when the races are over and when I'm due in."

Victoria laughed: "We'll leave *now!* We'll go to a motel!"

"Well, sure," said Ted . . .

They cashed their tickets and walked out to the parking lot. "We'll take my car. I'll drive you back when we're finished," Victoria said.

They found her car, a blue 1982 Fiat, it matched her dress. The license plate read: VICKY. As she put her key in the door, Victoria hesitated. "You're really not one of those kind, are you?"

"What kind?" Ted asked.

"A belt-whipper, one of those. My mother had a terrible experience once . . . "

"Relax," said Ted. "I'm harmless."

They found a motel about a mile and a half from the track. The Blue Moon. Only The Blue Moon was painted green. Victoria parked and they got out, went in, signed in, were given Room 302. They had stopped for a bottle of Cutty Sark on the way.

482 • CHARLES BUKOWSKI

Ted peeled the cellophane from the glasses, lit a cigarette, and poured a couple as Victoria undressed. The panties and the bra were pink, and the body was pink and white and beautiful. It was amazing how now and then a woman was created who looked like that, when all the others, most of the others, had nothing, or next to nothing. It was maddening. Victoria was a beautiful, maddening dream.

Victoria was naked. She came over and sat on the edge of the bed next to Ted. She crossed her legs. Her breasts were very firm and she looked as if she was already aroused. He really couldn't believe his luck. Then she giggled.

"What is it?" he asked.

"Are you thinking about your wife?"

"Well, no, I was thinking about something else."

"Well, you *should* think about your wife . . . "

"Hell," said Ted, "*you* were the one who suggested fucking!"

"I wish you wouldn't use that word . . . "

"Are you backing out?"

"Well, no. Listen, you got a cigarette?"

"Sure . . . "

Ted pulled one out, handed it to her, lighted it as she held it in her mouth.

"You've got the most beautiful body I've ever seen," said Ted.

"I don't doubt that," she said, smiling.

"Hey, are you backing out of this thing?" he asked.

"Of course not," she answered, "get your clothes off."

Ted began undressing, feeling fat and old and ugly, but he also felt lucky—it had been his best day at the track, in many ways. He draped his clothes over a chair and sat down next to Victoria.

Ted poured a new drink for each of them.

"You know," he told her, "you're a class act but I'm a class act too. We each have our own way of showing it. I made it big in the construction business and I'm still making it big with the horses. Not everybody has that instinct."

Victoria drank half of her Cutty Sark and smiled at him. "Oh, you're my big fat Buddha!"

Ted drained his drink. "Listen, if you don't want to do it, we won't do it. Forget it."

"Lemme see what Buddha's got . . . "

Victoria reached down and slid her hand between his legs. She got it, she held it.

"Oh oh . . . I feel something . . . " Victoria said.

"Sure . . . So what?"

Then her head ducked down. She kissed it at first. Then he felt her open mouth and her tongue.

"You *cunt!*" he said.

Victoria lifted her head up and looked at him. "*Please,* I don't like dirty talk."

"All right, Vicky, all right. No dirty talk."

"Get under the sheets, Buddha!"

Ted got under there and he felt her body next to his. Her skin was cool and her mouth opened and he kissed her and pushed his tongue in. He liked it like that, fresh, spring fresh, young, new, good. What a god damned delight. He'd rip her! He played with her down there, she was a long time coming around. Then he felt her open up and he forced his finger in. He had her, the bitch. He pulled his finger out and rubbed the clit. You want foreplay, you'll get foreplay! he thought.

He felt her teeth dig into his lower lip, the pain was terrible. Ted pulled away, tasting the blood and feeling the wound on his lip. He half rose and slapped Victoria hard across the side of her face, then backhanded her across the other side of the face. He found her down there, slid it in, rammed it in her while putting his mouth back on hers. Ted worked away in wild vengeance, now and then pulling his head back, looking at her. He tried to save it, to hold back, and then he saw that cloud of strawberry hair fanned across the pillow in the moonlight.

Ted was sweating and moaning like a high school boy. This was it. Nirvana. The place to be. Victoria was silent. Ted's moans lessened and then after a moment he rolled off.

He stared into the darkness.

I forgot to suck her tits, he thought.

Then he heard her voice. "You know what?" she asked.

"What?"

"You remind me of one of those quarterhorses."

"What do you mean?"

"It's all over in 18 seconds."

"We'll race again, baby," he said . . .

She went to the bathroom. Ted wiped off on the sheet, the old pro. Victoria was rather a nasty number, in a way. But she could be handled. He had something going. How many men owned their own home and had 150 grand in the bank at his age? He was a class act and she damn well knew it.

Victoria came walking out of the bathroom still looking cool, untouched, almost virginal. Ted switched on the bedlamp. He sat up and poured two more. She sat on the edge of the bed with her drink and he climbed out and sat on the edge of the bed next to her.

"Victoria," he said, "I can make things good for you."

"I guess you've got your ways, Buddha."

"And I'll be a better lover."

"Sure."

"Listen, you should have known me when I was young. I was tough, but I was good. I had it. I still have it."

She smiled at him, "Come on, Buddha, it's not all that bad. You've got a wife, you've got lots of things going for you."

"Except one thing," he said, draining his drink and looking at her. "Except the one thing I really want . . . "

"Look at your *lip!* You're bleeding!"

Ted looked down into his glass. There were drops of blood in his drink and he felt blood on his chin. He wiped his chin with the back of his hand.

"I'm going to shower and clean up, baby, be right back."

He walked into the bathroom, slid the shower door open and began to run the water, testing it with his hand. It seemed about right and he stepped in, the water running off him. He could see the blood in the water running into the drain. Some wildcat. All she needed was a steadying hand.

Marie was all right, she was kind, kind of dull actually. She had lost the intensity of youth. It wasn't her fault. Maybe he could find a way to stay with Marie and have Victoria on the side. Victoria renewed his youth. He needed some fucking renewal. And he needed some more good fucking like that. Of course, women were all crazy, they demanded more than there was. They didn't realize that making it was not a glorious experience, but only a necessary one.

"Hurry up, Buddha!" he heard her call. "Don't leave me all alone out here!"

"I won't be long, baby!" he yelled from under the shower.

He soaped up good, washing it all away.

Then Ted got out, toweled off, then opened the bathroom door and stepped into the bedroom.

The motel room was empty. She was gone.

There was a distance between ordinary objects and between events that was remarkable. All at once, he saw the walls, the rug, the bed, two chairs, the coffee table, the dresser, and the ashtray with their cigarettes. The distance between these things was immense. Then and now were light years apart.

On an impulse, he ran to the closet and pulled the door open. Nothing but coat hangers.

Then Ted realized that his clothes were gone. His underwear, his shirt, his pants, his car keys and wallet, his cash, his shoes, his stockings, everything.

On another impulse he looked under the bed. Nothing.

Then Ted noticed the bottle of Cutty Sark, half full, standing on the dresser and he walked over, picked it up and poured himself a drink. And as he did he saw two words scrawled on the dresser mirror in pink lipstick: "GOODBYE BUDDHA!"

Ted drank the drink, put the glass down and saw himself in the mirror—very fat, very old. He had no idea what to do next.

He carried the Cutty Sark back to the bed, sat down heavily on the edge of the mattress where he and Victoria had sat together. He lifted the bottle and sucked at it as the bright neon lights from the boulevard came through the dusty blinds.

He sat, looking out, not moving, watching the cars passing back and forth.

—*Hot Water Music*

cornered

• •

well, they said it would come to
this: old. talent gone. fumbling for
the word

hearing the dark
footsteps, I turn
look behind me . . .

not yet, old dog . . .
soon enough.

now
they sit talking about
me: "yes, it's happened, he's
finished . . . it's
sad . . . "

"he never had a great deal, did
he?"

"well, no, but now . . . "

now
they are celebrating my demise
in taverns I no longer
frequent.

now
I drink alone
at this malfunctioning
machine

as the shadows assume
shapes

I fight the slow
retreat

now
my once-promise
dwindling
dwindling

now
lighting new cigarettes
pouring more
drinks

it has been a beautiful
fight

still
is.

Trollius and trellises

of course, I may die in the next ten minutes
and I'm ready for that
but what I'm really worried about is
that my editor-publisher might retire
even though he is ten years younger than
I.
it was just 25 years ago (I was at that *ripe*
old age of 45)
when we began our unholy alliance to
test the literary waters,
neither of us being much
known.

I think we had some luck and still have some
of same
yet
the odds are pretty fair
that he will opt for warm and pleasant
afternoons
in the garden
long before I.

writing is its own intoxication
while publishing and editing,
attempting to collect bills
carries its own
attrition
which also includes dealing with the
petty bitchings and demands
of many
so-called genius darlings who are
not.

I won't blame him for getting
out
and hope he sends me photos of his
Rose Lane, his
Gardenia Avenue.

will I have to seek other
promulgators?
that fellow in the Russian
fur hat?
or that beast in the East
with all that hair
in his ears, with those wet and
greasy lips?

or will my editor-publisher
upon exiting for that world of Trollius and

trellis
hand over the
machinery
of his former trade to a
cousin, a
daughter or
some Poundian from Big
Sur?

or will he just pass the legacy on
to the
Shipping Clerk
who will rise like
Lazarus,
fingering new-found
importance?

one can imagine terrible
things:
"Mr. Chinaski, all your work
must now be submitted in
Rondo form
and
typed
triple-spaced on rice
paper."

power corrupts,
life aborts
and all you
have left
is a
bunch of
warts.

"no, no, Mr. Chinaski:
Rondo form!"

"hey, man," I'll ask,
"haven't you heard of
the thirties?"

"the thirties? what's
that?"

my present editor-publisher
and I
at times
did discuss the thirties,
the Depression
and
some of the little tricks it
taught us—
like how to endure on almost
nothing
and move forward
anyhow.

well, John, if it happens enjoy your
divertissement to
plant husbandry,
cultivate and aerate
between
bushes, water only in the
early morning, spread
shredding to discourage
weed growth
and
as I do in my writing:
use plenty of
manure.

and thank you
for locating me there at
5124 DeLongpre Avenue
somewhere between

alcoholism and
madness.

together we
laid down the gauntlet
and there are takers
even at this late date
still to be
found
as the fire sings
through the
trees.

my first computer poem

have I gone the way of the deathly death?
will this machine finish me
where booze and women and poverty
have not?

is Whitman laughing at me from his grave?
does Creeley care?

is this properly spaced?
am I?

will Ginsberg howl?

soothe me!

get me lucky!

get me good!

get me going!

I am a virgin again.

a 70-year-old virgin.

don't fuck me, machine

do.
who cares?

talk to me, machine!

we can drink together.
we can have fun.

think of all the people who will hate me at this
computer.

we'll add them to the others
and continue right
on.

so this is the beginning
not the
end.

Dinosauria, we

• •

born like this
into this
as the chalk faces smile
as Mrs. Death laughs
as the elevators break

as political landscapes dissolve
as the supermarket bag boy holds a college degree
as the oily fish spit out their oily prey
as the sun is masked

we are
born like this
into this
into these carefully mad wars
into the sight of broken factory windows of emptiness
into bars where people no longer speak to each other
into fist fights that end as shootings and knifings

born into this
into hospitals which are so expensive that it's cheaper to die
into lawyers who charge so much it's cheaper to plead guilty
into a country where the jails are full and the madhouses closed
into a place where the masses elevate fools into rich heroes

born into this
walking and living through this
dying because of this
muted because of this
castrated
debauched
disinherited
because of this
fooled by this
used by this
pissed on by this
made crazy and sick by this
made violent
made inhuman
by this

the heart is blackened
the fingers reach for the throat
the gun

the knife
the bomb
the fingers reach toward an unresponsive god

the fingers reach for the bottle
the pill
the powder

we are born into this sorrowful deadliness
we are born into a government 60 years in debt
that soon will be unable to even pay the interest on that debt
and the banks will burn
money will be useless
there will be open and unpunished murder in the streets
it will be guns and roving mobs
land will be useless
food will become a diminishing return
nuclear power will be taken over by the many
explosions will continually shake the earth
radiated robot men will stalk each other
the rich and the chosen will watch from space platforms
Dante's Inferno will be made to look like a children's playground

the sun will not be seen and it will always be night
trees will die
all vegetation will die
radiated men will eat the flesh of radiated men
the sea will be poisoned
the lakes and rivers will vanish
rain will be the new gold

the rotting bodies of men and animals will stink in the dark wind

the last few survivors will be overtaken by new and hideous diseases
and the space platforms will be destroyed by attrition
the petering out of supplies
the natural effect of general decay

and there will be the most beautiful silence never heard

born out of that.

the sun still hidden there

awaiting the next chapter.

Luck

....

once
we were young
at this
machine . . .
drinking
smoking
typing

it was a most
splendid
miraculous
time

still
is

only now
instead of
moving toward
time
it
moves toward
us

makes each word
drill
into the
paper

clear

fast

hard

feeding a
closing
space.

the bluebird

• •

there's a bluebird in my heart that
wants to get out
but I'm too tough for him,
I say, stay in there, I'm not going
to let anybody see
you.

there's a bluebird in my heart that
wants to get out
but I pour whiskey on him and inhale
cigarette smoke
and the whores and the bartenders
and the grocery clerks
never know that
he's
in there.

there's a bluebird in my heart that
wants to get out
but I'm too tough for him,
I say,
stay down, do you want to mess
me up?
you want to screw up the
works?
you want to blow my book sales in
Europe?

there's a bluebird in my heart that
wants to get out
but I'm too clever, I only let him out
at night sometimes
when everybody's asleep.
I say, I know that you're there,
so don't be
sad.

then I put him back,
but he's singing a little
in there, I haven't quite let him
die
and we sleep together like
that
with our
secret pact
and it's nice enough to
make a man
weep, but I don't
weep, do
you?